D0497765

WITHDRAWN

THE DARK SIDE
of Guy de Maupassant

THE DARK SIDE
OF Guy de Maupassant

A selection and translation by
Arnold Kellett
with introduction and notes

Foreword by Ramsey Campbell

Carroll & Graf Publishers, Inc.
New York

To my French teacher, Dr. J. H. Hird,
and to the successive years of Sixth Formers
with whom it was always such a pleasure to
read Maupassant in the original.

This selection and Introduction copyright © Arnold Kellett 1989
These translations copyright © Arnold Kellett 1972, 1976, 1989
Foreword copyright © Ramsey Campbell 1989

All rights reserved.

First published in Great Britain by Xanadu Publications Limited 1989.
First published in the United States of America by Carroll & Graf
Publishers, Inc. 1989, by arrangement with Xanadu Publications Ltd.

Carroll and Graf Publishers, Inc.
260 Fifth Avenue,
New York, NY 10001

Library of Congress Cataloging-in-Publication Data

Maupassant, Guy de, 1850–1893
  The dark side

  1. Maupassant, Guy de, 1850–1893—Translations, English.
  2. Horror tales, French—Translations into English.
  3. Horror tales, English—Translations from French.
  4. Supernatural—Fiction. I. Title.
  PQ·2349.A4E5 1989 843′.8 89–511

ISBN 0-88184-459-4

Manufactured in Great Britain

Contents

Foreword

By Ramsey Campbell

Of all forms of fiction, the fantastic and macabre allow the subconscious to speak most freely. This can mean that the fiction tells truths about the writer which he would prefer not to admit to himself, or even that it prefigures how the writer's personality will develop. Occasionally (as in the case of Arthur Machen) the writer attempts to create some awesome vision and then experiences it directly himself, but Machen is a benign exception, who had to turn to the occult in order to control what was happening to him. Imagine the possibility that the most intense and disturbing horror fiction may be the writer's own psychological experience, remembered or foreseen, and you should appreciate why I say that the writing of some horror fiction is an act of courage.

It involves inhabiting the dark side of the mind, whether in the act of imaginatively living through the tale as it is written or drawing on one's own experience to make the story psychologically true (which amounts to the same thing). Sometimes the fiction may be an attempt by the author to objectify an experience he is suffering, in order to place it outside himself. All three modes seem to be present in the macabre tales of Guy de Maupassant, and this leads me to regard him as one of the more courageous writers in this field.

'I'm afraid of myself! I'm afraid of fear, afraid of my panic-stricken mind, afraid of that horrible sensation of incomprehensible terror . . . I'm afraid of the walls, of the furniture, of familiar objects, which seem to me to take on a kind of animal life. Above all, I am afraid of the horrible confusion of my thoughts, of the way my reason becomes blurred and elusive, scattered by a mysterious, invisible anguish . . . '

So writes the narrator of *He?*, who later walks into his apartment and finds 'him' sitting in his chair, and one is tempted to hope that Maupassant is inventing these sensations for the sake of the story, even though he was to say of his own literary method: 'We must *feel* – that is everything . . . But we must not say, must not write – for the public – that we have been so shaken.' In his horror fiction it seems that he abandons understatement, and it won't do to dismiss passages such as the lines from *He?* as simple exaggeration. 'On certain days,' he wrote in a letter, 'I experience the horror of everything that is, to the point of longing for death.' But that is not all.

'Every other time I come home, I see my double. I open my door, and I see him sitting in my armchair. I know it for a hallucination, even while experiencing it. Curious! If I didn't have a little common sense, I'd be afraid.'

That is not a quotation from *He?*; that is Maupassant himself talking to his friend Paul Bourget. Maupassant, like Alfred Hitchcock, was addicted to practical jokes, and perhaps that was one; it might be comforting to think so. At the very least it displays an artist's poise, and the same may be said of his most famous horror story, *The Horla*, not least because he published three drafts of it. *Letter from a Madman* rounds off an essay on extraordinary perceptions with the first sight of the Horla, the second version distances the story by having a doctor at an insane asylum investigate it without reaching a conclusion about the narrator's sanity, and the last and best-known version appears herein. All this may be evidence of Maupassant's willingness to work at the story until it satisfied him – but perhaps it is also evidence of an obsession, particularly since the telling of the tale becomes progressively less distanced from the vision of the narrator.

'Thinking becomes an abominable torment when the brain is but a sore. There are so many bruises inside my head that my ideas cannot stir without making me want to scream. Why? Why? . . . And there are days when I do not think these things, but suffer anyway, for I am one of those who have been skinned alive . . . '

So Maupassant wrote in a letter some years before his death. Can his mental condition have been partly the result of the strain of writing – of attempting to render his experiences objective or to preserve his poise in writing about them? Or must we conclude that at least some of his horror fiction understated his lived experience?

'*I am absolutely lost. I am even dying.* I have a softening of the brain, the result of washing out my nasal passages with salt water. A saline fermentation has taken place in my brain, and every night my brain runs out through my nose and mouth in a sticky paste. This is imminent death and I am *mad* . . . '

This is from a letter Maupassant wrote at the end of December 1891 to his friend Dr Henry Cazalis (who wrote poetry as Jean Lahor). On New Year's Day Maupassant cut his own throat and called for

help. He had lost his poise at the edge of sanity. He lived, insane,
for another nineteen months.

How eloquent a description of the process leading up to the end
of his life this collection of stories represents is for the reader to decide.
Colin Wilson has suggested that Maupassant's short stories 'should
be swallowed in dozens, like oysters; this is the only way to get the
true Maupassant flavour', but I would not advise that in the case of
these tales. Their terrible clarity may not be to everyone's taste, but
it is an achievement to be respected, especially in these faithful yet
fluent translations by Arnold Kellett.

Be warned: the light of these tales may shine into your own dark.

Ramsey Campbell,
Merseyside

Introduction

In selecting and translating these powerful tales from a total of 311 by that acknowledged master of story-telling, Guy de Maupassant, I have found myself thinking, again and again, that this book really ought to carry a health-warning. It is certainly not for those with a tendency to depressive illness, or even for insomniacs, and other victims of an over-active imagination. Here is stuff that really *could* keep you awake at night.

My own addiction to Maupassant began long years ago as a Sixth Former, when in French classes I first read *Le Horla* – which is one reason why I place this unique spell-binder first. Though the author's other *contes* (short stories) and *nouvelles* (longer tales) cover a great variety of topics, I always found those dealing with fear and horror to be the most compelling, and eventually, in 1969, I published an annotated selection of such stories, *Contes du Surnaturel* (Pergamon Press), and later translated these and others for two Pan Books, *Tales of Supernatural Terror* and *The Diary of a Madman*. I also prepared a selection for Oxford University Press in simplified English, mainly for students in the Far East, *A Night on the River, and other Strange Tales*. First published in 1976, this has remained popular ever since, and has even appeared in a bilingual version in Chinese.

This present volume brings together most of the stories I first prepared for Pan, all thoroughly revised from Maupassant's original text. It constitutes, as far as I am aware, the first hardback collection of its kind in English – that is, one which deals exclusively with the dark side of Maupassant.

There is, of course, a brighter side to this famous writer, as we might expect from the period in which he lived. To the average English-language reader the France of the late nineteenth century was a time of elegant frivolity and sexual licence – all that is brought to mind by 'gay Paree', Toulouse-Lautrec, the Moulin Rouge, the Folies Bergère, and the somewhat earlier music of Jacques Offenbach, notably his famous can-can, a dance originally performed in the brothels of Algeria – done to death, yet still retaining its fresh Parisian vivacity.

Much of this is indeed reflected in the stories of Guy de Maupassant, written between 1875 and 1891. So many of them are light-hearted, full of *joie de vivre*, describing carefree boating-parties on the Seine, for example, in which Maupassant is himself depicted in a painting by Renoir. They abound in lively scenes of eating, drinking, and making merry – especially with prostitutes. Even in what is surely his best-known story, *La Parure* (The Necklace), the struggling poverty of the heroine results from her romantic ambition to be the belle of a high-society ball.

Moreover Maupassant had such a keen sense of humour that whether he was depicting the hard life and miserly ways of Normandy peasants, the brutality of the Franco-Prussian War, the world of obsequious civil servants, pompous officials, petty politicians, nagging wives, drunken husbands – and almost every facet of his contemporary society – he so often wrote as a terse and cynical raconteur, who could scarcely resist constant touches of dry, ironical humour, and who sometimes indulged in frank and rollicking Gallic fun.

Yet beneath the fashionable public exterior of wit and pleasure-seeking, there was a private Maupassant, whose desperate unhappiness and inner world of morbidity and terror he reveals to us in stories such as those presented in this book. There are others, too – some so unsavoury, or so grim and obsessive – that we lose nothing by excluding them. But those which follow are, I believe, absolutely characteristic, and sufficiently varied.

To understand the mind of Maupassant it is obviously helpful to know a little about his life. Henri René Albert Guy de Maupassant was born on the 5th August, 1850 in the château of Miromesnil, near Dieppe. When Guy was only six, soon after his brother Hervé was born, the father left Laure de Maupassant to bring up the boys on her own. She moved further down the Normandy coast to picturesque Étretat, where Guy was allowed to mix freely with seamen and peasants, developing a great enthusiasm for life in the open air, including fishing, hunting, and a love of dogs.

At thirteen he was sent to a strict Catholic boarding-school at Yvetot, where he was unhappy, badly behaved, and from where he was eventually expelled. When the family moved to Rouen the brothers went to a small private school, then in 1868 Guy became a boarder at the Collège Impérial, passing his *baccalauréat* the following year. From this period an important influence was Gustave Flaubert, author of *Madame Bovary* (1857), who was a close friend of Guy's mother, and lived at Croisset, near Rouen.

In October 1869 Maupassant joined his stock-broker father in Paris, and started to study for a degree in law at the Sorbonne. The following year, 1870, the Franco-Prussian war broke out, and Maupassant enlisted in the army. Though he saw little fighting, he experienced many hardships, including the siege of Paris, and developed a hatred for war in general, and Prussian officers in particular.

After demobilization in November, 1871, the young Maupassant, warned by Flaubert that it was too soon to risk writing for a living, started work as a poorly-paid civil servant, first with the Ministère de la Marine, later in the Ministère de l'Instruction Publique (Education). He hated office-life as much as the army, but kept physically fit by boating on the Seine, and mentally active by joining the circle of successful writers who had gathered round Flaubert.

He later testified how much he owed to Flaubert, '*mon cher maître*', who for seven years had made constructive criticism of his attempts at writing, teaching him his own disciplined, objective style. By 1880 Flaubert was satisfied that Maupassant could be safely launched on a literary career, declaring his *Boule de Suif*, published in a collection by Émile Zola, to be a masterpiece. From his busy pen there now poured a stream of successful work, including six novels and numerous articles, but mainly short stories, which first appeared in papers and periodicals such as *Le Figaro*, *Le Gaulois* and *Gil Blas*.

Calling himself an *industriel des lettres* (literature manufacturer), writing mainly for money, his financial success meant that he could build a villa at Étretat, buy a house for his mother at Nice, and a yacht for cruising on the Mediterranean. He travelled widely, visiting Switzerland, Corsica, Italy, Sicily and Algeria, with a short stay in England in 1886. Everywhere he went, everybody he met, provided material for his short stories.

Yet underneath this flamboyant, bohemian life-style was a man fighting a losing battle against an insidious and devastating disease. Maupassant had always led an immoral and promiscuous life, detesting women, yet constantly attracted to them. It is not surprising that not only is he said to have fathered three illegitimate children, but he also became infected with syphilis, probably during his twenties. This led to drug-taking – hashish, cocaine, morphine, and especially ether – and gave him blinding headaches and eye-trouble. Towards the end of his short life the disease began to attack his brain, producing hallucinations.

After firing revolver shots at an imaginary enemy at his home in Cannes, he attempted suicide by cutting his throat. Like his younger brother before him, Maupassant was now declared to be insane, and taken to an asylum in Paris, where, after suffering the most bizarre hallucinations and exhibiting the strangest behaviour, he died on 6th July, 1893, not quite forty-three years old.

The question immediately arises: are these tales of supernatural terror and gruesome horror simply the work of an author who was mad? Absolutely not. All those who have studied Maupassant take the view that until this suicide-attempt at Cannes, he was perfectly lucid and rational. What is more, he made a point of saying this himself, in his letters, and it is confirmed by his neatly-written manuscripts in the Bibliothèque Nationale.

The position, in fact, was this: he wrote, not as a psychotic, but as a man *approaching* the frontiers of madness, terrified at the prospect of losing his reason, obsessed with the thought of premature death. This is perfectly demonstrated in the first story of this volume, *The Horla*, where the diary discloses a mounting dread of incipient insanity, and by the final story, *Who Knows?*, in which Maupassant anticipates his own tragic fate.

Far from being insane when he wrote these stories, Maupassant, the *naturaliste*, writing in the new age of photogaphy, trained by Flaubert to search for *le mot juste* (the right word) as an impassive and precise recorder of human society, simply turned his analytical gaze inwards. Instead of writing about the outside world (where, in any case, he had always probed beneath the surface) he now became increasingly introspective, scrutinizing everything produced by his terror-stricken imagination. This is why these pages contain some of the finest descriptions ever penned of what it is like to be scared to death.

In addition to his relentless, incurable disease, other factors led Maupassant to choose these sombre topics. From an early age he had a morbid streak, encouraged by the poet Swinburne, who once presented the fourteen-year-old Maupassant with the mummified hand of a parricide, as a reward for helping to rescue him from drowning near Étretat. His morbidity was further encouraged by his reading of the fantastic tales of E. T. A. Hoffman and Edgar Allan Poe, the latter translated into French by Baudelaire by 1865. He was also greatly influenced by the atheistic philosophy of Arthur Schopenhauer (1788–1860), with its pessimistic emphasis on the inevitability of suffering. Though there is ample evidence that Maupassant knew how to enjoy himself, the majority of his stories are tinged with pessimism and misanthropy.

Then, of course, Maupassant wrote stories of this kind because he knew they would be popular. E. A. Poe's *Tales of Mystery and Imagination* and J. B. D'Aurevilly's *Les Diaboliques* had whetted the appetite for more stories of horrific, unsolved murders with overtones of the supernatural. There was also a renewed interest in all kinds of occult topics, especially F. A. Mesmer's 'animal magnetism', which was being revived by the physician J. M. Charcot, whose popular lectures on hypnotism Maupassant actually attended.

Our author was certainly a man of his time, but his themes are universal. It is no surprise that he has been enthusiastically acclaimed by writers with such differing backgrounds as Turgenev, Somerset Maugham and William Saroyan, and translated into so many different languages. It is not just a matter of his skill, but of his eye for a subject. He knew what his readers wanted – and what they always want. The public still has the same insatiable appetite for the mysterious and the shocking, for blood and death, and dread of the nameless unknown.

But is it right to feed this appetite? Is there any ethical justification for bringing together these potent tales of gloom and horror? I believe there is. In my view, here is so much that is downright honest and compassionate that the final effect is positive, even therapeutic. It is the old Greek idea of *catharsis*: to witness the suffering of someone else purges us through pity and fear. It makes us feel better, because it could so easily have happened to us, and has not. These stories were cathartic for Maupassant himself – he was working it out of his system, as it were. They can also be cathartic for us.

The element of compassion is even more important. Many of these stories involve, for example, some harrowing death, especially the loss of an only child. '*Pauvre vieille!*' exclaims the doctor, moved by the sight of the grief-stricken mother of Louise Roque, raped and murdered at the age of twelve. With such simple ingredients as this comment Maupassant moves his readers to compassion, and arouses our revulsion for man's inhumanity to man. There is, I believe, a hidden depth in these stories. They are cries of anguish and of protest. Maupassant, the allegedly dispassionate reporter, holding a mirror up to life, is really saying: Look at this! These things should not be allowed to happen!

So now let him speak for himself, button-holing us, holding our attention, usually by speaking in the first person, through a diary, a letter, or an anecdote told by somebody else, arising out of a chance remark – but always keeping our interest to the end. Then, without moralizing, without any gloating, he rapidly lowers the curtain, and is gone.

As for the translation itself, Maupassant is easy to read, but notoriously difficult to translate, mainly because of his compression and strict economy of style. His habitual brevity constantly challenges the translator to search for an adequate English equivalent, especially when certain of his characters speak an authentic, comically-clipped Normandy dialect.

I can only say that in all these stories I have tried to keep the flavour of the original, and especially to reflect the amazing clarity of this writer agonizing on the fringe of madness. As Rivarol remarked: *'Ce qui n'est pas clair, n'est pas français'* – what isn't clear, isn't French. I trust you will find that Maupassant is a supreme example of this happy French tradition, even in his darkest moments.

Arnold Kellett,
Knaresborough, North Yorkshire.

The Horla

May 8th. What a glorious day! I have spent the whole morning lying in the grass in front of my house under the great plane-tree which towers above it, providing complete shelter and shade . . . I love this district, and I love living here, because this is where I have my roots, those deep yet delicate roots which bind a man to the soil where his forefathers lived and died, roots which bind him to the way local people think, to what they eat, to the customs, the dishes, the dialect, the intonation of the country folk's voices, the smell of the soil, of the villages, of the very air.

I love this house of mine in which I have grown to manhood. From my windows I can see the Seine which flows past my garden, on the other side of the road, almost on my doorstep – the great, broad Seine which flows from Rouen to Le Havre, laden with passing ships.

Away to my left is Rouen, the city where blue roof-tops lie beneath a bristling throng of Gothic spires. These belfries seem innumerable – some slender, some sturdy, all of them dominated by the tall iron spire of the cathedral; and they are filled with bells which ring out in the blue sky of fine mornings, sending me their gentle, faraway hum of iron and their chimes of bronze, carried to me through the air, now louder, now fainter, rising and falling with the swell of the breeze.

What a lovely morning it has been! At about eleven o'clock a long line of ships sailed past my gate, pulled along by a tug which looked the size of a fly, wheezing away as it struggled, and belching forth dense clouds of smoke.

These were followed by two British schooners, with their red ensign fluttering in the breeze, and then came a magnificent Brazilian three-master, completely white, remarkably clean, and gleaming all over. For some reason or other I waved to it – probably just out of the sheer pleasure of seeing it.

May 12th. I have had a bit of a temperature for a few days. I don't feel at all well – or, to be more accurate, I feel depressed.

Where do these mysterious influences come from – the influences which change our happiness into despondency and our self-confidence into misery? You would think that the air, the unseen air, is full of incomprehensible powers, whose mysterious proximity has an effect on us. I wake up full of the joys of life, ready to burst into song . . . Why? . . . I walk along the river-bank and suddenly, after walking just a short distance, I come back feeling terribly depressed, as though some misfortune were waiting for me at home . . . Why? . . . Is it because a breath of cold air, passing over my skin, has upset my nerves and brought this gloom into my heart? Is it the shape of the clouds, or the tone of the daylight, or the ever-changing colour of the world around me, which has entered my eyes and disturbed my thoughts? Who can tell? Everything around us, everything we see without really looking at, everything we brush against without really noticing, everything we touch without really feeling, everything we encounter without really observing – all these things have on us, on our organs of sense, and through them, on our thoughts and feelings, an effect that is swift, amazing, impossible to account for.

How deep it is, this mystery of the Invisible. We cannot plumb its depths with our wretched senses, with our eyes, which are incapable of perceiving things that are too small, things that are too big, things too far away, the inhabitants of a star – or the inhabitants of a drop of water . . . And our ears deceive us, because they convey to us vibrations in the air in the form of sounds – they are like fairies performing this miracle of changing movement into sound, and through this transformation they give birth to music, turning into melody the silent rhythms of nature . . . And what of our sense of smell, inferior to that possessed by a dog . . . And our sense of taste, which can scarcely detect the age of a wine!

Ah! If only we had other sense-organs to work other miracles for us, who can tell how many more things we should discover in the world around us?

May 16th. I am ill – there's no doubt about it. And yet I felt so well last month. I have a fever, a terrible fever, or rather a feverish irritation of my nerves which afflicts my mind just as much as my body. I constantly have this dreadful sensation of being threatened by some danger, this feeling of imminent disaster or encroaching death, this state of apprehension which is no doubt caused by the onset of some hitherto unknown disease incubating in my blood and flesh.

May 18th. I have been to see my doctor, for I am getting no sleep at all. He found my pulse rapid, my pupils dilated, my nerves on edge – but no symptom of anything seriously wrong. He has advised me to have cold showers, and take potassium bromide.

May 25th. No change. My condition is really most peculiar. As evening approaches I feel myself being overcome by an unaccountable state of anxiety, as if the night concealed some terrible menace, destined for me. I eat my dinner hurriedly, then I try to read; but I can't understand the words I am reading; I can hardly make the letters out. Then I walk up and down my drawing-room, oppressed by a vague but overmastering fear – fear of sleep, and fear of my bed.

At about two o'clock in the morning I go up to my bedroom. The minute I get inside I double-lock the door and shoot the bolts. I'm afraid . . . But what am I afraid of? I never used to be afraid of anything before . . . But now I open my cupboards, look under my bed, and listen . . . and listen . . . What is it I expect to hear? . . . Isn't it strange that a simple indisposition – perhaps some disturbance of the circulation, an irritation of the nervous system, some slight inflammation, just a tiny irregularity in the imperfect, delicate working of this living machine of ours – isn't it strange that it can turn the most cheerful of men into a pessimist and the bravest of men into a coward? . . . Well, then I go to bed, and wait for sleep, just as a condemned man might wait for the executioner. I wait for it, terrified at the prospect of its arrival, with my heart pounding and my legs trembling – and the whole of my body lies shuddering in the warmth of the sheets, up to the moment when I suddenly drop off to sleep – like someone falling into a deep pool of stagnant water, and getting drowned. I never feel it coming over me, as I used to, this treacherous sleep which seems to lurk quite near me, spying on me, ready to pounce on my face, close my eyes and destroy me.

I sleep for a comparatively long time – perhaps two or three hours – then a dream – no, a nightmare – seizes me in its grip. I am fully aware that I am lying down and that I am asleep . . . I am aware of this, and I actually see it . . . and I am also aware that somebody is coming up to me, looking at me, running his fingers over me, climbing on to my bed, kneeling on my chest, taking me by the throat and squeezing . . . squeezing with all his strength, trying to strangle me.

I struggle desperately to get free, but I am tied down by that appalling feeling of helplessness which paralyses us in our dreams. I want to cry out – but I can't. I want to move – and I can't. Gasping for breath, making terrible, strenuous efforts, I try to turn on my side, try to throw off this creature who is crushing and choking me – but I can't!

Then, suddenly, I wake up, panic-stricken, drenched in sweat. I light a candle. I am all alone.

After this attack, which comes upon me every night, I am able to enjoy a peaceful sleep until dawn.

June 2nd. My condition has got even worse. What on earth is the matter with me? The bromide has done no good; neither have the cold showers . . . The other day, just to tire out my body – which in a sense is already exhausted – I went for a walk in the Forest of Roumare. At first I thought that the fresh air – so light, sweet, and full of the fragrance of grass and foliage – would somehow pour new blood into my veins, and give my heart a new burst of energy. I walked along one of those big tracks used by hunters, then I made for La Bouille, turning down an avenue which runs between two dense rows of enormously tall trees whose branches shut out the sky above me by forming a thick roof of dark green.

Suddenly a curious shudder ran through my body – not a shiver caused by the cold, but a strange shudder of terror.

I quickened my pace, ill at ease because I was all on my own in this wood, afraid for no particular reason, frightened, rather stupidly, by the absolute solitude. Then, suddenly, I got the feeling that somebody was following me, walking just behind me, nearly treading on my heels, close enough to touch me.

Abruptly, I stopped and turned round. I was entirely alone. All I could see were the tall trees of the straight, broad avenue, terrifyingly empty. And when I turned round again I could see the avenue continuing in front of me, stretching as far as I could see, empty in exactly the same way, and frightening to behold.

I shut my eyes – I don't know why. And I started to spin round on one heel, very rapidly, like a top. I made myself so dizzy I nearly fell. When I opened my eyes the trees seemed to be dancing about and the ground was swaying. I had to sit down . . . And then – oh, it was terrible! I couldn't remember which direction I had come from. What an uncanny feeling it was! How strange! How very strange! I simply had no idea. I set off down the part of the avenue which was on my right, and eventually found myself back in the hunter's track which had brought me into the heart of the forest.

June 3rd. What a horrible night I've had! I'm going to go away for a few weeks. A little trip will probably do me good . . .

July 2nd. Back home again. I'm cured! What's more I've had a really nice holiday. I've been to Mont Saint-Michel, which I'd never visited before.

What a sight when you arrive in Avranches as I did, towards the end of the day! The town stands on a hill, and I was directed to the park on the outskirts. When I got there I gave a cry of astonishment. An enormous bay stretched out before me as far as the eye could see, and the two widely separated coastlines were gradually lost in the faraway mist. In the middle of this great, yellow bay, under a sky of brilliant gold, there rose from amidst the sands a strange mountain, dark and sharply pointed. The sun had just gone down, and on the horizon, which was still ablaze with light, there stood the stark outline of this fantastic rock with the fantastic old building on its summit.

The following day, as soon as it was light, I went out there. It was low tide, as it had been the previous evening, and as I drew nearer I could see this astonishing abbey looming up before me. After several hours of walking I reached the huge rocky mass which is the foundation of the little fortified town and the church which rises above it. Having climbed the steep, narrow street I entered the most magnificent Gothic house that men have ever built for God, as big as a town, full of low halls, looking almost squashed under their vaulted roofs and their high galleries supported by slender columns. I entered this gigantic jewel made of solid stone, yet as delicate as lace-work, all covered with towers and delicate little belfries wrapped round with twisted stairways, and which thrust up into the blue sky of day and the black sky of night their bizarre heads, bristling with gargoyles, demons, fantastic animals, monstrous flowers, all interlinked by delicately ornamented arches.

When I got to the top I said to the monk who was my guide. 'Well, Father, you must enjoy living here.'

He replied: 'It's terribly windy up here, monsieur.' And we began to chat as we looked down on the rising tide which was flowing across the sand, covering it with a breastplate of steel.

The monk told me all kinds of stories concerning Mont Saint-Michel – one old legend after another.

There was one of them which impressed me very much. Local people claim that at night you can hear voices on the sands, that you can even hear the bleating of two goats, one loud, the other fainter. Sceptics say that it's only the cries of seabirds, which sometimes do sound like the bleating of a goat, and sometimes like a human voice. But fishermen, coming home late, swear that they have seen an old shepherd roaming about on the sands at low tide, wandering near this little town that has sprung up here, far from civilization. They say that no one has ever seen his face, as it is covered by his cloak, and that they have seen him walking in front of them, leading a he-goat with a man's face, and a she-goat with a woman's face. Both of them have long white hair and they keep up a long conversation, quarrelling with each other in a strange language – then suddenly they stop, and bleat for all they are worth.

I said the the monk: 'Do you believe that legend?'

He muttered: 'I don't know.'

I went on: 'If beings other than ourselves exist on the earth, how is it that we have never actually come across them in all this time? How is it that *you* have never seen them? How is it that *I* have never seen them?'

He replied: 'Can we see even a hundred-thousandth part of what actually exists? Take the wind, for example, the greatest force in nature: it can bowl men over, blow down their buildings, uproot trees, heap up the sea into mountains of water, break down the cliffs, toss great ships on to the reefs . . . This wind capable of killing, shrieking, moaning, roaring – have you ever seen it? Could you ever see it? And yet, there's no doubt that it exists.'

This simple argument reduced me to silence. This monk was either a wise man – or perhaps just naïve. I couldn't really be sure which – but I didn't argue. The point he had just made had often occurred to me before.

July 3rd. I've had a very poor night. There's no doubt that there's some kind of fever in the air round here, because my coachman is suffering from the same disease as I had. When I got back home yesterday I noticed how unusually pale he was, and I asked him: 'What's the matter with you, Jean?'

'The trouble is I can't get any proper rest, monsieur. My nights seem to eat into my days. Ever since you went away, monsieur, it's been hanging over me like a spell.'

At any rate, the other servants are all well. But I'm afraid that I might fall ill again myself.

July 4th. There's no doubt about it: this horrible disease has attacked me again. My old nightmares are back. Last night I felt that somebody was crouching on top of me, putting his mouth against mine, sucking my life out through my open lips. Yes, I really felt he was draining my life away through my throat, just like a leech sucking blood. Then, having gorged himself, he got off me – and I woke up, so battered, bruised and exhausted, that I couldn't move . . . If this goes on much longer, I shall certainly have to leave my house again.

July 5th. Am I going out of my mind? What happened last night – what I actually saw – was so strange that I go dizzy when I think about it.

I had locked my bedroom door, as I do every night now; then, as

I was feeling thirsty, I drank half a glass of water, and I happened to notice that my decanter was full right up to the glass stopper. I then went to bed, and soon dropped off into one of my dreadful slumbers, from which I was roused a couple of hours later by an even more terrible shock than usual.

Imagine a man being murdered in his sleep; he wakes up with a knife in his lungs, and he lies there covered in blood, struggling for breath, with gurgling sounds coming from his throat; he is on the point of dying – and yet he is unable to grasp why . . . Well, that's what I dreamt.

When I finally came to my senses, I realized that I felt thirsty again. I lit a candle and went over to the table on which my water decanter was standing. I lifted it up and tilted it over a glass. Nothing came out . . . It was empty! It was absolutely empty! At first I simply didn't understand. Then, suddenly, such a dreadful sensation came over me that I had to sit down – or rather, I collapsed into a chair. Then I jumped up again, looking all round the room. And then I sat down once again, gazing in terrified astonishment at the empty vessel before me. I stared hard at it, trying to puzzle out just what had happened – and my hands were trembling! So somebody had drunk this water. Who? Had *I* drunk it? Surely it was me – it could only have been me . . . Then I must be a sleepwalker, I must be leading that mysterious double life which makes us wonder whether there are two beings inhabiting one body – or whether there is some alien, undetected, invisible being which occasionally takes over when our spirit is quiescent, forcing our body to obey its orders, just as *we* might give orders to our body – only this being does it more effectively.

Oh, who will ever understand the overwhelming anguish I felt? Who can be expected to understand the feelings of a man who is sane, wide awake, with his mind working logically – and yet he sits here staring in terror through the glass sides of a decanter, looking for the water which has disappeared during his sleep? I sat there until daylight came, without daring to go back to bed.

July 6th. I must be going mad. Last night somebody drank all the water from my decanter – or rather, *I* must have drunk it!

But *was* it me? *Was* it me? Who else could it be? Who else? Oh, my God! Am I really going mad? Will nobody help me?

July 10th. I've just carried out some remarkable experiments . . . It certainly looks as though I'm insane – and yet!

On July 6th, before going to bed, I put on my table some wine, some milk, some water – and some strawberries.

Somebody drank – or maybe *I* drank – all the water and a little of the milk. Both the wine and the strawberries were left untouched.

On July 7th I repeated the same experiment, and it gave the same result.

On July 8th I did not put out the water or the milk. Nothing was touched.

Finally, on July 9th I placed only the milk and the water on my table, and this time I took the precaution of wrapping the decanters in white muslin and tying the stoppers with string. Then I got some black-lead and rubbed it all over my lips, my beard and my hands. Then I lay down.

The same, irresistible sleep took possession of me, soon to be followed by the horrible awakening . . . When I woke up I saw that I hadn't moved: the sheets hadn't been marked by the black-lead at all. I got up and rushed over to the table . . . the muslin which I had wrapped round the decanters was absolutely spotless . . . Quivering with terror, I untied the string round the stoppers . . . Every drop of water had been drunk! Every drop of milk had gone! – Oh, my God!

In a short while I shall be on my way to Paris.

July 12th. Paris. I really must have been out of my mind these last few days! I must have been the victim of my over-excited imagination, unless I really happen to be a sleepwalker or under one of those well-established but unexplained influences connected with hypnotism. In any case, my state was certainly verging on insanity, but twenty-four hours in Paris have been enough to restore my self-possession.

Yesterday, after shopping and visiting friends, which was like letting fresh air into my soul, I finished my evening by going to the Théâtre Français. They were giving a play by Alexandre Dumas the younger, and this writer's sharp and powerful wit helped to complete my cure. There's no doubt about it: solitude is dangerous for people with active imaginations. We need to have people around us who can think and talk. When we are alone for a long time, we fill the emptiness with phantoms of our own creation.

I walked along the boulevards on the way back to my hotel in a very happy frame of mind. Jostling through the crowds, I thought rather scornfully of my terrors and suppositions of the past week, when I had convinced myself – yes, really convinced myself! – that some invisible being was living under my roof. What a frail thing our mind is, and how easily it gets bewildered and dismayed as soon as it is faced with some little fact that is beyond its comprehension!

Instead of simply saying: 'I don't understand this because I cannot find the cause,' we immediately start imagining all sorts of fearful mysteries with supernatural powers to provide an explanation.

July 14th. The French national holiday. I went walking in the streets. Fireworks and flags still delight me just as much as they did when I was a boy. Of course, I realize that it is quite idiotic to rejoice on certain dates fixed by government decrees. Ordinary people are a silly herd, sometimes stupidly docile, and sometimes fierce and rebellious. When they are told: 'Enjoy yourselves!' they enjoy themselves. When they are told: 'Go and fight your neighbours!' they go and fight. When they are told: 'Vote for the Emperor!' they vote for the Emperor. And when they are told: 'Vote for the Republic!' they vote for the Republic.

Those in charge are also fools, but instead of obeying other men, they obey principles that can also only be inane, sterile and false just because they are principles, that is to say, well-established, certain, immutable notions in a world in which we can be sure of nothing, since both light and sound are nothing but illusions.

July 16th. Yesterday I saw certain things which troubled me a good deal.

I had dinner with my cousin, Madame Sablé, whose husband commands the 76th Regiment of Fusiliers stationed in Limoges. At my cousin's house I met two young ladies, one of whom was the wife of Doctor Parent, who specializes in nervous disorders and in the extraordinary phenomena discovered recently through experiments in hypnosis and suggestion.

He spent a long time talking about the fantastic results obtained by English scientists and by doctors at the Nancy School of Medicine.

The things he told us struck me as being so odd that I told him I simply couldn't believe them . . .

My cousin, who was also very sceptical, was smiling. Doctor Parent said to her: 'Would you like me to try to put you to sleep, madame?'

'Yes, I would.'

She sat down in an armchair, and he began to stare at her, and to hypnotize her. I suddenly felt rather uneasy: my heart beat faster, my throat went dry. I could see Madame Sablé's eyes gradually close, her mouth grow tense and her breast heave.

Ten minutes later, she was asleep.

'Will you sit down behind her?' the doctor asked me.

I sat down behind her. He put a visiting card into her hand and said to her: 'This is a mirror. What do you see in it?'

She answered: 'I can see my cousin.'

'What is he doing?'
'He's twirling his moustache.'
'And what is he doing now?'
'He's pulling a photograph out of his pocket.'
'What sort of a photograph is it?'
'It's a photograph of him.'

It was true. And this photograph had been delivered to me that very evening in my hotel.

'What does he look like in this picture?'
'He is standing up, holding his hat in his hand.'

She could apparently see what was going on behind her as though the white piece of cardboard were a mirror!

Very nervous, the young women were saying: 'Oh, that's enough! That's enough!'

But the doctor gave her this order: 'You will get up tomorrow morning at eight o'clock; you will then go to the hotel where your cousin is staying, and you will beg him to lend you five thousand francs, which your husband will expect you to give him when he gets back to Paris.'

Then he woke her up.

As I walked back to my hotel, I thought about the curious scene I had witnessed and doubts began to assail me – not about the absolute and unquestionable good faith of my cousin, whom I had known like a sister ever since she was a child, but about whether there hadn't been some trickery on the doctor's part. Had he concealed a mirror in his hand and shown it to the hypnotized woman at the same time as the visiting card? Professional conjurers, after all, can do far more baffling tricks of this type.

I reached my hotel room and went to bed.

At half past eight in the morning I was awakened by a servant.

'It's Madame Sablé, monsieur,' he said, 'and she wants you to see her right away.'

I dressed hurriedly and asked her in.

She sat down, looking very upset, and keeping her eyes lowered. Without raising her veil, she said: 'My dear cousin, I must ask you a very great favour.'

'What is it, cousin?'

'It's terribly embarrassing to have to tell you this, but I have no choice. I need – need quite desperately – five thousand francs.'

'Oh, surely not! You? Five thousand francs?'

'Yes, me . . . or rather, my husband. He has asked me to get hold of that amount.'

I was so astonished that I hardly knew what to say to her. I began to wonder seriously whether she hadn't been in league with the doctor to have fun at my expense, whether it wasn't just a well-planned and well-rehearsed practical joke.

But when I looked at her closely, all my doubts vanished. She was trembling and distressed; the step she had taken was obviously very painful to her. I could see that she was about to break down and start sobbing.

I knew that she was very well off, and I said: 'How is it your husband can't get hold of five thousand francs? Now look! Just think for a moment. Are you really sure he asked you to come to me for this money?'

She hesitated for a few seconds as if searching hard for something buried in her memory, after which she replied: 'Yes . . . Yes . . . I'm quite sure.'

'Has he written to you?'

Again she hesitated, stopping to think. I could imagine the tortured labour of her thoughts. She didn't know. All she knew was that she had to borrow five thousand francs from me for her husband. So she decided to tell a lie: 'Yes, he's written to me.'

'When? You never even mentioned it yesterday.'

'I got the letter this morning.'

'Could you show it to me?'

'Oh no, I couldn't . . . There were personal things in it . . . far too personal . . . I've . . . I've burnt it.'

'Ah! So your husband's got into debt!'

Again she hesitated, then mumbled: 'I don't know.'

Then I said quite abruptly: 'The fact is, dear cousin, I can't possibly get hold of five thousand francs right now.'

She gave a cry of pain. 'Oh, please, please, I beg you, I beg of you . . . Get it for me!'

She was beginning to lose control. She even clasped her hands as though she were praying to me. Her voice had changed. She was sobbing and stammering, tormented, subdued by the irresistible order she had received. 'Oh! I implore you to help me . . . If you knew how miserable I am! . . . I must have the money today!'

I took pity on her. 'You'll receive the money today,' I said.. 'I give you my word.'

'Oh, thank you! Thank you!' she exclaimed: 'You're so kind.'

I then asked her, 'Do you remember what happened yesterday at your house?'

'Yes, I do.'

'Do you remember being put to sleep by Doctor Parent?'

'Yes.'

'Well, he ordered you to come to me this morning and ask me for five thousand francs, and now you are obeying the suggestion he put into your mind.'

She thought for a few moments, then replied: 'But it's my husband who needs the money!'

For an hour I kept trying to convince her of the truth, but without success.

When she had gone I rushed off to the doctor's house. He was about to go out. He listened to me with a smile and said:

'Well, do you believe me now?'

'Yes, how can I help believing?'

'Then let's go to your cousin's house.'

She was dozing on a couch, apparently quite exhausted. The doctor felt her pulse and looked at her for a few moments with his hand raised to the level of her eyes, which gradually closed under the unbearable pressure of that hypnotic power.

When she was asleep, the doctor said: 'Your husband does not need the five thousand francs any longer. So you will forget that you have asked your cousin to lend you that sum, and even if he mentions it to you, you will not understand.'

Then he woke her up. I drew a wallet from my pocket and said: 'Here you are, cousin, here's what you asked me for this morning.'

She showed such surprise that I didn't dare insist on her taking it. However, I tried to get her to recall that morning's scene, but she vigorously denied it all, thought that I was pulling her leg, and finally almost lost her temper . . .

Well, that's what happened. I've just got back to my hotel, and this business has so shaken me I've not been able to eat any dinner.

July 19th. Many people to whom I have told the story have laughed in my face. I no longer know what to think. The wise man says: 'Maybe it's true, maybe it isn't.'

July 21st. I had dinner at Bougival, then spent the evening at the party thrown by the boating club. There's no doubt that everything depends on the placed and the atmosphere. To believe in the supernatural when you're on the island of La Grenouillère would be sheer lunacy . . . But what about when you're on the top of Mont Saint-Michel? . . . Or what if you were out in India? . . . It's terrifying the way we are so easily influenced by our environment.

Next week I shall be going back home.

July 30th. I got back yesterday. Everything is all right.

August 2nd. Nothing has happened. The weather is marvellous. I spend all my time watching the Seine flow past the garden.

August 4th. Squabbling amongst my servants. They claim that glasses are being broken in the cupboards during the night. The butler blames the cook, and she blames the washerwoman, who accuses the two others. Who is the culprit? It would take a clever man to get to the bottom of all this.

August 6th. This time I'm absolutely sure I'm not mad. I've *seen* something! I've *seen* something! . . . I've *seen* something! . . . There can be no doubt about it any longer . . . I've *seen* something! . . . It's left me chilled to the very fingertips . . . Deep down inside I'm still scared . . . I've *seen* something!

At about two o'clock, in bright sunlight, I was walking in my rose-garden . . . near the bed of late roses which are just coming into bloom.

As I stopped to look at a 'Géant des Batailles' which bore three magnificent flowers, I saw – saw very distinctly, just in front of me – the stem of one of these roses bend – just as if it were being pulled by an invisible hand – and then it snapped, as if this hand had plucked it! Then the flower moved upwards, in the kind of arc that would have been made by a hand carrying the flower to a mouth. And there it stayed, poised in thin air, all by itself, absolutely motionless – a terrifying splash of red, a few feet in front of my eyes.

In a frenzy I rushed forward to try to grab it. There was nothing there! It had disappeared! Then I became furious with myself, for it is intolerable that a sensible, serious-minded man should have hallucinations of this kind.

But *was* it a hallucination? I turned to look for the broken stem on the rose-bush and I found it straight away. There it was, a freshly broken stem, between the two other roses still on the bush.

Well, I came back to the house feeling terribly shaken. I'm certain now – as certain as that night follows day – that living near me is an invisible being, who feeds on water and milk, who can touch things, pick them up and move them about, and who therefore has a material nature, even though it cannot be perceived by human senses, and who is actually living, as I do, under the same roof . . .

August 7th. I've had a good night's sleep. He drank the water from my decanter, but he didn't disturb my sleep in any way.

I wonder if I *am* mad. When I was out walking just now, going along the river in the bright sunlight, I began to have doubts about my sanity – not vague doubts, like those I have had before, but well-defined, definite doubts. I have seen madmen, and I have known some who remained intelligent, lucid, and who had a clear appreciation of everything around them – except in one particular respect. They would talk on any subject with clarity, ease and penetration – and then, suddenly striking the reef of their madness, their thoughts would be torn to pieces, would scatter and then sink in that terrifying, furious ocean full of leaping waves and fog and sudden squalls – the ocean we call 'insanity'.

Certainly I would think I was mad, quite mad, if I had not been fully conscious of my surroundings, if I had not had a perfect understanding of my state, and been able to assess it and analyse it with perfect lucidity. So what it boils down to, I suppose, is that I experience hallucinations, but my reason is unaffected. Some strange disturbance must have taken place in my brain – one of those disorders which physiologists are now trying to track down and define – and I suppose that this disturbance will have caused a great gap in the logical progression of my thoughts. Similar phenomena occur in our dreams which take us through the most incredible regions of fantasy, and we never experience any surprise over it, because the part of us which verifies and controls is asleep, whereas the imaginative part of us is wide awake and active. In my case might it not be that one of the imperceptible keys of the cerebral keyboard has become stuck? Some people, as the result of an accident, find that they cannot remember proper nouns, verbs or figures – or perhaps just dates. It has now been proved that various mental functions are located in particular areas of the brain. So what is there so surprising about the possiblity that, in my case, there is at present a kind of sluggishness in the faculty which can distinguish between reality and delusion?

These were my thoughts as I walked along the river-bank . . . The sunlight was clothing the water with its brilliance, making the countryside a glorious sight, so that everything I looked upon filled me with a realization that I loved life – the swallows whose swift grace is a delight to behold, the reeds along the river-side whose gentle rustling is a joy to hear.

Gradually, however, an unaccountable uneasiness came over me. I felt that some kind of power – an occult power – was slowing me down, restraining me, preventing me from going any farther, pulling me back . . . I experienced the uncomfortable feeling that I ought to get home as quickly as possible – the sort of feeling you experience when you have left someone in the house who is ill, someone you love, and you have the sudden conviction that their illness has taken a turn for the worse.

So I came back, in spite of myself, convinced that as soon as I got back in the house I should find some bad news waiting for me, a letter or a telegram, perhaps. There was nothing like that, and I stood there feeling more surprised and more worried than if I had had another of these fantastic delusions.

August 8th. I spent an awful evening yesterday. He doesn't actually show himself now, but I can feel him near me, spying on me, staring at me, penetrating me, dominating me – and when he hides himself like this he is more frightening than if he were to draw attention to his continual invisible presence by using supernatural phenomena.

Even so, I managed to sleep.

August 9th. Nothing. But I'm afraid.

August 10th. Nothing. But what will happen tomorrow?

August 11th. Still nothing. I can't stay at home any longer with this fear and this attitude of mind taking possesion of me. I'm going to leave.

August 12th. Ten o'clock at night. The whole day I've been wanting to get off, but I can't. I've been wanting to perform this easy, straight-forward exercise of my freedom – just to go out and get into my carriage to drive to Rouen – but I've not been able to do it. Why?

August 13th. When you are afflicted by certain physical diseases all the springs of your physical being seem shattered, all the sources of energy reduced to nothing, all the muscles flabby; the bones seem as soft as flesh, and the flesh as fluid as water. This is the way I feel in my spiritual being, and it is all so strange and distressing. I don't seem to have any more strength, any courage, any control over myself, not even the ability to exercise my will-power. I can no longer will anything . . . But somebody else wills for me – and I obey!

August 14th. I am done for! Somebody else possesses my mind and controls all my movements, all my thoughts. I count for nothing now; I am no more than the enslaved and terrified spectator of everything I do. I want to go out – and I can't. *He* doesn't want me to. So I stay there, bewildered, trembling, sitting in my armchair, where he holds me fast. I just feel I would like to stand up or raise myself a little from the chair, so that I can prove to myself that I am still my own master. I can't do it! I seem riveted to my chair, and my chair seems glued to the floor, in such a way that no power on earth could possibly move us.

Then, all of a sudden, I have to go – *have* to, *have* to – down to the bottom of my garden to pick some strawberries and eat them! And off I go. I pick some strawberries and eat them. Oh, my God! My God! My God! . . . *Is* there a God? If there is a God, deliver me, Lord, rescue me, help me! Oh, forgive me! Take pity on me! Have mercy on me! Save me! Oh, what suffering! What torment! What horror!

August 15th. There's no doubt that this is exactly the way in which my poor cousin was possessed and dominated when she came to borrow five thousand francs from me. She was submitting to an alien will that had got inside her, like another soul, another parasitic, tyrannical soul. Is the world about to come to an end?

But who is he, this invisible, unknowable being who is controlling me, this prowler from some supernatural realm?

So invisible beings really do exist! Then why is it that, since the beginning of time, they have never manifested themselves as unmistakably as they are doing to me now? I have never read about anything in the least like what has been happening in my house. Oh, if only I could get away from this place, escape from here and never come back! I would be safe then . . . But I can't.

August 16th. Today I've been able to escape for a couple of hours, just like a prisoner who finds that the door of his dungeon has been accidentally left open. I felt that I had suddenly been made free, and that he had gone far away from me. I ordered my servants to harness the horses to my carriage as quickly as possible, and I drove to Rouen. Oh, what a joy it was to be able to say to a man: 'Drive to Rouen!' – and find that he obeyed me.

I told him to stop outside the library, and there I asked them to lend me the long treatise by Dr Hermann Herestauss on mysterious inhabitants of the ancient and modern world.

Then, just as I was getting back into my carriage, and was intending to say: 'Drive to the station!' I found myself shouting – not saying, but shouting, in a voice so loud that passers-by turned round: 'Drive me home!' Then, overwhelmed with anguish, I collapsed on to the cushions of the carriage-seat. So he had found me and taken me captive once again!

August 17th. Ah! What a night! What a night! And yet, in a sense, I suppose I ought to be glad. Until one o'clock in the morning I was reading a book. Hermann Herestauss, doctor of philosophy and theogony, has written an account of the history and the manifestations of all the invisible beings which haunt mankind or appear in dreams. He describes how they originate, the regions they inhabit, the power they possess. But not one of them is in the least like the thing which is haunting me.

From reading this book I have the impression that man, ever since he has had the ability to think, has had the foreboding that a new creature would appear, someone stronger than himself, who would be his successor on earth. And, feeling that his arrival was imminent, but not being able to see what form this new master would take, man has created, out of sheer terror, a whole race of imaginary occult beings, vague ghosts born of fear.

Well, having read this book until one o'clock in the morning, I went and sat down by the open window in order to cool my brow and my fevered brain in the tranquil night air.

The weather was very pleasant and mild. How I would have loved such a night if things had been different!

There was no moon. In the black depths of the sky the stars were glittering tremulously. Who inhabits those faraway worlds? What forms of life, what kinds of beings, what animals and plants live out there? And if there are thinking beings in those distant universes how much more do they know than we do? How much more can they do than we can? What things can they see which we do not even suspect? Just suppose that one of them were to travel through space one of these days and come to this earth to conquer it, rather like the Normans in the olden days crossing the sea to enslave weaker races! We are so feeble, so helpless, so ignorant, so tiny, we creatures on this whirling speck of mud and water . . .

With my mind occupied by thoughts like these I dozed off in the cool night air.

Now, when I had been asleep for about forty minutes I opened my eyes, and kept absolutely still. I had been wakened by some vague, strange feeling I couldn't account for. At first I saw nothing; then, suddenly, I thought I saw a page of the book – which I'd left open on my table – turn over, all by itself. Not a breath of air had come in through my window. Puzzled, I sat and waited. About four minutes later I saw – I really saw, saw with my own eyes – another page turn over and take its place on top of the previous one, just as if it had been turned over by a finger. My armchair was empty – or at any rate, seemed empty. But I knew full well that *he* was there, sitting in my place, reading my book.

With one furious leap, like that of some enraged beast turning to disembowel its tamer, I crossed the room to grab hold of him, throttle him and kill him! . . . But just before I reached my chair it fell over, as though someone had jumped up out of the way. The table rocked, the lamp fell off and went out, and the window slammed shut, just as if some burglar, taken by surprise, had grasped the shutters with both hands and rushed out into the darkness.

So he had run away! *He* had been frightened – frightened of me! Well, then . . . maybe tomorrow . . . or the day after . . . at any rate, some day or other, I shall be able to get hold of him, and pound him with my fists and squash him into the ground! Isn't it true that occasionally dogs turn on their masters and bite them , and tear out their throats?

August 18th. I've been thinking about it all day. Oh, yes! I'll obey him, all right. I'll comply with all his whims, carry out all his wishes, make myself humble, submissive, servile. He is stronger than I am, but one day, the hour will come.

August 19th. Now I know! I know the truth at last! I have just read this in the *Revue du Monde Scientifique*:

> A rather strange report has reached us from Rio de Janeiro. An outbreak of madness, a veritable epidemic of madness, similar to the infectious waves of insanity which attacked European populations in the Middle Ages, is raging at the present moment in the province of Sao Paulo. The panic-stricken inhabitants are leaving their homes, abandoning their villages and farms, claiming that they are being pursued, possesed and controlled, like human cattle, by beings who are invisible and yet tangible – vampires of some kind, which feed on them while they are asleep, and also drink water and milk, but apparently touch no other kind of food.
>
> Professor Don Pedro Henriquez, accompanied by several other distinguished medical authorities, has left for the province of Sao Paulo in order to make an on-the-spot investigation into the causes and symptoms of this strange madness, and to suggest to the Emperor the most suitable means of helping these hysterical people recover their sanity.

Ah, now I remember! I remember the handsome Brazilian three-master which sailed past my windows as it went up the Seine on May 8th. I thought her such a pretty, white, pleasant ship. The Being was on board, newly arrived from that place overseas where his race had originated. And he saw me! He saw my house, white like the ship – and he jumped ashore. Oh, my God!

Now I know. Now I can see what it means. The reign of humanity has come to an end.

He has arrived, the One awaited in terror by the primitive people of long ago, the One who used to be exorcized by anxious priests, the One summoned by witches in the gloom of night, even though he was still hidden from their eyes, the One to whom we, the apprehensive, temporary masters of the earth, attributed all kinds of monstrous or graceful forms – those of gnomes, spirits, genies, fairies, hobgoblins, and so on. Then, following these crude imaginings of primitive terror, men with greater insight have pictured him more accurately. Mesmer came very near to seeing him, and during the last ten years doctors have given a precise demonstration of the nature of his power, even before he made use of it himself. They have been playing with this weapon which belongs to the new lord of the world, the mastery of a mysterious will-power over the enslaved human soul. They have called it animal magnetism, hypnotism, suggestion – all kinds of things. I have seen them toying with this horrible power, like irresponsible children! Woe betide us! Woe betide man! He has arrived . . . The . . . the – what is his name? . . . the . . . it's just as though he is shouting his name to me, and I can't catch it . . . the . . . Yes! He's shouting it . . . Say it again! . . . the . . . Horla . . . I've got it! . . . the Horla . . . that's who he is . . . the Horla . . . the Horla is here!

Ah! The vulture has eaten the dove; the wolf has eaten the sheep; the lion has devoured the buffalo with his sharp-pointed horns; man has killed the lion with arrow, spear and gun . . . But the Horla is going to do to man just what man has done to the horse and to cattle: he is going to use him as his property, his servant, and his food – simply by exercising his will-power. Woe betide us!

And yet, sometimes an animal rebels and kills the one who has tamed it . . . That's what I want to do . . . and I shall manage it . . . provided I can get to know him, touch him and see him. Scientists tell us that an animal's eye is different from ours, that it doesn't see the same things as the human eye . . . And my own eyes cannot perceive the newcomer who is tyrannizing me.

Why? Ah! Now I remember what the monk said on Mont Saint-Michel: 'Can we see even a hundred-thousandth part of what actually exists? Take the wind, for example, the greatest force in nature: it can bowl men over, blow down their buildings, uproot trees, heap up the sea into mountains of water, break down the cliffs, toss great ships on to the reefs . . . This wind capable of killing, shrieking, moaning, roaring – have you ever seen it? Could you ever see it? And yet, there's no doubt that it exists.'

And further points occurred to me: for example, my eye is so weak, so defective, that it cannot even perceive solid bodies if they happen to be transparent – glass, for example. Suppose a sheet of plate-glass were placed across my path, my eye would cause me to bump into it just as a bird which has got into a room will bang its head against the window panes. What about the thousands of other things which deceive and mislead the eye? And what is there surprising about its inability to perceive a new kind of body through which light can pass?

A new being! And why not? Surely he was bound to come! Why should we be the last in all that has been created? Why is it that we can't see him, in the way that we can see all the other beings who were created before us? It's because his nature is nearer perfection, because his body is more delicate, and more complete than ours . . .

Why shouldn't there be one more order of creation? For that matter, why shouldn't there also appear new kinds of trees bearing gigantic, brilliant flowers whose scent would fill great tracts of countryside. And why shouldn't there be other elements besides fire, air, earth and water? There are supposed to be four, just four, of these basic sources of life. What a pitifully small number! Why shouldn't there be forty – four hundred – four thousand? How poor, miserly and wretched life seems – so mean and dull and clumsy. What grace can you see in an elephant, or a hippopotamus? What elegance is there in a camel?

But you may point out that I have forgotten such creatures as the butterfly. Ah, the butterfly – a winged flower! I can imagine a butterfly the size of a hundred universes, with wings whose shape, beauty, colour and movements I could not find words to describe. But I can picture it . . . it flies from star to star, leaving in the light, harmonious wind of its wake refreshment and fragrance! And the inhabitants of those worlds out there watch it pass by in an ecstasy of delight . . .

What's the matter with me? It's him, him – the Horla who is haunting me, filling my mind with these insane ideas! He is now deep within me, taking over my personality! . . . I will kill him!

August 20th. Yes, I will kill him! I've seen him now! Last night I sat down at my table and pretended to be completely absorbed in what I was writing. I knew very well that he would come and prowl round me, quite close to me, so close that I might be able to touch him and take hold of him. And then! Why, then I would have the strength of a desperate man! I would use my hands, my knees, my chest, my head, my teeth to strangle him, crush him, bite him, tear him to pieces!

And I sat there, lying in wait for him, with all my senses quivering with excitement.

I had lit my two lamps and the eight candles on my mantelpiece, as though, in this bright light, I imagined I might actually be able to see him.

In front of me stood my bed, an old oak four-poster; on my right was the fireplace; on my left was the door, which I had locked very carefully after leaving it open for a long time in order to entice him inside; behind me was a very tall wardrobe, with a full-length mirror which I used every day for shaving and getting dressed, and in which I had the habit of looking when I passed in front of it.

Well, I was sitting there pretending to write in order to deceive him, for *he* was spying on *me* too – when, all of a sudden, I sensed – indeed, I was certain – that he was reading over my shoulder, that he was there, almost brushing against my ear.

I stood up, with my arms outstretched, turning round so quickly that I nearly fell over . . . Now, with all those lights burning, my room was as well-lit as if it were broad daylight – and yet I couldn't see myself in the mirror! . . . It was clear, bright, filled to its depths with light! My reflection was simply not there . . . and yet I was standing right in front of it! I could see every inch of the tall expanse of glass, crystal-clear from top to bottom. And I stood there, staring at it with panic-stricken eyes. I hadn't the courage to take a step forward or to make any kind of movement, although I felt sure that he was there – this creature whose immaterial body had swallowed up my reflection – and I knew that he would escape me once again.

How terrified I was – absolutely terrified! Then, suddenly, I was astonished to see my reflection begin to form: it was all misty, as though I was seeing it through deep water – and I had the impression that this water was slowly moving away, from left to right, so that, second by second, my reflection gradually became clearer. It was like the passing of an eclipse. Whatever had been concealing me apparently had no sharply defined outline, but what I can only describe as an opaque transparency which was now clearing away little by little.

At last I was able to see my full reflection perfectly clearly, just as I can every day when I look in the mirror . . .

I had seen him! The terror of it is still with me, and I shudder every time I think about it.

August 21st. Kill him? How can I kill him if I can't get at him? Would poison be any use? No. He'd see me putting it in the water. In any case, would our poisons have any effect on his imperceptible body? No, of course not . . . Then what can I do? What can I do?

August 22nd. I have sent for a locksmith from Rouen, and I have got him to make me some iron shutters for my bedroom, the sort they have on the ground floor of big houses in Paris to keep out burglars. He's also going to make me one for the door, of the same type. It will look as though I'm a real coward – but what do I care!?

September 10th. Rouen, Hotel Continental. I've done it! I've done it! . . . But is he dead? I'm still terribly upset at what I've seen.

Yesterday, after the locksmith had fixed up the shutters on my window and door, I left them wide open until midnight, even though it was starting to get chilly.

All at once I knew he was there – and I was overcome with an insane feeling of delight. Very slowly I stood up, and began to walk around the room, so that he wouldn't suspect anything. Then I took off my boots, and casually put on my slippers. Next I closed the shutters on the window, and strolling over to the door in a leisurely manner, I shut that too, and locked it securely. I then went back to the window, fastened it with a padlock, and put the key in my pocket.

Suddenly, I realized that he was hovering round me, in a state of great agitation. Now it was *his* turn to be afraid, and he was ordering me to open the door for him. At first I thought I was going to give in to him – but I didn't. Instead, I stood with my back towards the door; then opened it a little, just wide enough for me to squeeze through the gap backwards. As I am very tall, my head almost touched the top of the frame. I was certain that he'd not been able to get out, and that I'd locked him in, all by himself! All by himself!

Marvellous! Now I had him! I ran downstairs and went into my drawing-room, which is just under the bedroom. I took my two big lamps and emptied the oil out of them all over the carpet and the furniture – everywhere. Then I set light to it, went out, double-locked the front door and got clear.

I went and hid at the bottom of the garden in a clump of laurel-bushes . . . What a long time it was taking! What a long time! Everything was black, silent, motionless. There was not the slightest breeze, not a star in the sky – only mountainous masses of unseen clouds which seemed to weigh so heavily on my heart.

I fixed my gaze on the house, and waited. What a long time it was taking! I was beginning to think that the fire had gone out – or that *he* had managed to put it out – when one of the downstairs windows burst open with the pressure of the blaze inside, and a tongue of flame, a great red and yellow tongue of flame, long, soft, caressing, leapt along the white wall of the house, licking it all the way up to the roof. A glow of light spread over the trees, along their branches and through their leaves, like a shudder of fear. The birds were waking; a dog started to howl; it was so light I felt as though dawn was breaking. Two more windows were shattered, and I saw that the whole of the lower storey of my house was now a terrifying, raging inferno.

But there was a scream! A horrible, piercing, heart-rending woman's scream rang out into the night. Two attic windows flew open! I had forgotten my servants! I saw their terror-stricken faces, and their arms frantically waving . . .

Sick with horror, I ran off towards the village, yelling: 'Help! Help! Fire! Fire!' I met people already on their way to the house, and I went back with them, to see what was happening.

By this time the house was one horrible, magnificent funeral-pyre, a monstrous funeral-pyre in which human beings were being burnt alive, and in which *he* was burning too – my prisoner, the new Being, the new Master, the Horla!

Suddenly, the whole roof fell in, and from between the walls flames shot up into the sky, as though from the mouth of a volcano. Through every window I could see the seething cauldron of fire, and I thought of him in there, in that fiery furnace, dead . . .

Dead? Possibly. But what about his body – his body which daylight could pass through? What if it could never be destroyed by the kind of thing which would destroy a human body?

Suppose he's not dead . . . Perhaps only time has any power over the Invisible Terror. Why should he have this transparent, incomprehensible body, this spirit-body, if he, too, must live in fear of disease, injuries, infirmities and premature death?

Premature death! All human terror comes from that! After man, the Horla. After the creature who may die on any day, at any hour, at any minute, through any little accident, there comes the one who will die only at his appointed time, when he has reached the limit of his existence!

No . . . No . . . there's not the slightest doubt about it, not the slightest doubt . . . He's not dead . . . Then . . . then . . . there's nothing left but to kill . . . *myself!*

The Devil

The peasant stood there facing the doctor, with the dying woman lying on the bed before them. The old mother was fully conscious, and she was looking calmly at the two men, perfectly resigned, listening to their conversation. She knew she was going to die. But it was something she accepted. Her time was up. She was ninety-two.

The July sunshine flooded in through the open door and window, casting hot rays over the uneven floor of brown earth which had been beaten hard by the clogs of four generations of peasants. Into the room gusts of a suffocatingly hot breeze carried the smell of the fields, the smell of grass, corn and leaves, all scorching in the noontide heat. The grasshoppers sounded as though they were chirping themselves hoarse, filling the countryside with a clear, crackling noise rather like that made by those toy wooden crickets which are sold at fairs.

The doctor was speaking in a louder voice now.

'Honoré,' he said, 'you can't leave your mother all on her own in the condition she's in. She could go at any moment.'

And the peasant, looking very upset, replied: 'But I've got to get mi corn in, yer know. It's been standin' in t' fields too long already. An' it's just t' weather for it, an' all. What do you think, Mother?'

The old woman who lay there dying was also tormented by the pangs of avarice, typical of Normandy, and so with a nod and a narrowing of her eyes she silently answered 'Yes', indicating that her son should go ahead and get in the corn, even if it meant leaving her to die all alone.

But the doctor became angry and, stamping his foot, he said:

'I tell you, Honoré, you're nothing but a brute! And I'll not allow you to do any such thing! Do you hear? If you've simply got to harvest your corn today, than you can damn well send for the Rapet woman and get her to look after your mother. I insist on it! Do you understand me? And I'll tell you this: if you don't do as I say, then when it's your turn to be ill I shall let you die like a dog. Understand?'

The peasant, a tall, lean, slow-moving fellow, was in a torment of indecision. Torn between his fear of the doctor and his passionate desire never to waste anything, he hesitated, started making calculations, then finally stammered out:

'How much does the Rapet woman charge for sitting up with people?'

'You don't expect *me* to know, do you?' shouted the doctor. 'It'll depend on how long you'll need her. Good Lord, man, you'll have to come to some arrangement with her. But I want you to get her here within the hour. Do you understand?'

'All right, I'll get 'er, I'll get 'er,' said Honoré, finally making his mind up. 'Don't be cross with me, doctor.'

'Well, just you watch out,' the doctor shouted as he left the house, 'because when *I* get annoyed, it's a serious matter!'

As soon as the doctor had gone the peasant turned towards his mother and said in a voice full of resignation:

'I'll go and find Mother Rapet, if it's what this doctor chap wants. Don't worry, I won't be long.'

And he went out of the house.

Mother Rapet was an old woman who earned her living by ironing clothes and by sitting up with the dead and the dying, both in the parish and the surrounding district. As soon as she had sewn her customers up in the sheet they would wear as a shroud for ever she would return to her task of ironing sheets for the living. Her face was as wrinkled as one of her last year's apples. She was spiteful, envious, and phenomenally mean and greedy. Always bent double, as though she had broken her back with the perpetual running of her iron over linen, you would have thought that she had developed a hideous, shameless passion for death-beds. Her only topic of conversation was the people she had seen dying, the various kinds of death throes she had witnessed. And she described them all in the most minute detail, never varying a single word, just in the way that a hunter describes how he has shot his game.

When Honoré Bontemps entered her cottage he found her busy preparing a tub of blue water for the collars she was washing for the village girls.

'Hello there, Mother Rapet,' he said. 'Everythin' all right, then?'

She turned her head to look at him, and said:

'Not so bad. How about you?'

'Oh, I'm all right. It's mi mother. She's not so good.'

'Your mother?'

'Aye, mi mother.'

'What's wrong with your mother?'

'She's breathin' 'er last, that's what's wrong with 'er.'

The old woman withdrew her hands from the water, and the blue-tinted, transparent drops trickled down her fingers to fall back into the tub.

Her interest suddenly aroused, she asked him:

'Is she as bad as that?'

'Doctor says she'll not last the night.'

'Ah, she's in a bad way, then.'

Honoré hesitated. He really needed to make some preliminary small-talk before getting round to the proposition he was going to put to her. But as he could not think of anything else to say he came straight to the point.

'How much will you charge me for sittin' up with 'er until the end? You know I've not got a lot o' money. Can't even afford to keep a single servant. It's that what's done for mi poor old mother – too much worry, too much work. She used to do the work of ten, even though she was ninety-two. You don't find women made o' that sort o' stuff nowadays!'

Mother Rapet answered him in very solemn tones:

'I've two different prices. For rich folks I charge forty sous a day and three francs a night. For ordinary folk I charge twenty sous a day and forty sous a night. You can 'ave it at the second price.'

But the peasant was thinking hard. He knew his mother's constitution. He knew how she clung to life and how tough and resilient she was. She could last another week, in spite of the doctor's opinion.

He replied very firmly:

'No. I'd rather you did it for a fixed price – one price for the whole job. I stand to lose by it just the same as you do. Doctor says she'll go any minute. If that 'appens, so much the better for you, so much the worse for me. But if she lasts until tomorrow – or even longer – then so much the better for me, and so much the worse for you!'

The death-bed attendant looked at him in surprise. She had never done her work by contract before. She hesitated, tempted by the notion of a little speculation. Then she suddenly became suspicious. Perhaps she was being tricked.

'I can't say until I've seen your mother,' she replied.

'Come an' see 'er, then,' said the peasant.

She dried her hands and followed him out of the cottage.

On the way they said nothing to each other. She trotted along and he kept up with her by taking great strides with his long legs, just as though he was stepping over roadside gutters.

The cows were lying in the fields, quite overcome by the heat. With an effort, they raised their heads and lowed feebly, as if to ask for some fresh grass from the two human beings who passed by.

As he came in sight of his house Honoré Bontemps muttered to himself:

'What if it were all over by now?'

And the tone of his voice indicated his unconscious hope that this should be the case.

The old woman was not dead. She was lying on her back in the curtained bed, with her hands resting on the bed-cover of purple calico. Her hands were horribly thin and bony, reminiscent of strange creatures – rather like crabs – and they were clenched and contorted as a result of rheumatism, hard work, the chores of almost a century.

Mother Rapet went up to the bed and took a good look at the dying woman. She felt her pulse, ran her fingers over her chest, listened to her breathing and asked her a few questions so she could hear how strong her voice was. Then, when she had gazed at her intently once again, she went out of the house, followed by Honoré. She had made up her mind: in her opinion the old woman wouldn't last the night.

'Well?' asked Honoré.

'Well. She'll last two days – maybe three. I'll charge you six francs for the whole job.'

'Six francs!' he exclaimed. 'Six francs! 'Ave yer lost yer senses? I tell you she's got five or six hours left – not a minute more!'

For a long time they engaged in a heated discussion. But as the old nurse was threatening to go back home, and as time was being wasted, and as his corn would not be harvested all by itself, he finally gave in.

'All right then,' he said. 'We'll call it six francs for the whole job. And that includes everythin', right up to the funeral.'

'Right, then. Six francs.'

Off he went, striding out in the direction of his fields where the reaped corn was lying under the oppressive sun which ripens harvests.

Mother Rapet went back into the house. She had brought plenty of work, because it was her custom when she sat by the bedside of the dying and the dead to keep on working, sometimes for herself, and sometimes for the patient's family, provided they paid her something extra.

Suddenly she said to the dying woman:

'Of course, I suppose you'll have received the Sacrament, Madame Bontemps.'

The old peasant moved her head to signify 'No'.

Mother Rapet, who was very religious, jumped up and exclaimed:

'Lord God Almighty! Would you credit it?! I must go and fetch the priest!'

And she ran to the vicarage in such haste that the urchins playing in the market place thought that something serious must have happened.

The priest came along straight away, wearing his surplice and accompanied by a choir-boy who walked in front of him ringing a little bell to announce that the Host was being carried through the calm and sweltering countryside. Men working in the distant fields took off their broad-brimmed hats and stood motionless until the white-clothed figure was lost from sight behind a farmhouse. Women who were gathering sheaves of corn stood to make the sign of the cross. Some black hens, frightened by the little procession, scurried along the ditches and disappeared into some favourite hiding-place. A foal, tethered in one of the meadows, took fright when he saw the surplice and started galloping round and round at the end of the rope, kicking up his heels. The choir-boy, dressed in his red cassock, walked very quickly, and the priest, wearing his square-shaped biretta, and with his head tilted to one side, was close behind him, mumbling prayers. Last of all came Mother Rapet, head bowed and almost bent double, as if to prostrate herself in prayer as she walked, and with her hands clasped just as if she was in church.

From a distance Honoré saw them passing by. He called out:
'Where's t' vicar going?'

His farmhand, who was quicker than he was, answered:
'He's takin' the Sacrament to yer mother, of course!'

Honoré showed no surprise at this.

'Aye, maybe 'e is,' he commented, and went on with his work.

Old Mother Bontemps made her confession, received absolution and took communion. Then the priest went away, leaving the two women alone in the suffocating cottage.

Mother Rapet now began to look closely at the dying woman, wondering if it would take long.

Daylight was fading. The air was cooler now, and a stronger draught came into the room, disturbing a cheap coloured print so that it flapped against the wall to which it was attached by a couple of pins. The little curtains across the window, once white, but now yellow and fly-spotted, fluttered as though they were trying to fly away, as though they were struggling to free themselves, like the old woman's soul.

Mother Bontemps lay there motionless, with her eyes open, apparently waiting with calm indifference for a death which was so near and yet so slow to arrive. She was taking short breaths now which made a kind of whistling sound in her constricted throat. Very soon her breathing would cease altogether, and there would be one woman less in the world, whom nobody would miss.

It was dark when Honoré got back home. Going up to the bed he saw that his mother was still alive and he asked her – exactly as he used to do when she was a little out of sorts:

'Feelin' any better?'

Then he told Mother Rapet she could go, adding:

'Tomorrow at five. Without fail.'

She replied that she would be there at five.

She was, in fact, there the next day at the crack of dawn. When she arrived Honoré was having a meal of soup before going out to the fields.

'Well,' she asked. 'Has your mother gone yet?'

He replied, giving her a sly look out of the corner of his eye:

'If anything, she's a bit better.' And off he went.

Mother Rapet, really worried now, went up to the dying woman, who looked in exactly the same state as the day before. She was lying there short of breath, but unconcerned, with her eyes wide open and her clenched fingers on the bedcover.

And the old nurse realized that it could go on for two days, four days – even a week. Her miserly heart felt the grip of fear and there rose within her a furious anger against this cunning fellow who had tricked her, and against this woman who refused to die.

Nevertheless she got on with her work and prepared to wait, with her eyes staring at the wrinkled face of Mother Bontemps.

Honoré came in for some lunch. He looked pleased. There was almost a look of mockery in his face. Then he went out again. It was certain now that he would get his harvest in under ideal conditions.

Mother Rapet was becoming exasperated. Each minute that slipped by seemed to her now like stolen time, like stolen money. She felt an insane desire to put her fingers round the throat of this wretched creature – this stubborn, unyielding old woman – and give the little squeeze that would put a stop to this quick, shallow breathing which was robbing her of her time and her money.

Then it occurred to her that this would be a risky thing to do. With quite a different idea forming in her mind she drew nearer to the bed – and asked this question:

'Have you seen the Devil yet?'

Madame Bontemps murmured that she had not.

Then her nurse began to chatter away, telling her stories calculated to terrify the enfeebled mind of this dying woman.

A few minutes before the end, she said, the Devil always appears to someone who is dying. He carries a broomstick in his hand; he has something like a cooking-pot on his head; and he utters loud yells. Once you've seen him, it's all over – there are only a few seconds left to live . . .

And she told her the names of all those she had sat with and to whom the Devil had appeared that very year. There was Joséphin Loisel, Eulalie Ratier, Sophie Padagnau, and Séraphine Grospied.

Madame Bontemps was calm no longer. She was becoming very agitated, fidgeting with her hands and trying to turn her head so she could peer into the dark corners of the room.

Suddenly Mother Rapet disappeared behind the curtains at the foot of the bed. From the wardrobe she took a sheet and wrapped it round herself. Then she picked up the cooking-pot and put it on her head, so that its three short, curved legs stuck up looking like three devil's horns. With her right hand she seized a broom, and with ther left hand she took a tin bucket and threw it into the air so that it would fall with a clatter.

It hit the floor, making a terrifying racket, and at that very moment she jumped onto a chair, pulled back the curtain at the foot of the bed, and stood there waving her arms about, uttering shrieks from inside the iron pot which covered her head, and like the demon in a Punch and Judy show she brandished her broomstick at the old peasant woman who was lying there on the brink of death.

Utterly bewildered, with an expression of insane terror on her face, the dying woman made a superhuman effort to raise herself and escape from the bed. She even managed to get her shoulders and chest out of the bedclothes. But it was too much for her, and she fell back with a deep sigh. It was all over.

Mother Rapet calmly put back the objects she had used – the broom in the corner, the sheet in the wardrobe, the cooking-pot in the hearth, the bucket on the shelf, the chair against the wall. Then, with professional dexterity, she closed the dead woman's great, staring eyes, placed a dish on the bed, poured into it some holy water, and dipped into this the sprig of boxwood which had been nailed over the chest of drawers. Then she got down on her knees and, with great fervour, began to recite the prayers for the dead, prayers which she knew by heart as a necessary part of her trade.

When Honoré came home that evening he found her still busy praying. Immediately he made a rapid calculation and realized that she had made a whole franc out of him, for she had only put in three days and one night, which came to five francs, instead of the six he had agreed to pay her.

Two Friends

Paris was under siege, in the grip of famine, at its last gasp. There were few sparrows on the roof-tops now, and even the sewers were losing some of their inhabitants. The fact is that people were eating anything they could get their hands on.

One bright January morning Monsieur Morissot was strolling dejectedly along one of the outer boulevards, with an empty stomach and his hands in the pockets of his old army trousers. He was a watchmaker by trade and a man who liked to make the most of his leisure. Suddenly, he came upon one of his close friends, and he stopped short. It was Monsieur Sauvage, whom he had got to know on fishing expeditions.

Every Sunday before the war it was Morissot's custom to set off at the crack of dawn with his bamboo rod in his hand and a tin box slung over his back. He would catch the Argenteuil train and get off at Colombes, from where he would walk to the island of Marante. The minute he reached this land of his dreams he would start to fish – and he would go on fishing till it got dark.

And it was here, every Sunday, that he met a tubby, jolly little man by the name of Sauvage. He was a haberdasher from the Rue Notre-Dame-de-Lorette, and as fanatical an angler as Morissot himself. They often spent half the day sitting side by side, rod in hand, with their feet dangling over the water. And they had become firm friends.

There were some days when they hardly spoke to each other. On other occasions they would chat all the time. But they understood each other perfectly without needing to exchange any words, because their tastes were so alike and their feelings identical.

On spring mornings at about ten o'clock, when the rejuvenated sun sent floating over the river that light mist which moves along with the current, warming the backs of the two enthusiastic fishermen with the welcome glow of a new season, Morissot would say to his neighbour:

'Ah! It's grand here, isn't it?'

And Monsieur Sauvage would reply:

'There's nothing I like better.'

This simple exchange of words was all that was needed for them to understand each other and confirm their mutual appreciation.

In the autumn towards the close of day, when the sky was blood-red and the water reflected strange shapes of scarlet clouds which reddened the whole river, and the glowing sun set the distant horizon ablaze, making the two friends look as though they were on fire, and touching with gold the russet leaves which were already trembling with a wintry shudder, Monsieur Sauvage would turn to Morissot with a smile and say:

'What a marvellous sight!'

And Morissot, equally taken up with the wonder of it all, but not taking his eyes off his float, would answer:

'It's better than walking down the boulevards, eh?'

As soon as the two friends had recognized each other they shook hands warmly, feeling quite emotional over the fact that they had come across each other in such different circumstances. Monsieur Sauvage gave a sigh and remarked:

'What a lot has happened since we last met!'

Morissot, in mournful tones, lamented:

'And what awful weather we've been having! This is the first fine day of the year.'

And, indeed, the sky was a cloudless blue, brilliant with light.

They started to walk on together side by side, pensive and melancholy. Then Morissot said:

'And what about those fishing trips, eh? *There's* something worth remembering!'

'When shall we be able to get back to it?' mused Monsieur Sauvage.

They went into a little café and drank a glass of absinthe. Then they resumed their stroll along the boulevards.

Morissot suddenly stopped and said:

'What about another glass of the green stuff, eh?'

'Just as you wish,' consented Monsieur Sauvage, and they went into a second bar.

When they came out they both felt very fuzzy, as people do when they drink alcohol on an empty stomach. The weather was very mild. A gentle breeze caressed their faces.

Monsieur Sauvage, who felt even more fuddled in this warm air, stopped and said:

'What about it, then? Shall we go?'

'Go where?'

'Fishing!'

'But where can we go?'

'To our island, of course. The French front-line is near Colombes. I know the colonel in command – fellow called Dumoulin. I'm sure we'd have no trouble in getting through.'

Morissot began to quiver with excitement.

'Right!' he said. 'I'm your man!'

And the two friends separated and went off to get their fishing tackle. An hour later they were striding down the main road together. They reached the villa in which the colonel had set up his headquarters. When he heard their request he smiled at their eccentric enthusiasm, but gave them permission. They set off once again, armed with an official pass.

They soon crossed the front-line, then went through Colombes, which had been evacuated, and now found themselves on the fringe of the area of vineyards which rise in terraces above the Seine. it was about eleven o'clock.

On the opposite bank they could see the village of Argenteuil which looked deserted and dead. The hills of Orgemont and Sannois dominated the horizon, and the great plain which stretches as far as Nanterre was empty, completely empty, with nothing to be seen but its leafless cherry trees and grey earth.

Pointing towards the high ground Monsieur Sauvage muttered:

'The Prussians are up there.'

And as the two friends gazed at the deserted countryside they felt almost paralysed by the sense of uneasiness which was creeping through them.

The Prussians! They had never so much as set eyes on them, but for four months now they had been aware of their presence on the outskirts of Paris, occupying part of France, looting, committing atrocities, reducing people to starvation . . . the invisible yet all-powerful Prussians. As they thought of them a kind of superstitious dread was added to their natural hatred for this unknown, victorious race.

'What if we should happen to run into some of them?' said Morissot nervously.

Monsieur Sauvage gave the sort of reply which showed that cheerful Parisian banter survived in spite of everything:

'Oh, we'll just offer them some nice fish to fry!'

Even so, they were so worried by the silence of the surrounding countryside that they hesitated about going any further.

It was Monsieur Sauvage who finally made up his mind.

'Come on!' he said. 'We'll go on – but we must keep a sharp look out!'

And they scrambled down the slope of one of the vineyards, bent double, crawling on their hands and knees, taking advantage of the cover afforded by the vines, keeping their eyes wide open and their ears on the alert.

All that now separated them from the riverbank was a strip of open ground. They ran across it and, as soon as they reached the river, they crouched amongst the dry rushes.

Morissot pressed his ear to the ground to see if he could detect the sound of marching feet. He could hear nothing. They were alone, competely alone.

They told each other there was nothing to worry about, and started to fish.

Opposite them the deserted island of Marante concealed them from the other bank. The little building which once housed the restaurant was closed and shuttered, and looked as though it had been abandoned for years.

It was Monsieur Sauvage who caught the first fish – a gudgeon. Morissot caught the second, and then, almost without a pause, they jerked up their rods time after time to find a little silvery creature wriggling away on the hook. This really was a miraculous draught of fishes.

They carefully placed each fish into a fine-meshed net which was suspended in the water at their feet. And as they did so they were overcome by a delightful sense of joy, the kind of joy you only experience when you resume something you really love after being deprived of it for a long time.

A kindly sun was shedding its warmth across their backs. They were so absorbed that they no longer heard, or thought, or paid the least attention to the outside world. What did anything matter now? They were fishing!

But suddenly, the bank beneath them shook with a dull rumble which seemed to come from underground.

The distant cannon were starting to fire again.

Morissot turned his head, and above the bank, over to the left, he saw the great bulk of Mont Valérien. On the mountainside was a white plume of smoke, showing where the gunpowder had just bellowed out.

Almost immediately another jet of smoke spurted from the fort on the summit, and a few seconds later the rumble of another detonation reached their ears.

Other cannon-shots followed, and every now and then the mountain spat out its deadly breath, exhaled its clouds of milky vapour, which rose slowly into the calm sky above.

'There they go again!' said Monsieur Sauvage with a shrug of his shoulders.

Morissot, who was anxiously watching the feather on his float as it bobbed up and down, was suddenly filled with the anger of a peace-loving man for these maniacs who indulge in fighting.

'They've got to be really stupid,' he growled, 'to go on killing each other like that!'

'They're worse than animals,' said Monsieur Sauvage.

Morissot, who had just caught another fish, called out:

'And it'll never be any different so long as we have governments!'

'Oh, no,' disagreed Monsieur Sauvage. 'The Republic would never have declared war . . .'

'Look!' interrupted Morissot. 'Under kings you have war against other countries. Under republican governments you have civil war.'

And they began to argue, in a calm and friendly way, sorting out all the world's great political problems with the commonsense approach of mild and reasonable men. On one point they were in absolute agreement: mankind would never be free. And as they talked Mont Valérien went thundering on without respite, demolishing French homes with its cannonades, pounding lives to dust, crushing human beings to pulp, putting an end to so many dreams, to so many long-awaited joys, so much long-expected happiness, tearing into the hearts of all those wives and daughters and mothers with pain and suffering that would never be eased.

'Such is life,' said Monsieur Sauvage.

'Better to call it death,' laughed Morissot.

But at that moment they both gave a start, scared by the feeling that somebody had been walking just behind them. They looked round and saw standing above them four men, four tall, bearded men, armed to the teeth, dressed like liveried footmen, with flat military caps on their heads – and rifles which they were pointing straight at the two friends.

The fishing rods dropped from their hands and went floating down the river.

In a matter of seconds they were seized, tied up, hustled along, thrown into a boat and carried across to the island.

Behind the building which they had thought deserted they saw a group of about twenty German soldiers.

A sort of hairy giant who was sitting astride a chair and smoking a large clay pipe asked them in excellent French:

'Well, messieurs, did the fishing go well?'

One of the soldiers placed at the officer's feet the net full of fish which he had been careful to bring along. The Prussian smiled and said:

'Well, well! I can see you didn't do badly at all! . . . But I have to deal with a very different matter. Now, listen to me carefully, and don't get alarmed . . . As far as I am concerned you are a couple of spies sent out here to keep an eye on me. I've caught you and I've every right to shoot you. You were obviously pretending to fish as a cover for your real purposes. It's too bad for you that you've fallen into my hands. But war is war . . . Now, since you've come out here past your own lines you're bound to have a password so you can get back. Just give me that password and I'll spare your lives.'

The two friends, ghastly pale, stood there side by side with their hands trembling. They said nothing.

'Nobody will ever get to know about it,' continued the officer. 'You will go back without any trouble, and the secret will go with you . . . If you refuse to cooperate, you'll die – straight away. So take your choice!'

They stood there motionless, keeping their mouths firmly shut.

The Prussian, who was still quite calm, pointed in the direction of the river and said:

'Just think! In five minutes you'll be at the bottom of that river. In five minutes! You must have families. Think of them!'

The rumbling of the cannon was still coming from Mont Valérien.

The two fishermen simply stood there, refusing to speak. The German now gave some orders in his own language. Then he moved his chair some distance away from the prisoners. Twelve men marched up and formed a line twenty yards from them with their rifles at their sides.

'I'll give you one minute to make up your minds,' called the officer. 'And not two seconds more.'

Then he jumped to his feet, went up to the two Fenchmen, took Morissot by the arm, and led him to one side. Then he said to him in a very low voice:

'Quick! Just let me have that password! Your friend won't know you've told.me. I'll make it look as though I've taken pity on you both.'

Morissot said nothing.

The Prussian then dragged Monsieur Sauvage to one side and made the same proposition to him.

Monsieur Sauvage said nothing.

So they were pushed together again, side by side.

It was then that Morissot happened to glance down at the net full of gudgeon which was lying in the grass a few yards away.

A ray of sunlight fell on the heap of glittering fish, which were still quivering with life. As he looked at them he felt a momentary weakness. In spite of his efforts to hold them back, tears filled his eyes.

'Farewell, Monsieur Sauvage,' he mumbled.

And Monsieur Sauvage replied:

'Farewell, Monsieur Morissot.'

They shook hands, trembling uncontrollably from head to foot.

'Fire!' shouted the officer.

Twelve shots range out simultaneously.

Monsieur Sauvage fell like a log onto his face. Morissot, who was taller, swayed, spun round, then collapsed on top of his friend, with his face staring up at the sky and the blood welling from where his coat had been burst open across his chest.

The German shouted out more orders. His men went off and came back with some lengths of rope and a few heavy stones which they fastened to the feet of the two bodies. Then they carried them to the riverbank.

All the time Mont Valérien continued to rumble, and now it was capped by a great mountain of smoke.

Two soldiers got hold of Morissot by the head and feet. Two others lifted up Monsieur Sauvage in the same way. The two bodies were swung violently backwards and forwards, then thrown with great force. They curved through the air, then plunged upright into the river, with the stones dragging them down, feet first.

The water spurted up, bubbled, swirled round, then grew calm again, with little waves rippling across to break against the bank. There was just a small amount of blood discolouring the surface.

The officer, still quite unperturbed, said, half aloud:

'Well, now it's the fishes' turn.'

As he was going back towards the building he noticed the net full of gudgeon lying in the grass. He picked it up, looked at the fish, then smiled, and called out:

'Wilhelm!'

A soldier came running up. He was wearing a white apron. The Prussian officer threw across to him the catch made by the two executed fishermen, and gave another order:

'Fry me these little creatures – straight away, while they're still alive.. They'll be delicious!'

Then he lit his pipe again.

Fear

After dinner we went up on deck. Before us lay the Mediterranean, shimmering with the tranquil reflection of the full moon. The big steamer was gliding along, sending up to the star-strewn sky a serpentine column of black smoke. And in our wake the water was ploughed up by the swift passage of the vessel and churned up by the propeller, and it foamed and writhed and emitted such brilliance that you would have thought that the moonlight itself was actually bubbling and boiling.

Six or seven of us stood there in silent admiration, gazing towards the distant shores of Africa, which was our destination. The captain, who had joined us to smoke an after-dinner cigar, suddenly resumed a conversation begun at the dinner-table.

'Yes, I knew what fear was that day. My ship lay for six hours with a rock through her hull and with the sea breaking over her. Forunately, towards evening we were sighted and picked up by, an English coal-ship.'

Then a man who had not yet spoken joined in the conversation. He was tall, sun-tanned, and serious-looking, the type of man you instinctively feel must have travelled through vast tracts of unexplored countries amidst constant danger, and whose steady eyes seem to retain in their depths something of the strange lands through which he has wandered – the sort of man you imagine will be steeped in courage.

'You say, Captain, that you knew what fear was. I don't believe it. You are mistaken both as to the term you used and the sensation you experienced. A strong, vigorous man has never any fear in the presence of actual danger. He may be excited, restless, and anxious, but fear is quite another matter.'

The captain laughed as he replied: 'Hang it all, man! I tell you, I really was scared!'

The bronze-faced man replied with deliberate slowness: 'Allow me to explain myself. Fear – and the boldest of men can experience fear – is a dreadful thing, an appalling sensation; it's as if your very soul were disintegrating; as if some frightful spasm convulsed the mind and heart. The mere recollection of it gives you a shudder of anguish. But a brave man never experiences fear at the prospect of facing an enemy, or when confronted by certain death, or any familiar form of danger. It comes upon him in certain abnormal conditions, when certain mysterious influences are at work, in the face of perils not clearly defined. Real fear has in it something of the memory of fantastic terrors of long ago. A man who believes in ghosts, and thinks he sees a phantom in the night, must experience fear in all its terrifying horror.

'About ten years ago I experienced real fear in broad daylight, and last winter it came upon me again, one December night. And yet I have often run risks and been very near to death. And I have seen a lot of fighting. I have been left for dead by bandits. I have been sentenced to be hanged as a rebel in America, and thrown into the sea from the deck of a ship of the coast of China. Each time I thought I was done for, but I immediately made my mind up to accept the situation without emotion, or even regret.

'But fear is a very different thing.

'I felt a first hint of it in Africa. And yet the North is its real home; the sun disperses it as though it were mist . . . This is an interesting point, gentlemen. Amongst Orientals life is of no account: they are immediately resigned to death. The clear eastern nights foster none of those gloomy forebodings which haunt the minds of those who dwell in cold countries. In the East there is such a thing as panic, but fear is unknown.

'Well, this is what happened to me over there in Africa.

'I was crossing the vast sandhills south of Ouargla, one of the strangest tracts of country in the world. You all know what the smooth level sands of a beach are like, running on and on, interminably. Well, picture in your minds the ocean itself turned to sand, in the middle of a hurricane. Imagine a silent tempest of motionless waves of yellow dust. They reach mountainous heights, irregular waves of all shapes and sizes, surging like the angry waters of the ocean, but vaster, and streaked like shot-silk. And the all-consuming southern sun, almost directly overhead, pours down its merciless flames on this raging sea, which nevertheless lies there silent and motionless. A journey across these waves of golden ash is one of continual ascent and descent, without a moment of respite or a vestige of shade. The horses gasp for breath and sink in up to their knees, and flounder down the slopes of these astonishing hills.

'Our party consisted of my friend and myself, with an escort of eight native soldiers or spahis, and four camels with their riders. Overcome with heat and fatigue, parched with thirst like the burning desert itself, we rode on in silence. Suddenly, one of our men gave a kind of cry.

Everyone halted; and we remained rooted to the spot, surprised by a phenomenon which, though familiar to travellers in those God-forsaken parts, has never been explained.

'From somewhere near at hand, but in a direction difficult to determine, there came the roll of a drum, the mysterious drum of the sandhills. Its beating was distinct, sometimes loud, sometimes soft, sometimes dying away, and then starting its fantastic rolling again.

'The Arabs looked at one another in horror, and one of them said in his own tongue: "Death is upon us!"

'And suddenly, as he spoke, my companion, my friend, who was almost like a brother to me, fell headlong from his horse, struck down by an attack of sunstroke.

'For two hours, while I laboured in vain to save his life, that mysterious drum filled my ears with its monotonous, intermittent, incomprehensible throbbing. And I felt fear, real fear, ghastly fear, creep into my bones, as I gazed at the body of the man I loved, there in that sun-baked hollow, between four sandhills, six hundred miles from the nearest French settlement, with that rapid, mysterious drumming echoing in our ears.

'That day I understood what it meant to be afraid. I understood even better on another occasion.'

The captain interrupted the story-teller: 'Excuse me, monsieur, but what was the explanation of the drumming?'

'I don't know,' the traveller replied, 'nobody knows. Officers who know the area and who have often been startled by this peculiar sound, are generally of the opinion that it is caused by sand scudding before the wind and brushing against tufts of dry grass, the echo being tremendously amplified and multiplied by the sand-dunes. It has been observed that the phenomenon always occurs where there are small plants scorched by the sun and hard as parchment. According to this theory, the drum was simply a sort of mirage of sound, that's all. But I didn't learn this till later.

'Let me tell you about my second experience.

'It was last winter in a forest in the north-east of France. The sky was so overcast that night fell two hours earlier than usual. My guide was a peasant, who walked beside me along a very narrow path beneath arching fir trees, through which the wind was howling. Above the tree-tops I saw the clouds scurrying past in wild confusion, as if fleeing in dismay and terror. Now and then, struck by a furious squall, the whole forest would sway in one direction and groan as if in pain. In spite of my rapid pace and my thick clothes, I was perishing with cold.

'We were to eat and sleep at the house of a forest-ranger which was now not far away. I was going to stay there to do some hunting.

'Occasionally my guide would look up and mutter:"Miserable weather!"

'Then he talked about the family with whom we were to stay. The father had killed a poacher two years before, and ever since he had seemed depressed as if haunted by the memory. His two married sons lived with him.

'The darkness was intense. I could see nothing before me or around me, and the branches of the trees, clashing together, filled the night with a ceaseless uproar. At last I saw a light, and my companion was soon knocking at a door. Shrill cries of women answered us. Then a man's choking voice asked! "Who's there?"

'My guide gave his name, and we entered. It was a scene I shall never forget.

'A white-haired old man with a wild gleam in his eyes stood waiting for us in the middle of the kitchen, with a loaded gun in his hand, while two tall lads, armed with axes, guarded the door. In the dark corners of the room I could make out two women kneeling, with their faces hidden against the wall.

'We explained why we had come. The old man replaced his weapon against the wall, and ordered my room to be got ready. As the women did not stir, he said to me abruptly: "You see, monsieur, two years ago tonight I killed a man. Last year he appeared and called me. I expect him to come again tonight."

'And he added in a tone which made me smile: "So we are rather uneasy."

'I did what I could to reassure him, and felt glad that I had come that particular evening, when I could see this curious display of superstitious terror. I told them stories, and more or less succeeded in calming them all down.

'By the fire lay an old dog, asleep with his head on his paws. He was nearly blind, and had a lot of whiskers – the sort of dog that reminds you of somebody you know.

'Outside the fierce storm was beating against the little house, and through a small square window, a sort of peep-hole near the door, I suddenly saw in a flash of vivid lightning a confused mass of trees, tossed about by the wind.

'In spite of my efforts, I realized these people were in the grip of some deep-rooted terror. Whenever I stopped talking, every ear was straining into the distance. Becoming tired of watching this silly exhibtion of fear, I was about to ask them if I could go to bed, when the old forest-ranger suddenly jumped up from his chair, seized his gun again, and stammered in a crazy voice: "There he is! There he is! I can hear him."

'The two women fell on their knees again in the corner and hid their faces, and the sons picked up their axes. I was preparing to make another attempt to calm them when the sleeping dog suddenly woke up, raised its head and stretched its neck and, looking into the fire with its almost sightless eyes, gave one of those melancholy howls which startle travellers who are going through the countryside at night. All eyes turned towards the dog. It stood there perfectly rigid, as if it had seen a ghost. And it began to howl again at something invisible, something unknown and, to judge from its bristling coat, something that terrified it.

'Pale with fear, the forest-ranger cried out: "He can scent him! He can scent him! He was with me when I killed him."

'And the two distracted women began to mingle their howls with those of the dog.

'In spite of myself, a cold sudder ran down my spine. That dog, seeing some kind of apparition, in that place, at that hour of the night, in the midst of those terror-stricken people, was a frightening thing to witness.

'For a whole hour the dog went on howling without stirring from where it stood. It howled as if in the agony of a nightmare. And fear, appalling fear, came upon me. Fear of what? I have no idea. It was fear. That's all I can say.

'We remained there motionless, pale with the expectation of some dreadful sequel, with ears straining and hearts pounding, shaken by the slightest sound. And then the dog started to roam about the room sniffing at the walls, and whining incessantly. The animal was driving us mad! Suddenly the peasant who had been my guide seized the dog in a sort of paroxysm of angry terror and, opening a door which led into a small enclosed yard, threw the animal outside.

'Immediately the dog stopped whining, and we remained engulfed in silence, which was even more nerve-wracking.

'Suddenly we all gave a start. Something was creeping along the outer wall on the side nearest the forest. It brushed against the door and seemed to fumble there with hesitating touch. Then we heard nothing for two minutes, and it nearly drove us out of our minds. Then the thing returned, brushing against the wall as before, and it began to scratch on it lightly, like a child scratching with its fingernail. Suddenly a face appeared at the small window near the door – a white face with gleaming eyes, like those of a wild beast. And from its mouth came a vague sound like a plaintive moan.

'There was a tremendous explosion in the kitchen. The old forest-ranger had fired his gun. Immediately the two sons rushed to block up the window with a big table, which they reinforced with the sideboard.

'And I assure you that, at that unexpected bang from the gun, I was filled with such an agony of heart and soul and body, that I was ready to faint, ready to die with fear.

'We stayed there till dawn, unable to stir or utter a word, in the grip of an indescribable state of terror.

'No one ventured to move the barricade till we saw, through a chink in the shutter, a slender ray of daylight.

'At the foot of the wall, close against the door, lay the old dog, its mouth smashed by a bullet. He had got out of the yard by digging a hole under the fence.'

The man with the sun-bronzed face stopped speaking. Then he added: 'You know, that night I was in no danger whatever. But I would rather re-live all the occasions when I have faced the most terrible perils than go through that single moment when the gun was fired at that hairy face at the window.'

The Hand

They had gathered in a circle round Monsieur Bermutier, the magistrate, who was expressing his opinion of the mysterious Saint-Cloud affair. For a whole month this inexplicable crime had been the talk of all Paris. Nobody could make head or tail of it.

Standing with his back to the fireplace, Monsieur Bermutier was talking away, marshalling evidence, discussing the various theories, but not reaching any conclusion.

Several women had got up and drawn nearer. They stood round him, their eyes fixed on the magistrate's clean-shaven lips which were uttering such solemn words. They shuddered and trembled, thrilled by that combination of fear and curiosity, that eager and insatiable love of being frightened, which haunts the minds of women, and torments them like a hunger.

There was a moment of silence. Then one of them, paler than the others, said: 'It's terrifying! It seems like something supernatural. We shall never get to the bottom of it.'

The magistrate turned towards her.

'Yes, madame. We probably never shall. But as for this word "supernatural" that you've just used, it doesn't apply in this case. We are dealing with a crime that was so cleverly thought out – and so cleverly carried out – so thoroughly wrapped up in mystery, that we cannot disentangle it from the baffling circumstances which surround it. But I once had to deal with a case which really *did* seem to have something supernatural about it. We had to abandon it, as a matter of fact, because there was simply no way of clearing it up.'

Several of the women-folk suddenly exclaimed, all at the same time: 'Oh, *do* tell us about it!'

Monsieur Bermutier smiled the serious smile which befits an investigating magistrate, and went on:

Now you mustn't imagine for a moment that I personally give a supernatural explanation to anything in this story. I believe only in natural causes. It would be much better if we simply used the word 'inexplicable' instead of the word 'supernatural' to describe what we do not understand. In any case, in the affair I am going to tell you about it was the circumstances which led up to it which I found so fascinating. At any rate, here are the facts . . .

At that time I was the investigating magistrate in Ajaccio, a little white town situated in a wonderful bay in Corsica, surrounded on all sides by high mountains.

My particular job there was the investigation of vendettas. Some of them are sublime, ferocious, heroic, incredibly dramatic. In them you come across the finest stories of revenge imaginable, hatreds that have lasted for centuries – dying down for a while, but never extinguished – detestable trickery, murders amounting to massacre and almost becoming something they take a pride in. For two years I had heard talk of nothing else but the price of blood, and this terrible Corsican tradition which compels a man who has been wronged to take his revenge on the man who has wronged him, and on his descendants and relations. I have seen old men, children, cousins – all slaughtered. I used to have my mind filled with incidents of this kind.

Now, one day I heard that an Englishman had just rented a little villa at the far end of the bay – and had taken a lease for several years. He had brought with him a French manservant he had taken into his service whilst passing through Marseilles.

Soon everybody was taking an interest in this strange character who lived alone, and never went out, except to go hunting and fishing. He never spoke to anybody, never came into town, and every morning he would spend an hour or two in shooting-practice, with pistol and rifle.

Legends began to grow round him. It was claimed that he was a person of some importance who had fled his homeland for political reasons. Then people asserted that he was in hiding because he had committed some dreadful crime. They even supplied particularly horrible details.

In my official capacity I tried to obtain some information about this man, but I found it impossible to learn anything – except that he called himself Sir John Rowell.

So I had to remain content with keeping a close watch on him – though, in fact, I had never received reports of anything suspicious concerning him.

However, as the rumours grew worse and became more widespread, I made up my mind to see this stranger for myself, and I started to make regular shooting expeditions in the neighbourhood of his property.

It was a long time before I had my opportunity, but at last it presented itself in the form of a partridge which I shot at and killed, right under the Englishman's nose, as it were. My dog brought the bird to me, but I took it straight away to Sir John Rowell and asked him to accept it, at the same time apologizing for having disturbed him with my shooting.

He was a big man with red hair and a red beard, tall and broad-shouldered, a sort of calm, well-mannered giant. He had none of the so-called British stiffness, and he thanked me warmly for being so civil, speaking with a strong English accent. During the following month we chatted together five or six times.

Then one evening, as I was passing his gate, I saw him smoking his pipe, sitting astride a chair in the garden. I greeted him, and he invited me into the garden to drink a glass of beer. I didn't need asking twice!

He received me with all the meticulous courtesy typical of the English, was full of praise for France and Corsica and said, in very bad French, how fond he was of '*cette* pays' (this country) and '*cette* rivage' (this stretch of coast).

Then I began to inquire about his past life and his plans for the future, asking my questions very tactfully and making a show of genuine interest in his affairs. He replied without any sign of embarrassment, and told me that he had travelled a good deal in Africa, India and America. He added, with a laugh: 'I've had plenty of adventures. I have indeed!'

When I brought the conversation back to the subject of hunting he began to tell me all sorts of interesting things about the hunting of hippos, tigers, elephants – and even gorillas.

'Those are all fearful brutes,' I said.

'Oh, no!' he said, with a smile. 'The worst brute of all is man!' And he gave the hearty laugh of a big, genial Englishman, then he added: 'I've often hunted man, too.'

Then he began to talk about guns and he invited me to come into the house and see the various types of guns he had.

His drawing-room was draped in black – black silk, embroidered with big golden flowers which were scattered over the sombre material, gleaming like flames.

'This silk is from Japan,' he said.

But in the middle of the largest panel a strange object attracted my attention: it was black and stood out clearly against a square of red velvet. I went up to it. It was a hand, a human hand – not the hand of a skeleton, all white and clean, but a black, withered hand, with yellow nails, exposed muscles, and with traces of congealed blood, looking like dirt. The bones had been chopped off at about the middle of the fore-arm, as though they had been severed by an axe.

An enormous iron chain was riveted and welded into the wrist of this filthy limb, and at the other end was attached to the wall by a ring strong enough to hold an elephant.

I asked him: 'What's that?'

The Englishman calmly replied: 'That's my worst enemy. It came from America. It was chopped off with a sabre, skinned with a sharp bit of stone, and then dried in the sun for a week. And a damn good job it was, too!'

I touched this human relic. It must have belonged to a man of gigantic size. The fingers, which were abnormally long, were held in place by enormous tendons which had fragments of skin still clinging to them. The hand – flayed like this – was a frightening thing to see. You could not help thinking that it was the result of some barbaric act of vengeance.

I remarked: 'This man must have been very strong.'

The Englishman replied in a gentle voice: 'Oh yes. But I was stronger than he was. I fixed that chain on his hand to prevent it from escaping.'

I thought he must be joking, so I said: 'That chain won't be much use now. The hand won't run away!'

Sir John Rowell then said in a very serious voice: 'It's *always* trying to get away. That chain is necessary.'

I took a quick glance at his face, saying to myself: 'Is the fellow a madman – or a practical joker?'

But his face remained inscrutable, with its placid, benevolent expression. So I changed the subject and began to admire his guns.

I noticed, however, that three loaded revolvers had been placed on various items of furniture, as if this man were living in constant fear of being attacked.

I made several more visits to his home, and then I stopped going there. We had become accustomed to his presence, and people now paid little attention to him.

A whole year went by. Then, one morning, towards the end of November, my servant woke me with the news that Sir John Rowell had been murdered during the night.

Half an hour later I was entering the Englishman's house along with the chief magistrate and the captain of the local police. Sir John's manservant, bewildered and in despair, was standing at the door in tears. At first I suspected this man – but he turned out to be innocent. We never did discover who the murderer was.

When I entered Sir John's drawing-room the first thing I saw was the corpse lying on its back in the middle of the room.

His waistcoat had been torn; a sleeve of his jacket had been ripped away; everything pointed to the fact that a terrible struggle had taken place.

The Englishman had been choked to death! His face was black and swollen – a terrifying sight – and the expression on it suggested that he had experienced the most appalling horror. There was something between his tightly clenched teeth, and in his neck, which was covered with blood, there were five puncture-marks. They looked as though they had been made by fingers of iron.

A doctor arrived. He spent a long time examining the imprints of the fingers in the flesh, and then came out with the strange remark: 'You'd think he'd been strangled by a skeleton!'

A shudder ran down my spine, and immediately I looked at the place on the wall where I had previously seen the horrible flayed hand. It was no longer there. The broken chain was hanging down.

Then I bent over the corpse. In his twisted mouth I found one of the fingers of the missing hand. It had been cut off – or rather sawn off – by the dead man's teeth, exactly at the second joint.

We got on with our investigations. But we could discover nothing. No door or window had been forced, nothing had been broken into. The two guard-dogs had not even wakened.

Very briefly, this is the statement made by the servant. He said that for the past month his master had seemed very upset. He had received a lot of letters which he had burnt as soon as they arrived. Often he had picked up a horse-whip and, in a display of anger which bordered on insanity, he had furiously beaten that withered hand, which had been riveted to the wall and which had, somehow or other, been removed at the very hour the crime was committed. Sir John used to go to bed very late, and he would carefully lock all the doors and windows. He always kept fire-arms within easy reach. Often, at night, he had been heard talking in a loud voice, as though he were quarrelling with someone . . .

On that particular night, as it happens, he had not made a sound, and it was only when he came to open the windows the next morning that the servant had found Sir John lying there, murdered. There was nobody this servant could think of as a suspect.

I told the magistrates and police officers everything I knew about the dead man, and the most detailed inquiries were made over the whole island. Nothing was discovered.

Now, one night, three months after the murder, I had a dreadful nightmare. I thought I saw the hand, that horrible hand, running like a scorpion, or a spider, all over the curtains and walls of my room. Three times I woke up, three times I fell asleep again, three times I saw that hideous human relic crawling rapidly round my bedroom, using its fingers as a creature uses its legs.

In the morning this hand was brought to me. They had found it in the cemetery, lying on Sir John's grave. He had been buried on the island because they had not been able to trace his family. The hand had the index-finger missing.

Well, ladies. There's my story. That's all I know.

The women who had been listening were horrified, and looked pale and trembling. One of them exclaimed: 'But that's not a proper ending! You haven't given us an explanation! We shall not be able to get to sleep tonight unless you tell us your opinion of what really happened.'

The magistrate gave his austere smile: 'Oh, ladies, I'm afraid I am going to deprive you of your nightmares! I simply think that the lawful owner of the hand was still alive, and that he came to get back his severed hand by using the one that remained. The only thing is, I just haven't been able to find out how he did it. It was obviously a sort of vendetta.'

One of the women murmured: 'No. That *can't* be the real explanation.' And the magistrate, still smiling, finally remarked: 'Well, I warned you my theory wouldn't satisfy you!'

Coco

The farm belonging to the Lucas family was known throughout the district as *la Métaire*. Nobody could have told you exactly why. The peasants probably associated it with the *métayage* system – the payment of rent in kind – and the name carried with it a feeling of wealth and prosperity, for this farm was certainly the largest, the richest and the most efficiently run in the whole district.

The farmyard was enormous and encircled by five rows of magnificent trees which sheltered the little, tender apple trees from the fierce winds which blew from the plain. Surrounding it were long buildings with tiled roofs which were used to store fodder and grain, fine cowsheds built in flint-hard stone, stables big enough for thirty horses, and a red-brick farm-dwelling which looked like a small château.

The manure heaps were always tidy, the watchdogs had kennels, and a multitude of poultry could be seen running amongst the tall grass.

Every day at noon fifteen persons – masters, farmhands and servants – all sat down at the long table in the kitchen, round a big earthenware tureen decorated with blue flowers, which was filled with steaming hot soup.

All the farm animals – horses, cows, pigs and sheep – were well fed and well looked after, and Maître Lucas, a tall man who was developing quite a paunch, used to make his round of inspection three times a day, to keep an eye on things and see that all was in order.

In a corner of the stables was a very old white horse, which they kept simply out of charity. The farmer's wife wanted to have him fed and looked after until he died of old age because she had reared him herself and had grown very attached to him – and many happy memories were associated with him.

This pensioned-off horse was looked after by a farm lad called Isidore Duval, known simply as Zidore. In the winter months he would give him is ration of oats and hay, and in the summer he was supposed to go four times a day to the hillside where the horse was tethered, and move him round so that he would have plenty of fresh grass to eat.

The animal was crippled with rheumatism, and it was with difficulty that he raised his heavy legs, which were swollen at the knees and just above the hoofs. His coat, which nobody ever groomed nowadays, looked as though it was made of white human hair, and very long lashes gave his eyes a sad expression.

When Zidore took him out to graze the horse moved so slowly that he had to pull hard on the rope, and the lad, bent double and panting away, used to curse and swear at him, exasperated that he had to look after such an old nag.

When the farmhands realized how furious Zidore was with Coco, they began to make fun of him and constantly teased him about the horse. His pals made jokes at his expense, and in the village they nicknamed him 'Coco-Zidore'.

The lad used to fume with anger, and he began to feel a growing desire to avenge himself on the old horse. He was a thin, long-legged boy, always very dirty, with a dense thatch of bristling reddish hair. He gave the impression that he was stupid, because he spoke with a stammer and a great deal of effort, as though ideas were very slow to form in his dull, brutish mind.

For a long time now he had not been able to understand why they kept Coco, and he was very indignant to see good food wasted on this useless creature. Since Coco had stopped working it seemed quite unfair to go on feeding him. He thought it a shocking thing to waste oats – oats which cost a lot of money – on this paralytic old dobbin. In spite of the strict instructions he had received from Maître Lucas he would often economize on the horse's food, giving him only half a measure of oats, and being very sparing with his straw and hay. And in the rudimentary mind of this lad there grew a hatred for the horse, the hatred of a greedy peasant, a cunning, ruthless, brutal, cowardly peasant . . .

When summer came round again he had to go and move the horse so that it could graze on different parts of the hillside. It was quite a distance. Every morning the lad became more and more furious as he plodded his way through the cornfields. The men who were out working used to call out to him in fun:

'Hello, there, Zidore! Give my kind regards to Coco!'

He never replied, but he would break off a long branch as he passed along the hedgerows, and when he had moved the stake to which the old horse was tethered, he would wait until he had started grazing again, then he would sneak up from behind and whip the back of his legs with the branch. The poor animal would try to run away, try to kick out, try to dodge the blows, and he would move round and round the stake to which he was tethered, like an animal in a circus ring. And the lad would run round after him, lashing out furiously, his teeth clenched in anger.

Then he would slowly walk away without looking round, whilst the horse watched him out of his senile eyes, with his bony flanks heaving, breathless from the exertion of having been made to trot. And he would never lower his bony white head to the grass until he had seen the young peasant's blue smock disappear from sight.

As the nights were warm now they let old Coco sleep out in the open, near the edge of the ravine, just beyond the wood. Zidore was the only one who went out to see him.

The boy now amused himself by throwing stones at him. He would sit down on the slope, about ten yards above him, and for as long as half an hour at a time he would keep throwing sharp-edged stones at the poor old dobbin, who stood there, tethered in front of his enemy, keeping his eyes on him all the time and never daring to start grazing again until he had gone.

One thought dominated the farm lad's mind: Why should he go on feeding this horse which no longer did any work? It seemed to him that this wretched old nag was stealing food which rightly belonged to others, stealing what belonged to men and what the Good Lord provided, stealing even from him, Zidore, who had to work for his living.

And so, gradually, day by day, the lad reduced the area on which the horse could graze, moving the wooden stake by shorter and shorter distances.

The animal was now starving, growing thin, wasting away. He was too weak to break his tether, so he stretched his head in an effort to reach the tall green grass which was gleaming in the sunlight, so close that he could smell its sweet scent – and yet just out of his reach.

But one morning Zidore had a better idea. He decided he would not move Coco at all. He had had as much as he could stand of walking all that way just to look after an old skeleton.

Nevertheless, he went out to see him – so he could enjoy his revenge. The poor creature stared at him anxiously. But on this particular day Zidore did not hit the horse. He simply strolled round and round him, hands in pockets. He even pretended he was going to change the position of the stake. But he banged it firmly back into exactly the same hole, and then he went off, delighted with his new trick.

When the horse saw him going away he neighed as though to call him back, but the farm lad broke into a run, leaving the old nag all alone in the little valley, securely tethered, without a single blade of grass within reach of his jaws.

Ravenous, he tried to reach the lush green pastures which he could only touch with the tip of his nostrils. He went down on his knees, craned his neck, and reached as far as he possibly could with his loose, frothing mouth. But it was no use.

During the whole of that day the old animal exhausted himself in useless, frantic efforts. He was tortured by the pangs of hunger, a torture made even more terrible by the sight of succulent green food stretching into the distance.

The farm lad did not come back at all that day. He was wandering through the woods, looking for birds' nests.

He turned up the following day. Coco, utterly worn out, was now lying on the ground. When he saw the boy he got up, thinking that perhaps he would at last be moved to a different place.

But the young peasant did not even touch the mallet used for moving the stake. Instead he came close, glared at the animal, and threw a clod of earth which crumbled when it struck his white old head. Then he walked away, whistling a tune.

The horse managed to say on his feet as long as the boy was in sight, then, knowing that it would be useless to attempt to reach the nearby grass, he lay down again on his side and closed his eyes.

The next day Zidore did not turn up.

When he came the following day and went up to Coco, who was still lying on his side, he saw that the horse was dead.

He stood there, looking down at him, very pleased with his achievement – even though he was surprised that it had happened so quickly. He poked the horse with his foot, then lifted up one of the animal's legs, let it drop again, and finally sat down on the carcass, staring at the grass for a while, his mind a blank.

When he returned to the farm he said nothing about what had happened because he wanted to make sure he would still be free to wander through the woods during the period when he was supposed to be looking after the horse.

He went out to see him the next day. As he approached, a few crows flew away from the carcass. Thousands of flies were crawling all over it, and buzzing round it.

When he got back to the farm he told them. As the animal was so old nobody was in the least suprised. The farmer said to two of his men:

'Get your spades. You'd better dig a hole and bury him just where he's lying.'

And the men buried the horse in the very place where he had died of hunger.

The grass there grew thick, lush and vigorous, fertilized by his poor old body.

The Mannerism

The diners were slowly entering the large hotel dining-room, and taking their places. The waiters began serving without undue haste in order to give the latecomers a chance, and so that they would not have to start serving dishes a second time. The experienced visitors to the spa, the ones who came here regularly to take the waters, and who were getting towards the end of their stay, were watching the door, looking with great interest each time it opened, hoping to see some new faces.

That is the chief form of entertainment in spa-towns. You look forward to dinner, when you can inspect the day's new arrivals, guess who they are, what they do, and what opinions they hold. A hope lingers in our minds, a hope that we shall meet somebody pleasant, make good friends, perhaps fall in love. In this bustling society neighbours and strangers take on a special significance. Curiosity is aroused, sympathy ready, sociability active.

Well, this particular evening, just as we did every other evening, we were wating for new faces to appear.

Two newcomers arrived, a man and a woman – father and daughter – but they were very unusual. They immediately reminded me of characters from the tales of Edgar Allan Poe, and yet they had charm, a kind of melancholy charm. They seemed to me to be victims of some misfortune. The man was very tall and thin, a little round-shouldered, with hair that was completely white – too white for his face, which was still young-looking. There was something grave in his bearing and in his person – that stern manner which Protestants have. The girl, who was perhaps about twenty-four or five, was short, very thin, too – and very pale, with a weary, tired-out, worn-out look about her. You sometimes meet people like this, who seem too weak for the tasks of everyday life – too weak to move about, to walk, to do all the ordinary things we do every day. She was quite pretty, this girl, pretty with a translucent, ghost-like beauty. She ate her food extremely slowly, as if she were almost incapable of moving her arms. She was obviously the one who had come to take the waters.

They were sitting opposite me, at the other side of the table, and

I noticed straight away that the father had a very curious mannerism, like that of a spastic.

Each time he wanted to reach something his hand would make a rapid swerving movement, a kind of uncontrolled zig-zag, before it could take what it wanted. After a few moments his spasmodic mannerism got on my nerves so much that I turned my head away, so as not to see it. I also noticed that the girl kept a glove on her left hand, all the time she was eating.

After dinner I went for a stroll in the grounds of the spa. We were in the little Auvergne watering-place of Châtel-Guyon, tucked away in a gorge at the foot of a high mountain-range, out of which flow many hot springs whose source is the deep core of extinct volcanoes. Over there, far above us, the *dômes*, peaks which are extinct craters, raised their stubby heads above the long range of mountains, for Châtel-Guyon is situated at the beginning of the *dôme* country.

It was very warm that evening. I was walking up and down the shady path on the hillock which overlooks the grounds, listening to the music from the casino, which had just started.

I noticed the father and daughter walking slowly in my direction. I said 'Good evening' to them in the way you do when you meet people from the same hotel in a spa. The man immediately stopped and asked: 'Could you possibly suggest a short walk, monsieur? A nice one that doesn't require too much effort, if possible. Forgive me for troubling you.'

I offered to take them to the valley where there was a stream, a deep valley forming a narrow gorge between craggy, wooded slopes. They accepted, and as we walked together we naturally began to talk about the virtue of spa water.

'Oh,' said the man, 'my daughter has a strange disease whose cause has baffled the doctors. She suffers from an unaccountable nervous condition. Sometimes they think she has heart disease, sometimes they think it's her liver, and sometimes they say it's her spinal cord. At the moment they put it down to some stomach condition – and that's why we are here. I personally think it's her nerves . . . Whatever it is, it's very distressing.'

I suddenly remembered the spastic mannerism of his hand and I asked: 'But isn't it hereditary? Haven't you a certain amount of nervous trouble yourself?'

Without showing any emotion he replied: 'Me? Oh, no. My nerves have always been very steady.'

Then suddenly after a moment of silence, he said: 'Oh, you're referring to the spasm I have each time I reach out with my hand. That is the result of a terrible experience I once had. Just imagine! This child here has been buried alive!'

All I could find to say was 'Ah!'. I was stunned with surprise, and rather moved.

He went on to tell me about it:

This is the story – quite a simple one, really. For some considerable time Juliette had been suffering from what seemed to be heart attacks. We believed her heart was seriously diseased, and we were prepared for the worst.

One day she was carried back into the house, cold, lifeless, dead. She had apparently collapsed in the garden a few moments before. The doctor certified that she was dead. I sat up with her corpse for two nights and a day. With my own hands I laid her in the coffin, and I went with it to the cemetery where it was placed in the family vault. This was in the heart of the country, in Lorraine.

At my request, she was buried wearing all her jewellery – bracelets, necklaces, rings – all presents she had received from me – and wearing her first party-dress.

You can easily imagine my state of mind when I got back home. She was all I had in the world; my wife had died a long time before . . . all on my own, half mad with grief, completely exhausted, I went up to my room and dropped into an armchair, incapable of thinking, too weak to move. I was no more than a wretched, quivering machine, a thing that had been skinned alive. My heart was like an open wound.

My old valet, Prosper, who had helped me to lay Juliette in her coffin and adorn her for her final sleep, silently entered the room and asked: 'Would monsieur like something to eat?'

I shook my head, but said nothing. He went on: 'Monsieur is wrong. You ought to look after yourself, monsieur. Would monsieur like me to help him to bed?'

'No,' I said. 'Just leave me.'

And my old servant went away.

How many hours passed I have no idea. Oh! what a night! What a night! It was cold; the fire in the big fireplace had gone out, and the wind, a bitterly cold winter wind, was hurling itself against the window-panes with sinister regularity.

How many hours went by? All I know is that I sat there, without sleeping, prostrate, overwhelmed, with my eyes wide open, my legs stretched out before me, my body limp and dead, my mind numb with despair. Suddenly there was a loud peal from the bell by the front-door in the entrance-hall.

I gave such a start that I heard the chair creak beneath me. The solemn, ponderous sound echoed through the empty château as if in a vault. I turned round to see what time it was by the big clock. It was two o'clock in the morning. Who could it possibly be at this hour?

The bell rang again, twice. It looked as though the servants were too frightened to get up and answer it. I took a candle and went downstairs. I was going to stop and call out: 'Who's there?' but I felt ashamed of such cowardice, and I slowly drew back the heavy bolts. My heart was pounding hard, for I was afraid. I opened the door abruptly, and I saw standing there in the darkness a white figure, like a ghost.

I reeled back, petrified with terror, stammering: 'Who . . . who . . . who . . . are you?'

A voice replied: 'Father – it's me.'

It was indeed my daughter. I really thought I had gone mad, and I retreated before this spectre as it came forward into the house. As I moved backwards I tried to ward it off, making that gesture with my hand which you noticed just now – and which has stayed with me as a nervous mannerism ever since.

The apparition spoke again. 'Don't be afraid, father. I was not dead . . . Somebody came to steal my rings, and to get them they cut off one of my fingers . . . The blood started to flow, and this has brought me round.'

And then I saw that she was, in fact, covered in blood. I fell down on my knees, choking, sobbing, gasping for breath.

Then, when I had regained a little self-control – though I was still too distraught to comprehend the terrible good fortune that had befallen me – I took her up to my room and got her to sit down in my armchair. Then I rang the bell urgently to summon Prosper, so he could light the fire again, fetch something for her to drink, and go to get help.

The man entered, stared at my daughter, opened his mouth in a gasp of fear and horror, then fell over on his back, stone-dead.

It was he who had opened the tomb, who had mutilated and then abandoned my child. He had not even bothered to put the coffin back into its recess in the vault, he was so sure that I would not suspect him, since I had always shown complete trust in him. So you see, monsieur, we've had a lot of misfortune.

Night had come, enveloping the little valley which now seemed so sad and lonely, and a sort of mysterious fear came over me in the presence of these strange beings – this dead girl returned from the grave, and the father with his alarming mannerism.

I could find nothing to say. I simply murmured: 'What a horrible thing to happen!'

Then, after a moment of silence, I added: 'What about going back? I think it's getting rather chilly.'

And we went back to the hotel.

The Madwoman

You know, talking about shooting woodcock (said Monsieur Mathieu d'Endolin) reminds me of a very unpleasant story from the Franco-Prussian war.

You know the house I have out at Cormeil. I was living there when the Prussians arrived.

At that time I had as my neighbour a woman who was more or less insanc. Her mind had given way as the result of a series of calamities. When she was twenty-five she had lost her father, her husband and her new-born child – all in the space of a single month . . . When death has once entered a house, it almost always pays a return visit: you have the feeling that it knows its way around.

The poor young woman, struck down by sorrow, took to her bed and was in a state of delirium for six weeks. Then a sort of calm lassitude followed this violent disturbance, and now she lay there motionless, hardly eating anything, and moving only her eyes. Each time anyone tried to make her get up, she screamed out as though they were trying to kill her. So they left her lying in the bed all the time, only taking her from between the sheets when it was necessary to wash her, change the bed-clothes and turn the mattress.

An old servant woman looked after her. Every now and then she would give her something to drink or get her to eat a little cold meat. What was going on within this anguished mind? Nobody ever knew, because she no longer spoke. Was she thinking of those who had died? Was she in a kind of melancholy daydream, without any precise recollection of what had happened to her? Or was her mind so stunned by grief that it was as still as a pool of stagnant water?

For fifteen years she stayed like this, withdrawn and inert.

The war broke out, and during the first few days of December the Prussians advanced as far as Cormeil.

I remember it as clearly as if it happened yesterday. It was freezing hard outside, and I was lying back in my armchair hardly able to move because of an attack of gout. I heard the heavy, rhythmic tread of their feet, and from my window I watched them marching by.

They went past in an apparently endless file, all looking exactly the same and marching with that puppet-like motion which is so typical of them. Then the officers billeted their men on the local inhabitants. I had to take in seventeen soldiers. My neighbour, the madwoman, had twelve of them, one of whom was a major – a real old soldier, brutal and surly.

For the first few days everything went smoothly. They had told this major that the lady who owned the house was ill, and he hardly seemed to bother about the fact. But soon this woman whom nobody ever saw began to get on his nerves. He made enquiries about the nature of her illness, and he was told that his hostess had taken to her bed fifteen years ago following a terrible calamity. He probably did not believe a word of this story, and he assumed that the poor insane woman was staying in bed out of pride, so she would not have to face the Prussians, or speak to them, or have any kind of contact with them.

He insisted that she should see him, and he was shown into her bedroom. He said to her in a very gruff manner:

'I ask you, madame, to get up and come downstairs so that everybody can see you.'

She looked at him with her vague and vacant eyes, but made no reply.

'I'll not stand any insolence,' he said. 'If you don't get up of your own accord, I'll soon find a way of getting you to walk on your own two feet!'

She did not make the slightest reaction or movement. It was as though she did not even see him.

He was becoming furious. This calm silence he took to be an indication of utter contempt. All he could do was add:

'If you've not come downstairs by tomorrow . . .'

And he left the room.

In the morning the old servant, in a state of panic, tried to dress the madwoman, but she started to scream and struggle. The officer immediately ran upstairs and the servant, throwing herself at his feet, cried out:

'She won't, monsieur! She won't! Forgive her. She's so unhappy!'

The soldier stood there, somewhat embarrassed. Angry though he was, he did not dare order his men to drag her out of bed. Then, suddenly, he started to laugh, and he gave some orders in German.

Soon a party of soldiers was seen coming out of the house carrying a mattress, just as they would carry a wounded man on a stretcher. In the bedclothes, which had not been disturbed, there lay the mad woman, still not speaking, calm and completely indifferent to what was going on, so long as they allowed her to lie there. A soldier walked behind them carrying a bundle of woman's clothes.

The officer rubbed his hands together and remarked:

'Now we'll see whether you can't get dressed by yourself, and take a nice little walk!'

And then the procession was seen to move off in the direction of the forest of Imauville.

Two hours later the soldiers came back without the madwoman. And she was never seen again. What had they done with her? Where had they taken her? Nobody every knew.

The snow now began to fall both night and day, covering the plain and the woods with a shroud of frozen foam. The wolves came and howled right outside our doors.

The thought of the woman who had disappeared began to haunt me, and I made several representations to the Prussian authorities, trying to get some information. I was so persistent that I nearly got myself shot by a firing squad.

Spring returned. The army of occupation withdrew. My neighbour's house remained shut, and the grass grew thickly in the garden paths.

The old servant woman had died during the winter, and nobody took any more interest in this affair. I alone thought about it constantly.

What had they done with this woman? Had she fled through the forest and escaped? Had she been picked up somewhere, and then been looked after in a hospital without anybody having been able to get any information out of her? Nothing happened to alleviate my anxiety, but gradually the passing of time eased the concern I felt for her.

Now, the following autumn woodcock flew over the district in great numbers, and as my gout was somewhat better, I managed to get as far as the forest to do some shooting. I had already shot four or five of these long-billed birds, when I hit one which fell into a ditch full of branches. So I had to go down into the ditch to recover the bird.

I found it, and saw that quite close to where it had fallen was a human skull. Immediately I thought of the madwoman, and the memory came to me like the blow of a clenched fist punching me in the chest. Lots of other people had no doubt perished in these woods during that dreadful year, but somehow or other I was certain, absolutely certain, I tell you, that I had stumbled upon the skull of that poor demented wretch.

And suddenly I understood what had happened, guessed the whole truth. They had simply abandoned her on that mattress in the cold and lonely forest. Loyal to her obsession she had allowed herself to die under the deep, light counterpane of snow, without so much as stirring an arm or a leg.

Then the wolves had devoured her. And the birds had made their nests from the fragments of her tattered bed.

I have kept this pitiful human skull – and I constantly pray that our sons may never see war again.

Mohammed-Fripouille

'Shall we have our coffee out on the roof?' asked the captain.

'Yes. By all means,' I replied.

The captain got up from his chair. It was already dark in the room, for it received its light only from the inner courtyard, as is usual in old Moorish houses. Half covering the lofty windows with pointed arches, creepers drooped down from the large roof-terrace where it was the custom to spend the warm summer evenings. The table had been cleared except for various kinds of fruit – the enormous fruit of Africa: grapes as big as plums, soft figs with purple flesh, yellow pears, long, plump bananas, and dates from Tougourt in a basket made from esparto grass.

The Moor who was waiting on us opened the door, and I started to climb the staircase whose sky-blue walls were lit up from above by the soft glow of sunset.

When I reached the terrace I breathed a deep sigh of contentment. We had a wonderful view of the port of Algiers and the whole roadstead and distant coastline.

The house which the captain had bought had previously been an Arab dwelling, and it was situated in the centre of the old part of the town, in the midst of those labyrinthine alleys which swarm with the strange, teeming population of the African coast.

Beneath us the flat, rectangular roofs went down like giant steps until they reached the sloping roof-tops of the European quarter. Beyond the latter we could see the masts of ships at anchor, and then the sea, the open sea, blue and calm under the calm, blue vault of heaven.

We lay back on straw mats, with our heads supported by cushions, and as I slowly sipped that delicious Algerian coffee I watched the stars come out one by one in the deepening blue of the sky. At that point they could only just be seen, and looked so far away, so faint, that it seemed as though they were not properly lit.

A gentle wave of warmth, as soft as the caress of a bird's wing, brushed against our skin. And occasionally we felt hotter, heavier gusts of air which seemed to carry a vague smell, the smell of Africa, and seemed like the close breath of the desert, coming to us from over the peaks of the Atlas Mountains.

'What a country, my dear fellow!' remarked the captain as he lay reclining on his mat. 'How sweet is life here! How delightful it is to relax here! It's a relaxation with a very special quality about it. How perfect these nights are for dreaming!'

I was still watching the stars appear. My interest in them was a little sleepy, but at the same time alert. I was enjoying a state of drowsy happiness.

'You know,' I said. 'You really ought to tell me something about your life out here.'

Captain Marret was one of the oldest officers in the French army in Africa. He was a soldier of fortune and had risen from the ranks where he served as a spahi, fighting his way up with the cut and thrust of his sword.

It was thanks to him – and to his contacts and friends – that I had been able to enjoy such a splendid trip through the Sahara, and that evening I had come to express my gratitude to him before returning to France.

'What sort of story would you like?' he asked. 'I've had so many adventures during my twelve years in the desert sand that it's difficult to think of any particular one that stands out from the rest.'

'Tell me something about Arab women,' I suggested.

He did not answer at first, but lay there with his arms folded back and his hands under his head. Now and then I caught a whiff of fragrance from his cigar, which was sending its thin column of smoke almost vertically into the still night air.

Suddenly he burst out laughing.

'Ah! Yes! I'll tell you about a curious experience that I had in my very earliest days out here.'

In those days we had in the African army some really extraordinary characters – the sort of men you never see nowadays, the sort we never seem to breed nowadays – characters that would have interested you so much that you might well have decided to spend the rest of your life in this country.

At that time I was just a spahi, a little infantryman, twenty years of age. I had fair hair, and a bit of a swagger, and I was strong and muscular, I can tell you, a real Algerian soldier. I was stationed at the military post at Boghar. You know Boghar, the place they call the balcony-window of the south. From the top of the fort you'll remember seeing the beginning of that burning stretch of desert, eroded, naked, tormented, strewn with reddish rocks. It would be true to describe it as the antechamber of the Sahara, the superb, blazing frontier of that immense extent of yellow wilderness.

Well, there were about forty of us spahis at Boghar, as well as a company from the African Battalion and a squadron of cavalry. One day we heard that the Ouled-Berghi tribe had murdered an English traveller who had somehow or other got into this territory – you know what adventurous devils the English are.

Somebody had to be brought to justice for this crime committed against a European, but the commanding officer was reluctant to send out a full punitive expedition, being of the opinion that the death of a solitary Englishman hardly justified such a movement of his troops.

Now, while he was discussing the matter with his captain and lieutenant, one of the sergeants who happened to be there to give a routine report suddenly volunteered to go and punish the tribe himself, with a squad of half-a-dozen men.

As you know, in southern Algeria the army is more free-and-easy than in the town garrisons, and there is a kind of comradeship between officers and men that you don't find anywhere else.

'You, my lad?' said the captain with a laugh.

'Yes, sir. And if you like, I'll bring back the whole tribe as prisoners.'

The commanding officer, who was no stickler for tradition, decided to take him at his word.

'Very well. You'll set out tomorrow morning with six men. You can pick them yourself. And if you don't keep your promise, woe betide you!'

The sergeant was smiling beneath his moustache.

'Don't worry, sir! My prisoners will be here by Wednesday noon at the very latest.'

This sergeant, who went by the name of Mohammed-Fripouille, was a really astonishing character. He was a Turk, a true-blooded Turk, who had enlisted in the French army after an obscure and chequered career. He had travelled all over the place – Greece, Asia Minor, Egypt, Palestine – and he must have left a trail of vicious crimes in his wake. He was a real *bashi-bazouk*, the typical Turkish mercenary. He was fearless, debauched, ferocious and cheerful, with the placid gaiety of an Oriental. And he was stout, extremely stout, yet was as nimble as a monkey, and also a marvellous horseman. His moustache was incredibly long and thick, and always vaguely reminded me of the crescent moon and scimitar. He hated the Arabs like poison, and he treated them with cunning, appalling cruelty, constantly thinking out new ways of tricking them, constantly performing terrible acts of cold-blooded treachery.

In addition to all this he was a man of prodigious strength and quite incredible bravery.

'Go and choose your men, my lad,' said the commanding officer. And I was one of those he picked. The gallant sergeant clearly had faith in me, and I became devoted to him body and soul, just because he had chosen me. I tell you, it gave me more pleasure than when I was awarded the *croix d'honneur* years later.

Well, we set out at dawn the next day. Just the seven of us. The other soldiers were real villains, the sort of gangsters and pirates who, having plundered and tramped through every land under the sun, end up by joining a foreign legion. At the time our army in Africa was full of ruffians like this – excellent soldiers, but utterly unscrupulous.

Mohammed had given us some lengths of rope to carry. We each had about ten of them, and they were about a metre long. In addition, because I was the youngest and lightest, he made me carry a huge coil of rope a hundred metres in length. When we asked him what he intended to do with all his bits of string he replied in his usual sly, unperturbed way:

'We're going to fish for Arabs.'

And he gave a wicked and knowing wink, a mannerism he had picked up from a Parisian who had once hunted in Africa.

He rode at the head of our little patrol, wearing the red turban he invariably wore when going out for some action. Beneath his enormous moustache we could see that he was grinning with sheer delight.

He really was a handsome fellow, this burly Turk, riding along with his great torso, his colossal shoulders, and his calm and collected manner. He was mounted on a sturdy white horse which was of average size, but which looked ten times too small for its massive rider.

We had just entered a little sandy ravine, full of stones and devoid of vegetation, which eventually enters the Chélif valley. We were talking about our expedition, and the conversation was in all kinds of foreign accents, for the group consisted of a Spaniard, two Greeks, an American and three Frenchmen. As for Mohammed-Fripouille, he rolled his 'r's in a way you wouldn't believe possible.

The sun – that terrible southern sun which is never experienced by anybody living north of the Mediterranean – was beating down on our backs, and we rode on at a walking-pace as is the custom in that sort of territory.

We rode for a whole day without seeing either a tree or a single

Arab. At about one o'clock in the afternoon we halted near a tiny
spring which trickled through the rocks. We ate the bread and dried
meat which we had in our haversacks, and then, after a rest of twenty
minutes, we set off again.

At last, round about six in the evening, after Mohammed had made
us take a long detour, we discovered a tribe of Arabs camped at the
other side of a small hill. The low, brown tents showed as dark patches
against the yellow ground and looked like big mushrooms sprouting
up at the base of the red, sun-baked hill.

It was the very tribe we were looking for. Their horses were grazing
a short distance away at the edge of a strip of dark green esparto grass.

'Charge!' ordered Mohammed, and we descended like a whirlwind
into the middle of the camp. The women, panic-stricken, with their
ragged white clothes fluttering about them, quickly retreated into their
canvas lairs, bending double to crawl in, shrieking like hunted animals.
The men, by contrast, appeared on all sides of us ready to defend
themselves.

We went straight for the tallest of the tents, the one that belonged
to the chieftain.

We kept our sabres in their scabbards, following the example of
Mohammed who made a strange sight as he galloped up to the tent.
He was sitting in the saddle bolt upright, not moving a muscle, with
the poor horse struggling frantically beneath him to carry his great
bulk. And the frantic activity of the horse contrasted strangely with
the statuesque calm of the heavily moustached rider.

The native chieftain came out of his tent just as we reached it. He
was a tall, thin, dark-skinned man, with glistening eyes set under a
bulging forehead and arching eyebrows.

'What do you want?' he shouted in Arabic.

Mohammed pulled up his horse with a jerk and answered him in
his own tongue.

'Was it you who killed the English traveller?'

The chieftain replied in a loud, clear voice:

'I don't have to submit to being questioned by you!'

All round us it seemed as if we could hear the rumble of a gathering
storm. Arabs were coming from all directions, were jostling us,
hemming us in, yelling furiously.

They had the look of birds of prey, with their large, curved noses,
their thin faces and prominent cheek-bones, their ample robes flapping
about them as they waved their arms in fierce gesticulation.

Mohammed was smiling. His turban was tilted to one side, and his eyes were gleaming with excitement. As I looked at him I distinctly saw his rather fleshy, sagging and wrinkled cheeks quiver with pleasure.

He spoke again, this time in a thunderous voice which silenced the surrounding clamour.

'Death to him who has caused death!'

He raised his revolver towards the chieftain's dark face. I saw a little puff of smoke come from the barrel. Then a pink froth of brain and blood spurted from a hole in the chieftain's forehead. As though struck down by lightning he fell over onto his back, flinging wide his arms, so that the billowing robes of his *burnous* opened like wings.

I tell you, the uproar that broke out all round us was so terrible that I thought my last hour had come.

Mohammed had unsheathed his sword, so we followed his example. Whirling the sabre round him like the arms of a windmill, he drove away the Arabs who were standing closest, and shouted:

'We'll spare the lives of those who surrender. Death to the others!'

And seizing the nearest Arab in his giant's grip he lifted him up, flung him across his saddle, started to tie his hands together, and yelled to the rest of us:

'Do exactly as I'm doing, and slaughter any man who resists.'

Within five minutes we had captured about twenty Arabs and tied them firmly by the wrists. Then we set off in pursuit of those who had run away, because the sight of our naked swords had created a tremendous panic. We brought back about another thirty of them.

All over the desert we could see fugitives clothed in white. It was the women, dragging along their children and uttering shrill cries of lamentation. The yellowish dogs, which looked like jackals, were barking all round us, baring their white fangs.

Mohammed, deliriously happy, leapt from his horse and, taking hold of the long rope I had carried, he called out:

'Pay attention, lads! First, I want two of you to dismount.'

Then he set about making a strange and terrible object: a necklace of prisoners, or rather a necklace of hanged men. He firmly bound the wrists of the first prisoner, then used the long rope to make a slip-knot round his neck. He then continued with the same rope, first tying the hands of the next prisoner, who stood behind, then making a slip-knot round his neck. Soon our fifty prisoners were tied one behind the other in such a way that if any one of them made the slightest attempt to escape he would strangle both himself and the man in front and behind him. The slightest movement could tighten the rope round their necks, and they would have to walk at a steady pace, keeping an exact distance from each other, otherwise they would have choked to death like hares in a noose.

When this curious task was complete Mohammed started to laugh that silent laugh of his: you could see his belly shake with mirth, but no sound came from his mouth.

'This,' he said, 'is the Arab Chain.'

When we saw the scared, pitiful expressions on the faces of the prisoners we also started shaking with laughter.

'Now, lads,' roared our leader, 'let's have a stake driven into the ground at the end of the chain, and the rope fastened to it.'

So we fixed a stake at each end of this string of captives, who were standing there like ghosts in their white robes, and keeping so still that they might have been turned into stone.

'And now for dinner,' announced the Turk.

We lit a fire and roasted a sheep, which we tore to pieces with our bare hands. Then we ate some dates we had found in the tents, and drank some milk which we also found there. We even picked up a few items of silver jewellery which the fugitives had left behind.

We were quietly finishing our meal when I noticed a strange multitude gathered on the hillside above the camp. It was entirely composed of the women who had run away a short while before. Now they were running down the slope towards us, and I pointed them out to Mohammed Fripouille. He gave a smile and said.

'Here comes the sweet course!'

Ah, yes! What a dessert we had at that dinner!

They came charging down on us like raving lunatics, showering volleys of stones upon us as they ran. And then we saw that they were armed with knives, tent-stakes and old pots and pans.

'Mount your horses!' shouted Mohammed – and only just in time. The onslaught was tremendous. They were determined to free the prisoners, and already were trying to cut the rope. Realizing the danger the Turk bellowed out in a furious voice:

'Use your sabres! Slaughter them! Slaughter them!'

Not one of us stirred. We were taken aback by an order of this kind, and we hesitated, reluctant to kill women. But single-handed, he rushed to deal with the mob of attackers.

All alone he charged into the midst of this ragged battalion of women. And he started to cut them down with his sabre, the swine, wielding his sword as though demented, and with such wild fury, with such passionate enthusiasm, that every time his arm swept down a white-robed body fell to the ground.

The mere sight of him inspired such terror that the women fled in a panic as quickly as they had arrived, leaving behind them a dozen dead and wounded, whose white robes were now stained with the red of their blood.

When Mohammed came back to us there was an expression of dismay on his face. He kept saying:

'Come on lads! Let's get out of here! Let's get out of here! They'll soon be back!'

And so we started our retreat, riding along very slowly, leading our string of prisoners, who were all half-paralysed with the fear of strangulation.

When we reached Boghar the next day it was just striking twelve as we came in with our chain of throttled men. Only six of them had died on the way, but we had frequently had to loosen the slip-knots along the whole length of the rope, for each jerky movement threatened to strangle a dozen prisoners at a single stroke . . .

The captain had finished his story. I made no comment. I was thinking about the strange country in which this kind of thing could happen. And I looked up into the black sky and gazed at the countless myriads of glittering stars.

The Blind Man

Why is it that the first real sunshine of the year seems so delightful? Why is it that we are filled with the sheer joy of being alive when this radiance is shed upon the earth? The sky is a cloudless blue, the countryside a perfect green, the houses gleaming white – and we look on with pleasure, drinking in these vivid colours which gladden our very souls. And we feel a sudden urge to start dancing, or running about, or to burst into song. Our thoughts become cheerful and light-hearted, and we experience such a feeling of universal friendliness that we could embrace the sun itself.

The blind men sitting on the doorsteps, impassive in their eternal darkness, remain as calm as ever in the midst of this new-found gaiety, and unaware of what is happening, they are for ever telling their frisky dogs to keep still. When they return home at the end of the day, if the young brother or little sister who is guiding them happens to remark: 'What a lovely day it's been!' they will reply: 'Yes, I could easily tell it was a lovely day because Loulou wouldn't keep to heel.'

I once knew a blind man like this, and his life was one of the most cruel martyrdoms you could possibly imagine.

He was a peasant, the son of a Normandy farmer. As long as his father and mother were alive he was looked after quite well, and he hardly knew any suffering except that caused by his dreadful affliction. But as soon as the old parents were both dead his appalling existence began. He was given a home by one of his sisters, and everybody on the farm treated him as a beggar who eats the bread which rightly belongs to others. They begrudged him his food at every meal he ate. They called him a layabout and a half-wit. And although his brother-in-law had taken possession of his share of the inheritance they provided his meals with great reluctance, giving him just sufficient to keep him from starving.

His face was very pale and his great white eyes looked like two of those circular wafers used for sealing letters. He remained unperturbed in spite of all the insults he received, and was so withdrawn that nobody knew whether he felt anything or not. Even before this period he had never known any real kindness: his mother had always browbeaten him and shown him hardly any affection, for amongst countryfolk those who cannot work are regarded as detrimental to the community and, if they could, peasants would cheerfully do as poultry do – and kill off the weak ones in the brood.

As soon as he had gobbled up his soup he would go and sit down – in the doorway in summer, by the fireside in winter – and never stir till bed-time. He never made a single gesture or any kind of movement, except that occasionally his eyelids, afflicted by some kind of nervous disease, would flicker over the white blotches which were his eyes. Did he have a mind, with coherent thoughts and a clear awareness of his life? Nobody was sufficiently interested to wonder whether he had or not.

For a few years this was how he existed. But his inability to do any kind of work, as well as his imperturbable, long-suffering nature, finally got on the nerves of his relatives. He now became the butt of cruel jokes, a sort of martyred buffoon, a kind of hunted animal preyed upon by the natural ferocity and savage gaiety of the brutes who surrounded him.

They thought up all kinds of cruel practical jokes for which his blindness made him an easy target. And so that they might get some sort of payment for the food he ate they turned his meals into feasts of fun for all the neighbours, and into hours of torment for the helpless wretch.

The peasants from all the surrounding farms would gather together for this entertainment. Details of what happened had spread from door to door, and now the kitchen was full of people every day. Sometimes, when the blind man was just about to dip his spoon into his soup, they would put a dog or a cat on the table, just in front of his plate. The animal would instinctively sense that the man was incapacitated and would very cautiously approach the plate, and eat away without making a sound, lapping up the soup with extreme delicacy – and when its tongue happened to make a somewhat louder noise and the poor devil's attention had been aroused, the animal would smartly jump out of the way to avoid being hit by the spoon with which the blind man struck out at random.

At this all the spectators who were crowded round the walls would burst out laughing, and they would nudge each other and stamp their feet with glee. As for him, he would never say a word, but would start eating again, with the spoon in his right hand and with his left hand held out to shield and defend his plate.

Sometimes they got him to eat corks, bits of wood, leaves, or even excrement, simply because he could not perceive what was being offered to him.

Then they even grew weary of the jokes, and his brother-in-law, furious that he constantly had to feed him, started hitting him and was for ever boxing him on the ears, and laughing at the blind man's futile attempts to ward off the blows or hit him back. So now they had a new game: the slapping game. The plough-boys, the farmhand and the servant girls would slap his face, time after time, and set his eyelids flickering rapidly. He could never find a hiding place, and he stood there with his arms continually outstretched trying to keep them away from him.

Finally, they forced him to go out and beg. They took him and made him stand on the roadside every market day. As soon as he heard the sound of approaching footsteps or the rumble of a cart he would hold out his hat and mutter the words: 'Your charity, if you please!'

But peasants are not lavish with their money and, for weeks on end, he never brought back a single copper.

Then they unleashed a torrent of merciless hatred against him. And here is the story of how he died . . .

It was during a winter when the countryside was covered with snow and there was a bitterly keen frost. Now, his brother-in-law had taken him a considerable distance away one morning and put him on a main road to make him beg for alms. He left him out there all day, and when it was dark he told everybody on the farm that he had not been able to find him.

'Anyway,' he added, 'we needn't bother about 'im. Somebody'll 'ave taken 'im in because 'e was cold. He won't 'ave got lost – that's for sure! He'll be back 'ere tomorrow, all right, guzzlin' 'is soup!'

The next day he did not come back.

After interminable hours of waiting, overwhelmed by the cold, and knowing that he was close to death, the blind man had started to walk. Unable to make out the road, which was buried under that frozen foam of snow, he had wandered on haphazardly, falling into ditches, climbing out again, never complaining, hoping he would find a house.

But the torpor of the snowy wastes had gradually entered his being, and since his weak legs could no longer carry him he had sat down in the middle of a field. He never got up again.

The white snowflakes were falling steadily, and soon he was buried beneath them. His stiffened body simply disappeared under their incessant accumulation, under this infinite multitude of tiny particles. And there was nothing now to indicate the presence of a corpse.

His relations made a show of making inquiries about him and of searching for him for a whole week. They even shed a few tears.

The winter was hard, and it was a long time before the thaw came. Then, one Sunday, when they were on their way to mass, the farmers noticed a great flock of carrion crows wheeling round and round, high above the plain. Then they swept down like a shower of black hail, descending in a heap onto a single spot, then rising into the sky only to swoop down again.

The following Sunday the sombre birds were still there. The sky was darkened by such a huge flock of them that it looked as though they had gathered there from every point of the compass. And with a tremendous clamour they kept swooping down into the dazzling snow, making curious black patterns against the white background as they persistently rummaged into it.

A farm lad went across to see what they were doing – and he discovered the body of the blind man, already half eaten away, torn to shreds. His white eyes had gone, pecked out by the long, voracious beaks . . .

And I can never experience the intense cheerfulness brought by the first sunshine of the year without a melancholy remembrance of that poor wretch, so utterly underprivileged in this life that his horrible death came as a relief to all who had known him.

At Sea

I recently came across the following item in the papers:

Boulogne-sur-Mer. 22 January.
A terrible disaster has just struck the population of this coastal area, which has already been so sorely tried during the past two years. The fishing boat commanded by Captain Javel was carried off its course in a westerly direction, just as it was entering the harbour, and was dashed against the rocks at the foot of the breakwater.

In spite of the efforts of the life-boat crew and the lines sent out by life-saving rockets, four men and the cabin-boy were lost.

The bad weather continues, and further disasters are feared.

Who was this Captain Javel? Could he be the brother of the man with one arm?

This poor fellow engulfed by the waves and perhaps killed under the shattered wreckage of his own ship — was he the Javel I am thinking of? If so, he was once involved in another tragedy at sea — a terrible but simple drama, like these tragedies at sea always are. It must have been about eighteen years ago . . .

In those days the elder of the two Javel brothers was the owner of a trawler.

Those trawlers are the ideal fishing boat. So sturdy that they can tackle any kind of weather, round-bellied, bobbing up and down on the waves like a cork, constantly out at sea, constantly lashed by the biting salt winds of the Channel, they tirelessly work the fishing-grounds, with their sails full and a great trawl-net trailing from the side, raking the sea-bed, detaching and gathering all the creatures dormant in the rocks — the flat fish hugging the sand, the ponderous crabs with their jagged claws, the lobsters with their bristling whiskers.

When the breeze is fresh and the waves choppy, the trawler begins to fish. Its net is fixed to a long iron-sheathed wooden rod which is lowered over the side by means of two cables running on two pulleys, one at each end of the boat. And the trawler, driven along by wind and tide, drags with it this tackle designed to ravage and plunder the bed of the sea.

As his crew, Javel had taken along his younger brother, four other men and a cabin-boy. He had set out from Boulogne on a fine, clear day, intending to start trawling. But soon the wind got up, and an unexpected squall drove the boat off its course. They came in sight of the English coast, but angry seas were pounding against the cliffs and breaking over the land, and it was quite impossible to get into any harbour. The little ship took to the open sea again and approached the French coast. The storm was still so bad that they could not risk approaching the break-waters, and the entrance to every harbour and haven was engulfed in foaming, roaring, dangerous waves.

The trawler set out onto the open sea again, riding on the waves, tossed, shaken, drenched, battered by heavy seas, but cheerful in spite of everything. She was, after all, quite accustomed to this kind of rough weather, which sometimes had kept her wandering about for five or six days between these two neighbouring countries, without being able to put into port in either of them.

Eventually the storm abated, and since they were out on the open sea the skipper ordered them to lower the trawl, even though the waves were still running high.

So the massive net was passed over the side and, with two men in the bows and two in the stern, they started to let the cables to which it was attached run over the pulleys. Suddenly the net touched the bottom, and at that very moment a great wave hit the boat, tilting it in the direction of the net. Javel's brother, who was in the bows supervising the lowering of the trawl, lost his balance, and his arm got caught between the wood of the pulley and the cable: the latter had slackened for a moment under the impact of the wave but had now tightened as the boat righted itself. Young Javel made a desperate attempt to ease the cable with his free hand, but the trawl was now being dragged along, and the rope was so taut that it would not budge.

Writhing in pain he cried out, and they all came running to his aid, including his brother who had been at the helm. They grabbed hold of the cable, struggling to slacken it in an attempt to free the arm it was crushing. It was hopeless.

'We'll 'ave to cut it,' said one of the sailors, and he produced a broad-bladed knife which in a couple of slashes could have saved young Javel's arm.

But cutting the rope would mean losing the trawl-net, and this trawl-net was worth a lot of money, something like fifteen hundred francs – and it belonged to Javel the elder, who took good care of his property. It was he who called out in an agonized voice:

'No! Don't cut it! Wait! I'll try to turn t'boat into t'wind.' And he ran to the helm and put all his weight against the wheel.

The boat hardly responded. It was held rigid by this great net and, in addition, it was being driven on a fixed course by the wind and the current.

By this time young Javel was on his knees. His teeth were clenched and his face was haggard, but he said nothing. His brother came back, still worried that one of the sailors might cut the rope:

'Wait a minute,' he said. 'Wait a minute! Don't cut it! We'll 'ave to drop anchor.'

They dropped the anchor which ran to the full extent of the chain. Then they began to heave at the capstan so they could slacken the cables holding the trawl-net. At last the rope eased sufficiently for them to free the lifeless arm which hung limply in its bloody, woollen sleeve.

Young Javel was staring idiotically before him. They took off his jersey and saw a horrible sight: there was a pulpy mass of flesh with the blood gushing from it in great spurts, just as though it were being driven out by a pump. The sailor looked at his arm and said:

'I'm done for!'

Then when they realized that the blood was coming out so fast that it was making a pool on the deck, one of the men shouted:

''E'll bleed to death! We must tie 'is arm.'

They got a piece of twine — a strong piece that was brown and tarred — and they fastened it round his arm above the injured part and pulled it as tight as they could. The spurting of blood gradually grew less, and finally stopped altogether.

Young Javel stood up, with his arm hanging at his side. He took hold of it with his other hand, lifted it up, moved it about, even shook it. Everything had been squashed and the bones completely broken: only the muscles kept this useless arm attached to the rest of his body. He looked at it gloomily and appeared to be deep in thought. Then he sat down on a heap of folded sail, and his shipmates told him he ought to keep wetting the injured part to prevent gangrene from developing.

They got a bucket of water and put it next to him. Every minute or so he dipped a glass into it and bathed the horrible wound by pouring onto it a thin, clear trickle of water.

'You'd feel better if you went below,' said his brother. He went below, but an hour later he was back on deck again; he had not felt so good all by himself — and besides, he preferred to be in the fresh air. So he sat down on the sail and once more started to bathe his arm.

The fishing was going well. Big white-bellied fish were lying next to him, threshing about in the throes of death. He watched them as he continued to sprinkle water on his arm that had been crushed to pulp.

Just as they were about to return to Boulogne, another strong wind got up, and the little fishing boat started off on its crazy course again, bouncing up and down and pitching about, tossing the wretched injured man.

Night came, and the sea remained rough until daybreak. When the sun rose they found themselves once again in sight of the English coast, but as the sea was a little calmer they made for France, beating into the wind.

Towards evening young Javel called his shipmates and showed them some traces of black, the sinister signs that gangrene had developed in the part of the limb which no longer belonged to him.

The sailors examined it, and each voiced his opinion.

'It could easily be t' Black Rot,' said one of them.

'I reckon it needs salt water pourin' on it,' declared another man.

They brought a bucket of sea water and poured it over the gangrenous arm. The injured man went ghastly pale, gritted his teeth and writhed in agony – but he did not cry out.

Then as soon as the burning pain caused by the salt water had faded a little, he said to his brother:

'Give me your knife.'

His brother handed his knife to him.

'Now just 'old mi arm up. That's it! Keep it straight – and pull on it.'

They did as he asked them.

Then he began to cut at it all by himself. He cut away gently, attentively, severing the remaining tendons with this razor-sharp knife, until soon he was left with just the stump of an arm. He gave a tremendous sigh and said:

'I 'ad to do that. Otherwise I'd 'ave been done for.'

He seemed relieved, and was now taking deep breaths. Once more he started to pour water onto the stump which remained.

That night the weather was rough again, and they still could not land.

When day broke young Javel picked up his severed arm and examined it for a long time. It looked as though putrefaction was setting in. The rest of the crew came up to look at it, and they passed it round, poking it, turning it over, sniffing at it.

The older brother said:

'I think it's time we chucked that overboard.'

But young Javel exclaimed angrily:

'No, you'll not! Not on your life! It belongs to me – don't it? It's *my* arm, and I'll do what I like with it!'

He took it back from them and put it down between his feet.

'Fair enough,' said the older brother, 'but it'll still go rotten.'

Then the injured man had an idea. When they were at sea for any length of time they used to preserve the fish by putting them into barrels of brine.

'I'll tell you what,' he said. 'It wouldn't go bad if we put it in brine.'

'Yes. That's an idea,' said the others.

So they emptied one of the barrels which was already filled with fish they had caught in the last day or two. They put the arm right at the bottom, poured salt over it, then one by one replaced the fish.

One of the sailors cracked a joke:

'We'd better make sure we don't auction it off in t' fish market!'

And everybody laughed – except the two Javel brothers.

The wind was still blowing hard, and though within sight of Boulogne, they had to beat windward until ten o'clock the next day. And all the time the injured man continued to pour water over the wound.

From time to time he would get up and walk from one end of the boat to the other.

Standing at the wheel, his brother watched him, shaking his head as he did so.

They finally got back to Boulogne.

A doctor examined the injury, and said it was healing well. He dressed and bandaged it, then told the patient to take a complete rest. But Javel refused to go to bed until he had got his arm back. As fast as he could he returned to the harbour and found the barrel, which he had carefully marked with a cross.

They emptied it while he watched, and he picked up his severed limb, which had been nicely preserved in the brine, though it was all wrinkled and looked curiously clean and fresh. He wrapped it in a towel which he had brought with him for the purpose, and went back home.

His wife and children spent a long time inspecting this object which had once been part of father. They handled the fingers, poking out crystals of salt which had got stuck under the nails. Then they asked a carpenter to make a tiny coffin for it.

The next day the full crew of the trawler joined the funeral procession behind the severed limb. In front walked the two brothers, side by side. Then came the parish sexton, carrying the corpse under his arm . . .

Young Javel never went back.to sea. He managed to get a job in the harbour,and in later years whenever he spoke about his accident, he would say in a very quiet voice, as though telling his listener something in confidence:

'You know, if my brother 'ad been willing to cut that trawl loose, I'd still 'ave my arm, that's for sure . . . But 'e wasn't one for partin' with 'is property.'

Apparition

They were talking about sequestration in connexion with a recent law-suit. It was at the close of a friendly gathering one evening in the rue de Grenelle, and each of them had told a story – a story he claimed to be true.

Then the old Marquis de la Tour-Samuel got to his feet, a man eighty-two years of age. He went across to lean on the mantelpiece, and told his story in a rather shaky voice:

I know a strange case myself, a case so strange that it has been an obsession all my life. It is now fifty-six years since this incident occurred, and yet not a month has passed in which I have not seen it again in my dreams. A sort of mark, an impression left by fear – if you understand me – has remained with me every since that day. For ten minutes I experienced such appalling terror that, ever since, a sort of constant fear has possessed my soul. Unexpected noises make me shudder to the depths of my being, and objects half-hidden in the gloom of evening fill me with a crazy desire to run away. I'm afraid of the dark, in fact.

Oh, I wouldn't have admitted this before reaching my present age! Now I can tell you anything. When you're eighty-two you're not obliged to be brave in the presence of imaginary dangers. I can assure you, ladies, that I have never flinched in the face of real danger.

This affair upset me so completely, and caused me such deep, mysterious, terrible distress, that I have never spoken about it to anyone. I have kept it in the depths of my innermost being, in those depths where we hide the painful secrets, the shameful secrets, all the unconfessed weaknesses of our lives.

I am going to tell you about it, exactly as it happened, without attempting to explain it. There is no doubt that an explanation could be found – unless I happened to be mad at the time. But, no! I was not mad, and I'll prove it to you. You may think what you like. Here are the simple facts:

It happened in 1827, in the month of July. I was then stationed in Rouen.

One day, as I was walking along the quay-side, I met a man whom

I thought I recognized, without being able to recall exactly who he was. I made an instinctive movement, as if to stop. The stranger noticed this, looked at me, then rushed up and flung his arms round me.

He was a friend of my youth to whom I had been deeply attached. In the five years that had elapsed since I had last seen him he seemed to have aged half a century. His hair was completely white, and he walked with a stoop, as though exhausted. He realized how surprised I was, and began to tell me his life-story. He had been shattered by a terrible misfortune.

Having fallen madly in love, he had married the girl in a state of ecstasy, but after a year of superhuman bliss and unquenchable passion she had suddenly died of some heart condition – killed by love itself, no doubt.

He had left his château on the very day of her burial, and had come to live in his house in Rouen. There he existed, lonely and desperate, consumed by grief, so wretched that he thought of nothing but suicide.

'Now that I have met you like this,' he said, 'I will ask you to do me a great favour. I'd like you to go to my former home and get me some papers which I need urgently. I cannot send a junior officer or a solicitor on a job of this kind; I need someone who is the soul of discretion and who will keep absolute silence about it. As for myself, there's nothing on earth would induce me to go back into that house.

'I will give you the key to this bedroom, which I locked myself when I left, and the key to my desk. In addition, I'll let you have a note to give to my gardener, so he will open the château for you. But come and have breakfast with me tomorrow, and we'll have a chat about it.'

I promised to do this small favour for him. It was, in fact, only a short outing for me, as his property was about twenty kilometres from Rouen. It would take me an hour on horseback.

At ten o'clock the next morning I went round to see him. We had breakfast together, just the two of us, but he hardly spoke. He asked me to forgive him, and explained that he was upset by the thought that I was about to visit the room which had once been the scene of his happiness. He really did seem strangely agitated and preoccupied, as though some mysterious struggle were taking place in his soul.

Eventually he explained to me exactly what I had to do. It was very simple. I had to get two bundles of letters and one of papers, which were locked away in the first drawer on the right of the desk for which I had the key. To his instructions he added the remark: 'I needn't ask you not to look at them.'

I was rather hurt by these words, and I told him so, rather sharply. He stammered: 'Forgive me – I'm so upset.' And he started weeping. I left him at about one o'clock, and set out on my mission.

The weather was glorious, and I rode through the meadows at a steady trot, listening to the singing of the larks, and the rhythm of my sword tapping against my boot.

Then I entered the forest and slowed my horse down to a walking-pace. As I rode on, branches brushed lightly against my face, and occasionally I would catch a leaf between my teeth and chew it greedily in one of those moments when you feel full of the joys of life, when for some reason or other you are filled with a tumultuous, elusive happiness, a kind of rapture of strength.

As I drew near the château I felt in my pocket for the letter I had for the gardener, and I was astonished to find that it was sealed. I was so surprised and annoyed that I nearly went back without completing my errand. But it occurred to me that if I did so I would be displaying an ill-mannered susceptibility. In the state he was in, my friend might easily have sealed the note without paying any attention to what he did.

His country house seemed to have been deserted for twenty years. The open gate was rotten, but standing upright, somehow or other. The paths were all overgrown with grass; the flower-beds were no longer distinguisable from the lawn.

In response to the noise I made by kicking on a shutter, an old man came out of a side-door, and looked at me in astonishment.

I jumped down from my horse and handed him the letter. He read it, re-read it, turned it over, look at me furtively, put the folded paper in his pocket, and said:

'Well? What do you want?'

I replied abruptly:

'You ought to know. You've just received your master's orders, I want to enter the château.'

He seemed stupefied.

'Then . . . you're going . . . into her room?'

I began to lose patience.

'I certainly am! Do you by any chance intend to cross-examine me?'

'No, monsieur,' he stammered, 'but the trouble is . . . the trouble is it's not been opened since . . . since the . . . death. If you'll just give me five minutes, I'll go . . . I'll go and see if –'

I interrupted him angrily. 'Now, look here! What do you take me for? You can't get into the room because I've got the key here!'

He could think of nothing to say to this, except: 'Very well, monsieur. I'll show you the way.'

'Show me the staircase, and then leave me. I shall easily be able to find the room on my own.'

'But . . . monsieur . . . even so—'

This time I became really angry. 'Now, just be quiet!' I snapped, 'or there's going to be trouble!'

I pushed him roughly aside, and went into the house.

First of all I passed through the kitchen, then through two small rooms where this man and his wife lived. Next I crossed a large hall, went up the stairs, and found the door which my friend had described to me.

I opened it without any difficulty, and went in.

The room was so dark that at first I could see nothing clearly. I stopped short, my nostrils assailed by that stale and musty odour of rooms which are unused, locked up, condemned to death. Then, gradually, my eyes became accustomed to the darkness and I saw fairly clearly that I was in a large bedroom, left in disorder. The bed was without sheets, but it still retained the mattress and pillows, in one of which I noticed a deep impression, as though made by an elbow or a head which had just been resting on it.

The chairs seemed to have been moved out of their places. I noticed that a door, probably leading to a store-room, had been left half open.

I first went over to the window in order to let in some daylight. I opened it, but the fastenings of the shutters outside were so rusty that I could not move them. I even tried to break them with my sword, without success. As I was getting irritated by my useless efforts, and as my eyes had by now become completely accustomed to the semi-darkness, I gave up hope of getting proper light into the room and went over to the desk.

I sat down in an armchair, let down the lid of the desk, and opened the drawer indicated by my friend. It was completely full of letters and papers. I only needed the three bundles whose description I had been given, and I started to look for them.

I was straining my eyes, trying to read the details, when I thought I heard – or, rather, thought I sensed – a kind of rustling behind me. I paid no attention to it, thinking that a draught might have moved a curtain or some other material in the room. But a minute later another sound, barely audible, sent a strange and unpleasant tingling sensation all over my skin. It was so silly of me to be nervous, even though I was only slightly nervous, that I felt it a point of honour to

to resist the impulse to turn round. By this time I had just found the
second of the bundles I needed, and I was about to take out the third
when I heard – just behind my shoulder – a long, heavy sigh. I jumped
out of the chair like a madman, and found myself standing a couple
of yards away. As I jumped I had turned round, instinctively grasping
the hilt of my sword – and, I assure you, if I had not felt it by my
side I should have fled like a coward.

A tall woman, dressed in white, was staring at me. She was standing
behind the chair in which I had been sitting a second or two earlier.

Such a shudder ran through my limbs that I nearly fell over
backwards! Oh, nobody can possibly understand, unless he has
actually experienced it, this kind of appalling, unreasonable terror.
Your very being seems to melt away, your heart seems to have stopped
beating, your whole body becomes as soft as a sponge, and you feel
as though your innermost self is crumbling away.

I do not believe in ghosts – and yet I was ready to faint with that
hideous fear of the dead, and – oh, I suffered more in those few
moments than in all the rest of my life, from the irresistible anguish
of supernatural terror.

If she had not spoken, I might have died with fright! But she did
speak – in a gentle, grief-stricken voice which made my nerves quiver.
I would not dare claim that I recovered my self-control and began
to think clearly again. No! I was so shaken that I hardly knew what
I was doing. But this self-respect of mine, and also a bit of my
professional pride as an officer, made me put on a brave face – almost
in spite of myself. I was putting it on for my own benefit, and no
doubt for hers, whoever she was, woman or ghost. I only realized
this later on, for I can assure you that when I saw the apparition, I
could think of nothing. I was simply terrified.

She said: 'Oh, monsieur! You can do me a great favour!'

I tried to reply, but I found it impossible to utter a single word.
Just a vague sound came from my throat.

She continued: 'Will you? You can save me, you can cure me. I
am suffering terrible pain. I am in such pain – oh, such pain!'

She slowly sat down in the armchair, and still looking at me, she
said: 'Will you?'

I nodded 'Yes'. My voice was still paralysed.

Then she held out a tortoise-shell comb, murmuring:

'Comb my hair! Oh, just comb my hair! That will cure me. All
I need is someone to comb my hair. Look at my face . . . You can
see how much I am suffering – and how much my hair is hurting me!'

Her loose hair, very long and black, it seemed to me, was hanging over the back of the chair and touching the floor.

Why did I do it? Why did I take hold of that comb, shuddering as I did so, and why did I take between my fingers her long black hair, which sent a horrible, chilly sensation all over my skin, just as though I were handling snakes? I've no idea why I did it.

I can still feel that sensation in my fingers, and it makes me shudder when I think about it.

I combed her hair. Somehow or other I handled those icy locks. I entwined her hair, tied it, and loosened it: I even plaited it, in the way that you plait a horse's mane. She kept sighing, leaning her head forward, and apparently was happy.

Suddenly she said: 'Thank you!', snatched the comb from my hand, and fled out of the room through the half-open door that I had noticed earlier.

Left alone, I experienced for a few seconds that confused feeling of dismay which you get when you wake up after a nightmare. Then I pulled myself together, ran to the window, and with a vigorous push burst open the shutters.

Daylight flooded into the room. I rushed over to the door through which this mysterious being had disappeared. I found it shut, and impossible to open.

I was suddenly overcome by a frenzied desire to escape, real panic, the kind of panic which is experienced on the battlefield. I grabbed the three bundles from the open desk, ran across the room, rushed down the stairs, four at a time, got out of the house somehow or other and, seeing my horse just a few yards away, jumped into the saddle and galloped off.

I didn't stop until I got back to my house in Rouen. Throwing the reins to my servant, I ran into my room and locked the door so I could be left in peace to think about what had happened.

For a whole hour I anxiously asked myself whether or not I had been the victim of a hallucination. Surely I had experienced one of those incomprehensible nervous upsets, one of those mental aberrations which give rise to miracles, and to which the supernatural owes its power.

And I was beginning to think it had been some kind of illusion, some error made by my senses, when I went over to the window and happened to glance down. The jacket of my uniform was covered with hairs – long hairs from the head of a woman, all entwined round the buttons!

I took them one by one and, with trembling fingers, threw them out of the window.

Then I called my servant. I felt too upset, too confused, to go to my friend's house straight away. And, moreover, I wanted time to think about exactly what I ought to tell him.

I sent him his letters, and he gave my servant a receipt for them. He apparently asked a lot of questions about me. My servant told him that I was not well, that I had got sunstroke, or something of the kind. He was apparently very worried.

I went round to his place the next day, as soon as it was light, having made up my mind to tell him the truth. He had gone out the previous evening and had not returned.

I went back again later in the day. But nothing had been seen of my friend. I waited a week. There was still no sign of him. Then I notified the authorities. They searched for him everywhere, but they were unable to discover any clue about how he had disappeared or where he was.

A thorough inspection was made of the empty château. They found nothing to arouse suspicion.

There was no indication that a woman had ever been concealed there.

As the inquiry never got anywhere the investigations were discontinued.

And in the fifty-six years since it happened I have heard nothing more. That's all I can tell you about it.

Saint-Antoine

They nicknamed him Saint-Antoine – Saint Anthony – partly because his name was Antoine, and also perhaps because he was such a jolly fellow, a man who enjoyed life, a man who enjoyed his food and drink, a practical joker and one with an eye for pretty servant girls – even though he was well over sixty.

He was a peasant from the Caux district, well-built, with florid cheeks, a broad chest and heavy paunch, all perched on top of his long legs, which looked too thin to support the great bulk of his body.

He was a widower, and except for a maidservant and two labourers, he lived alone on his farm, which he ran with a combination of friendliness and cunning, looking after his own interests, showing great skill in business matters and in the raising of cattle and the cultivation of crops. His two sons and three daughters had married well, and lived in the district. Once a month they would come and have dinner with their father. He was famous for his tremendous strength, and throughout the surrounding countryside they used to say, as a kind of proverb, 'He's as strong as Saint-Antoine.'

When the Prussian invasion took place, Saint-Antoine, who was in the village inn at the time, vowed that he would devour a whole army of Prussians. Like all true Normans he liked to boast, though in reality he was a braggart with a cowardly streak. On this occasion he thumped on the table with his fists, and he thumped so hard that it made cups and glasses dance about. With a sly gleam in his eyes he shouted with all the artificial anger of a jovial braggart: 'By God! I'll eat 'em alive!'

He was counting on the fact that nobody imagined the Prussians would ever get as far as Tanneville. From the moment he heard that they had reached Rautôt he never set foot out of the house, and kept a constant watch on the road from his little kitchen window, expecting to see the Prussian bayonets come past at any moment.

One lunchtime, when he and his farm hands were having their soup, the door opened, and in came Maître Chicot, the mayor of the parish, followed by a soldier wearing a black helmet with a brass spike. Saint-Antoine jumped to his feet, and all his servants looked on, expecting

to see him hack the Prussian to pieces. But all he did was shake the
mayor's hand and listen to him as he said:

'Now here's one for you to billet, Saint-Antoine. They arrived last
night. Whatever you do, don't cause any trouble. They've threatened
to shoot the lot of us and burn every building if the slightest thing
goes wrong. So don't say you haven't been warned . . . Give him
something to eat. He looks a decent sort of lad . . . Well, good-day
to you. I must go and see the others. Everybody's got to take a soldier.'

Off he went, and old Antoine, who had become quite pale, looked
at his Prussian. He was a stout young man with plump, white flesh,
blue eyes, fair hair and a full beard which covered his cheek-bones.
His appearance suggested that he was slow-witted, timid and good-
natured. The cunning Norman summed him up straight away, and,
with a sense of relief, motioned him to sit down. He then asked him:

'Do you want some soup?'

The foreigner did not understand. Suddenly becoming bold Antoine
thrust a large plateful of soup under his nose and said:

'There you are! Gobble that up, you fat pig!'

'*Ja!*' replied the soldier, and he started on the soup, eating it
greedily. The farmer, very pleased with himself, feeling that his
reputation had been saved, winked at his servants who were pulling
very odd faces, torn between genuine fear and the temptation to laugh.

As soon as the Prussian had gulped down his plateful of soup Saint-
Antoine gave him another, which he consumed just as greedily as the
first. But he refused a third helping, even though the farmer tried
to force him to eat it.

'Come on!' said Antoine. 'Stow that away in your belly! I'm going
to fatten you up, you pig, or I'll know the reason why!'

And the soldier, thinking simply that they wanted him to eat to
his heart's content, began to laugh good-naturedly and he made signs
to indicate that he was full.

Then Saint-Antoine, acting in a completely familiar and friendly
way, patted the Prussian on the stomach and shouted.

'My pig's got a real belly-full.'

Then he was suddenly so convulsed with mirth, that he was unable
to speak, and so red in the face that he looked as though he was about
to have an apoplectic fit. An idea had just struck him that almost
choked him with laughter.

'That's it! That's it!' he gasped. 'Saint Anthony and his pig – and
there's the pig!'

Now his three servants burst out laughing, and the old farmer was so pleased with himself that he sent one of them to bring in a bottle of his very best brandy for drinks all round. They drank to the Prussian, who smacked his lips to show them how excellent he considered the brandy.

'Now then! That's what you call brandy!' shouted the farmer within inches of the Prussian's face. 'I bet you don't get stuff like that in your country! Do you, pig?'

From that moment onwards old Antoine never left the house without his Prussian. This joke had now become his whole concern, his personal revenge, revenge such as could be taken only by a malicious practical joker. And, though they were all terribly scared, the folk of the surrounding countryside laughed till the tears ran down their cheeks at Saint-Antoine's farce, which he played behind the backs of the conquering soldiers. When it came to acting the clown there was nobody who could compare with old Antoine, nobody with his inventive turn of mind. What a comical rogue he was!

Every afternoon now he would call on his neighbours, linking arms with his German, whom he introduced to them with a cheerful remark, patting him on the shoulder.

'Look!' he would say. 'Here's my pig. Just look how nice and fat this animal's getting!'

And at this the peasants would grin with delight.

'He's a real comic, is old Antoine!'

'All right, Césaire,' he would say, 'I'll sell 'im to you for thirty francs.'

'It's a bargain, Antoine! And you can come and 'elp us eat the black pudding we'll make out of 'im!'

'What I like about 'im is 'is trotters.'

'Ah! Just you feel 'is belly. Nothing but fat!'

And they would all wink at each other and do their best not to laugh too much, in case the Prussian finally tumbled to the fact that they were making a laughing-stock out of him. Antoine, however, grew more and more daring as each day went by. He would pinch the soldier's thigh and call out: 'Nothing but solid fat!' He would slap him on the behind and yell out: 'What a lovely piece of pork crackling!' He would lift him off the ground in those old giant's arms capable of picking up a large anvil and he would announce: 'He weighs six hundred kilos – and it's all good meat, with no waste!'

Wherever he went it was his custom to get people to feed his pig, and this farce became the chief entertainment and the greatest delight of everyday life.

'Give 'im anything you want,' he used to say. 'He gobbles up anything!'

And they fed him with bread and butter, potatoes, cold stew – and pork sausages, which they set before him with the remark: 'Now there's a bit of your own kind. Prime quality pork!'

Apparently delighted by all the fuss that was being made of him, the slow-witted and docile soldier used to eat whatever they gave him. He would eat out of sheer politeness and make himself ill rather than refuse. And now he really was putting on weight and his uniform had become far too tight for him. This delighted Saint-Antoine. 'Well, now, my old pig,' he would say. 'We're going to have to get them to make you a new sty!'

And, really, these two had become the best of friends. When Antoine went away on business the Prussian always insisted on going with him, simply for the pleasure of his company.

The weather now became severely cold and it was freezing hard. That terrible winter of 1870 seemed to bring upon France every kind of trouble at once.

Old Antoine, who always looked ahead and never missed an opportunity, saw that he was going to be short of manure by the time it got to spring. So he bought some from a neighbouring farmer who needed the cash, and it was agreed that he would take his cart round each evening and load it up with manure.

Every evening, just as it was getting dark, he used to set out for the Les Haules farm, about a mile away, always accompanied by his human pig. And every evening the country folk flocked to the grand entertainment of stuffing the animal with food. They turned up as regularly as if it were High Mass on Sunday morning.

But the soldier was now beginning to suspect what was going on. When the laughter became too uproarious he would look all round him uneasily, and sometimes his eyes would flash with anger.

Now, one evening when he had eaten all he could possibly manage, he refused to touch another morsel. He tried to stand up and get away, but Saint-Antoine caught him in the grip of his wrist, and putting his two powerful hands on the Prussian's shoulders, he forced him to sit down again with such violence that the chair collapsed under him.

This incident evoked gales of laughter, and Antoine, beaming all over, helped his pig back onto his feet, and pretended to attend to his injuries.

'You may not want to eat,' he shouted, 'but I'll make sure you drink, by God!'

And they sent to the inn for some brandy.

The soldier looked round the room with a malevolent gleam in his eyes, but he drank the brandy nevertheless. What is more, he drank just as much as they required, and Saint-Antoine drank to keep up with him, to the great delight of the spectators.

With his face as red as a tomato, and his eyes flashing fire, the Norman kept filling up the glasses, clinking them in a toast and bawling out: 'Here's to you!' And the Prussian, without saying a word, gulped down glass after glass of cognac.

It was a contest, a battle, a kind of return match. They would see who could drink the most, by God! When the litre of brandy had been drunk dry they had both had as much as they could take. But neither would admit defeat. They were neck and neck, that was all. They would have to start again the next day!

The staggered out into the night and set off back home, following the cartload of manure which the two horses pulled slowly along.

It was beginning to snow. There was no moon, and the darkness of the night was relieved only by the melancholy, lifeless white that was covering the plains. The two men were feeling the intense cold, and this seemed to increase their state of intoxication. Saint-Antoine, annoyed that he had not won the drinking contest, relieved his feelings by pushing against the shoulder of his Prussian pig and trying to get him to fall into the ditch. The soldier managed to dodge aside, but each time he angrily uttered some words in German, which the peasant greeted with loud guffaws. Finally the Prussian lost his temper, and just as Antoine was about to give him another shove, he retaliated by giving him such a tremendous blow with his fist that the huge Frenchman staggered and almost fell.

Maddened by the brandy, the old man grabbed the soldier round the waist and shook him for a few moments as easily as if he had been a small child. Then he flung him clean across the road. Satisfied with this achievement he folded his arms and started laughing again.

But the soldier got to his feet very quickly. He had lost his helmet, and with his head bare and his sword unsheathed he came rushing towards old Antoine.

As soon as he saw him the peasant took hold of his whip by the middle. It was a big, straight whip made from a holly branch, tremendously strong and supple.

The Prussian came on with his head down and his sword held

straight in front of him, certain of killing the Frenchman. But with
one hand the old peasant grasped the blade which was pointing straight
at his stomach and thrust it aside. With the other hand he brought
the whip-handle down onto the Prussian's head, striking him a sharp
blow on the temple. His enemy collapsed at his feet.

Bewildered and dazed with shock Antoine stared at the body before
him. For a moment or two it writhed convulsively, then lay there
motionless, face downwards. He bent down, turned it over and gazed
at it for some time. The Prussian's eyes were closed and a trickle of
blood was oozing from a gash at the side of his forehead. Dark though
it was Antoine could make out the brown stain this blood was making
on the snow.

He stood there in utter dismay, and all the time his cart-load of
manure continued on its way, calmly pulled along by the horses.

What was he to do? . . . Now he would certainly be put before a
firing squad! They would burn down his farm! They would devastate
the countryside! . . . What could he do? What could he do? How could
he hide the body? How could he conceal the death? How could he
keep it from the Prussians?

The intense silence of the snow-covered landscape was broken by
the sound of distant voices. In a state of panic he picked up the helmet,
pushed it onto his victim's head, and taking hold of him round the
waist he hoisted him onto his shoulders, and ran after the cart. When
he caught up with it he threw the body on top of the manure. Once
he got home he would be able to work out what to do next.

He walked on, taking short, hesitant steps. He was racking his
brains, but could find no solution. He could only see himself as a
man who was doomed.

When he reached his farmyard he saw a light shining through the
attic window. This meant that the maidservant was still awake. So
he quickly backed the cart until it stood on the brink of the manure
pit. His idea was that by tipping out the load of manure the body
which lay on top would end up at the bottom of the pit underneath
the whole heap.

He tilted the cart, and, as he had guessed, the body was buried
under the manure. He smoothed the heap over with his pitch-fork
which he then stuck into the ground next to it. Calling out one of
the farmhands he ordered his horses to be stabled, and then went up
to his bedroom.

He got into bed, still thinking hard about what he ought to do. But he
could not see any way out, and his fear grew more and more appalling

as he lay motionless between the sheets. They would shoot him! . . .
There he lay, sweating in terror and listening to his teeth chattering,
until he could stand it no longer. Trembling from head to foot he
got out of bed and went down into the kitchen. He took the bottle
of brandy out of the sideboard and brought it back to his bedroom.
He drank two large glasses, one after the other, adding a new state
of intoxication to the one already there – but without finding any relief
from his anguish. What a mess he had made of things, God-forsaken
idiot that he was!

Now he began to walk up and down the room, very slowly, trying
to think of some trick, some plausible explanation, some clever
remark. And every now and then he would take another swig of
brandy to put some heart into him.

But he could find no way out of his predicament. No solution at all.

About midnight his watchdog – a mongrel with some wolf in him,
which he called Dévorant – suddenly started to howl as though he
sensed death. Antoine shivered to the very marrow of his bones. And
each time the dog repeated its long-drawn, mournful howl a shudder
of terror crept over the old man's skin.

By now he had collapsed into a chair. In a daze, exhausted, with
his legs apparently useless, he sat there anxiously waiting for Dévorant
to start another howl – and when it came he was shaken in every fibre
of his being, quivering with every tremor with which panic an afflict
the human frame.

The clock downstairs struck five. And still the dog continued to
howl. The sound was driving the old peasant mad. He go to his feet,
determined to let the animal off his chain in the hope that this would
silence him. He went downstairs, opened the door, and set out into
the darkness.

The snow was still falling. Everything was white except where the
walls of the farm buildings stood out as large, dark patches. Antoine
made his way to the kennel. The dog was pulling hard on his chain.
As soon as he released him Dévorant took a leap forward, then stopped
short, with his coat bristling, his legs rigid, his fangs bared, and his
gaze fixed on the manure heap.

'What's matter with you, you brute?' mumbled Saint-Antoine,
trembling from head to foot.

He took a few steps forward, straining his eyes to see into the gloom
of the vaguely outlined farmyard.

Then he saw a figure – the figure of a man sitting on the dung hill!

He stared before him, paralysed and breathless with terror. Suddenly he became aware of the handle of his pitch-fork sticking out of the ground quite close to him. He grabbed hold of it, and in one of those surges of fear which turn the biggest cowards into reckless men, he rushed forward to take a closer look.

It was him! It was his Prussian! Covered with filth he had crawled out from under his bed of manure, which had warmed and revived him. He had sat down on top of it automatically, and there he was, with the snowflakes settling upon him, daubed with dirt and blood, still stupefied with drink, still dazed from the blow on his head and weak from the wound.

He noticed Antoine, and although he was too besotted to understand anything of his situation, he made an effort to stand up. But as soon as the old man recognized him he started to foam at the mouth like a rabid animal.

'Ah! Pig! Pig!' he babbled. 'So you're not dead! Now you're going to give me away, aren't you! . . . Just you wait! . . . Just you wait!'

He charged upon the German, raising his pitch-fork like a spear. Holding it with both hands he drove it with all his might into the soldier's chest, burying the four steel prongs as far as they would go.

The Prussian fell flat on his back uttering a long-drawn sigh of death, but the old peasant pulled out his weapon from the four fatal wounds and thrust it into the body again and again – into the belly, the stomach, the throat – driving it home like a raving madman, riddling the twitching body from head to foot with terrible holes from which the blood welled out in great spurts.

Then he stopped and stood there, completely out of breath through the ferocity of his action, filling his lungs with big gulps of air, experiencing a sense of calm now that the murder had been accomplished.

From the hen runs he could hear the cocks crowing, and realizing that dawn was not far away he set about the task of burying the corpse.

He dug down into the manure heap until he reached the soil underneath; then he dug deeper still, toiling away in a frenzy, in a tremendous upsurge of energy, making furious use of his arms and his whole body.

When the hole was deep enough he used the pitch-fork to roll the corpse into it, filled it in with soil, stamped it down firmly, and replaced the manure on top of it. He smiled as he saw that his handiwork was being neatly finished off by the snow, which was coming down very thickly and covering up every trace of the crime with a veil of pure white.

Finally, he stuck the pitch-fork into the pile of manure and went back to his room. The bottle of brandy, still half full, was standing there on the table. He emptied it at a single draught, threw himself onto the bed, and fell into a deep sleep.

When he woke up he was perfectly sober and his mind was calm and clear, well able to assess the situation and to work out what should be done.

An hour later he was running all over the district asking everybody if they had any news of the whereabouts of his soldier. He went to see the Prussian officers and asked them why they had taken his soldier away from him.

As the closeness of his relationship with the Prussian was so well-known, the authorities never suspected him. He even went so far as to help them along with their investigations by telling them that every night the Prussian was in the habit of going out looking for girls.

A gendarme living in retirement, who kept an inn in the next village and who had a pretty daughter, was arrested and shot.

The Wolf

This was a story told to us by the old Marquis d'Arville after a dinner at Baron des Ravels' to celebrate the feast of St Hubert, patron of hunters.

That day they had brought a stag to bay. The marquis was the only guest who had not taken part in the day's chase, for he was a man who never went hunting.

During the whole of dinner, they hardly spoke of anything but the slaughter of animals. Even the ladies took an interest in the gory and often incredible tales, told in thunderous voices with gesticulated demonstrations of the fights between men and beasts.

D'Arville spoke well, with a good deal of poetic imagery which was rather sonorous, but really effective. He must have told the story often before, because it flowed very smoothly, and he did not have to grope for his words, which were skilfully chosen to give a vivid picture of what had happened:

Gentlemen, I have never gone hunting myself; neither did my father nor my grandfather nor my great-grandfather. But *his* father was a man who hunted more than any of you gentlemen. He died in 1764. Let me tell you how he died.

His name was Jean; he was married, and was the father of this child who was to become my great-grandfather; and he lived with his younger brother, François d'Arville, in our château in Lorraine which stands in the middle of the forest.

François d'Arville was so fond of hunting that he had remained a bachelor. The two brothers hunted from one end of the year to the other, without rest, or pause, or fatigue. Hunting was the only thing they loved and understood, the only thing they spoke of and lived for.

Deep in their hearts was this terrible, inexorable passion for hunting. It burned them, consumed their whole being, left no room for anything else.

No one was allowed to disturb them under any pretext whatever while they were out hunting. My great-grandfather was born while his father was hunting a fox, and when informed, my forbear shouted, without halting his horse: 'Ah, damn him! The little beggar could at at least have waited until we'd finished the hunt!'

His brother Francois seemed even more fanatical about hunting than he was. As soon as he was up in the morning he would go to inspect the hounds, and then the horses; then he would take a few shots at the birds around the château, just to while away the time until they went out to follow some bigger game.

They called them, in our district, Monsieur Le Marquis and Monsieur le Cadet. In those days the nobility made no attempt to establish a descending scale of rank, as do many of the aristocrats of today; for, after all, the son of a marquis is no more a count, or the son of a viscount, a baron, than the son of a general is a colonel – simply by birth. But then, the petty vanity of the present day finds advantage in this arrangement.

But let me get back to my ancestors . . . They were, I gather, exceptionally tall, big-boned, hairy, violent, and powerful. The younger one, who was even taller than his brother, had a voice so loud that, according to a legend in which he himself took pride, all the leaves in the forest shook when he shouted.

And when the brothers rode out to hunt, it must have been a great sight to see the two giants astride their big horses.

Now, towards the middle of the winter of 1764 the weather turned exceptionally cold, and the wolves became ferocious.

They even attacked peasants out late at night and they prowled around the houses, howling from sunset to sunrise and causing havoc amongst the cattle.

And soon a rumour spread. People were talking of a huge wolf with a greyish coat that was almost white; it had eaten two children, devoured a woman's arm, torn out the throats of all the guard-dogs in the area, penetrated fearlessly into fenced-off farmyards, and sniffed around the doors of the houses. All the local inhabitants claimed to have felt the animal's breath, a breath that made the light flicker. And soon panic spread throughout the whole province. No one dared to go out after dark any more, because the very shadows seemed to be haunted by the image of this beast.

The d'Arville brothers resolved to find it and kill it, and so they invited all the local nobility to great hunting parties.

It was no use. However hard they beat the forests and searched the thickets, they never found the beast. They killed wolves – but not that one.

And during the night following each hunting expedition the beast, as if to avenge itself, would attack some traveller or eat some farm animal – and always far from the place where they had been searching for it.

Then one night it broke into the pig-sty of the Château d'Arville and ate the two best prize hogs.

The brothers were really angry, regarding this attack as a piece of bravado on the part of the monster, a sheer insult and a challenge. So they gathered their strongest hounds, which were well accustomed to pursuing dangerous game and, with fury in their hearts, they set out to run down the wolf. From dawn until the time when the crimson sun went down behind the tall, bare trees, they beat the thickets – without finding a thing.

At last they rode home at a walking pace along a track bordered with brushwood, furious and frustrated, amazed at the way the beast had managed to thwart all their hunting lore, and with a mysterious fear suddenly filling their hearts.

The older brother said: 'There's something very strange about that wolf. He seems to think just like a man.'

The younger brother replied: 'Well, perhaps we ought to have a bullet blessed by our cousin the Bishop, or ask some priest to say whatever words are necessary.'

They were silent for a while.

Then Jean spoke again: 'Just look how red the sun is! The big wolf is going to cause some mischief tonight.'

No sooner had he uttered these words than his horse reared, and his brother's horse started kicking wildly. A thick bush covered with dead leaves seemed to open up suddenly in front of them and a colossal grey beast leaped out and dashed off through the wood.

Letting out a sort of growl of joy, the brothers bent over the necks of their big horses and urged the animals forward with shouts, gestures, and spurs – at such a pace that it looked as if the powerful riders had caught their heavy mounts between their thighs and were flying through the air with them.

They rode on like this at breath-taking speed, crashing through thickets, cutting through ravines, climbing slopes, hurtling down gorges, blowing their horns as loudly as they could to summon their men and their dogs.

Suddenly, during this frantic pursuit, my ancestor struck his forehead against a huge branch and fractured his skull. He fell dead to the ground, and his panic-stricken horse vanished into the darkness of the surrounding wood.

The younger d'Arville stopped short, jumped down from his

horse, took his brother in his arms, and saw the gaping wound through which blood and brain was oozing.

Then he sat down next to the body, placed the red, disfigured head on his knees, and waited there, staring at the motionless features of his elder brother. And, gradually, fear came over him, a strange fear such as he had never experienced before: fear of the darkness, fear of being alone, fear of the deserted forest, and fear too of the weird wolf which had just killed his brother to wreak vengeance on them.

The shadows deepened, and the sharp frost made the trees crackle. François stood up, shuddering, feeling he could stay there no longer, feeling almost ready to faint. Nothing more could be heard of either the baying of the hounds or the sound of the hunting-horns – everything was silence in the invisible world around him. And this dismal silence of the icy evening had something about it that was terrifying and uncanny.

He picked up the big body in his great arms, laid it across the saddle, ready to return to the château. He set off slowly, his head unclear, as if he had drunk too much, and he was haunted by horrible, peculiar visions.

Suddenly, down the path which was rapidly being invaded by the night, there flitted a great shadow. It was the wolf. A shudder of terror shook the hunter. Something cold, like a drop of water, slipped down the small of his back, and like a monk haunted by the Devil, he made a great sign of the cross, bewildered by this sudden return of the terrifying prowler. But then his eyes fell again on the lifeless body of his brother, tied to the saddle in front of him, and changing suddenly from fright to fury, he trembled with uncontrolled rage.

Then he spurred his horse on in hot pursuit of the wolf.

He followed it through copses, across ravines, amongst the ancient trees, passing through woods he had never been in before, his eyes fixed on the white patch that was racing through the descending darkness.

His horse, too, seemed driven on by an unaccountable strength and eagerness. It galloped with its neck stretched out, straight ahead, so that the head and feet of the dead man thrown across the saddle banged against trees and rocks. The briars tore at the dead man's hair; his forehead, bumping against the great tree-trunks, splattered them with blood; his spurs tore off strips of bark.

And, suddenly, just as the moon was rising above the hills, the horse and rider emerged from the forest and charged down into the gorge. It was a stony valley, blocked at one end by enormous rocks, with no possible way of escape. And the wolf at bay turned round.

François then let out a howl of joy that the echoes caught up, making it sound like a peal of thunder, and he jumped down from his horse, with his cutlass in his hand.

The beast waited for him, its coat bristling, its back arched, its eyes gleaming like stars. But before joining in combat the powerful huntsman grabbed his brother's body and sat it up on a rock. Propping up with stones the head which was now no more than a bloody lump, he shouted into the corpse's ear as if he were talking to a deaf man: 'Look, Jean! Watch this!'

Then he threw himself on the monster. He felt strong enough to overturn a mountain, to crush stones with his bare hands. The wolf tried to sink its fangs into him, to tear his belly open, but he had seized it by the throat and, without evening using his weapon, he strangled it with deliberate slowness, listening as the breathing in its throat and the beating of its heart grew fainter and fainter. And he laughed madly, jubilantly, tightening his tremendous grip harder and harder, and shouting with delirious delight: 'Look, Jean! Look!'

Then all resistance came to an end; the wolf's body became limp. It was dead.

François lifted the wolf up in his arms, carried it over to his brother's body, and threw it down at his feet, saying over and over again in a voice full of compassion: 'There, there, there Jean! There he is!'

And then he placed the two corpses, one on top of the other, across his saddle, and set off.

He arrived home laughing and weeping, like Gargantua when Pantagruel was born, yelling triumphantly and leaping about merrily as he told them about the death of the beast, moaning and tearing at his beard as he told them about the death of his brother.

And often, later, when he spoke of that night, he would say with his eyes full of tears: 'Ah, if only poor Jean had seen me strangle that beast he would have died content, I'm sure.'

My ancestor's widow instilled in her orphaned son a horror of hunting, which since then has been transmitted from father to son, down to me.

The Marquis d'Arville became silent. Then someone asked him: 'That story's just a legend, isn't it?'

The story-teller replied: 'I swear to you that it's absolutely true, from beginning to end.'

Then a woman said in a gentle little voice: 'Whether it's true or not, what a wonderful thing to have that kind of passionate enthusiasm.'

Terror

The train was travelling at full speed through the intense darkness. I was the only person in the compartment except for an old gentleman who was sitting opposite me, looking out of the window.

There was no moon, and the night was suffocatingly hot. You could not even see any stars, and as the train hurtled onwards it filled the carriage with a draught of air which felt like some hot, soft material, oppressive and stifling. We had left Paris three hours earlier and we were now somewhere near the centre of France – though we could glimpse nothing at all of the countryside through which we were travelling.

Suddenly, we saw something which seemed just like a supernatural vision – two men standing round a big fire in the middle of the forest.

We only saw the scene for a second or two, but we had a vivid impression of two wretched-looking tramps, clothed in rags, and aglow with red from their great blazing fire. Their bearded faces were turned towards us, and all round them, forming a kind of stage back-cloth, there were the green trees, bright and gleaming, with their trunks standing out vividly in the reflected blaze, and their foliage all suffused and drenched by the spreading firelight.

Then the vision disappeared, and everything was pitch-black again.

What a strange thing to see! What were these two vagabonds doing in that forest? Why had they lit this big fire on such a stifling night?

The old gentleman sitting opposite me pulled out his watch and remarked: 'It's exactly midnight, monsieur. What a remarkably odd sight we've just witnessed!'

I agreed with him, and we began to chat, speculating as to who these two strange men might be. Were they criminals burning the evidence – or sorcerers preparing some magic potion? After all, you don't light a fire like that in the middle of the night at the height of summer just to make soup. So what were they up to? We simply couldn't think of any likely explanation.

My travelling-companion now settled down to talk. He was an elderly man whose profession I never managed to discover. He was very well-educated and distinctly eccentric; I even had the feeling that he might have been a little unbalanced . . . But how can you tell who are the madmen in this world where reason and folly, madness and genius, are often confused?

'I'm glad I saw that,' he said. 'During those few moments I experienced a sensation to which mankind is now almost a stranger. How disturbing the world must have been in those far-off days when life was full of mystery!

'As one by one we lift the veils which conceal the unknown, we gradually depopulate the world of the imagination. Don't you agree with me, monsieur, that the night has become really empty – little more than a sort of commonplace blackness – now that men no longer believe it contains ghosts? People are saying: "No more weird visions, no more strange beliefs! All the things which were once inexplicable have now been explained." The supernatural is sinking lower and lower, like the water of a lake which is being drained away. With each new day science pushes back the frontiers of what was once marvellous and mysterious.

'Well, for my part, monsieur, I belong to the old generation, the one which likes to believe. I belong to the old, simple generation which is quite accustomed to not being able to understand, or investigate, or know for certain, a generation which has grown up surrounded by mystery, and which refuses to accept the simple, naked truth.

'Yes, monsieur, they've depopulated the world of the imagination by tracking down what was once invisible. Nowadays the earth seems to me like a forsaken world, empty and bare. All the beliefs which added poetry to life have now disappeared.

'When I go out in the dark, how I should love to shudder with that sense of mortal terror which has old women making the sign of the cross when they pass a graveyard, or which has the last remnants of a superstitious generation running away at the sight of strange mists rising from the marshes and the eerie dance of the will-o'-the-wisps! How I wish I could believe in some vague horror which people used to imagine they could sense lurking in the darkness!

'How grim and terrifying the dark shadows of evening must have been in the old days when the dark was full of strange, legendary beings! Hovering there were these evil spirits, and though people had no idea of what they looked like, their presence was so real that it froze the heart with dread, their occult power so great that it seemed beyond the measures of the human mind, and their realm so extensive that it was impossible to escape from them.

'When the supernatural disappeared from the earth, fear – in the true sense of the word – went with it. We are truly afraid only of things we do not understand. Visible dangers can move us, upset us, startle us – but what is that sort of thing compared with the overwhelming terror which engulfs your very being when you think that you are about to meet some walking ghost, experience the repulsive embrace of a corpse, or see charging towards you one of those ghastly mythical creatures invented by man in his terror? The darkness seems light to me, now that it is no longer haunted.

'And what proves my point is this: if we suddenly found ourselves alone in that forest we should be haunted by the vision of those two strange men whom we saw just now in the flare of their fire – and we should dread them far more than any kind of actual danger . . . Yes, we are truly afraid only of things we do not understand.'

At that moment there came into my mind a story which Turgenev had told us one Sunday at Gustave Flaubert's place . . . I've no idea whether or not he has ever included it in any of his published work.

This great Russian novelist has no equal when it comes to being able to thrill the reader with a shudder from the veiled unknown. In the twilight atmosphere of some strange story he can give us a glimpse into a whole world of disturbing, mysterious, ominous things.

In his stories you can really feel that vague fear of the Invisible, the fear of something strange behind a wall, behind a door, something lurking beneath the visible world. In his writing he suddenly sheds upon us an uncertain gleam of light – but only sufficient of it to increase our sense of dread.

Sometimes Turgenev seems to show us that there is a meaning behind curious coincidences, an unexpected connexion between circumstances which appear to be due to chance, and yet which are controlled by a hidden, sinister force. He shares with us the feeling that there is an imperceptible thread mysteriously guiding us through life, rather like being guided through some hazy dream whose meaning constantly escapes us.

He never rushes boldly into descriptions of the supernatural, like Edgar Allan Poe or Hoffmann. He tells us straightforward stories in which there is just the hint of something mysterious and disturbing. On that particular day he, too, happened to remark: 'We are truly afraid only of the things we do not understand.'

There he was in that big armchair, not so much sitting in it as flopping in it, with his arms hanging over the sides, his legs stretched out before him, limp and relaxed, and with his head clothed in white, his face almost submerged in that great flowing beard and long silvery

hair, which made him look like the Almighty Father, or one of the
River Gods described by Ovid.

He spoke slowly, with a kind of indolence which lent a charm to
the phrases he used, and a kind of hesitating heaviness in his speech
which seemed to emphasize the vivid accuracy of his words. He
seemed to re-live every moment of his strange experience, and his
pale eyes would occasionally open wide and light up with excitement,
just as children's eyes do when they are telling a story.

This was what he told us on that occasion . . .

In his younger days he used to go hunting in the Russian forests.
One day he he had done a lot of strenuous walking, and towards the
end of the afternoon he came to the banks of a peaceful river.

It was flowing along – under the trees and amongst the trees – full
of floating weeds, and the water was deep, cold and clear.

The hunter felt an irresistible urge to jump into this crystal-clear
water. He got undressed and dived in. He was a very tall and strong
young man, and a powerful and adventurous swimmer.

He allowed himself to float gently along, enjoying the feeling of
peaceful relaxation as the water-weeds and roots and hanging
vegetation brushed lightly against his flesh.

Suddenly he felt a hand on his shoulder.

He immediately turned round, with the instinctive reaction of shock,
and saw a horrifying creature staring at him with greedy eyes.

It looked like a cross between a woman and a she-ape. There was
a huge, wrinkled, contorted face, grinning at him, and two loathsome
objects – probably the creature's breasts – were floating in front of her;
a mass of long, tangled hair, which looked as though it had been
scorched by the sun, hung round her face and floated on the water
above her back.

Turgenev felt himself being overcome by a hideous dread, by the
icy terror of the supernatural.

Without a moment's thought, without any kind of reflection or
comprehension, he started to swim frantically for the river-bank. But
the monster swam even faster, and it kept touching his neck, his back
and his legs, giving little cackles of delight.

The young man, beside himself with terror, finally reached the
bank, and ran off as fast as he could through the wood, without even
thinking of trying to find his clothes and his gun.

The horrible creature came after him, running just as fast as he did,
and growling at him all the time.

Utterly exhausted, and terrified out of his wits, the fugitive was on the point of collapsing, when a child, who was looking after some goats, came on the scene. He was holding a whip, and with it he began to hit the fearsome human freak, which ran away howling with pain. And Turgenev saw it disappearing into the foliage, looking like a female gorilla.

It was, in fact, a crazy old woman, who had lived in this wood for more than thirty years, living on food provided by the kindness of the herdsmen, and spending half her time swimming in the river.

The great Russian author added this remark: 'I've never been so terrified in the whole of my life – and it was all because I just couldn't understand what this monster could be.'

Well, I told this story to my travelling-companion, and when I had finished, he said once more:

'Ah, yes. We're only afraid of the things we don't understand . . . You can experience that appalling spasm of the soul – the thing we call sheer terror – only when fear is touched with a little of the superstitious dread which men knew in the olden days. I once had a personal experience of the full force of this terror, and it was caused by such a simple, silly thing, that I am almost too ashamed to tell you about it . . .

'At the time I was on a walking tour through Brittany, all by myself. I had just finished walking across Finistère, a place of desolate moorland and barren earth, where nothing grows except gorse-bushes, from the midst of which arise great sacred stones that give you the impression that the place is haunted. The previous day I had visited the sinister promontory of Raz, that land's-end of the old world where two seas, the Atlantic and the English Channel, clash in an eternal conflict. My mind was full of legends and stories that are written or told about this region of strange beliefs and superstitions.

'It was night-time, and I was walking back from Penmarch to Pont l'Abbé. Do you know Penmarch? There's a flat coastline, completely flat and low-lying, so low, in fact, that it seems to be below sea-level. Wherever you look you can see that grey menacing sea, bristling with rocks which slaver with foam, like ferocious beasts.

'I had dined in a fisherman's tavern and was now walking along the road, which ran in a perfectly straight line across the moorland. It was very dark.

'Every now and then a stone monument erected by the Druids would loom out of the darkness like a motionless ghost, and seem to be staring at me as I passed. Gradually, I felt myself becoming vaguely apprehensive. I couldn't really say why . . . There are evenings when you have the sensation of being lightly touched by the spirits of the dead, when you shudder to the depths of your being for no particular reason, when your heart beats faster because you experience that indefinable terror of the invisible – that mysterious invisible which I personally wish were still part of life.

'How long this road seemed! – interminably long and lonely.

'There was no sound except the thunder of the distant waves somewhere behind me, and sometimes this monotonous and menacing sound seemed quite close to me, so close, in fact, that I imagined the waves were almost touching my heels, rolling and foaming towards me over the plain, and I felt as though I ought to break into a run, and flee before the encroaching tide as fast as my legs would carry me.

'The wind was not very strong, but it was blowing in short gusts, whistling through the gorse-bushes all round me. And though I was walking at quite a pace, my legs and arms were cold – with that vile cold which comes from a sense of dread. Oh, how I longed to meet another human being!

'It was now so dark that I could hardly make out the road.

'Suddenly I heard a rumbling noise, coming from a considerable distance ahead of me. I thought: "Hello! That sounds like a cart." Then I heard nothing more.

'A minute or so later I distinctly heard the same noise again, only this time it was getting nearer.

'I could see no light of any kind, but I said to myself: "I suppose they've no lantern on the cart. There's nothing surprising about that in this primitive district."

'The noise stopped once more, then started again. It didn't seem to come from anything as heavy as a cart – and, besides, I couldn't hear the sound of a horse trotting, which rather surprised me, because the night was quiet enough for me to have heard this.

'I began to ask myself: "What on earth can it be?"

'It was now coming rapidly towards me – very rapidly! I was certain now that the noise was being made by a single wheel. There were no hoof-beats, no running footsteps – nothing. What on earth was it?

'It was now very close, almost upon me. With the instinctive movement of fear I jumped out of the way into a ditch, and I saw passing right in front of me . . . a wheel-barrow . . . running along all by itself, with nobody pushing it . . . Yes . . . a wheel-barrow . . . all by itself . . .

'My heart started to beat so violently that I fell back into the grass and lay there listening to the rumbling of the wheel gradually fading away as it went towards the sea. And I was too terrified to stand up, or walk, or make any kind of movement, for if it had come back, if it had come after me, I should have died of sheer terror.

'It was a long time before I recovered – a very long time. And I completed my journey along the road in such a state of mental anguish that the slightest unexpected sound took my breath away.

'It was silly of me, I know. But I was absolutely terrified! When I thought it over, some time afterwards, I realized what it must have been. The wheel-barrow was being pushed along by some bare-footed child – whereas I had expected to see a man pushing it, and had looked for his head at the normal height.

'Just try to imagine how I felt . . . My mind was already being influenced by the supernatural atmosphere of the place . . . Then there was this-barrow, running along . . . all by itself . . . I was absolutely terrified!'

The Diary of a Madman

He had died a high-court judge, an honest and incorruptible magistrate, whose impeccable life was held up as an example in every court in France. Senior barristers, junior counsel, even judges, used to bow very low, as a token of profound respect, every time they saw his imposing, pale, thin face, which was illumined by two bright, deep-set eyes.

He had spent the whole of his life in bringing criminals to justice and in protecting the rights of the weak and innocent. Crooks and murderers had never known a more redoubtable enemy, for it seemed as though he could penetrate deep into their souls, read their innermost thoughts, and unravel – at a single glance – the mysterious secrets of mind and will.

Well, now he was dead, at the age of eighty-two, showered with praise and honour, and mourned by the whole nation. Smart soldiers in red breeches had escorted him to the tomb, and men in white cravats had sprinkled upon his coffin words of grief and tears of sorrow which seemed absolutely genuine . . .

Now, here is the strange document discovered by an astonished solicitor in the desk where this judge locked away his dossiers on all the great criminals.

It is entitled 'Why?' and is reproduced as follows . . .

20th June 1851. Just left the court. I have condemned Blondel to death! Why *did* this man kill his five children? Why? So often one comes across these people for whom the destruction of life is a physical pleasure. Yes. Yes, it must be a pleasure, perhaps the greatest thrill of all. For is not murder the act which bears the closest resemblance to creation? Create and destroy! These two words sum up the history of every universe, the history of every world that ever was, of everything that exists, everything! Why is it so exhilarating to kill?

25th June. To think that a living being is there – a being which exists, which walks and runs . . . A being? What is a being? It is no more than an animated thing which carries within it the principle of movement, and a will which controls this movement! It has no connection with anything, this being. Its very feet have no relation ship to the ground they touch. It is simply a speck of life moving on the surface of the earth. I have no idea how this speck of life came to be here – but it can be destroyed in all kinds of ways. Then there's nothing. Nothing at all. Just putrefaction, then it's all over.

26th June. So why is it a crime to kill? Yes, why? Far from being a crime it is the law of Nature. Every creature is destined to kill. It kills in order to live, and it kills for the sake of killing – killing is in our nature: we simply *have* to kill! Animals kill continuously, all day long, every moment of their existence – Man kills continuously in order to feed himself, but, as he also experiences the necessity to kill for sheer pleasure, he has invented the sport of hunting! A child will kill the insects he finds, or small birds, or any little creature he happens to get his hands on. But none of this could satisfy the overwhelming need to murder, which lies within us. It is not enough to kill animals; we also experience a need to kill human beings.

In olden times this need was fulfilled by human sacrifices. Today the necessity of living in society has turned homicide into a crime. We condemn and punish the murderer. But because we cannot live without yielding to this natural, overmastering instinct to kill, we obtain relief, every now and then, by means of wars in which a whole nation slaughters another nation. Then we have a real orgy in blood, a drunken orgy, which sends armies wild and intoxicates even respectable citizens and womenfolk – even the children, who read in the evening lamplight the thrilling stories of massacre.

And you might imagine that people would despise those who have the task of butchering human beings! Not a bit of it! Honours are heaped upon them. They are attired in gold and resplendent garments. They wear plumes on their heads, decorations on their chests, and they are presented with crosses, awards, and titles of every kind. They are proud, respected, loved by women, acclaimed by the crowds – and all this simply because they are men dedicated to the task of shedding human blood! They parade through the streets with their instruments of death, which the drably-clothed passer-by looks upon with envy. For slaughter is the one great law implanted by Nature at the very core of existence. There is nothing more glorious or more honourable than killing!

30th June. Killing is decreed by law, but Nature loves eternal youth. Whatever she does, however unconscious and unfeeling the act, she seems to cry out: 'Quick! Quick! Quick!' And the more she destroys, the more she is renewed.

2nd July. A human being – what *is* a human being? Everything and nothing. Through the power of thought it can mirror everything it experiences. Through memory and knowledge it becomes a microcosm, carrying the world within itself. A mirror of things, a mirror of facts, each human being becomes a little universe within the universe!

But do some travelling. Consider the teeming populations of the earth – and man becomes nothing! Nothing at all! Nothing! . . . Get on board a ship, sail away from the crowds upon the shore, and soon you will see nothing but the coast-line. The microscopic human being simply disappears: he is so tiny, so insignificant . . . Or take an express-train and make a journey through Europe. Look out of the carriage window and you will see people, people, always people, so many they cannot be counted – and all utter strangers – swarming in the fields, swarming in the streets. You see stupid peasants who only know how to till the ground; you see ugly women who only know how to cook for their men-folk and bear children . . . Go to India, go to China, and you will see yet more teeming billions who live and die without leaving behind them any more sign of their existence than would an ant squashed underfoot. Go to the countries inhabited by the blacks, who live in mud huts, or to the countries inhabited by the Arabs, who shelter under brown canvas flapping in the wind, and then you will understand that the isolated, individual human being is nothing, absolutely nothing . . .

Yes. Travel round the world and look at the teeming masses of countless anonymous human beings. Did I say anonymous? Ah! There's the key to the whole problem! Murder is a crime only because we have put labels on human beings. As soon as they are born we register them, give them names, have them baptized. The law takes them over. And there we are! But the human being who is not registered counts for nothing: kill him out on the moors or in the desert, kill him in the mountains or on the open plain – and what does it matter? Nature delights in death! She never punishes a murderer!

As an example of what is really sacred take the official register of births, marriages and deaths. This is the thing which defends the human race. The life of an individual is only sacred so long as his name has been registered! Show your respect for the register of births, marriages and deaths! Down on your knees!

Oh yes, the state can kill, because it has the right to change the official register. When it has attended to the slaughter of two hundred thousand men in a war, it crosses out their names in the register, it arranges for the registrar to annihilate them at the stroke of his pen.

And that's all there is to it . . . But we who cannot change what is inscribed in the town hall must respect life . . . Ah, register of births, marriages and deaths, glorious goddess enthroned in the temples of our town councils, I salute you! You are stronger than Nature! Ah, yes! Ah, yes!

3rd July. It must be a peculiarly delicious pleasure to kill someone, to have there, just in front of you, a living, thinking human being – and then to make a little hole in him, just a little hole, and to see that red, life-giving stuff we call blood flow out of the hole, and to end up with nothing in front of you but a heap of cold, limp, lifeless flesh, incapable of thought.

5th August. What if I – I who have spent my life passing judgement, condemning people to death, killing people by the mere utterance of a few words, killing by the guillotine those who had killed by the knife – what if I, yes, what if I were to act in the same way as the murderers I have condemned? If *I* were to do it, who would know?

10th August. Yes, who would ever know? Would anbody ever suspect *me* – especially if I choose a victim that I have no particular reason to want out of the way?

15th August. Temptation! Ah, temptation has eaten into me, like some loathsome grub crawling about inside me. It crawls around my whole body. It crawls into my mind which can now only think one single thought. I must kill! It crawls into my eyes, which are eager to see the shedding of blood, eager to witness death. It crawls into my ears, which constantly hear the echo of something mysterious, horrible, heart-rending, unnerving – the victim's last cry! It crawls through my legs, which tremble with eagerness to go – to go to the place where the thing will happen. It crawls through my fingers, which quiver with the intensity of the desire to kill. How enjoyable this experience must be, how rare – an experience worthy of a free man, a man a cut above his fellows, a man who is master of his feelings – and yet who is seeking an exquisite, new sensation!

22nd August. I could resist it no longer! I have killed a small creature, just as an experiment, just to make a start.

My valet, Jean, kept a goldfinch in a cage hanging by the pantry window. I sent him off on an errand, and then I took the tiny bird in my hand. In the palm of my hand I could feel its heart beating, and I could feel the warmth of its body. I went up to my bedroom. Every now and then I squeezed it more tightly. I could feel its heart beat faster.

The experience was atrocious, yet delightful! I nearly squeezed the life out of it – but if I had done that I would not have seen blood.

So I picked up some scissors, small nail-scissors, and cut open the bird's little throat, in three snips, ever so gently. It opened its beak, struggled to get away from me. But I held it firm! Oh, yes! I held it, all right! I felt so strong I could have held a mad dog . . . And I saw the blood flow! How beautiful it is – red, glistening, brilliant blood! It was so beautiful that I wanted to drink it. I tasted it on the tip of my tongue. Delicious! But there was so little of it in this poor, tiny bird! I did not have time to feast my eyes on this sight as much as I would have liked – Ah! What a wonderful thing it must be to see a bull bleed to death!

Next, I did what murderers usually do – real murderers. I washed the scissors, I washed my hands, and threw away the blood-stained water. Then I took the body, the little bird's corpse, down into the garden, in order to bury it. I dug a hole under a strawberry plant, and buried it there. Nobody will ever find it. Every day I shall eat a strawberry from this plant. Really, what enjoyment you can get out of life – once you know how!

My servant has been weeping. He thinks his bird escaped from the cage and flew away. How could he possibly suspect me? Ha! Ha!

25th August. I must kill a human being! I *must!*

30th August. I've done it! How easy it was!

I had set out to walk through the Bois de Vernes. I had no thought of murder in mind. No. Nothing like that. Then I saw a child walking along the woodland path, a little boy who was eating a sandwich . . .

He stood still to watch me go by, and as I passed he said:

'Bonjour, M'sieu le Président!'

And a thought suddenly entered my head: What if I were to kill him?

'Are you all by yourself, child?' I asked.

'Yes, m'sieu.'

'All on your own in this wood?'

'Yes, m'sieu.'

The desire to kill him flooded through me, intoxicating me like wine. I went up to him very gently, convinced that he would run away. And suddenly, I found my fingers round his throat . . . I squeezed and squeezed as hard as I could. He stared at me with terrifying eyes. Ah, those eyes! So round, so intense, so crystal clear, so terrible! I have never experienced such a feeling of brutality – but it was all over so quickly. He clung to my wrists with his little hands, and his body writhed and squirmed – just like a feather does when you throw it on the fire.

My heart was beating madly. Ah! It reminded me of the goldfinch's heart! I threw the body into a ditch, then covered it with grass.

I came back home. I had a good dinner. How easy it was!

This evening I have been very cheerful, very light-hearted, as though rejuvenated. I have spent the evening with the chief of police. Everybody thought I was very witty.

But I have not yet seen human blood! I shall have no peace till I do.

31st August. The body has been discovered! They are looking for the murderer! Ha! Ha!

1st September. Two tramps have been arrested. But there is no evidence against them.

2nd September. The little boy's parents have been to see me. They were in tears! Ha! Ha!

6th October. The case is still unsolved. It is presumed that the crime was committed by some vagrant . . . Ah! If only I had seen his blood flow. How much easier in my mind I should be!

18th October. The lust to kill thrills me to the very marrow. It's comparable to one of those passionate love affairs which torment you at the age of twenty.

20th October. I've done it again! After breakfast I went for a walk along the river. I passed a fisherman asleep under a willow tree. It was about twelve o'clock. In a potato field close to the river there was a spade which had been left stuck into the ground. It was as though it had been put there on purpose.

I took hold of it, retraced my steps, then I rasied the spade above my head like an axe, and with a single blow from the sharp edge I split the fisherman's head in two. Oh! Now, this one really *did* bleed! Lots and lots of blood, quite pink, all mingled with brain! It slithered into the water, ever so gently . . . And I walked away with slow and solemn tread . . . If only they could have seen me! Ha! Ha! I would have made a first-rate murderer.

25th October. The case of the murdered fisherman is causing a great stir. His nephew, who had gone fishing with him, has been accused of the crime.

26th October. The examining magistrate confirms that the nephew is guilty. Everybody in town believes it. Ha! Ha!

27th October. The nephew is putting up a very weak defence. He has stated that he had gone to the village to buy some bread and cheese. He swears that his uncle was killed during the time he was absent . . . Who's going to believe his story!?

28th October. They have got him into such a state that the nephew has almost confessed he did it! Ah! Justice! Justice!

15th November. They now have overwhelming evidence against the nephew. It has been discovered that he was to inherit his uncle's estate. I shall be the presiding judge at the assizes.

25th January. To death! To death! To death! I have had him condemned to death! Ha! Ha! The prosecuting counsel spoke with the eloquence of an angel! Ha! Ha! So I've another one to my credit. I shall go and see him executed!

18th March. It's all over. He was guillotined this morning. It was a lovely death, quite lovely. What a pleasure to watch! How splendid it is to see a man's head sliced from his body! The blood gushed out in a great flood, a great flood! Oh, if only I could have taken a bath in it! How exhilarating it would have been to lie under the guillotine and feel all that blood running through my hair, streaming down my face – and to get up again covered in red, covered in red. Ah! If only I knew just what it was like!

For the present, I shall wait. I can afford to wait . . . It would only need one little slip – and I should be found out . . .

There were many more pages in the diary, but none of them described any further crime.

The psychiatrists who are now studying this manuscript say that there are many unsuspected madmen at large, just as clever and terrifying as this monstrous maniac.

A Vendetta

Paolo Saverini's widow lived with her son in a little house on the outskirts of Bonifacio. The town is built on a mountain promontory, and in places it even overhangs the sea. It looks out over the narrow passage bristling with reefs, onto the southernmost coast of Sardinia. Immediately below, almost surrounding the town, there is a deep cleft in the mountain, like a gigantic corridor. This serves as a harbour, providing access to the lowest houses and bringing in, after their long, circuitous voyage between two sheer walls of rock, the little Italian and Sardinian fishing boats and, once a fortnight, the wheezy old steamer from Ajaccio.

On the white mountainside, the tiers of houses make an even whiter patch. They look like birds' nests, clinging like this to the rock, and overlooking this terrible passage through which ships rarely venture. The wind constantly lashes the sea, constantly erodes the stark, almost grassless coastline, and rushes through the narrow strait, ravaging the land on each side. The trails of pallid foam streaming from the black tips of countless rocks, which everywhere pierce the waves, look just like shreds of cloth floating and bobbing up and down on the surface of the sea.

Mother Saverini's house, built into the very edge of the cliff, had three windows, each of which looked out onto this wild and desolate scene.

There she lived, all alone, except for her son, Antoine, and their bitch, Sémillante, a large, skinny creature, with a coarse, shaggy coat, and with some sheepdog in her. The young man always used to take her as his gun-dog when he went hunting.

One evening there was a quarrel, and Antoine Saverini was treacherously stabbed to death by Nicolas Ravolati, who managed to get across to Sardinia the same night.

When they brought the body back to the old widow she did not shed any tears, but stood there for a long time, absolutely motionless. Then she stretched out her wrinkled, old hand over the corpse, and promised her son a vendetta. She did not want anyone to stay with her, and she shut herself in with the body, accompanied only by the bitch, which was howling, standing at the foot of the bed, with its head cocked on one side, looking at its master, and with its tail between its legs. It made no more movement than the mother, who was now bending over the body, staring hard, and shedding great, silent tears as she gazed.

The young man, lying on his back and wearing his rough jacket, which was torn and slashed about the chest, looked as though he were asleep. But there was blood all over him – on his shirt, which had been torn when they had tried to give first aid, and on his waistcoat, his trousers, his hands, his face. Clots of blood had congealed in his beard and his hair.

The old mother began to talk to him. At the sound of her voice the bitch stopped howling.

'There, there! You'll be avenged, my dear . . . my son . . . my poor child. Go to sleep now, go to sleep. You'll be avenged . . . do you hear me? It's your mother who is promising revenge! And she always keeps her promise, does your mother – you know that, don't you?'

And slowly she bent closer to him, and pressed her cold lips against the dead lips of her son.

Then Sémillante started to howl again – a long, monotonous wailing sound, heart-rending and horrible.

They both remained there, the woman and the dog, until dawn.

Antoine Saverini was buried that day, and eventually the people of Bonifacio were no longer talking about him.

He had left behind neither brother nor any near cousins – no man at all who could carry out the vendetta. But, all alone, his old mother was thinking about it . . .

From morning till night she stared at a white point on the coast on the other side of the strait. It was the little Sardinian village of Longosardo, where Corsican bandits take refuge when they are hard pressed. They form almost the entire population of this hamlet which looks across to the coast of their homeland, and there they wait until it is safe to come back and resume their life in the *maquis*. She knew very well that it was in this village that Nicolas Ravolati had taken refuge.

All alone, all day long, she sat by her window, looking across at the village, thinking of revenge. How would she be able to manage it, with no-one to help her, and with so little strength and such a short time to live? But she had made a promise, had sworn an oath over the corpse. She could not forget – and she could not wait. How could she manage it? She never slept at night now; she could find neither rest nor ease:

she was searching for a solution, refusing to give up. At her feet the bitch lay dozing, but sometimes she would raise her head and howl into the distance. Ever since her master's death she often howled like this, as if she were calling to him, as if her disconsolate animal soul also retained a memory which nothing could erase.

Now, one night, just as Sémillante was starting to howl again, the old mother suddenly had an idea, the idea of a revengeful, ferocious barbarian. She thought about it all night long, and then as soon as it was light she got up and went to the church. She prayed, lying prostrate upon the stone foor, humbling herself before God, imploring Him to help her, to sustain her, to give to her poor, worn-out body the strength she would need to avenge her son.

Then she went back home. She had in her yard an old barrel which collected water from the gutters. She turned it over on to its side to empty it, then fixed it firmly to the ground, holding it in position by means of stones and wooden stakes. Then she chained Sémillante to this kennel, and finally went indoors.

Now she restlessly paced up and down her room, never taking her eyes off the Sardinian coastline. There was the murderer – just over there!

The bitch howled all day long and throughout the night. In the morning the old woman brought her some water in a bowl – but nothing else: no soup, no bread, nothing.

Another day went by. Sémillante, weak and exhausted by now, spent the time sleeping. The next morning her eyes were gleaming, her coat was bristling, and she was tugging frantically on her chain.

Once again the old woman gave her nothing to eat. The animal was now vicious, and it was barking hoarsely. Another night went by.

Then, as soon as it was light, Mother Saverini went round to her neighbour's to ask if she might have two bundles of straw. She took some old clothes which her husband had once worn, and stuffed them with the straw until they looked like the body of a man.

She then stuck a pole in the ground in front of Sémillante's kennel, and tied this dummy to it so that it looked as though it was standing up. Then she made a head for it out of a bundle of old underclothes.

The bitch, surprised and puzzled, stared at this man of straw, and stopped barking, even though she was ravenously hungry.

Now the old woman went to the pork-butcher's and bought a long piece of black-pudding. When she got back home she took some sticks and lit a fire in her yard near the kennel, and then grilled her black-pudding on it. Sémillante, crazy with hunger, started jumping about, foaming at the mouth, and all the time her eyes were on the grilling black-pudding whose savoury, appetizing aroma was entering her very stomach.

Then the old mother took this steaming food and with it made a neck-tie for the straw dummy. She spent a long time fastening it around the neck, threading it so that it actually went inside. When she had finished, she unleashed the dog.

In one tremendous leap the animal reached the dummy's throat and began to tear it out, with its paws resting on the shoulders. It got down with a piece of the food in its mouth, then leaped up again, buried its fangs into the rope, tore out a few more fragments of food, got down again, then jumped up again, working away in a frenzy. With savage bites it demolished the face and reduced the whole of the neck to shreds.

Standing there motionless and silent, the old woman looked on, with a strange gleam in her eyes. Then she chained the animal up again, starved it for another two days, then started this strange performance all over again. For three months she accustomed it to this frantic struggle, to this meal which it could only obtain through the furious conquest of its fangs. Now she no longer needed to keep it on a chain. At the merest sign from its mistress it would leap upon the dummy.

She had taught the dog to tear the throat ravenously to pieces, even when there was no food concealed there. But as a reward she always gave it the black-pudding which she had just grilled.

As soon as Sémillante caught sight of the man of straw she would quiver with excitement, then look at her mistress, waiting for her to raise her finger and shout in her shrill voice: 'Now!'

When she thought that the time had come Mother Saverini went to church one Sunday morning, making her confession and taking communion with ecstatic fervour. Then she got some man's clothes and disguised herself as an old, ragged beggar. Next she struck a bargain with a Sardinian fisherman to take her and her dog across to the other side of the strait.

In a cloth bag she carried a large piece of black-pudding. Sémillante had been kept without food for two whole days. Every now and then the old woman let her smell the savoury food in order to excite her.

Soon they reached the village of Longosardo. The old Corsican widow went hobbling along until she came to a baker's shop where she asked if they could tell her where Nicolas Ravolati lived. He had gone back to his former trade, that of a carpenter, and he was working alone at the back of his workshop.

The old woman pushed open the door and called out:

'Hello, there, Nicolas!'

He turned round. Slipping the bitch from the lead she shouted:

'Now! Now! Food! Food!'

The half-crazed animal went for his throat. The man flung out his arms, then fell rolling on the floor, grappling with the dog. For a few seconds he lay there writhing, kicking out with his feet. Then he became absolutely still as Sémillante rummaged into his throat, tearing it to shreds.

Two neighbours, who had been sitting on their doorsteps, distinctly remembered having seen an old beggar leave the house. With him was a skinny black dog which was eating something brown, and being fed by its master as they went along . . .

By evening the old woman had got back home again. That night she slept well.

The Smile of Schopenhauer

He was drawing very near to death, rapidly losing ground in the way that consumptives do. Every day at about two o'clock I used to see him sit down on a seat on the promenade – just under the hotel windows – and look out on to the tranquil sea. For some time he would remain motionless, enjoying the warmth of the sun and gazing mournfully out over the Mediterranean. Occasionally he would turn to glance up at the hazy summits of the lofty mountains which lie behind Menton. Then, with a very slow, deliberate movement he would cross his long legs – legs so thin that they looked like two bare bones, with the trousers flapping loosely about them. After this he would open a book – always the same one. He would then continue to sit there, quite motionless, reading so intently that you felt that his eyes and his mind were absolutely concentrated on his book. The whole of his poor decaying body seemed to be reading; his very soul seemed to be buried in the book, totally absorbed by it, quite lost in it, until the time when the air became somewhat cooler and made him start to cough a little. When this happened he would get up and go back into the hotel.

He was a tall German with a blond beard. He used to take all his meals in his room, and never spoke to anybody.

I was attracted to him by a sort of vague curiosity, and one day when he was reading I sat down next to him, taking care to bring with me, for the sake of appearances, a book of Musset's poems.

My neighbour suddenly asked me, speaking in very good French: 'Do you know German, monsieur?'

I told him that I could not understand a word of the language.

'That's a pity,' he said. 'Since chance has brought us into contact I would have lent you and demonstrated to you a priceless treasure – this book that I am holding.'

'What book is it?'

'It is a copy of something by my teacher – Schopenhauer, with notes in his own handwriting. As you can see, he has filled all the margins with his notes.'

I took hold of the book with a certain reverence and looked at these letters, which though I could not understand a word of them, expressed the imperishable thoughts of the greatest destroyer of dreams who has ever walked the earth.

I suddenly remembered those lines written by Musset:

Dors-tu content, Voltaire, et ton hideux sourire
Voltige-t-il encore sur tes os décharnés?

Are you sleeping in peace, Voltaire, and does your
   hideous smile
Still hover around your fleshless bones?

And I couldn't help comparing the childish, anti-religious sarcasm of Voltaire with the irresistible irony of Schopenhauer, the German philosopher whose influence will never be eradicated.

A disillusioned pleasure-seeker, he has upset beliefs, hopes, poetry and flights of imagination. He has destroyed aspirations, devastated confidence, killed love, demolished the idealized worship of woman, burst the bubble of every human illusion, accomplished the most gigantic labour of scepticism that the world has ever known. His mockery has penetrated everything, and emptied everything of meaning. And even today, those who detest him seem, in spite of themselves, to carry in their minds little fragments of his thought.

'So you knew Schopenhauer personally, then?' I said to the German.

He gave a rather sad smile, and replied: 'Until the day he died, monsieur.'

And he began to tell me about him, mentioning in particular the almost supernatural impression which this strange being made on everybody who met him.

He told me about the interview the old iconoclast gave to a French politician, a doctrinaire republican, who was determined to see him and found him in a noisy beer-cellar sitting there in the midst of his disciples – dry-looking, wrinkled, smiling his unforgettable smile, taking ideas and beliefs and biting at them and tearing them to pieces with a single phrase, just as a dog tears things to shreds with a single bite.

He quoted what this Frenchman had shouted out as he went away, bewildered and terrified: 'I feel as though I've just spent an hour with the Devil!'

Then the German added this: 'You know, monsieur, he really did have a horrible smile, which frightened us even after he had died. There's a true story about this, which few people have heard – and I'll tell it to you, if you are interested.'

And in a tired voice he began to tell his tale, which was interrupted every now and then by violent fits of coughing:

Schopenhauer had just died, and it was decided that we should take turns to sit up with the body until the next morning.

He was laid out in a large, plainly furnished bedroom, which was very gloomy. Two candles were burning on the table by the bed.

It was midnight when my friend and I came to watch over the corpse. The two friends whom we were replacing left the house, and we went and sat at the foot of the bed.

The expression on the face had not altered at all. It was still smiling. The corners of the mouth were turned up in that grin we knew so well, and we almost expected him at any moment to open his eyes, move and speak. His mind, or rather his thoughts, seemed to surround us; more than ever before we felt ourselves overcome and possessed by the atmosphere of his genius. Now that he was dead his over-mastering spirit seemed more absolute than before. The power of his incomparable mind was now touched with mystery.

The bodies of men of his kind may disappear, but the men themselves remain. And I assure you, monsieur, that during the first night after their hearts have stopped beating, these men are terrifying.

In hushed voices we began to talk about him, recalling his words, his aphorisms, those remarkable maxims which seem like rays of light, shed by a few mere words, into the darkness of the Unknown.

'I have the feeling that he's just going to open his mouth and talk,' said my friend. And together, with an uneasiness bordering on fear, we looked at this motionless face, which went on smiling.

We gradually began to feel very ill at ease. The atmosphere seemed oppressive, and we were beginning to feel faint.

'I don't know what's the matter with me,' I said falteringly, 'but I can assure you that I'm not at all well.'

It was then that we noticed that there was an unpleasant smell coming from the body.

My friend suggested that we should go into the next room, leaving the bedroom door open, and I agreed.

I took one of the candles from the bedside table, and then went and sat down at the far end of the other room. From this position we could see the bed and the dead man lying on it, clearly visible in the light from the remaining candle.

But the spirit of Schopenhauer still seemed to haunt us. It was just as though his soul, now released from the body and therefore free, all-powerful, and all-masterful, was prowling about quite close to us. And occasionally we would also catch the filthy stench of the decomposing body, which seemed to fill our whole being with an indefinable nausea.

Suddenly, we experienced a violent shudder which went right through us . . . A sound, just a slight sound, had come from the room where the dead man was lying. We immediately looked at him, and we saw – yes, monsieur, we both saw, as plainly as could be – something white run across the bedclothes, drop on to the carpet, and disappear under a chair.

We jumped to our feet before we had time to think of anything: we were immediately overcome by senseless terror, ready to run away in sheer panic. Then we looked at each other. We were both ghastly pale. Our hearts were thumping away so furiously that you could almost see them beating under our clothes . . . I was the first to speak.

'Did you see it?'

'Yes, I saw it.'

'Do you think he's still alive?'

'How can he be? The body's started to putrefy.'

'What should we do?'

My friend replied, with some hesitation:

'We must go and take a look.'

I picked up our candle and led the way in, looking all round the big bedroom and peering into its dark corners. There was nothing moving now . . . I went towards the bed – then stopped short, petrified with astonishment and horror: Schopenhauer was no longer smiling. His face was contorted in the most horrible grimace, with his lips pursed, and his cheeks dreadfully hollow.

I stammered out. 'He's not dead!'

Yet the appalling stench was filling my nostrils, suffocating me . . . And I stood there, staring at him, as terrified as if I were seeing a ghost.

My friend picked up the other candle and leaned forward. Then, without saying a word, he touched my arm. I followed his gaze and saw lying on the floor, under the chair next to the bed, something which gleamed white against the dark carpet. It was Schoepenhauer's set of false teeth – wide open, as though preparing to bite.

The process of decomposition had loosened his jaws and had caused the dentures to jump out of his mouth.

I was really terrified that night, monsieur . . .

And now that the sun was low in the sky, almost touching the glittering sea, the consumptive German got up from the seat, gave a little bow, and went back into the hotel.

On the River

Last summer I rented a little cottage on the banks of the Seine, a good few miles from Paris, and every night I used to go out there to sleep. After a few days I got to know one of my neighbours, a man between thirty and forty years of age, who really was one of the most curious characters I have ever met. He was an old boating enthusiast, absolutely mad about boats, always near the water – or on it, or in it. He must have been born in a boat, and he will certainly die one day whilst taking his final trip on the river.

One evening when we were walking along the banks of the Seine I asked him to tell me something of his boating experiences. The old oarsman immediately came to life and his face lit up; he became eloquent, almost poetic. There was one great, all-consuming, irresistible passion in his life – his passion for the river.

Ah! [he said] how many memories I have of this river you see flowing past us! You folk who live in the city streets have no idea what the 'river' really is. But just notice the way a fisherman says the word. For him it is a thing mysterious, profound, strange – a world of mirage and fantastic shapes, a world in which you can see at night things which are not really there, hear noises you cannot account for, shiver for no particular reason, as if you were passing through a graveyard – and, you know, the river is the most sinister of all graveyards, because you can be buried here without a grave.

To a fisherman the dry land seems restricted, and in the twilight, when there is no moon, the river seems to be limitless. A sailor doesn't have the same kind of feeling about the sea. It's true that the open sea is often harsh and cruel, but it roars and howls, and you can tell exactly what it is going to do. The river is silent – and treacherous. It does not roar: it flows along in continual silence, and this eternal movement of flowing water is more terrifying to me than the great waves of the ocean.

Romantic dreamers have claimed that the sea conceals in its depths immense worlds of blue, where those who have been drowned float about amongst the great fish, in strange forests and crystal caves. The river has only black depths, where the drowned rot in the mud. Yet the river is beautiful when it is glittering in the light of the rising sun, and when its waters are gently lapping between banks clothed in rustling reeds.

The poet talks about the mournful tales that could be told by the waves of the ocean . . . Well, I think that the stories whispered by the slender reeds in their tiny soft voices must be even more sinister than those mournful tales told by the howling waves.

But since you ask me to tell you a few of my experiences on the river, I'll tell you about a peculiar thing that happened to me here about ten years ago.

In those days I lived – and I still do – at Mother Lafon's place, and one of my best friends, Louis Bernet who, incidentally, has now given up boating and his easy-going ways to become a councillor, had taken a cottage in a village about five miles down the river. We used to have dinner together every day, sometimes at his place, sometimes at mine. One evening I was coming back on my own, feeling rather tired, and with some difficulty rowing my heavy boat – a twelve-foot *océan* which I always use at night-time. I stopped for a few moments to get my breath back, just over there, near that little promontory formed by the reeds, about two hundred yards before you get to the railway bridge. The weather was magnificent; the moon was shining brightly; the surface of the river was gleaming in the moonlight, and the air was still and mild. This peaceful atmosphere tempted me: I thought to myself that it would be very pleasant to stop here and smoke a pipe of tobacco. Without any hesitation I picked up my anchor and threw it overboard.

The boat, which was being pulled back downstream by the current, slipped to the end of the chain, then stopped, and I sat down in the stern of the boat on my sheepskin rug, making myself as comfortable as possible. There was not a sound to be heard, not a sound – except that occasionally I thought I just caught an almost inaudible lapping of water against the river bank, and I could see clumps of reeds rising high above the bank, taking on strange shapes and apparently stirring every now and again.

The river was absolutely calm – and yet I felt disturbed by the extraordinary silence which surrounded me. Even the frogs and toads, creatures who normally make music in the swamps at night, were not making a sound. Then, suddenly, somewhere to my right, a frog croaked. The noise made me jump. It didn't croak again. I could hear nothing else, and so I decided to smoke a little, just to give myself something to do. But, you know, though I'm an inveterate pipe-smoker,

I couldn't do it. After a puff or two I felt sick, and stopped smoking. I started to hum a tune, but the sound of my voice somehow disturbed me, and so I lay down in the bottom of the boat and looked up at the sky.

For a while I felt calm, but soon I became worried by the slight pitching of the boat. The impression I had was that it was lurching violently, touching first one bank and then swinging over to the other. Then I got the idea that some invisible being or force was gently drawing the boat to the bottom of the river, then lifting it up and letting it drop again. I fancied I was being tossed about as if in the middle of a storm, and I could hear noises all round me. I leapt to my feet. The water was gleaming in the moonlight . . . and everything was calm.

I realized that what was the matter was that my nerves were a bit on edge, and I decided it was time to move on. I pulled on my anchor-chain. The boat started to move, and then I felt a resistance. I pulled harder, but the anchor wouldn't budge. It had caught on something at the bottom of the river and I simply couldn't get it up. I started tugging again, but it was no use.

Then, by using the oars, I turned my boat round and moved upstream a little in order to change the position of the anchor. It was no good: it held as firm as ever. I lost my temper and gave the chain a furious shaking – but it still wouldn't budge.

Very discouraged, I sat down and began to think about the mess I was in. I couldn't dream of breaking this chain or separating it from the boat. It was enormously thick, and riveted to the bows in a piece of wood that was thicker than my arm . . . But as the weather was still very good, I thought it would probably not be long before some fisherman would come to my rescue. This annoying discovery had calmed my nerves: I sat down and found that at last I could smoke my pipe. I had a bottle of rum with me. I drank two or three glasses, and began to laugh at the situation I was in. The weather was really very mild, so at a pinch I could spend the night in the open without coming to much harm.

Suddenly there was the sound of a bump against the side of my boat. I jumped to my feet with a start, and a cold sweat broke out all over my body. This sound had no doubt been made by some piece of driftwood carried along by the current, but it had been sufficient to upset me, and once again I felt myself in the grip of a strange nervousness. I grabbed hold of the anchor-chain, and pulled on it for all I was worth, in one final desperate effort.

The anchor held firm. I sat down once again, exhausted.

Meanwhile the river had gradually become covered with very dense, white mist which crept along close to the surface of the water, with the result that when I stood up I could no longer see either the river, or my feet, or my boat. All I could see were the tips of the reeds then, farther away, the meadows, all pale in the moonlight, with large, black patches reaching up into the sky, which were formed by groups of Lombardy poplars. It was just as though I was buried up to my waist in an expanse of incredibly white cotton-wool – and it conjured up all kinds of fantasies. I imagined that somebody was trying to get into the boat, which I could no longer see beneath me, and that the river, concealed by his opaque fog, must be full of strange creatures which were swimming all around me.

I experienced a horrible feeling of faintness; my temples were throbbing; my heart was pounding so hard I seemed to be short of breath and, losing all self-control, I seriously thought of jumping overboard and swimming to safety. Then, immediately, this idea made me shudder with fright. I pictured myself lost, floundering about haphazardly in this thick mist, struggling amongst the vegetation and reeds which I would surely become entangled in, gasping in terror, unable to see the bank, unable to find my boat – and I seemed to feel myself being dragged by my feet down into the depths of that murky water.

In fact, as I would have had to swim against the current for at least five hundred yards before finding a part free of water-weed and rushes, where I could get a proper foothold, I had a ninety-per-cent chance of losing my way in the fog, and of getting drowned – no matter how good a swimmer I might be.

I tried to reason with myself. I felt absolutely determined not to be afraid, but there was something within me other than my willpower, and that something else was experiencing fear. I asked myself what there was to be afraid of: the brave part of me jeered at the cowardly part – and never have I felt, as strongly as I did on that occasion, the struggle between the two beings which live within us, one willing something, the other resisting it, and each triumphing over the other in turn.

This stupid and unaccountable fear was still increasing, and was now becoming sheer terror. I stood there motionless, with my eyes open wide and my ears straining to catch any possible sound . . . waiting. What was I waiting for? I had no idea, but whatever it was it must have been something terrible. I think that if a fish had suddenly taken it into its head to jump out of the water, as fish frequently do, that would have been quite sufficient to make me fall flat on my face, unconscious.

However, by making a strenuous effort to control myself I finally managed to bring my state of mind gradually back to normal. Once again I took my bottle of rum and drank from it in great gulps. Then I had an idea: I started to call out at the top of my voice, successively turning to face the four points of the compass. When my throat hurt so much that I couldn't shout any more, I stood and listened . . . All I could hear was the distant howling of a dog.

I drank some more rum, then I lay down, stretching myself full length along the bottom of the boat. I stayed like this for maybe an hour – possibly two hours – without going to sleep, with my eyes wide open, and with nightmares hovering all around me. I didn't dare sit up, and yet I had an intense desire to do so. Each minute I kept putting it off, saying to myself: 'Come on, sit up!' – but I was too afraid to move. At long last I slowly began to raise myself – taking infinite care as I did so, as if my very life depended on the slightest sound I might make – and I looked over the side of the boat.

My eyes were dazzled by the most marvellous, the most astonishing sight it is possible to imagine. It was just like one of those phantasmagoric tableaux depicting fairyland, one of those fantastic scenes that travellers from distant countries describe to us, and we listen without really believing them.

The fog, which two hours before had been hanging over the water, had gradually lifted and settled over the banks. Leaving the river entirely clear, it had formed on each side a long, continuous hill, six or seven yards high, which shone in the moonlight with the superb brilliance of snow. The result was that nothing could be seen except this fire-spangled river flowing between these two white mountains, and overhead a full, brilliant moon set in a sky of milky blue.

All the inhabitants of the river-bank had come to life. The frogs were croaking away furiously, and every now and then, sometimes on my left, sometimes on my right, I could hear the short, slow, dismal note of a metallic-voiced toad, serenading the stars. Oddly enough, I was no longer afraid. I was surrounded by such extraordinary scenery that the most bizarre phenomena would not have surprised me in the least.

Just how long all this lasted I have no idea, because eventually I dropped off to sleep. When I opened my eyes again the moon had gone down and the sky was full of clouds. The water was lapping mournfully against the boat; the wind was blowing; it was cold, and pitch-dark.

I drank what was left of the rum, then, as I sat there shivering, I listened to the rustling of reeds and the sinister murmur of the river. I tried to see, but I could make out neither my boat, nor even my hands when I held them close to my eyes.

Gradually, however, the intense darkness diminished. Suddenly I thought I sensed a dark shape gliding along, quite near to me. I gave a shout, and a voice answered me. It was a fisherman. I called across to him, and he rowed up to me. I told him all about my misadventure, and then he brought his boat alongside mine and together we pulled on my anchor-chain. The anchor still would not budge.

The day was dawning, a gloomy, grey, wet, chilly day, one of those days which you feel is bound to bring you sorrow and misfortune. I caught sight of another boat and we shouted across to it. The man who was in it rowed up and added his efforts to our own, and finally, little by little, the anchor began to move. It came up very, very slowly, and was obviously carrying a considerable weight. At last we saw a black mass emerge, and we dragged it into my boat.

It was the corpse of an old woman, with a huge stone tied round her neck.

He?

My dear friend, you are completely baffled by it, aren't you? And I can easily understand why. I suppose you think I've gone mad. Perhaps I *am* a little insane – but not for the reasons you imagine.

Yes. I'm getting married. It's quite true.

And yet my ideas and convictions on this subject have not changed. I still consider legalized cohabitation to be foolish. I am certain that eight husbands out of ten have wives who are unfaithful – and that is just what they deserve for having been idiotic enough to fetter their lives, give up the freedom of love, the only good and cheerful thing in the world, and clip the wings of the romantic fancy which constantly urges us to take an interest in all women . . . More than ever I feel incapable of loving merely one woman, because I should always be too fond of all the others. I wish I had a thousand arms, a thousand lips, a thousand . . . personalities, so that I could embrace at the same moment, a whole regiment of these charming but insignificant creatures.

And yet, I am getting married.

I might add that I hardly know the girl who will become my wife tomorrow. I have only seen her four or five times. I know that I do not find her displeasing – and this is sufficient for the purpose I have in mind. She is short, fair and plump. After tomorrow I shall ardently wish for a woman who is tall, dark and slender.

She is not rich. She comes from an ordinary family. She is the sort of girl you can find by the hundred in the middle classes – very marriageable, with no outstanding characteristics, either good or bad. People say of her: 'Mademoiselle Lajolle is a very nice girl.' And tomorrow they will be saying: 'She's very nice, you know, is Madame Raymond.' In short, she belongs to that vast number of decent girls, whom you are 'glad you have married' – until the day when you discover that, in fact, you prefer all the other women to the one you have chosen.

'Then why on earth are you getting married?' you will say.

I hardly dare tell you the strange, incredible reason which is urging me to commit this senseless action.

I am getting married so I shall not have to be on my own!

I don't know how to tell you about it, how to make myself understood. I am in such a wretched state of mind that you will feel sorry for me, and also despise me.

I cannot bear to be alone any more at night. I want to feel some human being near me, touching me, a human being who can speak, say something – anything at all.

I want to be able to interrupt her sleep, suddenly ask her a question of some kind, even a silly question – just so I can hear a voice, feel that my home is lived in, feel that there is another soul awake, another mind alert – I want to see, when I hastily light the candle by my bed, another human face next to mine . . . because, you see . . . because – I'm so ashamed I dare hardly admit it – because . . . I am afraid of being on my own.

Oh, I don't suppose you will understand!

It's not that I'm afraid of any danger. If a burglar were to come into the room I would kill him without turning a hair. I'm not afraid of ghosts, and I don't believe in the supernatural. I'm not afraid of the dead – I believe they are completely annihilated when they leave the earth.

'Well, then!' you'll say. 'What are you afraid of?' Yes. I know . . . Well . . . I'm afraid of myself! I'm afraid of fear, afraid of my panic-stricken mind, afraid of that horrible sensation of incomprehensible terror.

Oh, you can laugh, if you like. But it's terrible – and incurable. I'm afraid of the walls, of the furniture, of familiar objects, which seem to me to take on a kind of animal life. Above all, I am afraid of the horrible confusion of my thoughts, of the way my reason becomes blurred and elusive, scattered by a mysterious, invisible anguish.

At first I feel a vague uneasiness which enters my soul and sends shivers all over my skin. I look all round me. There's nothing there. And yet I wish there were something there to be seen – something I could understand. The only reason I'm frightened is that I don't understand the cause of my fear.

I happen to say something aloud – and I'm frightened by the sound of my own voice! I walk about my room – and I'm afraid there might be something strange behind the door, behind the curtains, in the cupboard, under my bed. And yet I know very well that there is nothing there at all.

Sometimes I suddenly turn round because I'm afraid of what might be behind me – and yet there is nothing there, as I very well know.

I become agitated, feel the nervousness increasing, and so I lock myself in my room, bury myself in my bed and hide myself under the sheets. Then cowering there, all huddled up as round as a ball, I close my eyes in despair and stay like this for a long, long time, knowing full well that my candle is still burning on the bedside table, and that I really ought to put it out – and yet I haven't the courage to do so!

Isn't it dreadful, to be in this state?

I never used to feel in the least like this. I used to come home in a calm frame of mind. I used to walk around my flat without anything disturbing my serenity. If somebody had told me that one day I should be stricken by some disease characterized by unreasonable, stupid, ghastly fear, I would have laughed outright. When it was dark I used to open doors as calmly as you like. I used to take my time going to bed, and I never bothered to bolt the doors and windows. I never used to get up in the middle of the night – as I do now – to make sure that everything was properly fastened.

It all started last year, in a very curious way . . .

It was one damp evening in the autumn. I had finished dinner, the maidservant had left the flat, and I was wondering what I could do to pass the time. For a while I walked up and down my room. I was feeling very tired, worn out for no particular reason; I felt completely incapable of work, and had not even the energy to read a book. A fine drizzle was moistening the window-panes. I felt un-happy, overwhelmed by one of those unaccountable fits of depression which make you want to weep, make you wish you could talk to somebody – anybody at all – just to shake off the heavy burden of your thoughts.

I was feeling very lonely. My flat seemed emptier than it had ever been before. I felt myself immersed in a never-ending, heart-breaking solitude. What could I do? I sat down – and then felt a kind of nervous impatience seize my legs. I stood up and started to pace the room again. I was certainly a little feverish: I was holding my hands clasped behind my back – in the way you often do when you are walking slowly up and down – and I noticed that they felt hot to the touch. Then, suddenly, a cold shiver ran down my back. It occurred to me that the damp night air might be getting into my room, and I thought I would light a fire. I did so; it was the first I had lit that autumn. And I sat down once again, watching the flames. Soon, however, the feeling that I could not possibly sit still got me to my feet again, and I knew that I would have to get out, shake off my present mood, find a friend to keep me company.

I went out. I called to see three of my friends, but not one of them was at home. Then I went as far as the boulevards, determined to find some acquaintance to talk to.

Everywhere was depressing. The damp pavements were gleaming in the gaslight. The mild, humid air – the kind of air that chills you with sudden shivers, an oppressive humidity composed of rain which cannot really be felt – was lying heavily over the streets, where it seemed to weary the feebly-burning gas-lamps.

I walked languidly, saying to myself: 'I shan't find anybody I can talk to.'

Several times I looked in cafés, walking all the way from the Madeleine to the Faubourg Poissonnière. Melancholy people were sitting at tables, looking as though they had not even the strength to finish their drinks.

I wandered along like this for a long time, and towards midnight I set off back home. I was very calm now, but very tired. My concierge, who is usually in bed by eleven o'clock, opened the door straight away. This was not what I would have expected, and I thought: 'Hello! It looks as though another tenant has just gone upstairs ahead of me.'

Now, when I go out I always make sure my door is locked. When I got up to my flat I found that the door was only pulled to, and this struck me as rather odd. I assumed that the concierge had brought a letter up to my room during the evening.

I entered my flat. The fire was still burning sufficiently to light up the room a little. I picked up a candle with the intention of lighting it at the fire when, looking straight ahead, I noticed somebody sitting in my fireside chair, warming his feet, with his back towards me.

I was not frightened – not in the least. A very likely explanation immediately occurred to me: it was that one of my friends had come to see me. The concierge, to whom I had spoken on my way out, had told him I would be coming back and had lent him a key. And in a flash I remembered the things I had noticed on my return: the fact that the street-door was opened immediately, and that my own door was unlocked and on the latch.

I could only see the back of my friend's head. He had evidently fallen asleep in front of the fire, whilst waiting for me. So I went across in order to wake him. I could see him perfectly clearly: his right arm was hanging down, and his legs were crossed; his head, leaning back on the chair, a little to the left, gave an unmistakable impression of a man asleep.

I asked myself: 'Who can it be?' There was not much light in the room, and I still couldn't make out who he was, so I stretched out my hand to touch him on the shoulder . . .

My hand came into contact with the wood of the chair-back! There was no longer anybody sitting there! The chair was empty!

My God! How I jumped!

Instantly I drew back as though some terrible danger had confronted me.

Then I turned round, feeling sure that there was somebody standing behind me. Then, immediately overcome by an insistent need to see the chair again, I spun round on my heels – and I stood there, panting with terror, so bewildered that I could no longer think, so shaken that I was ready to collapse.

But I am by nature a man with self-control, and I soon recovered. I thought: 'I've just experienced some kind of hallucination, that's all.' And I immediately began to think of how this could have come about. Thoughts move very quickly in such moments as this.

I had experienced a hallucination – that was an indisputable fact. Now, throughout this experience my mind had remained crystal-clear, working normally and logically. So there was no confusion arising from the functioning of my brain. It was only my eyes which had been deceived – or rather, which had deceived my mind. My eyes had experienced a vision – one of those visions which lead simple folk to believe in miracles. What had happened was that there had been some nervous disturbance of the optical system, nothing more. My eyes were probably just tired and slightly inflamed.

So I lit my candle. As I bent down towards the fire I noticed that I was trembling – and I stood up again with a start, as though somebody had touched me from behind.

I had not been able to reassure myself – that was obvious.

I walked about a little, talked in a loud voice, and hummed a few tunes. Then I double-locked my door, and this gave me a little more reassurance. At any rate, nobody could get in.

I sat down, and for a long time I thought about the incident that I had experienced. Then I went to bed and blew out my candle.

For a few minutes all was well. I was lying on my back, feeling quite calm. Then I knew I simply had to look across the room, and I turned over on my side.

All that remained of my fire was a few glowing embers, the light from which faintly lit up the legs of my fireside chair – in which I thought I saw the man sitting again.

With a rapid movement I struck a match. I had been mistaken. There was nothing to be seen.

I got up, however, and went and hid the chair behind my bed.

Then I blew out my candle again, and tried to get to sleep. I had not been asleep for more than five minutes when I dreamt that I saw the whole thing again, as vividly as if it were reality. I woke up in a panic, and having lit the candle again, I stayed there, sitting up in bed, without even daring to try to get to sleep again.

Twice, however, I was overcome by sleep in spite of myself – just for a few moments. And twice I saw the thing again. I thought I was going mad.

As soon as daylight appeared I felt that I was cured, and I slept peacefully until noon.

It was all over, completely finished. I had been feverish, had a nightmare – something of that sort. I had been ill, in fact . . . Even so, I felt that I had made a real fool of myself.

I was very cheerful that day. In the evening I went out for a meal, and afterwards went to the theatre. I set off to walk back home, but as I got near the house I was overcome by a strange uneasiness. I was afraid of seeing 'him' again. I was not actually afraid of 'him', not afraid of his presence, in which I simply did not believe, but I was afraid that my eyes might play tricks on me again, afraid of another hallucination, afraid of the terror which would then come upon me.

For more than an hour I walked up and down the pavement in front of the house. Then I eventually decided that my behaviour really was too ridiculous for words, and I went in.

I was so short of breath that I could hardly get up the stairs – and stood for another ten minutes, waiting on the landing outside my flat. Then, suddenly, I had a spurt of courage, and pulled myself together. I pushed my key into the keyhole, and rushed in with a candle in my hand. I kicked open the inner door, which was standing ajar, and took a terrified glance at the fireplace. There was nothing to be seen. Ah! What a relief! What a delight! What a deliverance! I walked about the room cheerfully and confidently. Yet I was not entirely reassured. I kept turning round with a jerk. I was bothered by the shadows in the corners of my room.

I did not sleep very well, and was constantly waking up because I imagined I heard something . . . But I did not see 'him'. It was all over!

Ever since that time I have been afraid when I have been alone at night. I feel that it's there, quite near me, round about me, this phantom. It has not appeared to me again. Oh, no! And, in any case, supposing it did, what does it matter, since I don't believe in it, since I know that it doesn't exist?

Yet it still bothers me, because I am constantly thinking about it . . . his right arm was hanging down, his head was leaning to the left, just like the head of a man asleep – Oh, stop it, for God's sake! I don't want to think about it any more!

And yet, why am I obsessed with this thing? Why is the image so persistent? . . . His feet were quite close to the fire!

He is haunting me – I know it sounds mad, but that's the way it is. *Who* is haunting me? 'He'? I know very well that 'he' doesn't exist, that there is nothing there! He only exists in my nervous imagination, in my fear, in my terror – Oh, I must stop talking about it like this!

Yes, but however hard I try to argue myself out of it and bolster my courage, I can no longer stay at home on my own, because '*he*' is there. I shall not see him again, I know. He won't show himself again – that's all over. But he is there all the same – in my thoughts. Even though he remains invisible, that does not prevent him from being there . . . He is behind the doors, in the wardrobe, under the bed, in all the dark corners, lurking in every shadow. If I open the door, if I open the wardrobe, if I take a candle and look under the bed, if I light up the shadowy corners . . . he is no longer there. But then I sense that he is behind me. I turn round – though with the certainty that I shall not see him, that I will never see him again. None the less he is behind me, still behind me.

It's ridiculous – but it's horrible. I'm sorry . . . I simply can't help it.

But if there were two of us in my flat – yes, I feel absolutely convinced – that he wouldn't be there any more. You see, he's there because I am alone – just because I am alone!

Old Milon

For a whole month the sun has been shedding its scorching heat over the countryside. Vigorous life is bursting forth under this fiery downpour, and the land is clothed with green as far as the eye can see. The sky is a perfect blue down to the very edge of the horizon. The Norman farmsteads, scattered here and there across the plain, look from a distance like copses because they are surrounded by hedges of tall and slender beech trees. When you approach one of them and open the worm-eaten old gate you feel that you are looking at some enormous garden, for all the ancient apple trees, standing there as gnarled as peasants, are covered in bloom. In the farmyard you see rows of their old, black, crooked, twisted trunks, displaying to the sky their brilliant canopies of white and pink. The sweet perfume of their opening blossom mingles with the rich smells which come from the open cowsheds and the steaming manure heap, where all the hens are picking.

It is noon. The family is dining in the shade of the pear tree which stands in front of the door: there are the father, the mother, the four children, the two maidservants and the three farmhands. There is not much conversation. They are busy finishing the soup, and they are starting on the casserole of potatoes and bacon.

Every now and then one of the servants gets up and goes to the storeroom to fill up the jug with cider.

The farmer, a tall fellow about forty years old, is gazing at a vine which is growing against the wall of his house. It is still leafless, and runs as tortuous as a snake up behind the shutters and along the whole length of the wall.

After a while he says: 'Father's vine is in bud early this year. There'll be a good crop.'

His wife turns round and also looks at the vine, but she says nothing.

This vine is growing on the exact spot where her husband's father was killed.

It happened during the 1870 war. The Prussians had occupied the whole district. General Faidherbe, with the French northern forces, was preventing any further advance.

Now, the Prussian headquarters had been set up on this farm. The old peasant who owned it, Pierre Milon, better known as Old Milon, had welcomed them and fixed them up to the best of his ability.

For a month the German advance-party had been using the village as a base for reconnaissance. The French had dug their heels in about forty kilometres away, and yet every night German soldiers were reported missing.

All the scouts they sent out on routine patrols, even when they went in twos and threes, never returned alive.

In the morning they would be found dead, lying in a field or a farmyard or a ditch. Even their horses were found lying at the roadside with their throats slashed open by a sabre.

All these killings seemed to have been carried out by the same group of people, but they were never discovered.

The Prussians terrorized the district. They shot peasants on the strength of a mere accusation; they put women in prison; they tried to terrify children into telling them who the killers were. But they were unable to find out anything at all.

Then one morning Old Milon was seen lying in one of his stables. There was a gash across his face made by a Prussian sword.

Two soldiers were found three kilometres from the farm. Their stomachs had been ripped open, but one of them was still holding a bloody sabre in his hand. He had obviously fought hard to defend himself.

A court-martial was immediately set up. It was held in the open air in front of the farmhouse, and the old man was brought before it.

He was sixty-eight years of age. He had a short, thin body which was somewhat twisted, and two huge hands which looked like the claws of a crab. His hair was lifeless, like the down on a duckling, and so thin and sparse that the skin of his head could clearly be seen beneath it. Running up his brown, wrinkled neck were large veins which disappeared under his jaws and seemed to reappear on his temples. In the surrounding villages he had the reputation of being a miser, and a man who struck a hard bargain.

They stood him with two soldiers on each side, making him face the kitchen table which had been brought out of the farmhouse. Five officers and the colonel sat down at the other side of the table. The colonel addressed him in French.

'Père Milon, ever since our arrival here we have had nothing but praise for you. You have always been obliging, and have even been especially considerate to us. But today a dreadful accusation hangs over you, and we simply must establish the truth . . . How did you receive the injury which you have on your face?'

The peasant did not answer.

'Your silence condemns you, Père Milon,' continued the colonel. 'But I want you to answer my question! Understand? Do you know who killed the two soldiers who were found this morning near the roadside calvary?'

The old man repled with very distinct articulation:

'It was me.'

The colonel, taken aback, remained silent for a few moments, staring at the prisoner before him. Old Milon stood there impassively, with the air of a stupid yokel, looking at the ground the way he did when talking to his priest. The only thing which might have indicated an inner anxiety was the fact that he kept swallowing his saliva, and doing so with a visible effort as though his throat was completely choked.

The old chap's family – his son Jean, his daugher-in-law and their two little children – stood looking on, about ten yards away, terrified and dismayed.

'Do you also know,' said the colonel, 'who killed the military scouts who have been found all over the countryside every morning for the past month?'

The old man answered him in the same impassive manner, as though he were a brute beast.

'It was me.'

'Was it you who killed all of them?'

'Aye. Every man-jack of 'em. It was me.'

'You? All by yourself?'

'All by myself.'

'Tell me how you went about it.'

This time the old man showed some emotion. It was obvious that he was bothered about having to speak more than a few words at a time.

'How do *I* know?' he muttered. 'I just did it t' way it 'appened to work out at t' time.'

'I warn you that you'll have to tell me everything,' said the colonel. 'It'll be best for you if you make up your mind to tell me now. What started it all?'

The old man glanced anxiously round at his family, who were standing behind him in rapt attention. He hesitated for a few seconds more, then suddenly made up his mind to talk.

.

'I was coming back 'ome one night. It 'ould be about ten o'clock – and it was t' day after you took over t' farm . . . You and your soldiers 'ad taken more than fifty crowns-worth of fodder from me, as well as a cow and two sheep. So I said to myself: "Every time they take twenty crowns-worth from me I'll see that they pay me back!" And then I'd other things on my mind, which I'll tell you about later . . . Anyway, I 'appened to notice one of your soldiers sittin' at the edge of mi ditch, just at t' back o' mi barn, smoking 'is pipe. I went and took down mi scythe and came and crept up behind 'im – so quietly that 'e never 'eard a thing. And I cut off 'is 'ead with a single stroke – a single stroke – just as if it 'ad been an ear o' corn. Do you know, 'e did'nt so much as say "ouch!" If you don't believe me, all you've got to do is to search t' bottom o' t' pond. You'll find 'im there in a coal sack, with a big stone from t' gate-post weighin' it down.'

'Well, that's when I got my idea. I took all 'is uniform and equipment – from 'is boots to 'is helmet – and went and 'id them in t' lime-kiln in Le Martin wood, just at t' back o' t' farmyard.'

The old man became silent. The officers looked at each other, dumbfounded. The colonel resumed his interrogation, and this is what they learnt . . .

Once he had committed this first murder Old Milon had only one thought in his head! 'I'll kill some Prussians!' He hated them with the crafty, fierce hatred of a covetous peasant who is also a true patriot. As he said, he had got an idea. He waited a few days before trying it out.

The Prussian authorities allowed him complete freedom to come and go as he pleased, to leave and return to the house whenever he felt like it – and they granted him this freedom because he had behaved towards the victorious army in such a humble and obliging way, causing no kind of trouble.

Now, each evening he used to see the troopers setting out on patrol. One night he overheard the name of the village where they were going, and he had already picked up from the soldiers the few German words that were necessary for his purpose.

He left the farmyard, slipped into the wood, reached the lime-kiln and went to the far end of the long tunnel. Here, lying on the floor, he found the uniform of the soldier he had killed. He took off his own clothes and changed into it.

Then he set off, prowling round the fields, crawling along the ditches, keeping hidden behind the grassy banks, straining his ears to catch the slighest sound, as cautious as a poacher.

When he thought the time had come, he got close to the road along which a soldier would be riding, and hid in the undergrowth. He had to wait a long time but at last, about midnight, he heard the sound of a horse galloping over the hard surface of the road. He put his ear to the ground and listened to make sure that only a single rider was approaching. Then he got ready.

The German cavalryman came galloping on at full speed, carrying military dispatches. As he rode he kept his eyes wide open and his ears on the alert. The moment he came within ten yards of where he was lying, Old Milon dragged himself out into the road groaning: 'Hilfe! Hilfe! Help! Help!'

The uhlan pulled up his horse, saw what appeared to be a dismounted German, assumed that he must be wounded, got off his horse, went up to him without suspecting anything was amiss, and as he was bending over the stranger – received right through the middle of his stomach the long curved blade of a Prussian sabre. He collapsed and died almost immediately, his body shuddering on the ground in a few final death-throes.

The Norman got up and, filled with the silent, unexpressed joy of an old countryman, he slit the throat of the corpse just for the fun of it. Then he dragged the body over to the ditch and threw it in.

The horse was patiently waiting for its master. Old Milon climbed into the saddle, and set off across the fields at full gallop.

An hour later he came upon two other soldiers riding side by side on their way back to headquarters. He rode straight up to them shouting once again: 'Hilfe! Hilfe!' The Prussians, seeing his uniform, allowed him to approach with complete confidence. But the old man flew past them like a cannon-ball, striking them both down, one with a fatal blow from his sabre, the other with a pistol-shot.

Then he slit the throats of the horses – German horses! And finally he quickly made his way back to the lime-kiln and hid the first horse at the far end of the dark tunnel. He took off his uniform, put on his own ragged clothes, and got back to his bed, where he slept soundly till morning.

He stayed indoors for four days until they had finished making enquiries. But on the fifth day he set out again and killed two more soldiers, using the same ruse as before. From then on there was no stopping him. Every night he would wander off, roaming all over the district, slaughtering Prussians, sometimes here, sometimes there, galloping by moonlight across the deserted fields, playing the part of a cavalryman who had lost his way – and who was out to hunt men.

Then, when his night's work was done, leaving behind him the corpses strewn along the roadside, the old rider would return to the lime-kiln to hide his horse and his uniform.

Towards noon he would calmly walk out to the kiln, carrying a supply of oats and fresh water for the mount he had left hidden in the underground passage. And as he was working the horse very hard he always made sure it had a particularly good feed . . .

But last night one of the two soldiers he had attacked had been on his guard, and had managed to slash the old peasant's face with his sabre.

He had killed both of them, even so! Once again he had got back, hidden the horse and put on his everyday clothes, but as he was returning to the farm he had been overcome by a feeling of faintness. Quite incapable of reaching the farmhouse, he had just managed to drag himself as far as the stable.

They had found him there, lying in the straw, covered in blood . . .

When he had finished telling his story he suddenly stood with his head held high, looking at the Prussian officers with an air of pride.

The colonel, who was tugging at his moustache, asked him:

'You've nothing else to tell us?'

'No. Nothin' else. I've settled the account now. I've killed sixteen of 'em. Not one more. Not one less.'

'You understand that you will have to die?'

'I 'aven't asked you to spare me.'

'Have you ever served as a soldier?'

'Aye. I've done service in my younger days – And, you know, it was your lot that killed my father. He served under Napoleon, t' first Emperor. So I've paid you back for that – and that's not countin' my youngest son, François. You killed 'im last month, somewhere near Evreux . . . Anyway, I owed you something, and I've paid it. We can call it quits.'

The officers looked at each other, and the old man continued:

'Eight for mi father, eight for mi lad. So we're quits . . . It's not that I've got any quarrel with you personally. I don't even know you. I don't even know where you come from . . . But 'ere you are on my farm, and you run everythin' as though it belonged to you . . . Well, I've taken my revenge – and I'm not sorry for anythin'.'

And holding his arthritic old body as erect as he could manage the old man folded his arms across his chest, looking the picture of simple heroism.

For some considerable time the Prussian officers held a discussion, speaking in low voices. A captain who had also lost his son the previous month was speaking in defence of this poor old farmer who showed such nobility.

Then the colonel stood up and walked over to Old Milon. Lowering his voice he said to him:

'Now, listen, old fellow. We might be able to find a way of saving your life. If we . . .'

But the old fellow was not listening to a word he said. With the breeze ruffling the downy hair on his skull he looked straight into the eyes of the all-victorious officer, and contorting his gaunt, sabre-slashed countenance into a horrible grimace, he swelled out his chest and, with all the strength he could muster, spat into the Prussian's face.

The colonel raised his hands in dismay, and for the second time the Frenchman spat into his face.

All the officers were now on their feet, all yelling out orders at the same time.

Within less than a minute Old Milon – still showing no sign of emotion – was stuck up against the farmhouse wall and shot. At the moment he died he was smiling across at Jean, his elder son, at his daughter-in-law and at the two little children who were looking on in utter bewilderment.

The Head of Hair

The walls of the cell were whitewashed and completely bare. This bright but sinister little room received its light through a narrow, barred window, high up and well out of reach. The madman, sitting on a wicker chair, was staring at us with a vague, terror-stricken look in his eyes.

He was very thin, with sunken cheeks. His hair was almost white – and you had the impression that it must have gone white within the space of a few months. His clothes seemed too big for his bony limbs and his hunched and shrunken body. You had the feeling that this man was being eaten alive, that there was some single thought gnawing away at him, just as a grub gnaws away at a fruit. His madness, his obsession was there in that head, relentless, aggressive, all-consuming, eating away his body, little by little. A single idea – a thing invisible, intangible, imperceptible – was burrowing into his flesh, drinking up his blood, destroying his life . . .

What a mysterious business it was – a man being destroyed by a dream! To see him sitting there, possessed of a devil, filled you with an uncomfortable mixture of fear and pity. What strange, terrifying, mortal delusion occupied that brow of his, furrowed by deep wrinkles which were continually twitching and shifting.

'He has terrible fits of rage,' said the doctor. 'He's one of the strangest cases I have ever seen. His affliction is a form of insanity which is both erotic and macabre. He's a sort of necrophiliac . . . What's more, he's kept a diary which depicts his mental illness for us with remarkable clarity. So his madness, in a sense, is something we can get to grips with . . . If you're interested you can look through what he's written.'

I followed the doctor into his office, and he handed me the diary kept by this poor wretch.

'Read it,' he said, 'and then you can tell me your opinion.'

This is what was written in the note-book . . .

Up to the age of thirty-two I led a very quiet life, and had never been in love. Life seemed to me to be very good. It was uncomplicated, easy to live. I had plenty of money. I was interested in so many different things that I never developed an overwhelming passion for any one of them. In those days it was good to be alive! Every morning I used to wake up happy, ready to do whatever took my fancy, and I used to go to bed content, calmly looking forward to the next day and to a future free from care.

I had had a few mistresses, but I never knew the madness of desire or the torments of love. It's good to live like that. It's better to be in love – but love can be a terrible thing. I suppose that the average person in love must experience a wonderful happiness, but it is probably a happiness not as great as mine, for love came upon me in an incredible way . . .

Having plenty of money I used to collect antiques, especially old furniture. And I often used to think about the unknown hands which had touched these articles, about the eyes which had gazed on them in admiration, about the hearts which had loved them – for people *do* love mere things!

I used to spend hour after hour staring at a little watch from the eighteenth century. It was so dainty, so pretty, with its enamel and its delicately-worked gold. And it was still going, just as it had done on the day when a woman had bought it and experienced the delight of owning a fine piece of jewellery. It had never stopped pulsating away as it lived out its mechanical life, and it had ticked away smoothly for a whole century.

Who, I wonder, was the first woman to wear it on her bosom, keeping it warm and cosy in the folds of her dress – the heart of the little watch beating close against the heart of a woman? What hand had enclosed it, had turned it over and over again with the tips of warm fingers, and then had wiped clean the porcelain shepherds whose image had been momentarily dulled by the moistness of human skin? What eye had gazed upon this little face decorated with flowers, watching for the long-awaited hour, the dear, divine hour of love?

How I wish I had known her, or even seen her, the woman who once chose this rare and exquisite object! Alas, she is dead! And I am possessed by the desire for women of long ago . . . I love – from a distance – all those women who once were in love! The thought of all these bygone passions fills my heart with longing. Oh! To think of all the beauty, all the smiles, all the caresses and hopes of youth! Should not such things live for ever?!

How I have wept – for a whole night, sometimes – over the poor women of olden days, women who were so beautiful, so tender, so gentle, women who opened wide their arms ready to receive a kiss – and now they are dead! The kiss itself is immortal. It travels from mouth to mouth, from century to century, from age to age. Men and women receive kisses, give kisses – and die.

I am attracted by the past, and terrified by the present, because all that the future holds is death. I long for everything that has already taken place, I weep for those who have already lived. I wish I could stop the passage of time, stay the fleeting hour. But on and on it goes . . . Time rushes by and, second by second, it steals a little bit of myself for the nothingness of tomorrow . . . And I shall never pass this way again.

Farewell, ladies of yesteryear! I love you all!

But I do not ask for pity. I have found the woman I have been waiting for, and through her I have tasted unimagined delights . . .

One sunny morning I was strolling through Paris in a very cheerful mood, walking along with a light step, and casually glancing into the shop windows. Suddenly I noticed in an antique shop an Italian bureau from the seventeenth century. It was very handsome, and very rare. I felt sure it was the work of a Venetian craftsman by the name of Vitelli who was very famous in his day.

Having looked at it, I walked on. Why did the image of this piece of furniture pursue me with such power that I had to turn round and retrace my steps? I stopped once again outside the shop, and as I stood looking at it, I felt that it was tempting me.

What a strange thing this kind of temptation is! You look at an object, and gradually it seduces you, disturbs you, invades your very being – just as a woman's face can do. You are penetrated by its charm, a peculiar charm which is composed of its shape, its colour, the countenance it possesses, even though it is a mere thing. And already you are in love with it, you want it, you must have it. You are overcome by a desire for possession, a desire which is sweet at first, like something timid, but then it increases and becomes violent, irresistible.

And shopkeepers seem to be able to sense this secret, growing desire when they see the gleam in the eyes of their customers . . .

I bought this piece of furniture and had it delivered to my home straight away. I put it in my bedroom.

Oh, I feel sorry for those people who do not know the honeymoon which the collector enjoys with an item he has just purchased! You let your eyes and your fingers run over it, just as if it were human flesh. You are constantly coming back to it, always thinking about it, wherever you go, whatever you do. The thought of this beloved object accompanies you when you walk down the street, when you mingle with the crowds, everywhere you go. And when you get back home, before you even take off your gloves and your hat, you go and gaze at it as tenderly as any lover.

For a whole week I really adored this piece of furniture. Every now and then I would open the doors and the drawers, handling it with sheer delight, savouring all the intimate joys of possession.

Now, one evening, as I was feeling the thickness of one of the sides I realized that it must contain a secret recess. My heart started pounding with excitement, and I spent the whole night in a vain attempt to find the hiding-place.

I managed it the next day by pushing the blade of a knife into a crack in the woodwork. A panel slid back, and I saw, lying on a background of black velvet, a magnificent head of hair – a woman's hair!

Yes, a head of hair, a great mass of braided hair! It was blond, with an auburn sheen, bound with a thread of gold, and it was so long that it must have been cut off close against the skin.

I stared at it in amazement, trembling and feeling uneasy. A perfume which was barely perceptible – so ancient that it seemed like the ghost of a perfume – was coming from this mysterious recess and the remarkable relic it contained.

I took hold of it, gently, almost reverently, and I drew it from its place of concealment. Immediately it uncoiled itself, spilling out in a golden wave which almost reached to the floor. It was thick, yet light, as supple and as brilliant as the fiery tail of a comet.

I felt myself in the grip of a strange emotion. What did this mean? When did it happen? How did it happen? Why had this hair been locked away in this piece of furniture? What adventure, what drama, could this memento reveal?

Who had cut off this hair? A lover, on the day he said farewell? A husband, on the day of vengeance? Or did the woman who had worn this hair cut it off herself, on a day of despair?

Or was it when she had taken her vows and become a nun that it had been tossed away like some love-token, bequeathed to the outside world? Or was it when they nailed her into her coffin, this beautiful girl who had died so young? Was it then that the one who loved her had kept the glorious adornment of her head, the only part of her which he could possibly keep, the only living part of her which would never decay in death, the only part of her which he could still love and caress and embrace in the frenzy of his grief?

Was it not strange that the hair had survived like this, when there remained not the merest fragment of the body to which it had belonged?

I let my fingers run through it and felt it brushing against my skin with a unique caress – the caress of a dead woman. I felt so overcome with emotion that I nearly started weeping.

For a long, long time I held it in my hands. Then I became convinced that it was exciting me, as though something of the woman's soul remained concealed within it. And I placed it back on the velvet which had become dull with age, and I slid back the panel and locked the bureau, then went out to walk through the city and think things over . . .

I walked on, feeling very melancholy – and very uneasy too, with the kind of uneasiness people experience when they have exchanged a passionate kiss. I had the impression that I had already lived in a previous age, that I must have known this woman in real life.

And I found my lips sobbing out some lines from the fifteenth-century poet François Villon:

Dictes-moy, où ne en quel pays
Est Flora, la belle Romaine . . .?
Et Jehanne, la bonne Lorraine
Que Anglais brûlèrent à Rouen?
Où sont-ils, Vierge souveraine?
Mais où sont les neiges d'antan?

Tell me, in which country now
Is Flora, the Roman beauty . . .?
And Joan, the good lass from Lorraine
Whom the English burnt in Rouen?
Where are they now, Virgin supreme?
Where are the snows of yesteryear?

When I got back home I experienced an overwhelming need to have another look at my strange find. I took hold of it and, as soon as I touched it, I felt a shudder run through the whole of my body.

For the next few days, however, I continued to live in my usual way, in my normal state of mine – though I was never free from the nagging thought of this head of hair.

Each time I returned home the moment I entered I simply had to see it and handle it. I used to turn the key in the bureau with the same thrill of expectancy a man has when he opens the door to the house of his beloved mistress, for in my hands and my heart I felt a constant need – a confused, peculiar, sensual need – to dip my fingers into that delightful stream of dead hair.

Then, when I had finished stroking it and locked it away in the bureau again, I used to experience a powerful impression of its presence in there, as though it were some human being I had hidden away and kept a prisoner. I lusted for it again, and felt a renewal of the overwhelming impulse to take it out, to fondle it, to excite myself almost to the point of exhaustion by handling this object which was cold, sleek, exciting, maddening – sheer delight!

I must have lived in this state for another month or two, though I can't remember just how long it lasted. All I know is that I became obsessed with the hair, and that it somehow took possession of me. I was happy, yet tormented, as though I was unable to express my love fully, as though I had declared my love and was now waiting for the physical embrace.

I used to shut myself up in my room with it so I could press it against my skin and bury my lips in it, kissing it and biting it. I would smother my face in it, drinking it in, drowning my eyes in its rippling waves of gold . . .

I was in love with it! Yes, I was in love with it! I could no longer do without it, nor go a single hour without seeing it.

And I was waiting . . . waiting for something . . . What was I waiting for? For *her*!

One night I suddenly woke up with the conviction that I was not alone in my room.

Of course, when I looked, there was no-one there. Yet I couldn't get back to sleep again, and after tossing and turning in a feverish insomnia I got out of bed in order to fondle the hair. It seemed to be more delightful than ever – and more full of life . . . Do the dead return?

The hot and passionate kisses I lavished upon it made me almost faint with bliss, and I took it back to bed with me, and lay there pressing my lips to it as if it were a mistress I was about to possess . . .

Ah, the dead do return! *She* has returned! Yes, I have seen her, I have held her in my arms, I have possessed her, just as she was in real life in the olden days – tall, blond, plump, with breasts which felt cold and hips which were shaped like a lyre. And as I caressed her my fingers ran over those divine undulations which go from the bosom to the feet, following all the curves of her flesh.

Yes, she was mine – every day, every night. She came back, the Dead Woman, the beautiful Dead Woman, the Adorable, the Mysterious, the Unknown – every night!

My happiness was so great that I could no longer conceal it. In her presence I experienced a superhuman ecstacy, the profound, inexplicable bliss of possessing the Intangible, the Invisible, the Dead Woman! No lover tasted more ardent or more terrible delights!

I could not find a way of concealing my happiness. I loved her so passionately that I could no longer bear to be without her. I took her with me wherever I went and whatever I did. I escorted her when I walked through the city, just as if she were my wife. I took her with me to the theatre and sat in a box with her, just as if she were my mistress . . .

But they saw her . . . They guessed my secret . . . And they have taken her from me! . . . They have thrown me into prison, like a common criminal . . . they have taken her from me! . . . Oh, how desperately unhappy I am! . . .

This was as far as the manuscript went . . . I was just turning to the doctor with a look of bewilderment on my face when, suddenly there rang out through the asylum a terrible cry – a howl of helpless rage and the anguish of frustrated desire.

'Just listen to him!' said the doctor. 'We have to cool this obscene madman down by giving him a cold shower – five times a day.'

I was so astonished and upset, so moved with the horror and pity of it all, that I simply blurted out:

'But . . . what about this hair? Does it actually exist?'

The doctor got up, opened a cupboard full of bottles and surgical instruments, and threw over to me a mass of gleaming blond hair which seemed to fly across the room like a golden bird.

I gave a shudder as I felt on my hands its delicate, tender caress. And I stood there with my heart beating faster, filled with disgust – and envy . . . With disgust, because I felt I was handling an object associated with something criminal . . . With envy, because I felt the powerful temptation of a thing outrageous and mysterious . . .

The doctor remarked, with a shrug of his shoulders:

'Ah, well. The mind of man is capable of everything.'

The Inn

Typical of all the wooden guest-houses which you find in the Hautes-Alpes, at the foot of the glaciers, in the bare, rocky gorges which cut into the white mountain-tops, the Schwarenbach Inn serves as a refuge for travellers attempting the Gemmi pass.

For the six summer months it remains open, with Jean Hauser's family in residence; then, as soon as the early snows begin to accumulate, filling the valley and making the descent to Leuk impracticable, the women-folk and the father, with the three sons, go away and leave the house in charge of the old guide, Gaspard Hari and his companion, and Sam, the big mountain dog.

The two men and the dog live in their prison of snow until the spring arrives. They have nothing to look at except the vast white slopes of the Balmhorn, surrounded by pale, glistening mountain-peaks. They are shut in, blockaded, buried under the snow, which rises all round them, enveloping, embracing, crushing the little house, piling up on the roof, covering the windows and walling up the door.

On the day on which the Hauser family left for Leuk, the winter was closing in, and the descent was becoming dangerous.

The three sons set off on foot, leading three mules laden with clothes and luggage. Behind them came the mother, Jeanne Hauser, and her daughter Louise, riding a fourth mule. Last came the father and the two caretakers, who were to accompany the family as far as the beginning of the track that leads down the mountainside.

The party first skirted the edge of the little lake, already frozen, in the great rocky hollow in front of the inn; then they proceeded along the valley, which lay before them, a bright sheet of snow, with snow-capped peaks dominating it on every side.

A flood of sunshine fell across this wilderness of white, lighting it up with a cold, blinding brilliance. There was no sign of life in this ocean of mountains; not a movement could be seen in the limitless solitude; not a sound disturbed its profound silence.

Gradually, the young guide, Ulrich Kunsi, a tall long-limbed Swiss, forged ahead of Hauser and old Gaspard Hari, and reached the mule on which the two women were riding.

The youngest daughter looked at him as he came up to her, and there was sadness in the glance with which she welcomed his approach. She was a little blonde peasant girl, with a complexion like milk, and flaxen hair so pale that you might imagine it had been bleached by prolonged residence among the snow and ice.

On reaching the mule on which she was riding, he placed his hand on its croup and slackened his pace. Mother Hauser began to talk to him, explaining in infinite detail her instructions about how they should spend the winter. It was the first time that Ulrich had stayed behind. Old Hari, on the other hand, had already spent fourteen winters under the snow that covered the Schwarenbach Inn.

Ulrich Kunsi listened, but without any appearance of grasping what was said, and never taking his eyes off the girl. Every now and then he would reply: 'Yes, Madame Hauser.' But his thoughts seemed far away, and his face remained calm and impassive.

They reached the Daubensee, whose vast surface, a level sheet of ice, lay at the bottom of the valley. On the right, the rocks of the Daubenhorn, dark and precipitous, rose above the vast moraines of the Lemmern Glacier, and the Wildstrubel towered still higher.

As they approached the Gemmi pass, from where the descent to Leuk begins, they suddenly beheld, across the deep, wide valley of the Rhône, the immense vista of the Valais Alps. They were a distant multitude of white peaks of unequal size, some flattened, some pointed, all glistening in the rays of the sun. There was the two-horned Mischabel, the powerful mass of the Weisshorn, the lumbering Brunnegghorn, the lofty and fearful Cervin, which has killed so many men, and that seductive monster the Dent-Blanche.

Then, below them in an enormous hollow at the foot of terrifying precipices, they caught sight of Leuk, its houses looking like grains of sand thrown down into the vast crevasse, which has at one end the Gemmi, and at the far end an opening onto the Rhône valley. The mules stopped at the edge of the path which winds in serpentine coils, fantastic and marvellous, all down the mountainside, until it reaches the almost invisible village at the foot.

The two women jumped down into the snow. The two old men had now caught up with them. 'Come along,' said old Hauser, 'we must say goodbye, and wish each other all the best till next year.'

Old Hari repeated: 'Till next year!' The men embraced. Madame Hauser gave her cheeks to be kissed, and her daughter followed her example.

When it was Ulrich Kunsi's turn to kiss Louise, he whispered in her ear: 'Don't forget those of us who are up there.'

'No,' she replied in a tone so low that he guessed, rather than heard, what she said.

'Come along. It's goodbye,' said Jean Hauser again. 'Take care of yourselves!'

And, going in front of the women, he led the way down.

All three were lost to view as soon as they rounded the first bend in the track.

The two men turned round and started back to the Schwarenbach Inn.

They walked slowly, side by side, without speaking. They had seen the last of their friends. They would be alone, just the two of them, for four or five months.

Gaspard Hari began to tell Ulrich about the previous winter. His companion then had been Michel Canol, who was now too old for this job: an accident could easily happen during the long period of solitude. Still, they had not been bored. The secret of the whole thing was to make up your mind to it from the first day. You soon learnt to make your own entertainment and games, and find things to while away the time.

With downcast eyes Ulrich Kunsi listened to his companion, but his thoughts were following the women, who were making their way to the village down the winding path on the Gemmi mountainside.

Soon they caught sight of the inn. It was so tiny it could only just be seen – a black dot at the base of the stupendous sweep of snow.

When they opened the door Sam the great curly-haired dog, started to frisk around them.

'Now then, Ulrich,' said old Gaspard, 'we've no women here now. We must get dinner ready ourselves. You can peel the potatoes.'

And, sitting on wooden stools, they began to prepare the soup.

The morning of the following day seemed long to Ulrich Kunsi. Old Hari smoked his pipe and spat into the fireplace, whilst the younger man looked through the window at the brilliant mountain which rose in front of the house.

In the afternoon he went out, and retracing the route they had taken the previous day, he followed the tracks of the mule on which the two women had ridden. When he reached the Gemmi pass he lay on his stomach to look over the edge of the precipice, and gazed down on Leuk.

The village, nestling in its rocky hollow, had not yet been obliterated by the snow. There was snow very near, but its advance had been arrested by the pine forests which protected the hamlet. Seen from this height, the low houses looked like paving-stones set in a meadow.

The little Hauser girl was now in one of those grey dwellings. Which one was it? They were too far away for Ulrich Kunsi to make out. How he longed to go down there, while it was still possible!

But the sun had disappeared behind the great peak of the Wildstrubel, and the young man went back. He found old Hari smoking. When he saw him enter, Hari suggested a game of cards, and the two men sat down on opposite sides of the table. They played for a long time a simple game called *brisque*. Then they had supper and went to bed.

The days that followed were like the first; clear and cold, without any fresh fall of snow. Gaspard used to spend his afternoons watching the eagles and the few birds which venture on to these frozen peaks. But Ulrich went regularly to the Gemmi to look down at the village. In the evening they played cards, dice, and dominoes, staking small objects to lend an interest to the game.

One morning Hari, who had been the first to get up, called out to Ulrich. A drifting cloud of frothy white, deep yet light, was coming down on them, settling all around them, silently, gradually burying them under a thick quilt of foam that deadened every sound. The snowfall lasted four days and nights.

They had to clear the doors and windows, dig a passage, and cut steps to enable them to climb out on to the surface of the icy powder, which twelve hours of frost had made harder than the granite of the moraines.

After that they lived like prisoners, hardly ever venturing outside their dwelling. The household tasks were shared between them, and were punctually performed. Ulrich Kunsi undertook the cleaning and washing and keeping the house tidy. He also chopped the firewood whilst Hari did the cooking and kept the fire going. These necessary, monotonous tasks were relieved by long games with dice or cards. Being both of a calm and placid temperament, they never quarrelled. They never even displayed impatience or bad temper, or spoke sharply to each other, both having made up their minds to make the best of their winter sojourn on the mountain-tops.

Occasionally, old Gaspard took his gun and went out hunting chamois; and when he had the good luck to kill one it was a great day in the Schwarenbach Inn, and there was a feast of fresh meat.

One morning he set out on one of these expeditions. The thermometer outside the inn showed eighteen degrees of frost. He had left before sunrise hoping to take the chamois by surprise on the lower slopes of the Wildstrubel.

Left to himself, Ulrich remained in bed until ten o'clock. He was by nature a good sleeper, but he would not have dared to give way to his inclination in the presence of the old guide, who was always full of energy and an early riser.

He lingered over his breakfast, which he shared with Sam, who spent his days and nights sleeping in front of the fire. Then he began to feel saddened, somehow frightened, by the solitude, and he longed for his daily game of cards, as people do when they are accustomed to something by an ingrained habit.

Then he went out to meet his companion, who was due to return at four o'clock.

The deep valley was now of a uniform level under its thick covering of snow, which filled the crevasses to the top, obliterated the two lakes and upholstered the rocks. Beneath the immense peaks, the valley was now one immense basin of symmetrical, frozen, blinding whiteness.

It was three weeks since Ulrich had been to the edge of the precipice from which he could look down at the village. He wanted to go there again, before climbing the slopes that led to the Wildstrubel. The snow had now covered Leuk, and the houses could scarcely be distinguished under their cloak of white.

Turning to the right, he reached the Lemmern Glacier. He strode along with the mountaineer's loping gait, driving his iron-pointed staff down into the snow, which was as hard as stone. With his keen eyes he looked for the small black dot which he expected to see moving in the distance on this vast expanse of snow.

On reaching the edge of the glacier he stopped, wondering whether old Hari had really come that way. Then, with quicker steps and mounting anxiety, he began to skirt the moraines.

The sun was sinking. The snow was suffused with shades of pink, and over its crystalline surface swept sharp gusts of a dry and icy wind. Ulrich called out with a long, shrill, resonant shout. His voice seemed to take flight in the death-like silence of the sleepy mountain. It rang far out over the deep motionless waves of frozen foam, like the cry of a bird over the waves of the sea. Then it died away. And there was no answer.

He walked on. The sun had sunk behind the distant peaks, and the purple glow of sunset still lingered about them. But the depths of the valley were becoming grey, and the young man suddenly felt afraid. He felt as though the silence, the cold, the solitude, were taking possession of him, were about to arrest his circulation and freeze his blood, stiffen his limbs and change him into a motionless, frozen object. As fast as he could, he ran back towards the inn. The old man, he thought, must have already got back home. He would have returned by a different route and he would find him sitting by the fire, with a dead chamois at his feet.

He soon came in sight of the inn. There was no smoke rising from the chimney. Ulrich ran still faster, and opened the door. Sam leaped up to greet him. But Gaspard Hari had not returned.

Nervously Kunsi kept turning round, as though expecting to find his companion hiding in a corner. Then he lit the fire again and made the soup, still hoping that he would soon see the old man coming in.

From time to time he went outside to see if there was any sign of him. Night had fallen, the pallid night of the mountains, illumined only by the slender, yellow crescent of a new moon, which was low on the horizon and would soon be sinking behind the mountain-tops.

Returning to the house the young man sat down by the fire, and while he was warming his hands and feet he began to think of the accidents which might have happened. Gaspard might have broken a leg, or fallen into a crevasse, or taken a false step and sprained his ankle. He would be lying in the snow, stiff with the cold, in agony of mind, lost, perhaps calling out for help, shouting with all the strength of his voice in the silence of the night.

Where could he be? The mountain was so vast, so rugged, the approach to it so dangerous, especially at this time of the year, that it would take ten or twenty guides, searching for a week in all directions, to find a man in that immensity.

Even so, Ulrich Kunsi made up his mind to take Sam and set out to look for Gaspard, if he had not come back by one o'clock in the morning.

And he made his preparations. He put two days' provisions into a bag, got his crampons, wound round his waist a long, thin, strong rope, and inspected his alpenstock and the little axe he used for cutting steps in the ice. Then he waited. The fire was blazing in the fireplace, the big dog lay snoring before it, lit up by its blaze. The steady ticking of the clock, in its resonant wooden case, sounded like the beating of a heart.

Still he waited, his ears straining to catch any distant sound. When the breeze lightly touched the roof and the walls, he shuddered.

The clock struck midnight. Feeling shivery and nervous, he put some water on the fire to boil, so that he might have some really hot coffee before setting out.

When the clock struck one he got up, woke Sam, opened the door, and set off in the direction of the Wildstrubel. He climbed for five hours, scaling the rocks with the help of his crampons, cutting steps in the ice with his axe, always moving steadily forward, and sometimes hauling the dog after him up some steep escarpment. It was just six o'clock when he reached one of the peaks to which Gaspard often came in search of chamois. And there he waited for the day to break.

The sky above him gradually became paler. Then suddenly a strange light from an unknown source rapidly lit up the great ocean of snow-clad peaks, stretching for a hundred leagues around him. It seemed as though this diffused brilliance was rising from the snow itself to lose itself in space. Gradually the highest peaks in the distance were suffused with a delicate flesh-like pink, and the red sun appeared from behing the great masses of the Bernese Alps.

Ulrich Kunsi set off again. Like a hunter, he bent down, searching for tracks and saying to his dog: 'Find him, old lad! Find him!'

He was now on his way down the mountain, scanning every chasm, and sometimes giving a long, loud call, which was quickly lost in the silent immensity. At times he would put his ear close to the ground to listen. He would imagine he heard a voice and he would start running again, shouting as he went. But he heard nothing more, and he would sit down, exhausted and in despair. About midday he had some food and fed Sam, who was as weary as he was. Then once again he set out on his search.

When evening came he was still walking, having covered fifty kilometres among the mountains. He was too far from the house to think of returning there, and too tired to drag himself along any farther. Digging a hole in the snow, he huddled up in it with his dog, under a blanket he had brought with him. Man and beast lay together, each body sharing the warmth of the other, but chilled to the bone none the less.

Ulrich hardly slept, his mind haunted by visions, his limbs shaking with cold.

When he got up, day was about to dawn. His legs felt as rigid as bars of iron; his spirits were so low that he almost called out in distress, and his heart beat so violently that he nearly collapsed with excitement whenever he fancied that he heard a sound.

The thought suddenly came to him that he too might perish of cold in this wilderness, and the terror at the prospect of such a death whipped up his energy and roused him to fresh vigour.

He was now making the descent towards the inn, falling down, picking himself up again, with Sam following far behind, limping along on three legs.

It was four o'clock in the afternoon before they reached the Schwarenbach Inn. There was nobody there. The young man lit a fire, had something to eat, and then fell asleep – so utterly overcome with fatigue that he could no longer think.

He slept for a very long time. It seemed as if nothing could disturb him. Then, suddenly, he heard a voice call out: 'Ulrich!' It shook him out of his deep torpor and made him sit up.

Had he been dreaming? Was it one of those strange voices that disturb the slumber of uneasy souls? No! He could hear it still. That ringing cry had penetrated his ears, had entered his body, thrilled him to the tips of his sinewy fingers. Beyond all doubt, somebody had shouted, somebody had called out: 'Ulrich!' Then someone must be out there, near the house. There could be no question about it. He opened the door and yelled with all his strength: 'Gaspard, is that you?'

There was no reply. Not a sound, not a murmur or groan – nothing at all. The snow had a ghastly pallor.

The wind had risen. It was that icy wind which splits the rocks and leaves nothing alive on these forsaken altitudes. It blew in sharp gusts, which were more withering and deadly than even the scorching winds of the desert. Again Ulrich called out:

'Gaspard! . . . Gaspard! . . . Gaspard!'

He waited a little. All was silent on the mountainside. Then it was that terror shook him to the very bone. He rushed back into the inn, shut the door, and pushed home the bolts. Trembling all over, he collapsed into a chair. He was now convinced that the cry for help had come from his friend, at the very moment when his spirit was leaving his body.

He was as certain of it as people are of being alive or of eating their meals. For two days and three nights old Gaspard Hari had been in the throes of death in some hollow in one of those deep immaculate ravines, whose whiteness is more sinister than subterranean darkness. For two days and three nights he had been dying, and a moment ago whilst he lay at the point of death, his thoughts had turned to his companion, and his soul, in the instant of gaining its freedom, had flown to the inn where Ulrich lay sleeping. It had called to him through that mysterious and terrible power by which the souls of the dead haunt the living. This voiceless spirit had called aloud to the weary soul of the sleeper; it had uttered its last farewell, or perhaps, its reproach, or its curse, on the man who had given up the search too easily.

And Ulrich felt its presence there, quite near the walls of the house, behind the door which he had just closed. The soul was prowling about like a bird in the night, whose feathers flutter against a lighted window. The distraught young man was ready to scream out in terror. He wanted to run away, but did not dare go out. He did not dare now – nor would he ever dare go outside, for the ghost would be there, day and night, hovering round the inn, until the corpse of the old guide had been recovered and laid in the consecrated earth of a cemetery.

When day broke Kunsi regained a little confidence in the brightness of the returning sun. He prepared his breakfast and gave the dog his food; but after that he remained sitting motionless in a chair, his heart in torment, his thoughts on the old man who was lying out there in the snow.

When night again descended upon the mountains new terrors assailed him. He paced the gloomy kitchen in the dim light of a tallow candle. He took great strides as he walked up and down the room, and always he was listening, listening for that cry, which had terrified him the night before. Might it not come again, piercing the mournful silence of the world outside? He felt alone, poor wretch; alone as no man had ever been before, alone in this vast wilderness of snow, alone two thousand metres above the inhabited world, above the dwellings of men, above busy, noisy, pulsating life – alone up here in the frozen sky. He was torn by a crazy desire to get away, in any direction, by any means – to get down to Leuk, even if he had to hurl himself over the precipice. But he did not dare so much as open the door; he was sure that the man outside, the dead man, would bar his passage, and prevent him from leaving him all alone in the mountains.

Towards midnight, weary with walking up and down, overwhelmed with agonizing fear, he finally succumbed to sleep, sitting on a chair – for he dreaded his bed just as he would have dreaded a place that was haunted.

Suddenly his ears were penetrated by the same strident cry that he had heard the previous night. It was so shrill that Ulrich stretched out his hands to ward off the ghost and, losing his balance, he fell backwards on to the floor, taking the chair with him.

Aroused by the noise, Sam began to howl in terror, and ran up and down the room, trying to find out where the danger came from. When he came to the door he sniffed at the bottom of it, and began snorting, snarling and growling, his coat bristling, his tail erect.

Beside himself with terror, Kunsi had got up and, grasping his chair by one leg, he shouted: 'Don't come in! Don't come in, or I'll kill you!'

And the dog, excited by these menacing tones, barked furiously at the invisible enemy whom his master was challenging.

Gradually Sam calmed down, and went back to lie on the hearth, but he was still uneasy; his eyes were gleaming, his head was alert, and he was baring his teeth and growling.

Ulrich, too, regained his senses; but feeling faint with terror, he went to get a bottle of brandy from the sideboard and drank several glasses of it in quick succession. As his mind became more hazy, his courage rose, and a feverish heat coursed through his veins.

On the following day he ate hardly anything, confining himself to drinking alcohol; and for some days after he lived like a drunken brute. The moment the thought of Gaspard Hari crossed his mind he would begin drinking, and would not leave off until he collapsed on the ground in a drunken stupor and lay there face downwards, snoring and helpless. Hardly had he recovered from the effects of the maddening, scorching liquor, when the cry 'Ulrich!' would rouse him – like a bullet penetrating his skull. He would start to his feet, staggering, stretching out his hands to keep himself from falling, and calling to Sam to help him. And the dog, which now seemed to share his master's madness, would hurl itself against the door, scratching at it with his claws, gnawing at it with his long white teeth, while the young man, with his head thrown back, swallowed great gulps of brandy as though he were drinking cold water after a climb in the mountains. Soon his thoughts, his memory, his frantic terror, would be drowned in drunken oblivion.

In three weeks he finished his entire stock of spirits. But the only effect of his intoxication was to lull his terror to sleep. When the drink was no longer available, his fears returned with new ferocity. His fixed idea, aggravated by a month of drunkenness, continually grew more intense in that absolute solitude and, like a gimlet, bored deeper and deeper into his being. Now he paced his room, every now and then putting his ear to the door, listening to see if the other man were there, shouting defiance at him through the wall.

And when, in utter weariness, he dozed off, he would hear the voice – and leap once more to his feet.

At last, one night, with the courage of a coward at bay, he rushed to the door and opened it, to see who it was who was calling him, and to force him to keep quiet.

The cold air struck him full in the face, and froze him to the marrow. He slammed the door shut and bolted it, not noticing that Sam had dashed outside. Shivering, he threw some more wood on the fire and sat down to warm himself. Suddenly he gave a start. There was someone scratching at the wall and moaning.

He cried out in a terror-stricken voice: 'Go away!' He was answered by a long, melancholy wail.

Now the last vestiges of reason were swept away by terror.

'Go away!' he cried again, and he turned round and round in an effort to find some corner in which he could hide himself. But the thing outside, continually wailing, passed along the front of the house, rubbing itself against the wall. Ulrich rushed to the oaken sideboard, which was full of provisions and crockery, and with superhuman strength he dragged it across the room and pushed it against the door to act as a barricade. Then he took all the remaining furniture – mattresses, palliasses and chairs – and blocked the window, as if he were in a state of siege.

But the thing went on groaning mournfully, and Ulrich himself began to reply with similar mournful sounds.

Days and nights passed like this, with these two constantly wailing at each other. One of them was for ever moving round the house, clawing at the walls, desperately trying to break a way through. The other, inside the inn, crouched with his ear close to the wall, following every movement of the thing outside, and answering all its appeals with horrifying shrieks.

One evening Ulrich heard nothing more from outside. He dropped into a chair, and he was so worn out that he fell asleep immediately.

When he awoke his mind and memory were a blank. It was as if that sleep of exhaustion had swept everything from his mind. He felt hungry, and took some food.

The winter was over. The Gemmi pass was open again, and the Hauser family set out on its journey to the inn.

At the top of the first long climb the two women got on their mule and talked about the two men whom they would soon meet again.

They were surprised that neither of them had come down a few days earlier, as soon as the Leuk road was passable, to give them the news of their long winter stay.

They came in sight of the inn, which was still covered with a thick mantle of snow. They saw that the door and window were closed, but old Hauser was reassured by the fact that a thin column of smoke

was rising from the chimney. As he drew nearer, however, he saw
on the threshold the skeleton of an animal. It was a large skeleton,
lying on its side, and the flesh had been torn off the bones by the
eagles.

They all looked at it.

'It must be Sam,' said Madame Hauser.

And she called out: 'Hello, Gaspard!' From inside the inn came
a shrill cry, like that of an animal. Old Hauser now shouted: 'Hello,
Gaspard!' A cry just like the first came from within.

Then the father and his two sons tried to open the door, but it
resisted their efforts. From the empty shed they took a long beam,
and used it as a battering-ram. They drove it with all their strength
against the door, which gave way with the loud crunch of splintering
planks. A great crash shook the house, and they saw that behind the
sideboard that had just fallen over, there stood a man. His hair came
down to his shoulders, a beard grew down to his chest, his eyes were
gleaming brightly, and his clothes were in tatters.

They did not recognize him. Then Louise Hauser exclaimed:
'Mother! It's Ulrich!'

And the mother acknowledged that it was indeed Ulrich, although
his hair had turned white.

He let them come up to him, let them touch him; but when they
asked him questions, he made no reply. He had to be taken down
to Leuk, where the doctors certified that he was insane.

And nobody ever found out what had happened to his companion.

That summer young Louise Hauser was dangerously ill with some
mysterious debilitating disease. They attributed it to the cold air of
the mountains.

Mother Savage

I hadn't been back to Virlogne for fifteen years. One autumn I went there to do some hunting on the estate of my friend Serval who had finally got his château rebuilt after it had been destroyed by the Prussians.

I used to be tremendously fond of this district. There are parts of the world so delightful that they have an almost sensual appeal to the eye. You love them with the love that is physical. And those of us for whom the earth has this kind of attraction recollect with a very special tenderness certain springs, woods, lakes, hills – these parts we have seen so often and which have moved us like so many happy events in our lives. Sometimes, even, our thoughts go back to a corner of the forest, or part of a riverbank, or an orchard carpeted with flowers – scenes we saw on just one occasion, one bright day, and which have remained in our hearts like those glimpses of women we have encountered in the streets on spring mornings, women in bright, flimsy dresses, who have left in our souls and our flesh an unfulfilled, unforgettable desire, the sensation of having brushed against perfect happiness . . .

At Virlogne I loved all the surrounding countryside, with its little woods scattered here and there, and the streams running through them, flowing across the ground like veins bringing blood to the earth. You could fish in these streams for crayfish, trout and eels. What bliss it was! You could swim in certain parts, and you could often shoot snipe in the tall grass which grew on the banks of these slender little rivers.

One day I was striding along, as sprightly as a mountain-goat, watching my two dogs searching the ground ahead of me. Serval, a hundred metres to my right, was beating a field of clover. I went round the clump of bushes which form the boundary of the Saudres wood, and I came upon a ruined cottage.

Suddenly I recalled the cottage just as it was when I had last seen it, in 1869. Then it had been clean and tidy, with vines growing up the walls, and hens feeding round the door. Can there be any sight as sad as that of a dead house, standing there like a skeleton, dilapidated and sinister?

I also recalled that in this cottage a kind woman had given me a glass of wine to drink, one day when I was particularly tired, and that Serval had later told me something about the family. The father was an old poacher who had been shot by the gendarmes. The son, whom I had seen on other occasions, was a tall, lean lad who was also regarded as a terrible poacher of game. They were known as the Savage family.

Was this their real name, or a nick-name?

I shouted to Serval to come across, and he came up to me taking his long stilt-like strides.

I asked him: 'What happened to the folk who lived here?'

And this was the story he told me . . .

When the Franco-Prussian war was declared the Savage lad, who was then thirty-three, joined the army and left his mother alone in the cottage. People were not particularly sorry for the old woman, as it was known that she was reasonably well-off.

So she stayed here, all by herself, in this isolated house which was so far from the village, on the fringe of the wood. And she was not in the least afraid, because she was of the same stock as her menfolk – a tough old woman, tall and thin, who hardly ever laughed and with whom nobody ever cracked a joke. Country women in general rarely seem to laugh. They leave humour to the menfolk. The women have sad, restricted souls as a result of their lives of unrelieved gloom. The peasant learns a little noisy gaiety in the tavern, but his wife sits seriously at home, wearing an expression of continuous severity. The muscles of her face never seem to have learnt to move in laughter.

Mother Savage went on living her normal life in her cottage, which was soon covered by the winter snow. Once a week she would go off to the village to get some bread and a bit of meat; then she would return home. As it was rumoured that there were wolves about she used to carry on her shoulder a gun, the one that belonged to her son: it was rusty, with the butt worn by constant handling. She was a curious sight, old Mother Savage, going along rather hunched-up, taking slow strides through the snow, with the barrel of the gun poking out from under her black shawl, which was tightly bound round her head, imprisoning her white hair, which nobody had ever seen.

One day the Prussian soldiers arrived. They were billeted out amongst the local people according to the wealth and income of each family. Mother Savage, who was known to be comfortably off, got four of them.

They were four big lads with pink flesh, blond beards and blue eyes.

They had remained plump in spite of the hardships they had already endured, and they were well-behaved in spite of the fact that they were in occupied territory. Isolated in the home of this aged woman they behaved with great kindness towards her, sparing her as much as they could both hard work and expense. In the mornings you could see all four of them getting washed round the well, standing there with their shirt sleeves rolled up in the harsh light of the surrounding snow, swilling water over pinky-white northern flesh, whilst Mother Savage went about her work, preparing the soup. Then you would see them cleaning the kitchen, polishing the window panes, chopping wood, peeling potatoes, doing the washing, undertaking all the household chores, like four good sons helping their mother.

But the old woman was constantly thinking of her own boy, her tall lean son with his hooked nose, brown eyes, and thick moustache which furnished his upper lip with a cushion of black hair. Every day she would ask one of the soldiers sitting round her fireside:

'Do you know where the 23rd Infantry Regiment has got to? That's the one my boy is in.'

They used to reply: 'No. Not know. Not know anything.'

And because they understood her trouble and anxiety – for they too had mothers back in their homeland – they would bestow upon her many little acts of kindness. And, besides, these four enemies of hers were really quite fond of her, for peasants hardly every know patriotic hatred; this is something you only find in those at a higher social level. Humble folk, the ones who pay the most because they are poor and because each new burden overwhelms them, the ones who are slaughtered wholesale, who provide the real cannon-fodder because there are so many of them, the ones, in fact, who suffer most cruelly the appalling miseries of war because they are the weakest and the least resistant – these humble folk hardly understand this ardour for fighting, this easily-roused sense of honour, and these so-called political alliances which in six months can exhaust two whole nations – the victor as well as the vanquished.

When the local people spoke of the Germans staying with Mother Savage they used to say:

'Those four have fallen on their feet.'

Now, one morning, when the old woman was alone in the cottage she noticed in the distant meadows a man coming towards her dwelling. Soon she recognized him: he was the soldier who had been given the job of delivering letters. He handed her a folded piece of of paper and she took out of their case the spectacles she used when sewing. Then she read the following:

Madame Sauvage,

I am writing to bring you sad news. Yesterday your son Victor was killed by a cannon-ball which practically cut him in two. I was close by him, because we served side by side in the company. He used to speak to me about you, and told me to let you know straight away if any misfortune should befall him.

I have taken from his pocket his watch, which I will bring back to you when the war is over.

Yours sincerely,

Césaire Rivot. (Private, 2nd Class, 23rd Infantry)

The date on the letter showed that it had been written three weeks ago.

She did not weep. She remained motionless, so overcome, so dazed, that she was not yet even suffering. She thought:

'Now Victor's gone and got killed.'

Then, gradually, her eyes filled with tears and her heart was flooded with grief. Thoughts came one after the other, dreadful, tormenting thoughts. She would never kiss him again, her child, her tall son, never again! The gendarmes had killed the father; the Prussians had killed the son . . . He had been cut in two by a cannon-ball. And it seemed to her that she could see it happening – and all the horror of it: his head falling, his eyes staring, as he chewed at the corner of his big moustache, just as he used to do when he was angry.

What had they done with his body afterwards? If only they had brought her child back to her, like they had brought back her husband, with a bullet through his forehead.

But she could hear the sound of voices. It was the Prussian soldiers coming back from the village. She quickly hid the letter in her pocket, and welcomed them calmly with a normal expression on her face, for she had had time to wipe her eyes properly.

All four of them were laughing, delighted with themselves, because they had brought back a fine rabbit, one they had probably stolen, and they were making signs to the old woman that they were going to have a good feast.

She immediately set to work to get the meal ready, but when it was time to kill the rabbit, she hadn't the heart to do it – even though she had killed so many in her time. One of the soldiers knocked it senseless by giving it a punch behind the ears.

Once the animal was dead she removed the skin from the red body, but the sight of the blood on her fingers, covering her hands, the warm blood which she felt cooling and congealing, made her tremble from head to foot. And she could still see her son, cut in two, and covered in red, just like this animal, which was still quivering.

She sat down at the table with the Prussians, but she could not eat, not even a mouthful. They greedily ate the rabbit without paying her any attention. She was watching them out of the corner of her eye, saying nothing, turning over an idea, and keeping such an impassive look on her face that they did not notice anything.

All of a sudden she said: 'You know, we've been together a month now and I don't even know your names.'

They understood what she meant – though not without difficulty – and they told her their names. That was not enough for her – and she made them write their names on a sheet of paper, together with the addresses of their families. Putting her spectacles on her big nose she gazed at this strange writing, then, folding up the sheet of paper, she put it into her pocket, next to the letter which had informed her of the death of her son.

When the meal was over she said to the men:

'I'm going to do something for you.'

And she started to carry hay up into the loft where they slept.

They were surprised at this, but when she explained that they would feel the cold less with the hay, they began to help her. They piled bundles of hay right up to the thatched roof, making a sort of large bedroom with four walls of fodder, warm and pleasantly scented, where they would be able to sleep in marvellous comfort.

At the evening meal, one of them was upset to see that Mother Savage was still not eating anything. She told them that she had a stomach-ache. Then she made up a good fire to warm herself by, and the four Germans climbed up into their bedroom by means of the ladder which they used every evening.

As soon as the trap-door was closed, the old woman took away the ladder, then silently opened the outside door, and went to get some bundles of straw with which she filled the kitchen. She went out into the snow barefoot, so gently that she did not make the slightest sound. From time to time she listened to the loud, irregular snoring of the four sleeping soldiers.

When she considered that she had made sufficient preparation she threw one of the bundles of straw into the fire, and as soon as it was alight she scattered it over the rest of the straw. Then she went outside and watched.

In a few seconds a tremendous brilliance lit up the whole of the cottage interior, then it became a terrifying inferno, a gigantic fiery furnace, the glow from which streamed through the small window and cast over the snow a brilliant beam of light.

Then a great shout came from the top of the house, followed by a clamour of human screams, of heart-rending cries of anguish and terror. Then, because the trap-door had collapsed, a swirling mass of flame shot into the loft, pierced the thatched roof, and rose into the sky like an immense blazing torch. The whole cottage then became one raging sea of flames.

Nothing could be heard from inside now except the spluttering of the fire, the cracking of the walls, the collapse of the beams. Suddenly the roof fell inwards, and the blazing carcass of the house sent up into the sky, out of the midst of a cloud of smoke, a great shower of sparks.

The white, snow-covered countryside, lit up by the fire, gleamed like a sheet of silver, tinged with red.

In the distance a bell began to toll.

Old Mother Savage stood there, in front of her ruined home, armed with her gun – the one that had belonged to her son – in case any of the men should try to escape.

When she saw that it was all over she threw her gun into the blaze and a brief explosion was heard.

People were now arriving, both peasants and Prussians.

They found the woman sitting on a tree-trunk, calm and contented. A German officer, who spoke French like a native, asked her: 'Where are your soldiers?'

She stretched out her thin arm towards the red heap of dying flames and replied in a loud voice:

'In there!'

They quickly gathered round her. The Prussian officer asked: 'How did the fire start?'

'*I* started it!'

They didn't believe her. They thought that the sudden disaster had driven her mad. Then, with everybody gathered round listening to her, she told the story from the very beginning to the very end, from the arrival of the letter to the last cry of the men who had been burnt alive with her house. She did not leave out a single detail of what she had felt or of what she had done.

When she had finished she took out of her pocket the two pieces of paper, and in order to make out which was which in the dying glow of the fire, she once more put on her spectacles. Then she said, pointing to one of them:

'This one, this is about Victor being killed.'

Pointing to the other, and giving a nod in the direction of the red ruin of her home, she added:

'This one, this is their names, so somebody can write and tell their families.'

And she calmly offered the white sheet of paper to the officer, who was shaking her by the shoulders as she went on:

'You'll write and tell them how it happened! And you'll tell their parents that it was *me* who did it. Victoire Simon, Mother Savage. Don't forget!'

The officer shouted out some orders in German. They grabbed hold of her, threw her up against the wall of her home, a wall that was still hot from the fire. Then twelve men briskly lined up opposite her at a distance of twenty metres.

She did not move. She had understood. She was waiting.

An order rang out, immediately followed by a volley of shots. A single shot went off on its own, just after the others.

The old woman did not actually fall. She collapsed as though her legs had been mown from underneath her.

The Prussian officer went up to her. The bullets had almost cut her in two – and in her clenched fingers she was still holding her letter, now soaked in blood.

My friend Serval added this remark: 'It was as a reprisal that the Germans destroyed the local château, which belonged to me.'

But I was thinking of the mothers of the four quiet lads who had been burnt to death in this cottage – and of the terrible heroism of that other mother who had been put up against this wall and shot.

And I picked up a little stone, still blackened by the flames.

Was he Mad?

When they said to me: 'I suppose you know that Jacques Parent has died insane, in an asylum,' a painful shudder, a shudder of fear and anguish, ran through my body; and I suddenly saw him again, this tall, strange fellow, mad for a long time perhaps, a disturbing, even frightening, maniac.

He was a man of about forty, tall, thin, a little round-shouldered, with the eyes of a man who sees visions, dark eyes – so dark that you could hardly distinguish the pupils, eyes which were always restless, always wandering, with their morbid and haunted expression. What a strange, disturbing creature he was, carrying with him and spreading all round him a vague uneasiness of body and soul, one of those incomprehensible nervous sensations which make you believe in the existence of supernatural powers.

He had an irritating mannerism: the peculiar habit of hiding his hands. He hardly ever let them wander over objects or furniture, as we might do. He never handled things which happened to be lying about, with the familiar gesture that nearly all men have. He never left those hands of his exposed to view – those long, bony, sensitive, rather feverish hands.

He would thrust them deep into his pockets, or under his armpits, when he folded his arms. You would have thought that he was afraid that, in spite of himself, they would do some forbidden deed, that they would perform some shameful or ridiculous action, if he left them free and masters of their own movements.

When he was obliged to use them for all the everyday tasks of life, he would use them in abrupt, jerky movements, with rapid sweeps of his arms, as if he dare not allow them time to act on their own, time to defy his will, time to do something completely different. When sitting at a table he would snatch his glass, his knife or his fork, so quickly that before you could foresee what he intended to do – it was all over.

Now, one evening, I got an explanation of the astonishing illness which afflicted his soul.

From time to time he used to come and spend a few days at my place, in the country, and this evening he seemed to be particularly nervous.

A storm was building up. The air was stifling and the sky black after a day of appalling heat. Not a breath of wind stirred the leaves. Humid air, as hot as if it came from an oven, passed over our faces, and made us gasp for breath. I felt uneasy, nervous, and I wanted to get to bed.

When he saw that I was getting up to leave, Jacques Parent took hold of my arm as though terrified.

'Oh, no! Please stay a little longer,' he said.

I looked at him in surprise, and murmured:

'It's this storm – it's getting on my nerves.'

He moaned, or rather he cried out: 'And what about *me*? Oh, stay here, I beg of you! I wouldn't want to be left alone.'

He looked to be in a state of panic. I simply said: 'What on earth's the matter with you? Have you taken leave of your senses?'

'Yes, I occasionally do – on evenings such as this, evenings when the atmosphere is full of electricity. I'm . . . I'm . . . I'm afraid – I'm afraid of myself . . . You don't understand, do you? The fact is I am endowed with an ability – no . . . a power – no, not that – a force . . . Oh, I don't know how to explain it, but I have within me such an extraordinary magnetic force that I'm afraid, I really am afraid of myself – as I was saying just now.'

And, shuddering uncontrollably, he hid his quivering hands under the lapels of his jacket. And I suddenly felt myself trembling all over, with a vague, powerful, horrible fear. I wanted to get out, to escape, never to see him again, never again to see his wandering eyes look me over, then turn away to gaze round the ceiling, looking for some dark corner of the room, into which they could stare – as if he were trying to hide his fearful gaze, as well as his hands.

I stammered: 'You've never told me about this before.'

He replied: 'Do you think I ever tell anybody about it? But, listen; tonight I cannot remain silent. And I would rather you knew all about it. Besides, you might be able to help me.

'Hypnotism! Do you know what it is? No. No one knows. Yet we know that such a thing exists. It is officially recognized, and doctors themselves practise it. One of the most famous of them, Monsieur Charcot, teaches it – so there's no doubt that it exists.

'A man, a human being, has the power, the terrifying and incomprehensible power, of putting another human being to sleep by sheer strength of his will and, while he is asleep, stealing his thoughts, just as you might steal a purse. He steals his mind, that is to say, his soul, his sanctuary, this secret place of the self, that deepest part of man once thought to be impenetrable, the soul, this secret retreat of thoughts that cannot be confessed, of everything a man hides, everything he loves, everything he would conceal from all other human beings – this sanctuary the hypnotist opens, violates, displays, and flings to the public! Is it not atrocious, criminal, infamous? . . . Why, and how, is it done? Does anyone know? What *can* anyone know?

'Everything is mystery. We only communicate with things by means of our wretched, incomplete, infirm senses, so weak that they scarcely have the power to perceive the world around us. Everything is mystery. Think of music, that divine art, the art that stirs the soul to its depth, ravishes, intoxicates, drives it to distraction. What is it? Nothing.

'You don't understand? Listen. Two bodies come into contact. The air vibrates. These vibrations are more or less numerous, more or less rapid, more or less violent, according to the nature of the contact. Now, we have in our ears a tiny membrane which receives these vibrations of the air and transmits them to the brain in the form of sound. Imagine a glass of water turning to wine in your mouth. The ear-drum accomplishes this incredible metamorphosis, the astounding miracle of turning movement into sound. Just like that!

'Music, this complex and mysterious act, precise as algebra and vague as a dream, this art made out of mathematics and air, is simply the result of the strange properties of a little membrane. If that membrane did not exist, sound would not exist either, since in itself it is merely vibration. Would we be able to detect music without the ear? Of course not. Well, we are surrounded by things whose existence we never suspect, because we lack the organs that would reveal them to us.

'Hypnotism is perhaps connected with these hidden things. We can only sense this power, only nervously approach this region of spirits, only catch a glimpse of this new secret of Nature, because we do not possess in ourselves the instrument capable of detecting it.

'As for myself . . . As for myself, I am endowed with a horrible power. You would think there was another being imprisoned within me, constantly trying to escape, trying to act in spite of me, continually moving about, gnawing at me, exhausting me. What is it? I don't know, but there are two of us in my poor body, and it is he, the other one, who is often the stronger, as he is tonight.

'I have only to look at people, and I send them to sleep, just as if I had given them opium. I have only to stretch out my hands, and I make things happen . . . terrible things . . . If only you knew! Yes, if only you knew! My power doesn't merely extend over people, but over animals too, and even . . . over objects . . .

'It tortures and terrifies me. I have often wanted to put out my eyes and cut off my hands.

'But I'm going to tell you . . . I want you to know everything. Look, I am going to demonstrate it for you – not on a human being, that is what you can see done anywhere, but on . . . on . . . an animal.

'Call Mirza.'

He was taking great strides round the room, looking like a man who suffers from hallucinations, and he took out his hands, which had been hidden away, tucked into his jacket. They looked terrifying to me – just as though he had unsheathed two swords.

I obeyed him mechanically, quite subdued, shaking with terror and consumed by a kind of impetuous curiosity to see this thing. I opened the door and whistled for my bitch, who was lying in the hall. I immediately heard the hurried sound of her paws on the stairs, and she arrived full of joy, wagging her tail.

Then I motioned to her to lie down in an armchair: she jumped in, and Jacques started to stroke her, staring at her whilst he did so.

At first she seemed restless; she was shivering, turning her head to avoid the man's stare; she seemed agitated by a growing fear. Suddenly, she started to tremble in a way dogs do. The whole of her body was quivering, shaken by long shudders, and she tried to get away. But he put his hands on the animal's head, and under his touch it uttered one of those long howls that you sometimes hear at night in the country.

I felt dazed, giddy, the sort of feeling you have when you board a boat. The furniture seemed to sway, the walls seemed to move. I stammered: 'That's enough, Jacques! Enough!'

But he was no longer listening to me; he was looking at Mirza in a steady, frightening sort of way. She had now closed her eyes, and her head was drooping as though she were going to sleep. He turned towards me:

'I've done it,' he said. 'Now look!' And throwing his handkerchief to the other side of the room, he called out: 'Fetch!'

The animal then got up, and staggering along and stumbling as if she were blind, moving her paws as paralytics move their legs, she went towards the piece of material which showed up as a white patch against the wall. She tried several times to pick it up in her mouth, but she bit at it towards one side, as though she could not see it. At last she seized it, and returned with the same swaying gait, like a dog walking in its sleep.

It was a terrifying thing to see. He ordered: 'Lie down!' She lay down. Then, touching her forehead, he said: 'There's a hare! After him, after him!' And the animal, still lying on her side, tried to run, stirred like a dog which is dreaming and, without opening her mouth, uttered strange little barking sounds, which sounded as though they had been made by a ventriloquist.

Jacques seemed to have gone mad. Sweat poured from his forehead. He called out: 'Bite him! Bite your master!' She made two or three terrible convulsive movements. You could have sworn she was resisting, struggling. He repeated: 'Bite him!' Then, getting up, my bitch came towards me – and I crouched back against the wall, shaking with terror, my foot raised ready to kick her, ready to keep her away.

But Jacques ordered: 'Come here! At once!' She turned round and faced him. Then, with his two great hands, he started to rub her head, as if to release her from invisible bonds.

Mirza opened her eyes. 'It's all over,' said Jacques.

I dared not touch her at all, and I pushed open the door to let her out. She left, slowly, trembling, exhausted, and again I heard her paws on the stairs.

But Jacques came towards me. 'That's not all. What frightens me most of all is this . . . Look! Objects obey me!'

There was on my table a sort of paper-knife which I used to cut the pages of new books. He stretched his hand towards it. It seemed to creep, to approach slowly, and suddenly I saw, I really saw, the knife itself begin to quiver. Then it slid gently, all on its own, across the table towards the poised hand which was waiting for it, and placed itself between his fingers.

I started to cry aloud in terror. I thought that I was going mad myself, but the shrill sound of his voice suddenly calmed me down.

Jacques went on: 'All objects come towards me like this. That is why I hide my hands. What is it? Hypnotism, electricity, magnetic attraction? I don't know – but it's horrible.

'And do you know why it's horrible. When I am alone, as soon as I am alone, I cannot prevent myself from attracting everything around me . . .

'I spend whole days moving things around, and I never grow weary of trying out this abominable power – it's as if I want to see whether it has left me.'

He had buried his great hands deep in his pockets, and he was looking out into the night. A slight sound, a light rustling, seemed to pass through the trees.

It was the rain starting to fall.
I mumbled: 'It's frightening!'
He said once again: 'It's horrible!'
A murmur ran through the foliage, like a gust of wind.
It was the torrential downpour of the storm.
Jacques started to take deep breaths which made his chest heave.
'Leave me,' he said. 'The rain will calm me. I want to be alone now.'

The Dead Girl

I had been madly in love with her. Why *do* people fall in love? How strange it is that in the whole world you can see only one creature, have in your mind only one thought, in your heart only one desire, and on your lips only one name – a name which constantly rises like water from a spring, up to the lips from the depths of the soul, a name which you say over and over again, which you constantly murmur wherever you go, just as though it were the words of a prayer.

I will not tell you our story. Love has only one story – and it is always the same. I had met her and loved her. That is all. And I had lived for a year in her tenderness, in her arms, in her caresses, in her gaze, in everything she wore, in everything she said, so utterly wrapped up and imprisoned in everything that was hers that I no longer knew whether it was day or night, whether I was dead or alive, whether I was on earth or in heaven.

And then she died. How? I don't know – I can't remember any more.

She came home wet through one rainy evening, and the next day she started coughing. The cough continued for about a week, then she took to her bed.

What happened? I can't really remember.

Doctors brought medicines; a woman gave them to her. Her hands were hot, her forehead burning and damp, her eyes gleaming and sad. I would speak to her and she would answer me. What did we say to each other? I can't remember. I've forgotten everything, everything!

She died – and I remember very clearly her little sigh, such a weak little sigh, her very last. The nurse said: 'Ah!' I understood! I understood!

I knew practically nothing after that. Nothing. I saw a priest who referred to her as 'your mistress'. It seemed to me that he was insulting her. Since she was dead nobody had the right to know that. I sent this priest away. Another came, and he was very kind, very gentle. I wept when he talked to me about her.

I had to attend to all kinds of things connected with the burial. I've forgotten it all now. But I still have a vivid memory of the coffin – and the sound of the hammering as they nailed her in. Oh, my God!

She was buried! Buried! *She!* In that hole! A few people had come to the funeral, girls who were friends of hers. I got away as quickly as I could. I walked the streets for a long time, then I returned home. The next day I went away . . .

Yesterday I arrived back in Paris.

When I saw my room again – *our* room, our bed, our furniture, the whole of this house in which there remained something of her, the sorrow came back to me with such violence that I nearly opened the window and threw myself out into the street. I could stay no longer in these surroundings, between these walls which had enclosed her and sheltered her and which surely retained in their tiniest cracks a thousand microscopic particles of her flesh and her breath. So I picked up my hat and went out.

In spite of myself, without realizing it, without intending it, I went towards the cemetery. I found her grave, a very simple one. It had a marble cross bearing these words:

She loved, was loved, and died.

She was there, under there, her flesh all rotting! How horrible! I started sobbing, with my forehead touching the ground.

I stayed there for a long, long time. Eventually I realized that it would soon be evening. And then it was that a strange, mad desire came upon me, the desire of a desperate lover. I wanted to spend the night with her – one last night, weeping over her grave.

But people would see me, would send me away. How could I arrange it? I was very cunning. I got up and began to wander around this city of the dead. I went on and on . . . How small it is, this city, compared with the one in which we live! And yet the dead are far more numerous than the living. We need tall houses, streets, plenty of room . . .

At the end of the main part of the cemetery I suddenly came upon a part that was not in use, the part in which the old corpses were completing the process of mingling with the soil, where even the tombstones were perishing, and where eventually they would put the newcomers. It was full of untended roses, flourishing black cypresses – a sad and superb garden, fed by human flesh.

I was alone, all alone. I huddled up in an evergreen tree, so that I was completely hidden in its lush and gloomy branches.

And I waited, clinging to the trunk like a shipwrecked sailor to a floating plank.

When it was dark, really dark, I left my hiding-place and began to walk about gently, slowly, with muffled tread, over this ground so full of the dead.

I wandered about for a long time – a long, long time . . . And I couldn't find her grave! With my arms outstretched, my eyes staring, bumping into the tombstones with my hands, my feet, my knees, my chest, even my head, I went on and on – and still could not find it. I handled things and fingered them, like a blind man trying to find his way; I felt headstones, crosses, iron railings, wreaths of glass and wreaths of withered flowers. I read the names with my fingers, running them over the letters. What a night! What a night! . . . I could not find it!

There was no moon. What a night! I was afraid, dreadfully afraid, in these narrow paths between two rows of graves. Graves everywhere! To my right, to my left, in front of me, surrounding me – graves everywhere! I sat down on one of them, for my legs were so weak, I could walk no longer.

I could hear my heart beating . . . And I could hear something else! What was it? An indistinct, loathsome sound. Was it in my terror-stricken head, or in the pitch-black night – or was this noise coming from under the mysterious ground, the ground crammed full of human corpses? I searched the darkness all around me . . .

How long did I stay there? I don't know. I was paralysed with fear, crazy with terror, ready to scream out, ready to die.

Then, suddenly, it felt as though the marble slab on which I was sitting had started to move. Yes! It was moving – just as though somebody was lifting it up. In one leap I was on the next grave. And then I saw – yes, with my own eyes I saw the tombstone I had just left stand straight up – and the dead man appeared, a naked human skeleton who, with his back bent double, was lifting up the stone slab. I could see, see very clearly, even though the night was so black. On the headstone I could read:

Here lies Jacques Olivant, who departed this life at the age of 51. He loved his family, was honest and kind, and died in peace.

Now the dead man himself was reading these things which had been written over his grave. He picked up a stone from the path, a little sharp-edged stone, and began with great care to scratch away the inscription. Slowly and thoroughly he removed the words, gazing with his empty eye-sockets at the place where they had been. Then, with the end of the bone which had once been his forefinger he wrote in luminous letters, in the kind of phosphorescent writing you can do with a match:

Here lies Jacques Olivant, who departed this life at the age of 51. Through his callous behaviour he hastened the death of his father, because he wanted his money. He tormented his wife, harassed his children, deceived his neighbours, robbed people whenever he could, and died in disgrace.

When he had finished writing, the dead man, motionless, contemplated his handiwork. And as I looked round I saw that *all* the graves had opened, that *all* the corpses had got out and that all of them had removed the lies written by their relations over their graves and that, instead, they were writing the truth.

And I saw that they had all been the tormentors of their families, that they had been full of hatred, dishonesty, hypocrisy, lying, cheating, back-biting, jealousy, that they had stolen, deceived, done every kind of shameful and abominable act, these good fathers, these faithful wives, these devoted sons, these chaste girls, these honest businessmen – all these men and women whose lives had been described as beyond reproach.

They were all writing – all at the same time – over the doorway of their eternal abode the cruel, terrible and holy truth which everybody on earth either does not know, or pretends not to know.

The thought struck me that *she*, too, must have been writing the truth over her grave. And, free from fear now, running through the midst of these half-opened coffins, through the midst of these corpses and skeletons, I went towards her grave, certain this time I would find it.

I recognized it from a distance, without needing to see the face wrapped in the shroud. And on the marble cross where only recently I had read: *She loved, was loved, and died*, I saw:

Having gone out one day in order to deceive her lover, she caught cold in the rain, and died.

At dawn the next day somebody apparently found me unconscious, lying near one of the graves.

Mademoiselle Cocotte

We were on our way out of the asylum when I noticed in a corner of the courtyard a tall thin man who was very carefully going through the motions of calling an imaginary dog. In a soft, gentle voice he was calling: 'Cocotte! Nice little Cocotte! Come here, Cocotte! Come here, my beauty!' And at the same time he kept patting his thigh in the way people do when they want to call a dog to heel.

'Who's that patient over there?' I asked the doctor.

'Oh, he's not a particularly interesting case,' he replied. 'He's a coachman. His name's François. He became insane after he'd drowned his dog.'

'Tell me about him,' I insisted. 'It's often the most simple and ordinary things which are the most moving.'

And here is the story the doctor told me, a story obtained from a groom who was this patient's friend.

On the outskirts of Paris there lived a wealthy bourgeois family. They owned a villa set in large grounds on the banks of the Seine. Their coachman was this François, a lad from the country. He was good-natured, but a little on the clumsy side, rather naïve, and easily taken in.

One evening, as he was returning to his employer's residence, a dog started to follow him. At first he took no notice of it, but the way the creature obstinately walked close to his heels soon made him turn round. He looked at the dog, wondering if it was one that he knew. No. He had never set eyes on it before.

It was a bitch, with teats hanging conspicuously down, and yet it was horribly thin. With a pitiful, half-starved look about her, she trotted along behind François, her tail between her legs, her ears lying close to her head, stopping when he stopped, setting off again when he set off.

He tried to get rid of this skeleton of an animal.

'Go away!' he shouted. 'Clear off! Do you hear?'

She went a few yards away, then sat down on her haunches, waiting. Then, as soon as the coachman started walking again, there she was, trotting behind him.

He pretended to pick up stones to throw at her. The bitch ran away, with her flabby teats swinging beneath her. But as soon as he turned his back she began to follow him again.

Then the coachman took pity on the bitch and called her to him. Timidly she came closer, with her back bent almost in a circle, and all the ribs showing under her skin. He stroked her, feeling these protruding bones. Quite upset by the wretched condition of the animal, he said to her:

'All right, then! Come on!'

As soon as he said this she started to wag her tail, as though she sensed that she was to be made welcome and given a home, and instead of trotting at the back of her new master's legs, she started to run on in front of him.

He found a place for her in the stable and made it comfortable with straw. Then he ran to the kitchen to get some food. When the bitch had eaten to her heart's content, she fell asleep, curled up as round as a ball.

The next day, when the coachman told his employers about the animal, they gave him permission to keep it. She was a nice bitch, affectionate and faithful, intelligent and gentle.

But soon they discovered that she had one terrible fault. She was madly in love from one end of the year to the other. In a short while she had made the acquaintance of every dog in the district, and they started to hang round her day and night. She bestowed her favours on them with the indifference of a prostitute, and seemed to be on good terms with each one of them. Trailing behind her she had a veritable pack of hounds, composed of every conceivable breed that barks – some so small they would go on the palm of your hand, others as big as donkeys. She took them out along the roads for marathon runs, and when she stopped to rest on the grass verge, they would gather round her in a circle and gaze upon her with their tongues hanging out.

The countryfolk regarded her as something of a phenomenon. They had never seen anything like it before. Even the local vet was baffled.

As soon as she got back to her corner in the stable each evening the crowd of dogs would besiege the house. They wormed their way in through every little gap in the garden hedge, they ruined the borders, uprooted the plants, dug holes in the neat, round flower beds, and drove the gardener to despair. They would howl the whole night long round the building inhabited by their lady-friend – and nothing could persuade them to go away.

During the daytime they even got into the house. It was nothing less than an invasion, a veritable plague, a real disaster. At any given moment the people of the house could meet on the stairs, even in the bedrooms, little yellow mongrels sporting bushy tails; there were hunting dogs, bulldogs, and vagabond Alsatians with dirty coats and neither house nor home; there were enormous Newfoundlands which terrified the children.

It reached the point where strange dogs turned up from as far as thirty miles around. Nobody knew where they came from, how they lived, or where they eventually disappeared to.

But in spite of all this François really loved Cocotte. He had called her Cocotte without any intention of criticizing her, though she certainly deserved to be called a coquette. Over and over again he would say: 'You know, that dog is almost human. All she lacks is the power of speech.' He had a splendid collar made for her. It was in red leather and bore these words, engraved on a brass name-plate: *'Mademoiselle Cocotte, owned by François the coachman.'*

She soon became a tremendous size. She was now as excessively fat as she had once been excessively thin, with an obese body under which still hung her long, swaying teats. She had put on weight all of a sudden, and now she walked with some difficulty, with her legs straddling outwards in the way very stout people walk, and she breathed with her mouth wide open, panting with exhaustion every time she tried to run.

In addition, she proved to be prodigiously fertile, and four times a year she would produce a litter of little pups belonging to every branch of the canine race. François, after choosing one for her to continue feeding, would gather up the other puppies into his apron and go and drown then in the river, without feeling the slightest pity.

But soon the cook started to bring her complaints, adding them to those of the gardener. She had even found dogs under the kitchen range, in the sideboard, and in the coal shed. What is more they were stealing everything they could find to eat.

The master of the house, now completely out of patience, ordered François to get rid of Cocotte. The poor fellow was heart-broken, but he tried to find her a home . . . Nobody would have her.

So he made up his mind he would try to lose her. He handed her over to a carter who had agreed to abandon her out in the country at the other side of Paris, somewhere near Joinville-le-Pont.

That same evening Cocotte was back.

Sterner measures were obviously necessary. On payment of five francs they persuaded a guard to take her with him on the Le Havre train. He was to let her loose as soon as they arrived.

Three days later she was limping back into her stable, out of condition, emaciated, scratched and grazed, utterly exhausted.

The master of the house felt so sorry for her that he allowed her to stay.

But soon the dogs were back again, in even greater numbers than before, and displaying more ardour than ever. One evening when the people of the house were giving an important dinner, a chicken stuffed with truffles was carried off by a great mastiff, right from under the nose of the cook who was too scared to argue.

This time the master of the house really lost his temper. He summoned François and angrily said to him:

'If you've not thrown that animal into the river by tomorrow morning – then I'll kick you out! Do you understand?'

François was shattered. And he went up to his room to pack his bags, feeling he would rather lose his job than drown Cocotte. Then it occurred to him that he would never be able to get a job anywhere else, so long as he had this nuisance of an animal trailing after him. He reflected that here he had a good employer, that he was well paid and well fed. He told himself that it was not worth giving up all this for the sake of a dog. Eventually he got quite carried away, and now was arguing vehemently in favour of his own interests. Finally he made a firm decision to get rid of Cocotte as soon as it was light.

Even so, he slept very badly. At the crack of dawn he was up and dressed. After finding a strong piece of rope he went to get the bitch. In a leisurely fashion she got up, shook herself, stretched her paws and then came and fussed round her master.

When this happened his courage failed him, and he started to stroke her very lovingly, smoothing back her long ears, kissing her on the muzzle, lavishing upon her all the tender names he could think of.

From somewhere close at hand a clock struck six. He could delay no longer. Opening the door he said: 'Come on!' The bitch wagged her tail, convinced that her master was going to take her for a walk.

They reached the riverbank, and he chose a place where the water looked deepest. Then he tied one end of the rope round the fine leather collar and, lifting up a heavy stone, fastened the other end of the rope round it. Next he took Cocotte in his arms and kissed her passionately, just as if he had been saying farewell to a human being. He held her close against his chest, started rocking her to and fro and calling her

'Nice Cocotte, sweet little Cocotte.' And she lay there, nestling in his arms, giving little growls of pleasure.

A dozen times he tried to throw her in, and each time he hadn't the heart to do it.

But, suddenly, he made up his mind. Using all his strength he flung her as far out as he could. At first she tried to swim, just as she used to do when François took her with him in the river, but her head, weighed down by the stone, plunged again and again beneath the surface. She kept giving her master a look of utter bewilderment, a look that was intensely human, and she struggled away like a person who is drowning. Then the whole of the front part of her body went under, and her hind legs thrashed about wildly above the surface of the water, until they too disappeared from sight.

For five minutes bubbles of air came to the surface, just as if the river had started to boil. And François, at his wits' end, with his eyes staring, his heart pounding, imagined he could see Cocotte, writhing in the mud of the river-bed, and he said to himself with the simplicity of the peasant that he was: 'What will she think of me now, the poor creature!'

He was ill for a whole month, and almost lost his reason. Every night he used to dream of his dog. He used to feel her licking his hands: he used to hear her barking. They had to call a doctor to him, but eventually he got better, and towards the end of June his employers took him for an outing to their estate at Biessard, near Rouen.

Here he was, on the banks of the Seine again, and he decided to go swimming. Every morning he went down to the river with his friend the groom, and they used to swim across to the other bank.

Then, one day, when they were enjoying themselves splashing about in the water, François suddenly called across to his friend:

'Look at that lot floating down the river. I'll treat you to a nice cut of meat, if you like!'

It was an enormous carcass, all bloated and decomposing, carried along by the current, with its feet sticking up into the air.

François swam towards it, still making jokes:

'Lord! It's not what you'd call fresh. But what a catch, lad! There's plenty of meat on it!'

He swam round it, keeping a safe distance from this great, putrefying carcass.

Then, suddenly, he stopped making jokes, and stared in rapt attention. He swam a little closer, as if he were going to risk touching it. Now he was staring at the collar. He stretched out his arm, took hold of the neck, then, swivelling the body round in the water, drew it towards him. Attached to the discoloured collar there was a brass name-plate, all green with verdigris, on which he could read:

'Mademoiselle Cocotte, owned by François the coachman.'

The dead bitch had found her master again – a hundred and fifty miles from home!

François let out a terrifying yell and started to swim for the bank as hard as he could, yelling all the time. As soon as he reached dry land he ran off into the countryside, stark naked, berserk – hopelessly insane.

A Night in Paris

(A nightmare)

I am passionately fond of the night. I love it in the way that men love their country or their mistress, with a love that is instinctive, profound, indestructible. I love it with every one of my senses – with my eyes which see it, with my sense of smell which breathes it in, with my ears which listen to its silence, with the whole of my body which feels the gentle caress of its darkness. The larks sing in the sunlight, in the blue sky, in the warm, light air of bright mornings. The owl wings through the night, a dark blotch amidst the blackness of space and, rejoicing in the black, exhilarating immensity, he utters his sinister, tremulous cry.

I am tired and bored by the daylight. It is brutal and noisy. I get up reluctantly, get dressed languidly, go out regretfully – and every movement, every gesture, every word, every thought wearies me as though I were lifting some great, heavy load.

But when the sun goes down, a strange joy fills my whole being. I wake up. I come alive. As the darkness increases I feel a different sort of person – younger, stronger, livelier, happier. I watch them intensifying, these gentle shades of night falling from the sky, watch them drowning the city like some impenetrable, intangible wave, concealing, removing, destroying all colours and shapes, enfolding people, houses, great buildings in their imperceptible embrace.

Then I feel like shrieking with delight, like the screech-owls, feel like running along the roof-tops, like the cats; and an urgent, irresistible desire for love courses through my veins.

I walk on and on, sometimes through the darkened Paris suburbs, sometimes through the neighbouring woods, where I can hear the prowling footsteps of my fellow-creatures – the nocturnal animals, and the poachers.

The thing that you love with a violent passion always kills you in the end. But how can I explain what it is that comes over me? How can I even make myself understood so that I can tell the story? I don't know. I simply don't know. All I know is that it's there.

Well, at any rate, yesterday – or was it yesterday? Yes, surely it was – unless it happened earlier, some other day, some other month, some other year – I don't realy know . . . Yet it must have been yesterday because there's been no dawn since it happened, there's been no sunrise. But how long has this night lasted? How long? Who can tell? Who will ever know?

Well, yesterday then, I went out after dinner, as I do every evening. It was fine; very mild; warm in fact. As I walked down towards the main boulevards I looked up at the black star-spangled river overhead, flowing along between the roof-tops, which seemed to curve and make this rolling stream of stars undulate like an actual river.

Everything shone brightly in the clear air, everything from the planets in the sky to the gas-lamps on earth. So many lights were burning up there and in the city that the very darkness seemed to be luminous. Bright nights like this are much more delightful than days of bright sunshine.

Along the boulevards the cafés were ablaze with light: people were laughing, moving about, sitting drinking. I went into a theatre for a short while. Which theatre was it? I can't remember. It was so brightly lit in there that it depressed me, and I came out again with my heart saddened by the harsh glare of light on the gilded balcony, by the artificial glitter of the great crystal chandelier, by the brilliance of the footlights, by the general melancholy effect of this false, crude light.

I walked to the Champs-Elysées where the open-air cafés looked like blazing hearths amongst the foliage. The chestnut trees, touched with yellow light, gave the impression of having been painted, and looked quite phosphorescent. And the electric-light globes – pale yet dazzling moons, moon-eggs fallen from heaven, living monster-pearls – made the thin flames of ugly, dirty gaslight with their garlands of coloured glass pale into insignificance beneath their mother-of-pearl radiance, mysterious and regal.

I stopped under the Arc de Triomphe and looked down the Champs-Elysées, the wonderful, long, star-lit Avenue going down the centre of Paris between two rows of lights, and with the stars overhead – those unknown stars, scattered at random in the immensity of space where they form those strange constellations, the source of so much dreaming and philosophizing.

I went into the Bois de Boulogne and walked in there for a long, long time. I experienced a most peculiar sensation, an unexpected and overpowering thrill, a kind of exaltation which seemed like the fringe of madness.

I walked about for a long, long time, then I came back towards the city. What time would it be when I passed under the Arc de Triomphe

˙again? I don't really know. The city was now asleep, and clouds, great black clouds, were slowly spreading across the sky.

For the first time I felt that I was about to witness something strange, something new. It seemed to be getting cold, and the air seemed somehow denser: I felt as though the night, my beloved night, was weighing heavily upon my heart.

The Avenue was deserted now. There were just two policemen – all alone – walking near the cab-stand. A row of carts laden with vegetables was on its way to the central markets, going along the roadway which was dimly lit by the dying flames of gas-lamps. The carts were moving along slowly, piled high with carrots, turnips and cabbages. The drivers were asleep, hidden from view, and the horses were walking at a steady pace, following the carts in front of them, making no noise on the wooden paving-blocks. As they passed each lamp at the edge of the pavement the carrots showed up red under the light, the turnips white, the cabbages green. As they passed along, one after the other, these carts of fiery red, silvery white and emerald green, I followed them, then I turned into the rue Royale and got back to the boulevards. There was nobody about now, no brightly-lit cafés – just one or two people who had stayed out late and were hurrying back home. I had never seen Paris so dead and deserted. I took out my watch. It was two o'clock in the morning.

Some kind of force was urging me on, compelling me to continue walking. So I continued as far as the Place de la Bastille. It was there that it occurred to me that I had never experienced a night as black as this. I couldn't even see the Colonne de Juillet, and the little golden god on top was lost in impenetrable darkness. A covering of cloud, infinitely thick, had blanketed out the stars and now seemed to be descending to annihilate the earth.

I retraced my steps. There was not a soul to be seen – except that when I got to the Place du Château d'Eau a drunk nearly bumped into me and then he, too, disappeared into the night. For some time I could hear his unsteady steps echoing through the darkness . . . I walked on . . . When I drew level with the Faubourg Montmartre a cab went past, going down towards the Seine. I shouted after it. The driver made no reply . . . There was a prostitute hanging about near the rue Drouot. 'Hey! Monsieur!' she called. 'Wait a minute!' I quickened my pace to avoid her outstretched hand. After that there was nothing . . . In front of the Vaudeville Theatre a rag-and-bone man was picking about in the gutter. His little lantern was swinging to and fro close to the ground. I asked him: 'What time is it, old chap?'

He muttered: 'How should I know? I haven't got a watch.'

Then I suddenly realized that all the gas-lamps had gone out. I know they turn them off early at this time of the year for the sake of economy. But they do it towards dawn, and dawn was still very far away.

'Come on!' I said to myself. 'Let's go to Les Halles. At least there'll be some life down in the markets.'

I set off, but I couldn't even see to find my way. I moved forward very slowly, as you do in the middle of a wood, recognizing the streets by counting them as I went.

In front of the Crédit Lyonnais bank a dog growled at me. I turned down the rue de Grammont, but then I got lost. I wandered about for a while, and then I realized that I had reached the Stock Exchange, because I recognized the iron railings which surround it . . . The whole of Paris was asleep, lost in a deep, terrifying slumber . . . But in the distance I heard a solitary cab rumbling along, probably the cab that had passed me not long before. I tried to reach it, going in the direction of the sound made by its wheels, feeling my way along lonely streets as dark as death.

I was lost again. Where was I? How idiotic to put the gas-lamps out so early! There was not a single passer-by, not a single person going home late, not a single suspicious character roaming the streets, not even the mewing of an amorous cat. Nothing at all.

Where on earth were the police? I thought: 'I'll call out. Surely a policeman will come and help me.' I called out. Nobody answered.

I called out even louder. My voice was lost in the darkness – weak, muffled, without any echo, as though stifled by the night, the impenetrable night.

I yelled out: 'Help! Help! Help!' My cry of despair remained unanswered. What time could it be, then? I pulled out my watch, but I had no matches with me so I could not see it. With a strange and unfamiliar pleasure I listened to the faint ticking of this little piece of mechanism. It seemed like something alive. I felt less lonely now. How strange! I set off again, groping my way like a blind man, tapping along the walls with my walking-stick, and every now and then I would look up at the sky, hoping to see some glimmer of dawn. But the heavens were black, intensely black, even blacker than the city.

What could the time be? I seemed to have been walking for ages: my legs were ready to give way under me, I was short of breath, and aching with the pangs of a terrible hunger.

I decided that I would ring the first door-bell I came to. I pulled the brass handle, and the ringing of the bell echoed through the house. It was a strange kind of ring, as though this quivering sound were the only thing alive in the house.

I waited, but there was no answer; nobody opened the door. I rang once again, and waited again . . . Nothing!

I became frightened. I ran to the house next-door, and twenty times in quick succession I rang the bell in the darkened entrance-hall where the concierge would be sleeping. But he did not wake up . . . And I went on and on, down the street, pulling the bells as hard as I could, banging with my hands and feet and my stick on these doors which remained so obstinately closed.

Then I suddenly realized that I had reached Les Halles. The great market was deserted. Not a sound, not a movement, not a cart, not a human being, not a bundle of vegetables or a bunch of flowers . . . The place was empty, petrified, abandoned, dead!

A horrible feeling of terror came over me. What was happening? Oh, my God! What was happening?

I set off again. But what time was it? What time was it? Who would tell me the time? Not a single clock had struck in any of the churches or public buildings. I thought: 'I know, I'll open the front of my watch and feel the position of the hands with my fingers.' I pulled out my watch . . . It wasn't ticking any more. It had stopped . . .

Nothing now. Nothing . . . Not a ripple of movement in the city, not a single gleam of light, not the slightest rustle of sound. Nothing! Nothing any more! Not even the distant rumbling of the cab! Nothing!

I had reached the quay-side, and I could feel the chilly damp rising from the river.

Was the Seine still flowing?

I had to know . . . I found the steps and went down . . . But I couldn't hear the water rushing under the bridge . . .

A few more steps . . . then there was sand . . . then mud . . . then water . . . I thrust my arm into it . . . Yes, it was flowing . . . flowing . . . cold . . . cold . . . cold . . . almost frozen . . . almost dried up . . . almost dead.

And I knew only too well that I should never have the strength to get back up again . . . that I, too, was going to die there . . . of hunger, fatigue, and cold . . .

The Case of Louise Roque

I

Médéric Rompel, the postman, who was known to everybody as 'Médéri', set out at his usual time from the post office of Roüy-le-Tors. He strode through the little town with the brisk step of an old soldier, then cut across the Villaumes meadows and reached the banks of the Brindille. By following the river he would come to the village of Carvelin, where his postal round began.

He walked quickly along the edge of the narrow river which was frothing and gurgling, winding its turbulent way through the grassy meadows and under the arching willows. Each big stone which impeded its course was surrounded by a kind of watery collar, like a necktie fastened with a knot of foam. Every now and then he passed waterfalls about a foot in height. Most of them could not be seen, but under their green canopy of leaves and intertwining foliage they were making their sound of subdued fury. Then, further along, where the river broadened out, there was a placid little lake where trout were swimming amongst those fronds of green water weed that wave to and fro in the depths of tranquil streams.

Médéric strode along, paying little attention to the scenery, and with only one thought in his head: 'My first letter is for the Poivron family, then I've got one for Monsieur Renardet. So I shall have to go through the wood.'

His blue smock, fastened round his waist by a black leather belt, moved along at a rapid, regular pace against the green background of the willow trees. His walking-stick, a stout one made of holly, kept perfect time with the steady march of his feet.

He crossed the Brindille by means of a bridge made from a single tree-trunk, which had been thrown across the water, with no other handrail than a rope fastened to two stakes driven into each bank.

The wood on the other side belonged to Monsieur Renardet, the mayor of Carvelin, who was the biggest landowner in the district. It consisted of enormous, ancient trees as straight as columns of stone, and stretched for about a mile along the left bank of the little river which served as a boundary to this immense dome of greenery. Near the water's edge large plants had grown in exposed places where they enjoyed the warmth of the sun; but in the depths of the wood there was nothing but moss – thick, soft, cushiony moss – which filled the motionless air with a faint smell of mustiness and dead branches.

Médéric slackened his pace, took off his peaked cap trimmed with red braid, and wiped the sweat from his forehead, for the morning was already very warm, even though it was not yet eight o'clock.

He had just recovered from the effects of the heat and had set off at his brisk pace once more, when he noticed at the foot of a tree a small knife – the kind that might have belonged to a child. As he was bending down to pick it up he also spotted a thimble, and a little further away there was a needle-case.

When he had picked up these three objects he thought: 'I'll hand them over to Monsieur le Maire.' And he continued on his journey. But now he kept a sharp look-out as he walked, expecting to find something else at any moment.

Suddenly, he stopped in his tracks – so suddenly that it was as if he had bumped into a wooden fence. A few yards ahead of him he saw the body of a young girl, completely naked, lying on her back in the moss. She would be about twelve years old. Her arms were outstretched, her legs were wide apart, her face was covered with a handkerchief. There were a few smears of blood on her thighs.

Staring hard, Médéric began to move closer, walking on tip-toe as though he were afraid of making a sound, as though he sensed some danger.

What did it mean? Perhaps the girl was simply asleep. Then it occurred to him that surely nobody would conceivably be sleeping like that, stark naked, at half-past seven in the morning, in the cool depths of the wood. She was dead, all right, and he had stumbled upon the scene of the crime. When the thought came home to him he felt a cold shudder run down the small of his back, old soldier though he was . . . And then, a murder was such a rare event in this part of the country, especially the murder of a child, that he could hardly believe his eyes. The odd thing was that she did not appear to have any injury, nothing other than the smears of congealed blood on her legs. So how had she been killed?

He had got quite close to her now, and he was looking at her, leaning on his walking-stick. There was no doubt that he knew the girl, since he knew every single person in the district. Not being able to see her face, however, he could not put a name to her. He bent down to remove the handkerchief which covered her features – then stopped, with his arm outstretched, held back by a thought which had just struck him.

Had he the right to interfere with the state of the corpse before the authorities had been informed? To his way of thinking the law was rather like a general in the army, a man who allows nothing to escape his vigilance and who attaches as much importance to a missing button as to a stab in the stomach. Under this handkerchief there might well be evidence that would lead to a death sentence. It was, at any rate, an important exhibit which might lose its value if disturbed by some clumsy hand.

So he straightened up, and was on the point of running off to the mayor's residence when he was held back by another thought. Supposing the girl by some chance was still alive; he could not run off and leave her like this . . . He got down on his hands and knees, and keeping a cautious distance from her, he gradually moved a little nearer and stretched out his hand to touch her foot. It was cold, icy cold, with that horrible chill feeling that makes dead flesh so terrifying and leaves no room for doubt. The moment he touched the foot Médéric felt his heart turn right over inside him – as he later described it – and all the saliva seemed to dry up in his mouth. Suddenly he jumped to his feet and set off running through the wood to Monsieur Renardet's house.

He ran as fast as he could, with his stick tucked under his arm, his fists clenched, his head thrust forward, and his leather mail-bag, full of letters and newspapers, bouncing rhythmically against the small of his back.

The mayor's residence was at the far end of the wood, which formed part of the grounds. A considerable part of the outer walls were washed by a small lagoon, which the Brindille had formed at this point. It was a large, square-looking house built of grey stone, and was very ancient. In the olden days it had withstood many a siege, and at one end there was still an enormous tower, twenty metres high, which rose straight out of the water.

From the top of this fortress the defenders of old would have a fine view of all the surrounding countryside. It was known as the Renard Tower – the Tower of the Fox – though nobody seemed to know exactly why. And from this, no doubt, the family name of Renardet had been derived, a name borne by all the owners of this land which had remained in the same family, it was said, for more than two hundred years. The Renardets belonged to that section of the bourgeoisie which was almost artistocratic, and which was often met with in country districts in the days before the Revolution.

The postman burst into the kitchen, where the servants were having breakfast, and shouted:

'Is the mayor up yet? I've got to speak to 'im – right now!'

They knew Médéric to be a man whose opinions carried weight, and who spoke with some authority, so they immediately realized that something serious had happened.

As soon as Monsieur Renardet was informed he ordered them to bring the postman up to his room. Médéric entered, pale and breathless, with his cap in his hand. He found the mayor sitting at a long table strewn with papers.

He was a tall, well-built man, with a florid complexion. He was as strong as an ox, and very popular with the local community, in spite of the fact that he had a violent temper. Aged about forty, he had been a widower for the past six months, and he lived on his estate just like a country gentleman. His fiery temperament had often got him into trouble, but the magistrates of Roüy-le-Tors, playing the part of discreet, indulgent friends, had always managed to get him out of the mess he was in. Had he not, one day, thrown the coachman from the top of the coach, because he had nearly run over his dog, the retriever he called Micmac? Had he not fractured the ribs of a gamekeeper who had accused him of breaking the law because he had walked across a neighbour's land with a gun under his arm? Had he not even grabbed hold of a sub-prefect by the collar because, although he had stopped in the village on an administrative tour of duty, Monsieur Renardet – who followed the family tradition of always opposing the government – was quite convinced that the fellow was doing some electioneering?

'What's the matter, then, Médéric?' asked the mayor.

'I've found a young girl lying dead in your wood.'

Renardet jumped to his feet, his florid face glowing brick-red.

'A young girl, do you say?'

'Yes, m'sieu. A young girl, stark naked, lying on 'er back, with blood on 'er. She's dead. No doubt about that.'

'By God!' exclaimed the mayor. 'I'll bet it's the young Roque girl! I've just been informed that she never got back home last night . . . Whereabouts did you find her?'

The postman described where he had found the body, giving the exact location, and offered to take the mayor to the place himself.

'No,' said Renardet brusquely, 'I don't need you. Go and tell the constable, the clerk and the doctor, that I want them here straight away. Then you can carry on with your postal round . . . Come along! Quickly! Off you go! . . . And tell them to meet me in the wood!'

The postman, who was a man accustomed to obeying orders, did as he was told, but went away furious, upset by the fact that he would not be present at the investigation.

The mayor followed him out of the room, picked up his hat, a big broad-brimmed hat of soft grey felt, and paused for a while on the threshold of his home. In front of him stretched a spacious lawn which set off three great splashes of colour, one red, one blue and one white – three large flower-beds in full bloom, one oppposite the house and the others at each side. In the background the first trees of the old wood stood against the sky, while to the left, above the point where the Brindille broadened out into a lagoon, the meadows could be seen. They made a level sweep of green country, relieved here and there by ditches, and by the hedges made of willows, which looked grotesque, like stocky dwarfs, with their branches all lopped off and with a tuft of slender new growth, quivering on top of their huge, thick trunks.

To the right, behind the stables, the coach houses and the various other buildings connected with the work of the estate, the mayor could see the beginning of the village, a prosperous place, mainly inhabited by dairy farmers.

Renardet slowly went down the stone steps in front of the house and, turning to the left, he soon came to the edge of the water, which he followed, walking slowly, with his hands clasped behind his back. As he walked his head was bent forward, but every now and then he raised his head and looked over his shoulder to see if there was any sign of the people he had sent for.

As soon as he was in the shade of the trees he stopped, took off his hat, and wiped the sweat from his brow, just as Médéric had done, for the blazing July sun was pouring down its fiery heat over the whole countryside. The mayor set off again, then stopped once more, and retraced his steps. He suddenly bent down and dipped his handkerchief into the river gliding past his feet, and then draped it over his head, under his hat. Drops of water ran down his forehead, down behind his ears – which were still flushed with crimson – down the back of his powerful, red neck, and trickled one by one underneath his white shirt-collar.

As nobody had appeared so far, he started to tap his foot against the ground with impatience. Then he called out: 'Hello, there!'

Now the doctor appeared from amongst the trees. He was a short, thin man, who had once been a medical officer in the army and who was regarded by the people of the district as very competent. A war-wound had left him with a limp, and he had to walk with the aid of a stick.

Then the police constable and the clerk appeared. They had received the message at the same time, and so arrived together. There was a look of consternation on their faces and they were hurrying along, panting away, walking a few yards, then running a few yards, in order to get there as quickly as possible, and moving their arms so vigorously that it seemed as though they were more essential to their progress than their legs.

Renardet said to the doctor:

'You know what it's all about, I suppose.'

'Yes. A child found dead in the woods by Médéric.'

'That's right. Come on!'

They set off walking side by side, followed by the two other men. As they walked over the moss their footsteps made no sound, and their eyes were searching the ground in front of them.

Doctor Labarbe suddenly stretched out his arm and pointed.

'Look!' he said. 'There it is!'

Some distance away they saw something bright under the trees. If they had not known what it was they would never have guessed. It looked so white and shiny that they might have taken it to be a sheet that somebody had dropped – for a ray of sunlight which had penetrated the foliage was illuminating the pale flesh, making a wide strip of light across the corpse. As they drew nearer they could gradually make out the figure, with its veiled face turned in the direction of the river and its two arms stretched out in an attitude of crucifixion.

'I feel damn hot!' said the mayor.

And, bending down at the edge of the Brindille, he dipped his handkerchief in the water once again and put it back on his head.

The doctor quickened his pace, his interest aroused. As soon as he reached the corpse he leaned forward to examine it, but did not actually touch it. He had put his glasses on, as people do when they are inspecting some curious object, and he was moving round the body very slowly, looking at it from different angles.

Still bending over it, he said: 'Rape, then murder, as we shall establish very shortly . . . What's more, this girl is almost a woman. Look at her bosom.'

The two breasts, already well developed, hung limply on her chest, relaxed by death.

The doctor gently removed the handkerchief and revealed her face. It was black – a hideous sight – with the tongue protruding and the eyes staring.

'My God!' said the doctor. 'As soon as it was over she was choked to death!'

He ran his fingers down the neck, then went on:

'Strangled by a pair of hands which have left no clues. There's neither a scratch from a finger-nail, nor the imprint of the fingers . . . Well, there we are. It's the Roque girl all right.'

Very delicately he replaced the handkerchief.

'There's nothing I can do. She's been dead for at least twelve hours. We'll have to inform police headquarters.'

Renardet, standing with his hands clasped behind his back, was staring hard at the body spreadeagled on the ground.

'What a wretch he must be!' he muttered. 'We ought to try to find her clothes.'

The doctor was busy examining the hands, arms and legs.

'She'd probably just been for a swim. Her clothes should be somewhere on the bank.'

They mayor started issuing orders. 'You, Principe (this was the clerk to the council) work your way along the river and find those clothes for me . . . You, Maxime (this was the police constable) run as fast as you can to Roüy-le-Tors and bring back the magistrate and the *gendarmerie*. They must be here within the hour. Do you understand?'

The two men quickly moved off, and Renardet turned to the doctor and said:

'What scoundrel could have done a thing like this in a district such as ours?'

'Who can say?' answered the doctor. 'Everybody is capable of it – nobody in particular, and everybody in general . . . I wouldn't worry about it. It must be some vagrant, some unemployed labourer . . . Ever since we became a Republic men like that have been tramping the roads.'

Both of them were Bonapartists.

'Oh, yes,' said the mayor. 'It could only be a stranger, somebody passing through, some tramp with no fixed abode.'

The doctor added, with the hint of a wry smile:

'And with no wife, either . . . He'd neither a decent supper, nor anywhere to stay, but he managed to get what he wanted here . . . There must be goodness knows how many men capable of committing a crime like this at some point in their lives . . . Were you informed that this girl had disappeared?'

As he spoke he was using the end of his walking-stick to touch the dead girl's stiffened fingers, pressing on them one by one, as though they were the keys of a piano.

'Yes,' replied the mayor. 'Her mother came to see me last night, at about nine o'clock, because the child had not turned up for the evening meal at seven. We were out looking for her on the roads right until midnight, but we never thought of the wood. In any case, we needed to wait until daylight before we could carry out a proper search.'

'Can I offer you a cigar?' asked the doctor.

'No, thank you. I don't feel like smoking. Seeing this has given me quite a turn.'

They both stood there gazing down at that slender adolescent figure, looking so pallid against the dark green of the moss. A big fly – a blue-bottle – was crawling up one of the thighs. When it reached one of the smears of dried blood it stopped, then started crawling again, working its way up the body, running up past the waist with its quick, jerky little movements. It crawled up onto one of the breasts, then crawled down again and began to explore the other, seeking some moisture from the dead girl. The two men were watching the progress of this wandering black dot.

The doctor remarked:

'How pretty it can be, a fly on the skin! The ladies of the eighteenth century were so right to stick black beauty-spots on their faces. I wonder why the fashion has died out.'

The mayor did not apparently hear him, and seemed lost in his own thoughts.

But, all of a sudden, he turned round, his thoughts interrupted by the sound of someone approaching. A woman wearing a bonnet and a blue apron was running towards them through the trees. It was the mother, Madame Roque. As soon as she saw Renardet she started to yell:

'My little girl! Where's my little girl?'

She was in such a distressed condition that she came straight towards them without so much as a glance at the ground.

Then, suddenly, she saw the body. She stopped abruptly, and, clasping her hands together, she raised her arms above her head and uttered a loud, heart-rending shriek, like the cry of an animal torn in a trap.

Then she ran up to the body, fell down on her knees before it, and snatched away the handkerchief covering the face. When she saw that frightful countenance, all black and distorted, she recoiled in horror, then fell forward, pressing her face into the ground and making a continuous, terrible, wailing sound, which was partly muffled by the thick cushion of moss.

Her tall, thin frame, in its tight-fitting clothes, was quivering uncontrollably, shaken by powerful spasms. They could see her bony ankles and skinny legs shuddering horribly. And she was clawing at the ground with her taut and crooked fingers – so frantically that it seemed as if she were trying to dig a hole in which to bury herself from sight.

'Poor old lass!' said the doctor, feeling very upset.

Renardet experienced a curious rumbling in his stomach, and then he gave a sort of loud sneeze, which came through his nose and mouth at the same time. Pulling out his handkerchief he started to weep into it, coughing, sobbing, and blowing his nose very noisily.

'Damn' . . . damn' . . . damn' swine,' he stuttered, 'to do a thing like that! I'd – I'd like to see his head roll under the guillotine!'

At that moment Principe, the clerk, appeared. But he was empty-handed. 'I can't find anything, M'sieu le Maire, nothing at all. I've looked everywhere.'

The mayor, startled by his arrival, answered him in a thick voice which seemed drowned in tears:

'What is it you can't find?'

'The girl's clothes.'

'Well – Well . . . Look again! . . . And – And you'd better find them . . . or you'll have *me* to deal with!'

Knowing that he could not argue with the mayor the man walked away dejectedly, taking a timid, sidelong glance at the corpse.

In the distance there was the sound of people amongst the trees, a confused babble of voices – the noise of an approaching crowd, for Médéric had spread the news from door to door on his postal round. The people of the district, astounded at first, had talked about the crime in the streets, then finally they had gathered together, gossiped, argued and expressed their opinions on the case for several minutes – and now they were coming to see for themselves.

They arrived in small groups, rather hesitant and uneasy at first because they were afraid of being shocked by what they might see. As soon as they saw the body, they stood still, not daring to come any closer, and they started talking in subdued voices. Then they grew a little bolder, came forward a few steps, stopped again, then moved closer once more. Soon they had formed a circle all round the dead girl, her mother, the doctor and Renardet, a tightly-packed circle of spectators who were excited and noisy, and who were constantly being pushed forward by the sudden pressure of the latest arrivals at the back of the crowd. Now those at the front were right up to the corpse. A few of them even bent down to feel it with their fingers . . . The doctor moved them back. And the mayor, suddenly rousing himself from his state of dazed melancholy, blazed into a fit of anger and, snatching the walking-stick from Doctor Labarbe's hand, he flung himself into the midst of the worthy people he served as mayor and spluttered: 'Get to hell out of here! . . . Clear off! You're nothing but a herd of animals! . . . Clear off!' Within a second or two the crowd of sight-seers had drawn back two hundred yards.

Madame Roque had got up from the ground, had turned away from the body and sat down. Now she was weeping, with her face buried in her hands.

The crowd was busy discussing the case, and some of the lads were avidly running their eyes over this naked young body. Renardet noticed this, and so he took off his jacket and threw it over the dead girl, who was then completely covered by this capacious garment.

The more inquisitive members of the crowd were gradually getting nearer again. The wood now seemed to be full of people and a continuous murmur of voices rose up into the dense foliage of the great trees.

The mayor was standing there in his shirt sleeves, with the walking-stick in his hand, looking prepared for battle. He seemed infuriated by the morbid curiosity of the crowd, and kept saying:

'If one of you comes a step nearer I'll smash his skull in just as easily as I'd kill a dog!'

The countryfolk were very frightened of him, and they held back. Doctor Labarbe, still smoking his cigar, sat down next to Madame Roque and spoke to her, trying to find something to say that might help. The poor woman immediately took her hands away from her face and answered him with a flood of tearful words, pouring out her sorrow and finding relief in the sheer torrent of speech. She told him her life-story, about her marriage, about how her husband had died, about how he had been a herdsman and had been gored to death by a bull . . She told him about her daughter's early childhood, about her own wretched life as a poverty-stricken widow with a little girl to support . . . Her little Louise was all she had in the world – and she had been killed, killed in this wood . . .

Then, all of a sudden, she wanted to see her again and, dragging herself on her knees over to the corpse, she lifted up a corner of the jacket which covered it. Then she let it fall and started to wail again . . . The crowd was silent now, watching with eager attentiveness every movement the poor mother made.

But then there was an unexpected stirring and swaying in the crowd, and people were calling out:

'It's the police! The police!'

In the distance two gendarmes on horseback appeared, galloping alongside their captain and a small gentleman with ginger side-whiskers, who was bobbing up and down like a monkey, perched on top of a big white mare.

The constable had found Monsieur Putoin, the magistrate, just as he was mounting his horse for his daily ride – for he fancied himself as an expert horseman, to the great amusement of the military officers.

He dismounted at the same time as the captain of the *gendarmerie*, and shook hands with the mayor and the doctor, taking a quick, ferret-like glance at the big jacket which made the body beneath it look enlarged and swollen.

When he had ascertained the facts of the case the first thing he did was order the gendarmes to get rid of the crowd. They were driven out of the wood, but soon they reappeared in the meadow, forming a kind of hedge, a long hedge of excited, bobbing heads all along the Brindille, on the opposite bank.

The doctor now stated the results of his examination, and these Renardet wrote down in pencil in his pocket-book. All the evidence was given, recorded and discussed, but nothing was discovered that might point to the culprit. In addition, Principe had come back without having seen any sign of the missing clothes.

The disappearance of these garments puzzled everybody. The only explanation seemed that they had been stolen, but as they would be little more than rags, worth only a few coppers, this explanation seemed most unlikely.

The magistrate, the mayor, the captain and the doctor set off in pairs to make another search, rummaging amongst every bit of undergrowth along the riverbank.

'Why on earth,' Renardet was saying to the magistrate, 'did this wretch hide or take away the clothes, and leave the body like that, out in the open, exposed to view?'

The magistrate, who was shrewd and discerning, replied:

'Ha, ha! Perhaps it was just a ruse. This crime was committed

either by a brutalized thug, or by a really crafty devil. Whichever it
was, we'll soon find him.'

The rumble of carriage wheels made them look round. It was the
deputy magistrate, the coroner and the clerk of the court who were
arriving in their turn. They resumed their search, now chatting in
a lively manner.

Renardet suddenly said:

'Do you realize that I'm expecting you all to have lunch with me?'

Everybody smilingly accepted his invitation, and the magistrate,
feeling that they had had done about as much as they could on that
particular day to solve the case of the Roque girl, turned to the mayor
and said:

'I suppose I can have the body taken to your place, can't I? You've
surely got a room you can keep her in until this evening.'

Renardet looked upset and stammered out:

'Er . . . Well, no . . . no, not really . . . To tell you the truth I'd
rather the body weren't brought into my house . . . because – because
of my servants. You know, they – they already say there are ghosts – in
my tower, in the Renard Tower . . . You know . . . I couldn't keep
a body there . . . No . . . I'd rather not have it in my house.'

The magistrate gave a smile.

'All right,' he said. 'I'll have it taken straight away to Roüy for
the forensic examination.

Turning to his deputy, he said:

'I can use your carriage, can't I?'

'Yes, of course.'

They all walked back towards the corpse. Madame Roque was now
sitting next to her daughter, holding her hand and staring into space
with a blank, bewildered expression in her eyes.

The two doctors tried to lead her away so that she would not see
the girl being removed. But she instantly understood what was going
to happen, and she threw herself across the body and encircled it with
her arms. As she lay on top of it she shouted:

'You'll not 'ave 'er!'

All the men stood round her, feeling very moved, but not knowing
what to do. Renardet got down on his knees and started to talk to her:

'Listen, La Roque. We have to do it. It's so we can find out who
killed her . . . If we didn't take her away we'd never know . . . We've
simply got to find him and punish him. She will be given back to
you as soon as we've found him. That I promise you.'

This argument made an impression on the woman, who said, with a gleam of hatred forming in her half-crazed eyes:

'So you'll catch 'im, then?'

'Yes. I promise you we will!'

She got up, having decided to let these men do as they wished. But when the captain muttered: 'It's odd we can't find her clothes,' an idea that had never occurred to her before suddenly entered the peasant woman's head.

'Where are 'er clothes?' she demanded. 'They belong to me. I want them. Where 'ave you put 'em?'

They explained to her that they had searched, but had not been able to find them. But then, with the obstinacy of despair, she insisted on having them. Weeping and moaning she cried out:

'They're mine! I want them! Where are they? I want them!'

The more they tried to calm her down, the more she sobbed and insisted. She was no longer asking to keep the body. What she wanted now was the clothes, her daughter's clothes – and wanted them perhaps as much through the unconscious thriftiness of a poor wretch to whom a few coppers mean a fortune, as through her love as a mother.

And when the little body, wrapped in blankets brought from Renardet's house, had been taken away in the carriage, the old woman was still there in the wood, supported by the mayor and the captain, shouting out:

'I've nothing, nothing, nothing left in all the world! Not even 'er little bonnet, 'er little bonnet! I've nothing, nothing. Not even 'er little bonnet!'

The curé had just arrived, quite a young priest, who was already putting on a little weight. He offered to take Madame Roque home, and they went off together in the direction of the village. The mother's grief became easier to bear as she listened to the minister expounding religious truths which promised her infinite compensations. But she still kept saying, again and again, obsessed by this single thought:

'If only I 'ad 'er little bonnet . . . '

They were some distance away when Renardet called out behind him:

'You'll come and have lunch with us, Monsieur l'Abbé? In an hour's time.'

The priest looked round and replied:

'With pleasure, Monsieur le Maire. I'll be with you at twelve.'

And the men all made their way to the house, whose grey frontage and great tower on the banks of Brindille they could glimpse through the trees . . .

The meal lasted a long time, as they were busy discussing the murder.

Everybody was of the same opinion: it had been committed by some vagrant, who happened to have passed through the wood when the girl was bathing in the river.

After the meal the officials set off back to Roüy, saying that they would return early the next day. The doctor and the priest went home, and Renardet, after taking a long stroll through the meadow, went back to the wood, where he walked about until it got dark, walking about with very slow steps and with his hands clasped behind his back.

He went to bed early and was still asleep the next morning when the magistrate entered his bedroom. The latter was rubbing his hands and looking very pleased with himself.

'Ah! So you're still asleep!' he said. 'Well, my dear fellow, we've a new development this morning.'

The mayor had sat up in bed.

'What's that?' he asked.

'Oh, something very strange. You will, of course, remember how the mother was insisting yesterday on having something to remember her daughter by, especially her little bonnet. Well, when she opened her door this morning she found on the threshold the pair of little wooden shoes that the child had been wearing . . . This proves that the crime was committed by somebody in the district, by somebody who took pity on the mother. What's more, Médéric the postman has brought me the thimble, knife and needlecase which must have belonged to the dead girl. It looks as though the murderer let these drop out of the pockets when he was hiding the clothes . . . My feeling is that the most important clue is the way he returned those shoes. It indicates that he was a man of some education, with a sense of morality and a capacity for sympathy. So if you have no objection we will both start working through the list of all the noteworthy inhabitants in your area.'

The mayor had now got up, and he rang for his servant, ordering him to bring in the hot water for his shave.

'Certainly,' he said. 'But it will take a long time, so we ought to begin straight away.

Monsieur Putoin had sat down with his legs astride the chair, giving the impression that even when he was in somebody's house he still kept up his mania for horsemanship.

Monsieur Renardet was now looking into a mirror, covering his chin with white lather. When he had honed his razor on the leather strop he continued:

'The most noteworthy inhabitant in the Carvelin area goes by the name of Joseph Renardet. He's the mayor, and a wealthy landowner – a gruff fellow who beats up gamekeepers and coachmen . . .'

The magistrate burst out laughing.

'That'll do for him,' he said. 'Let's move on to the next one.'

'The second most noteworthy inhabitant is Monsieur Pelledent, the deputy mayor, a farmer who raises cattle, an equally wealthy landowner, a cunning peasant, particularly sly, very devious when it comes to financial transactions – but quite incapable, in my opinion, of having committed such a crime.'

'Right,' said Putoin. 'Let's move on to the next.'

And so, as he continued to shave and wash himself, Renardet went on with this moral inspection of all the inhabitants of Carvelin. After a total of two hours of discussion their suspicions had eventually fallen on three rather dubious characters: a poacher, called Cavalle; a man who fished for trout and crayfish, called Paquet; and a herdsman called Clovis.

II

The investigations went on throughout the summer, but they still had not found the criminal. The men under suspicion had been arrested, but had easily been able to prove their innocence and police headquarters were compelled to call off the active search for the guilty person.

Yet this murder seemed to have affected the whole district in a very strange way. It had left in the minds of the local inhabitants a feeling of anxiety, a vague terror, a sense of mysterious dread, which was caused partly by the fact that it had been impossible to track down the murderer, and even more so by the fact of that strange find of the wooden shoes on Madame Roque's doorstep the day after the crime. The certainty that the murderer had been present in the crowd during the investigations, that he was probably still living in the village, haunted and obsessed every thinking person, and seemed to hang over the whole neighbourhood like a perpetual menace.

In addition, the wood had now become a place to be dreaded and avoided, a place that was supposed to be haunted. Before, the locals used to come for walks here every Sunday afternoon. They used to sit down on the moss beneath the gigantic trees, or walk along the edge of the water, watching the trout darting amongst the water-weed. In certain areas where the ground had been cleared and levelled, the lads used to play bowls, skittles and ball games; and the lasses used to walk about arm-in-arm, in groups of four or five, warbling in their shrill voices that grated on the ear, singing love songs whose discordant notes disturbed the calm air of the countryside and set the teeth on edge as surely as if they had been vinegar. Now nobody went under the lofty canopy of trees any more. It was as though people always expected they might find some corpse in there.

Autumn arrived, and the leaves started to fall. They fell day and night, circular and delicate, whirling round as they came down the length of the tall trees, and now the sky could just be seen through the branches. Sometimes, when a gust of wind passed through the tree-tops, the slow, continuous shower of leaves suddenly became heavier and changed into a rustling downpour, covering the moss with a thick yellow carpet which crunched when it was walked upon. And the almost inaudible murmur of these falling leaves, this wavering, incessant, gentle, melancholy murmur, seemed like a wail of sorrow, and these continually falling leaves seemed like tears, great tears shed by the tall, sad trees, which wept day and night because the summer had ended, because there would be no more warm sunrises and mild sunsets, no more warm breezes and bright sunlight – and they were also weeping, perhaps, over the crime they had seen committed in the shade of their branches, over the girl raped and murdered at their feet. They wept in the silence of the desolate, empty wood, the wood which no one visited and everyone dreaded, the wood in which there surely wandered the solitary little soul of the girl who had died so young.

The Brindille, swollen by the recent storms, was flowing more rapidly now, and its yellow, angry-looking waters rushed on between its dry banks and the hedges of thin, bare willow tress.

Then, one day, Renardet suddenly resumed his custom of walking in the wood. Every evening, just as it was getting dark, he would leave the house, walk slowly down the stone steps to the lawn and then saunter along under the trees with his hands in his pockets, looking as though he was lost in thought. He would walk for a long time over the damp and spongy moss, whilst overhead, a great flock of rooks which had gathered from all round to roost in the high tree-tops, would unfurl themselves across the sky like some enormous black veil of mourning floating on the wind, and as they did so they would utter their harsh and sinister cries.

Sometimes they would settle in the tangled branches, making a host of black patches against the red background of the sky, the blood-red sky of autumn twilights. Then, all of a sudden, they would fly again, cawing horribly and unfurling once more, high above the wood, the long and sombre fabric of their flight.

Then they would eventually settle on the topmost branches and their clamour would gradually cease, while the encroaching darkness mingled the black of their plumage with the black of the night.

Renardet would stay a little longer, strolling under the trees, taking his time. Then, when the darkness was so dense that he could no longer see where he was going, he would return home, collapse like a dead weight into his armchair, and sit in front of his blazing hearth, with his legs stretched forward and his damp boots steaming away in the heat of the flames.

Now, one morning, a startling piece of news ran through the whole neighbourhood: the mayor was having all his trees felled.

Twenty woodcutters were already working on it. They had started felling the trees which were nearest to the house, and were making rapid progress, with Renardet standing over them.

First of all, the men whose job it was to lop off the branches would climb up the trunk. Secured by means of a loop of rope each man put his arms round the tree, then kicked it soundly with the steel spike attached to the sole of his boot. With the spike firmly embedded in the wood he climbed up, using it as a kind of step, then kicked into the trunk with the spike on his other boot, and used this as his support while he started again with the first boot.

At each step he raised the loop of rope which secured him to the tree, and from his waist there dangled the hatchet of gleaming steel. Slowly and persistenly he climbed the trunk, like some parasitic creature attacking a giant, and he laboriously traversed the whole length of this huge column, embracing it and digging his spurs into it as he came to decapitate the tree.

As soon as he reached the lowest branches he stopped, detached from his belt the sharp-edged hatchet, and began to chop. He chopped slowly, methodically, lopping off the branch quite close to the trunk. Suddenly, it cracked, began to yield, bent over, tore itself away and fell to the ground, brushing against the other trees nearby. Then it crashed against the earth with a loud splintering noise, and all the little twigs could be seen trembling for a long time after.

The ground was soon covered with these branches, which other woodcutters trimmed in their turn and chopped into bundles of firewood, which they arranged in piles, like gigantic stakes, all amputated and shaven by the keen cutting-edge of the hatchets.

And when the man had finished his task of lopping off the branches he left his rope at the top of the straight and slender trunk, and came down by digging his spurs into the beheaded tree, which the lumbermen then attacked at the base, striking it with great blows which echoed through the remaining woodland.

When the wedge they had cut into the base of the trunk seemed deep enough, a few men, all shouting in rhythm, pulled hard on the rope that was attached to the loop round the top of the tree, and the huge mast suddenly gave a creak and fell to the ground with the muffled crash and rumble of a distant cannon.

And each day the mayor's wood grew smaller, losing its felled trees like an army losing its soldiers.

Renardet was there all the time now: he stood quite motionless, with his hands behind his back, surveying the slow death of his ancient wood. When a tree had been felled he would place his foot upon it, as though it were a corpse. Then he would turn his gaze on the next tree about to be felled, and look at it with a kind of inward, controlled impatience, as though he expected something, hoped for something, at the end of all this massacre of trees.

Eventually the felling drew near the place where the Roque girl had been found. At last they reached it – one evening when it was already twilight.

As the sky was overcast, and as it was really quite dark, the woodcutters wanted to stop work and wait until morning before they felled such an enormous beech tree. But the mayor objected, and insisted that they immediately set about lopping and felling this colossal tree in whose shade the crime had been committed.

When they had finished dressing it for execution by denuding it of its branches, and when the woodcutters had weakened its base, five men started to pull on the rope that was attached to the top of the trunk.

The tree would not budge. Even though its massive trunk had been cut half-way through by the axes it was as rigid as if it had been made of iron. Working as a team they pulled on the rope with a kind of regular jumping motion, leaning back until they almost touched the ground, and giving guttural, breathless shouts which both indicated the effort they were making and helped them to pull together.

Two of the woodcutters, standing next to the gigantic tree, were holding their axes like two executioners ready to strike the victim again.

Renardet was standing quite still with his hand on the bark, waiting anxiously and nervously for the great tree to fall.

'You're standing too near, Monsieur le Maire,' said one of the men. 'When it falls you could easily be injured.'

Renardet did not answer, and he did not move away. He looked as though he was preparing to fling his arms round the beech tree and throw it to the ground himself, like a man in a wrestling match.

All of a sudden there came from the foot of the tall column of wood a splintering sound which seemed to run up the trunk like a spasm of pain, and it bent over a little, ready to fall, yet still not yielding. The men, quite excited now, braced themselves and made an even greater effort. The tree broke, began to totter – and, suddenly, Renardet stepped in front of it, then stood there, rounding his back as he prepared to receive the overwhelming, fatal blow which would crush him into the ground.

But the great beech veered slightly to one side and simply struck him a glancing blow on the back, sending him sprawling onto the ground five yards away.

The workmen rushed forward to help him. He had already got to his knees, and was looking round, dazed and wild-eyed, passing his hand across his forehead as though he were waking up from some insane nightmare.

When they had got him to his feet again the men, astonished and quite baffled at why he had done this, started to ask him questions. He stammered out in reply that his mind must have wandered for a moment, or rather that for a second or two he must have been carried back to his childhood, and that he had imagined he had just the time to run in front of the tree, like lads do when they run in front of a horse-and-cart, that he had been gambling with danger, that for the past week he had felt this thing growing within him, and that every time he heard a tree splinter he wondered if there would be time to run under just before it crashed to the ground. It was a silly thing to do, he admitted it. But everyone has these odd moments of irrationality and feels tempted to do something stupid and childish.

He gave this explanation slowly, struggling for the words, and speaking in a strange faraway voice. Then he set off for home, saying: 'See you tomorrow, friends. See you tomorrow.'

As soon as he was back in his room he sat down at the table which was brilliantly illuminated by a lamp with a shade and, burying his face in his hands, he started to weep.

He wept for a long time, then he wiped his eyes and looked up at the clock. It was not yet six. He thought: 'I've still time before dinner'. And he went and locked the door of his room. Then he came and sat down again at his table. He opened the middle drawer and took out a revolver, which he placed on top of his papers in the bright lamplight. The steel of the weapon gleamed with reflected light and seemed to flash with fire.

Renardet stared at it for some considerable time with glassy eyes, as though intoxicated. Then he stood up and started to walk about.

He walked up and down the large room, pausing from time to time, only to start pacing again immediately afterwards. Suddenly, he opened the door of his dressing-room, dipped a towel into the water jug and wet his forehead, just as he had done on the morning of the crime. Then he set off pacing the room again. Each time he walked past his table the gleaming weapon attracted his attention, invited him to take it in his hand. But he kept looking up at the clock and saying: 'I've still time.'

When the clock struck half-past six he picked up the revolver, opened his mouth as wide as he could in one horrible grimace, and thrust the barrel right into it, just as though he were trying to swallow it. He stood like this for a few seconds, not making the slightest movement, with his finger round the trigger. Then, suddenly giving a shudder of revulsion, he spat the pistol out of his mouth and let it fall onto the carpet.

He collapsed into his armchair once again, sobbing away:

'I can't! I daren't! Dear God! Dear God! How can I find enough courage to kill myself?'

There was somebody knocking at the door. He got to his feet in a panic.

'Monsieur's dinner is ready,' called a servant.

'Very well. I'm coming down,' he replied.

He picked up the weapon from the floor, put it back into the drawer, and then looked at himself in the mirror above the fireplace to see whether his face betrayed how upset he was. It had its normal florid appearance; perhaps it was a little redder than usual, but that was all. He went downstairs and sat up to the table.

He ate very slowly, like a man who wants to make his meal drag out as long as possible, who wants to put off the time when he will be entirely alone. While they were clearing away he stayed in the dining-room and smoked a few pipes of tobacco, and finally went back up to his room.

As soon as he had shut the door, he looked under his bed, opened all the wardrobes, looked into every dark corner, searched through every item of furniture. Then he lit the candles on his mantelpiece and, turning round several times, he ran his terrified gaze all over the room, his face contorted in an expression of horror – for he knew very well that he was going to see her again, just as he saw her every night . . . he was going to see *la petite Roque*, the girl he had raped, then strangled.

Every night the revolting vision used to return. He started by experiencing in his ears a kind of rumbling sound, like that of a threshing machine or a train passing over a distant bridge. Then he started to pant, to feel short of breath, and he had to unbutton his shirt collar and loosen his belt. He used to walk about to try to improve his circulation; he would try to read, try to sing. But it was never any use: in spite of himself his thoughts always came back to the day of the murder, and he found himself compelled to go over everything again in the most intimate detail and the most powerful emotion, from the very first minute to the last.

When he had got up on that particular morning, the morning of the day of horror, he had experienced a little dizziness and headache, which he had put down to the heat. That was why he had stayed in his room until the servants had called him for lunch. After the meal he had taken a siesta, and then he had gone out towards the end of the afternoon to breathe in the fresh, soothing breeze which usually blew through the trees of the old wood.

But as soon as he had got outside, the heavy, stifling air from the plain oppressed him even more. The sun, still high in the sky, was pouring down its flood of scorching light over the parched, sun-baked, thirsty land. Not a breath of air stirred the leaves. Every kind of bird and beast was silent, even the very grasshoppers. Renardet came to the tall trees and started to walk over the moss under the immense canopy of branches, where the Brindille seemed to release a little of its evaporated coolness. But he felt ill at ease. It seemed as though a strange invisible hand was squeezing his throat. There was nothing in his thoughts to account for this, and, indeed, he was not a man given to much imaginative thinking.

Only one vague thought had been haunting him for the past three months, the thought of getting married again. Living alone was a source of real suffering to him, both psychological and physical. Having become accustomed over a period of ten years to feel a woman near him, to enjoy her continued presence, to know her daily embrace, he was now experiencing a need, an overmastering, embarrassing need for her incessant touch and her regular kiss. Since Madame Renardet's death he had constantly suffered without really understanding why: he suffered because he could no longer feel her dress brushing against his legs by day, and, above all, he suffered because he could no longer find peace and relaxation in her arms at night. He had been a widower for just under six months, and yet he was already keeping his eyes open for some local girl or widow whom he might marry once the period of mourning was over.

Though he possessed a soul that was chaste it dwelt in the powerful body of a Hercules, and fleshly fantasies began to disturb both his sleep and his waking thoughts. He drove them away, but they always came back, and he would occasionally murmur, smiling at his predicament:

'I'm getting just like Saint Anthony.'

Since he had had several of these obsessive fantasies that particular morning, he suddenly felt the urge to go and swim in the Brindille to refresh himself and cool the ardour of his blood. He knew a place a little further along, where the water was deep and spacious, and where the local folk sometimes came to bathe in summer. To this spot he now made his way. A dense screen of willows hid this clear pool of water in which the current seemed to halt and slumber a while before continuing on its journey downstream. As Renardet drew near he thought he heard a slight sound, a faint splashing, which was certainly not made by the stream lapping against the bank. He gently parted the leaves and looked. A young girl, completely naked, completely white in the crystal-clear water, was splashing and dancing about, beating the waves with both hands and going round and round in a graceful motion. She was no longer a child, but she was not yet a woman. She was plump and well-developed, at the same time having the look of a precocious lass, one who has suddenly spurted into growth and is almost mature.

He remained stock-still, petrified with surprise and the pangs of desire, his breath taken away by a curiously poignant emotion. He stayed there, with his heart pounding away as though one of his sensual dreams had just become reality, as though some impure fairy had conjured up before him this disturbing creature who was too young for him, this little peasant Venus rising from the waves of the river, just as the other, the adult Venus, had been born out of the waves of the ocean.

Suddenly, the girl came out of the water, and without seeing him, she walked in his direction to find her clothes and get dressed. As she came towards him, taking little cautious steps because of the sharp pebbles, he felt himself drawn towards her by an irresistible force, by a bestial surge of passion which roused his whole body, drove him demented, and set him trembling from head to foot.

She remained standing for a few moments behind the willow that hid her from view. Then, losing all control, he tore open the branches, rushed upon her, and took her in his arms. She fell to the ground, too startled to offer any resistance, too terror-stricken to cry out, and he took possession of her without realizing what he was doing.

He came round from his crime – just as people wake up from a nightmare. The girl started to weep.

'Be quiet!' he said. 'You must be quiet! I'll give you some money.'

But she was not listening to him, and she went on sobbing.

'Now you must be quiet!' he went on. 'You must be quiet!' You must be quiet!'

She started screaming and writhing about in order to get away from him.

It was then that it suddenly occurred to him that he was going to be ruined. And he grabbed her round the throat in order to stifle these terrible, ear-splitting shrieks. As she continued to struggle, with the desperate, frantic strength of a creature trying to escape death, he closed his giant's fingers round that little throat bursting with screams. He squeezed with such fury that in a few moments he had strangled her, even though he had not had the least intention of killing her, only of making her keep quiet.

He stood up, overwhelmed with the horror of what he had done.

She was stretched out before him, stained with blood, and with her face all black. He was on the point of running away when there rose within his panic-stricken soul the vague, mysterious instinct which seems to come to the help of all creatures in the hour of danger.

His first inclination was to throw the body into the water, but then he felt an urge to pick up the girl's clothes and make them into a small bundle, which he tied up with a piece of string from his pocket and hid in a deep hole in the riverbank, just under a tree whose roots went down into the waters of the Brindille.

Then he walked away, striding out as fast as he could. When he reached the meadows he took a long roundabout route so that he would be seen by some of the countryfolk who lived a great distance from the scene of the crime, at the far side of the district, and then he came back for dinner at his usual time, telling his servants the route he had taken on his long walk.

In spite of what had happened he had a good night's sleep. It was the profound sleep of a brute beast, such as men condemned to death must sometimes experience. He did not open his eyes until the first light of dawn, and then he waited until his normal time of rising, tormented by the fear that the crime would be discovered.

Then he had to be present at the investigation. He played his part in the manner of a sleepwalker, living through a series of hallucinations, which made both things and people seem part of a dream, clouded by the hazy state of his thoughts and that sense of unreality which disturbs the mind in times of crisis.

The only thing which really came through to him with the ring of truth was the heart-rending cry uttered by Madame Roque. At that moment he had nearly thrown himself at the old woman's feet and shouted: 'It was me!' But he had controlled himself. Even so, he went and found the dead girl's wooden shoes and took them to the mother's doorstep.

Just as long as the inquiry continued, as long as he had to guide and lead astray the course of justice, he remained calm, cunning, affable, master of all his actions. He quietly discussed with the magistrates all the theories they brought forward, disagreed with their opinions, demolished their arguments. He even took a certain bitter, morbid pleasure in upsetting their investigations, in bringing their ideas into confusion, in proving the innocence of the people they suspected.

But once the investigations were officially discontinued, he started becoming more and more nervous, more excitable than he had ever been before, even though he was able to control his fits of bad temper. Sudden noises made him jump with fright; he would start trembling at the slightest thing, would even shudder from head to foot when a fly unexpectedly settled on his forehead. Then he would be overcome by an urgent need for physical activity, which would send him out walking for tremendous distances, and keep him up for whole nights at a time, pacing up and down his room . . .

He was afraid of nightfall now, afraid of the shadows gathering round him. He did not yet understand why he was so terrified of the dark, but he had an instinctive fear of it, and felt that it was inhabited by terrors of every kind. Broad daylight does not encourage the apprehension of horror. You see things and people in the daytime, and so you only expect to see the kind of natural phenomena which can be seen in the bright light. But for Renardet, night was a very different matter. It was dense, thicker than the very walls, and it was empty, so black, so immense, that within it you could brush against appalling things and feel roaming and prowling around a strange mysterious horror. To Renardet the night seemed to conceal an unknown danger, lurking there so close and menacing. But what was it?

Before long he was to find out. Late one night he was sitting in his armchair, quite incapable of sleep, when he thought he saw the curtain of his window move. He waited anxiously, with his heart beating fast. The material did not move for a while then, suddenly, it moved once more – or, at least, he *thought* he saw it move. He dared not get up; he dared hardly breathe. And yet he was a man of courage: he had often been involved in a fight, and nothing would have pleased him more than to tackle burglars on his premises.

Had this curtain moved? He began to wonder if it had, and was beginning to think that his eyes had been deceiving him. After all, it had been such a slight movement, the merest ruffling of the material, a sort of trembling in the folds of the curtain, just a light rippling such as might be caused by the wind. Renardet stared hard at the curtain, craning his neck. Then, suddenly, he jumped up, ashamed of his fear. He strode forward, seized the curtain with both hands and flung it wide open. At first he saw nothing but the dark window-panes, which were as black as pools of gleaming ink. Beyond them stretched the night, the intense, impenetrable night, extending as far as the unseen horizon. He stood gazing at this limitless extent of blackness – and, all of a sudden, he noticed a glow of light which seemed to be moving about in the distance.

He brought his face close to the window-pane, thinking that perhaps it was some poacher searching for crayfish in the Brindille, for it was already past midnight, and this light seemed to be moving along the edge of the water in the old wood. As he still could not make out what it was Renardet concentrated his gaze by cupping his hands round his eyes. Suddenly, this gleam of light became a brilliant scene – and he saw the young Roque girl lying on the moss, naked and bloody.

He recoiled in horror, bumped against his chair, and fell over onto his back. He remained lying there for a few moments in a state of anguish. Then he sat up and started to think. He had experienced a hallucination, that was all. It was a hallucination which had originated in the fact that some prowler had been walking along the water's edge holding a lantern. There was nothing particularly surprising about the memory of his crime occasionally bringing the scene of the dead girl before him.

He got to his feet, drank a glass of water, then sat down. 'What am I going to do if this happens again?' he thought. And he felt that it *would* happen again. He was absolutely sure of it. Already the window was attracting his attention, appealing to him to turn and look at it. So he would not have to see it any more he turned his chair completely round, then picked up a book and tried to read. But soon it seemed that he could hear something moving behind him, and he spun his chair round again. The curtain was still moving. It had definitely moved this time, there could be no doubt of it. He rushed forward and grabbed hold of it with such violence that the whole curtain came down, complete with the rail. Then he eagerly pressed his face against the glass of the window . . . There was nothing to be seen. Everything outside was in absolute darkness. And he breathed freely, with the joy of a man whose life has just been saved.

So he went and sat down in his armchair again. Almost immediately, however, he was overcome by a need to look out of the window once more. Now that the curtain had fallen there was a kind of enticing, fearful black hole which opened out onto the dark countryside. In order to prevent himself from yielding to this dangerous temptation to look out, he got undressed, blew out the candles, and got into bed, where he lay with his eyes closed.

Lying quite still on his back, his skin hot and damp with perspiration, he waited for sleep. Through his closed eyelids there suddenly came a bright gleam of light. He opened his eyes, convinced that his house must be on fire. Everything was pitch-black. He got up on his elbow and tried to make out the position of the window which was still compelling his attention. By straining his eyes he could see a few stars, and so he got up and groped his way across the room. He felt for the window-panes with his outstretched arms and pushed his head against them . . . Down there, under the trees, the girl's body was glowing with a phosphorescent light, illuminating the surrounding darkness!

Renardet gave a shout and rushed back to his bed, where he stayed until morning with his face buried in the pillows.

From that moment his life became intolerable. He spent his days in terrified anticipation of what would happen at night. And each night the vision came back again. He had scarcely locked himself up in his room when he found himself trying to struggle against it. But it was always in vain. An overpowering force lifted him up and carried him towards the window, as though he simply had to call for the phantom to appear. And he saw it straight away now: first of all it would be lying in the place where the crime had been committed, lying with arms and legs outstretched, just as the body had been found. Then the dead girl would get up and come towards him, taking little hesitant steps – just as the child had done when she had come out of the river. She would glide gently towards him in a straight line, passing over the lawn and the bed of withered flowers, and then rise through the air towards Renardet's window. She was coming towards him, exactly as she had done on the day of the crime, coming towards the murderer . . .

And he drew back before the apparition, retreated as far as his bed, and threw himself onto it, knowing full well that the girl had entered the room, and that she was now standing behind the curtain which in a while would start moving again. And he would stare at this curtain until daylight came, expecting to see his victim come from behind it at any moment. But she did not show herself again. She simply stood there, behind this material which every now and then was disturbed by a trembling motion. Renardet would dig his fingers into the bedclothes, squeezing them just as he had squeezed the throat of the Roque girl. In the silence of the night he would listen to the clock striking the hours, would hear the ticking of the pendulum and the loud thudding of his heart . . . And during those nights the wretched man experienced suffering such as few men have ever known.

Then, as soon as a white line appeared on the ceiling, heralding a new day, he would feel deliverance, would feel that he was alone at last, that there was no one else in the room, and he would settle down in bed again. He would then sleep for a few hours. But it was an uneasy, feverish sleep during which he often saw in his dreams the terrifying vision of the previous night.

When he eventually went downstairs for some lunch he seemed to ache all over, as though he had done something tremendously strenuous and exhausting. And he hardly ate any food, oppressed and haunted by the constant terror of the girl he would see again the following night.

Yet he knew very well that it was not an apparition, that the dead do not come back to haunt the living. He knew that his sick mind, his mind obsessed by a single thought, by an unforgettable memory, was the sole cause of his torment. It was his mind which had brought the dead girl back to life, and called her forth, and set her before his eyes, in which her image remained irremovably imprinted. But he also knew that he would never recover from his sickness, that he would never be able to escape the savage persecution of his memory. And he came to the conclusion that he would rather die than put up with this torture any longer.

Now he began to look for a way in which he could kill himself. He wanted something simple and natural, which would not allow anyone to think that he had committed suicide. The fact was that he still cared very much about his reputation, about the good name he had inherited from his ancestors, and if anyone were to suspect that he had killed himself, people would no doubt think of the unsolved case, of the missing murderer, and it would not be long before they would be accusing him of the crime.

One very strange notion had formed in his mind – that of getting himself crushed to death by the tree underneath which he had murdered the Roque girl. So he made up his mind to have his wood felled and to try to simulate an accident. But the beech tree refused to break his back.

When he had returned home that day, in the grip of utter despair, he had taken his revolver, and then not had the courage to pull the trigger . . .

He would have to find something that would compel him to die, devise some kind of trick to deceive himself, so there would be no more hesitation, no more delay, no more regrets. How he envied the men condemned to death, who are led to the scaffold through crowds of soldiers. Oh, if only he could ask somebody to shoot him! If only he could confess the state of his soul, confess his crime to some trusted friend who would never divulge the secret, and then receive death at his hands! But of whom could he ask this dreadful favour? Who would do it? In his mind he reviewed the various friends he knew . . . What about the doctor? No. He would almost certainly talk about it afterwards . . .'

One night an idea suddenly struck him. He would write to Putoin, the investigating magistrate, who was a close friend, and denounce himself as the one who had committed the crime. In his letter he would tell him everything – the crime itself, the torture he was enduring, his determination to kill himself, his hesitation to do so, and the means he was now using to bolster his failing courage. He would beg him, in the name of their longstanding friendship, to destroy the letter as soon as he learnt that the guilty person had administered justice to himself. Renardet could count on this magistrate. He knew him to be trustworthy, discreet, quite incapable of an idle word. He was one of those men who have an inflexible conscience, governed, directed and controlled entirely by their reason.

As soon as this plan had formed in his mind he felt his heart possessed by a curious feeling of delight. Now he really was calm . . . He would write his letter, taking his time over it, then in the morning, as soon as it was light, he would drop it in the letter-box fixed on the outside wall of the farm. Then he would climb to the top of his tower, watch for the postman coming, and as soon as he saw the man in the blue smock going away with the letter, he would throw himself headlong from the tower, and be killed on the rocks which formed its foundations. He would first make sure he was in full view of the workmen who were felling his trees. He could then climb out onto the parapet to which the flag-pole was fixed, the one they used for unfurling a flag on special occasions. He would smash this pole at one stroke by throwing himself onto it, and he would fall to the ground still holding it. How could anyone suspect it was not an accident? Because of his considerable weight and the height of the tower he would be killed outright . . .

Immediately, Renardet got out of bed, went over to his table and started to write. He left nothing out, not a single detail of the crime, not a single detail of his anguished life or the torments of his heart, and he ended the letter by saying that he had passed sentence on himself, that he was going to execute the criminal, and he begged his friend, his old friend, to see to it that there would never be any stain attached to his memory.

As he finished off the letter he noticed that day was dawning. He closed the envelope, sealed it and wrote the address. Then he went downstairs with carefree footsteps, ran to the little white post-box fixed to the wall at the corner of the farm, and with trembling fingers pushed the letter into it. He then quickly returned to the house, bolted the front door, and climbed up to the top of the tower to wait for the arrival of the postman who would deliver his death-sentence.

He felt at peace now, somehow liberated and saved.

A cold, dry wind, an icy blast, struck him in the face, and with open mouth he breathed in the cold air, eagerly welcoming its chilling caress. The sky was red with the blazing red of winter, and the whole plain was glistening in the first rays of sunlight, looking as though it had been sprinkled with powdered glass. Standing there bareheaded Renardet gazed out over the vast extent of countryside: to his left he saw the meadows, to his right the village, whose chimneys were beginning to send up smoke as the folk within prepared the first meal of the day.

At his feet he could see the Brindille flowing amongst the rocks on which he would shortly be crushed to death . . . And in this beautiful, frosty dawn he somehow felt himself being born again, filled with new strength, filled with new life. The sunlight was immersing him, enveloping him, penetrating him with a renewal of hope. His mind was suddenly flooded with a thousand memories, memories of mornings like this when he had walked out over the hard earth which rang beneath his feet, and had happily gone on shooting expeditions along the shores of the lakes where wild duck lie concealed in the rushes. All the good things he loved, all the good things of life, came crowding into his memory, goading him with new desires, arousing all the appetites of his active, powerful physique.

And he was about to die? Why should he die? Was he going to kill himself on a sudden impulse, just because he was afraid of a shadow — afraid of nothing substantial at all? He was still wealthy, still in the prime of life! What madness to want to kill himself! Of course, he would need something to take his mind off things, go away somewhere, take some kind of a trip in order to forget . . . He had not seen the vision of the girl the previous night, simply because his mind had been preoccupied with other things. Perhaps he would never see her again. And even if she still haunted him in this house, she would surely not follow him elsewhere. The earth was wide, the future stretched out before him! Why should he die?!

His gaze wandered over the meadows — and he perceived a patch of blue moving along the path which followed the course of the Brindille. It was Médéric the postman, bringing letters from the town and coming to take away those posted in the village.

Renardet gave a start, and felt a painful shudder pass through his body. He rushed down the winding staircase to get his letter back, to ask the postman to return it to him. Little did it matter if anybody saw him now. He ran through the grass, which was still white with the hoar-frost of the previous night, and reached the post-box on the corner of the farm almost at the same time as Médéric.

The postman had opened the little wooden door and was taking out the few letters which had been posted by the people of the neighbourhood.

'Good morning, Médéric,' said Renardet.

'Morning, Monsieur le Maire.'

'I say, Médéric. I popped a letter in that post-box which I happen to need again. I've come to ask you to let me have it back.'

'No trouble, Monsieur le Maire. You can have it back, all right.'

At that moment the postman happened to look up, and he stared in amazement at Renardet's face. The Mayor's cheeks were suffused with purple, and his eyes were bleary, with dark lines under them, and they seemed to have sunk into his flesh. His hair was dishevelled, his beard unkempt, his tie unfastened. It was obvious that he had not had a proper night's sleep.

'Are you not well, Monsieur le Maire?' asked the postman.

Suddenly realizing that his appearance must be strange Renardet lost his composure and stammered:

'Er, no . . . No . . . The fact is I've just jumped out of bed to ask you for this letter . . . I was fast asleep . . . Do you understand?'

A vague suspicion was forming in the mind of the old soldier.

'Which letter do you mean?'

'The one you're going to give me back.'

Médéric now began to hesitate. The mayor's behaviour did not strike him as in the least natural. This letter perhaps contained an important secret, a political secret. He knew that Renardet was not a member of the Republican party, and he knew all the tricks and subterfuges employed during elections.

'Who's this letter addressed to, then?' he asked.

'To Monsieur Putoin, the magistrate. You know Monsieur Putoin, of course. He's a friend of mine!'

The postman searched through his mail and found the letter he was being asked to hand over. He started to examine it, turning it over and over in his hands. He was feeling very perplexed about what he should do, upset both by the fear of committing a serious offence and by the fear of making an enemy of the mayor.

Seeing that he was still hesitating, Renardet tried to snatch the letter from him. This rash gesture convinced Médéric that something important and mysterious was involved, and he decided he would do his duty, whatever it might cost him.

So he threw the envelope into his post-bag and fastened it up with the remark:

'No, I can't, Monsieur le Maire. As soon as I knew the letter was addressed to the magistrate I realized I couldn't let you have it back.'

Renardet felt his heart gripped by a horrible sensation of anguish.

'But . . . you know me very well personally,' he babbled. 'You can even recognize my handwriting when you see it . . . I tell you, I must have that piece of paper.'

'I can't let you have it.'

'Look here, Médéric. You know that I'm not the sort of man who'd deceive you. I tell you, I need it.'

'No, I can't.'

A burst of anger surged through Renardet's violent nature.

'Dammit, man! You'd better mind what you're doing! You know that I don't play games with people. You know that I can have you kicked out of your job, my fine fellow – and kicked out damn quick . . . And, after all, I am the mayor of this district, and now I'm ordering you to give me back that letter!'

The postman replied with very great firmness;

'No, I can't Monsieur le Maire.'

Then Renardet, losing all self-control, grabbed hold of the postman's arm and tried to take his post-bag from him. But Médéric freed himself with a powerful thrust and stepped back, raising his great stick made from a stout holly branch. Still keeping his composure, he said:

'Oh, you'd better not lay your hands on me, Monsieur le Maire, or I'll hit you with this. You watch yourself. All I'm doing is my duty!'

Sensing that now he was done for, Renardet suddenly became humble, gentle, imploring the postman like a snivelling child.

'Look, *mon ami*,' he whined. 'Look, give me back that letter and I'll reward you – I'll give you money. Listen! Listen! I'll give you a hundred francs. Do you hear? A hundred francs!'

The postman swung round on his heel and set off back to town. Renardet followed him, panting and stammering away:

'Médéric! Médéric! Listen to me! I'll give you a thousand francs! Do you hear? A thousand francs!'

The postman kept on walking and made no reply.

'I'll make your fortune for you,' persisted Renardet. 'Do you hear? You can have any amount you want . . . Fifty thousand francs for that letter! . . . What does it matter to you? . . . You still won't agree? . . . All right, then . . . A hundred thousand . . . What about that, then? . . . A hundred thousand francs . . . Do you understand? A hundred thousand francs . . . A hundred thousand francs . . . '

The postman turned round. There was a look of hardness on his face, an expression of utmost gravity in his eyes.

'That's quite enough of that. If you don't stop, I'll inform the authorities of everything you've just been saying to me.'

Renardet stopped in his tracks. It was all over. There was not a single hope left. He turned round and ran off in the direction of his home, bounding along like a hunted animal.

Now Médéric stopped and turned to watch the flight in amazement. He saw the mayor enter the house, and then he waited, convinced that something unusual was bound to happen.

Soon, in fact, the tall figure of Renardet appeared at the very top of the Renard Tower. He ran round the parapet like a madman, then took hold of the flag-pole and shook it furiously, but did not manage to break it. Then suddenly, like a swimmer taking a headlong plunge, he dived out into space, with both arms stretched in front of him.

Médéric rushed forward to get help. As he passed through the grounds he saw the woodcutters on their way to work. He called across to them, shouting out the details of the accident . . .

Beneath the walls they found a gory body whose head had been smashed against a rock. The Brindille, broadening out into a pool at this point, flowed past the rock, and they could see in the clear and tranquil water a long, pink trail of mingled brain and blood.

The Drowned Man

I

Everybody in Fécamp knew about Mother Patin. There's no denying that the old lass had been very unhappy with her husband. Throughout the marriage he used to beat her, just like a farmer who regularly threshes corn in his barn.

He was the master of a small fishing-boat, and a long time ago he had married her because she appealed to him, in spite of the fact that she was poor.

Patin was a good seaman, but he was also a brute. He used to spend his time in old Auban's tavern, where on the average day he would drink four or five tots of brandy, and on the days when he had brought in a good catch, nine or ten, and even more, depending on how jolly he felt, as he put it.

The brandy was served to the customers by old Auban's daughter, a rather attractive brunette. It was simply her good looks that encouraged trade, for there had never been any kind of talk about her morals.

When Patin used to come into the tavern in the evening he was content at first just to look at her, and make polite and respectable conversation. When he had drunk his first glass of brandy he was already finding her more attractive than usual. After the second glass, he would wink at her. After the third, he would say: 'If you wanted, you know, Mam'zelle Désirée . . . ' but he never finished the sentence. After the fourth glass he would try to catch hold of her by her skirt, so he could kiss her. And by the time he got to his tenth glass, old Auban used to take over the job of serving him with brandy.

The old liquor-merchant, who knew all the tricks of the trade, used to keep Désirée moving round the tables, to speed up the orders for drinks. And Désirée, who was not old Auban's daughter for nothing, used to swirl her skirt amongst the drinkers, and share in their jokes with a smile on her lips and a mischievous twinkle in her eye.

As a result of this habit of drinking glasses of brandy Patin grew so familiar with the sight of Désirée's face that he even imagined it when he was at sea, when he was casting his nets far from the shore, on windy nights and calm nights, on moonlight nights and dark nights. He imagined it as he held the tiller in the stern of his boat, while his four shipmates were sleeping with their heads resting on their folded arms. He always pictured her smiling at him, pouring out the yellow brandy with a little tilt of her shoulders, then walking away and saying: 'Well, there you are. Have you had enough now?'

Eventually, as a result of all this gazing at her, both in reality and in his mind's eye, he became so taken up with the idea of having her for his wife that one day, not being able to restrain himself any longer, he asked if she would marry him.

He was a wealthy man, the owner of his boat, his nets and a house at the foot of the hill on the Retenue, whereas old Auban had nothing. So his offer of marriage was eagerly accepted, and the wedding took place as soon as possible, both parties being anxious for its consummation – though for different reasons.

However, they had only been married three days when Patin began to wonder how on earth he could have formed the opinion that Désirée was different from any other woman. Of one thing he was now convinced: he must have been a real fool to get himself tied up with this penniless wench who had enticed him into marriage with her liquor. To think of all that brandy she'd plied him with – and what's more, she'd probably laced it with some filthy drug or other.

Whenever he was at sea now he never stopped cursing and swearing for hours on end. He would bite the stem of his clay pipe so hard that it broke. He would brow-beat his crew and, having cursed everything under the sun with every swear-word in his vocabulary, he would spit out the remnant of his rage on the fish and the lobsters, as he took them one by one from the nets, and tossed them into the creels to the accompaniment of oaths and foul language.

Then, when he got back home, there was his wife, old Auban's daughter, within reach of his sharp tongue and his heavy hand, and before long he came to regard her as the most contemptible creature on earth. Since she was used to being ill-treated by her father she listened to Patin's outbursts with patient resignation. He became so exasperated by her meekness that one evening he hit out at her. From then on there was a reign of terror in his house.

For the next ten years the chief topic of conversation amongst the folk who lived on the Retenue was the regular thrashing which Patin used to inflict on his wife, and his habit of swearing at her on every possible occasion. He had, in fact, a unique talent for swearing, with a wealth of vocabulary and a loudness of mouth which no man in Fécamp could equal. Whenever he returned from fishing, as soon as his boat came into view at the entrance to the harbour, they used to wait in keen anticipation for the first volley of curses which he would fire from his deck on to the jetty, the moment he saw the white bonnet of his better half.

They would see him coming in when there was a heavy swell, standing in the stern with one eye on the bows and the other on the sail, and in spite of the careful attention he had to pay as he piloted his boat through the narrow, difficult passage, in spite of the great waves which came rolling through the narrow entrance to the harbour, he would scan the group of women waiting for their menfolk on the sea-lashed jetty, and try to pick out his wife, old Auban's beggarly daughter.

The instant he saw her, he would launch above the roar of the waves and the wind such a torrent of abuse, delivered with such prodigious lung-power, that everybody used to burst out laughing, even though they really felt very sorry for the poor woman. Then, when his boat reached the quayside, he liked to get rid of his extra cargo of good manners, as he put it, which he was accustomed to do whilst unloading his haul of fish, surrounded by a crowd composed of all the urchins and idlers in the harbour.

This extra cargo issued from his mouth, sometimes like cannon-shots, very loud and brief, sometimes like the rumbling of thunder lasting as long as five minutes – a veritable hurricane of bad language, so violent that he seemed to have stored up in his lungs all the storms of the Almighty.

Then, when he stepped ashore and came face to face with the poor woman standing there amidst a crowd of inquisitive bystanders and fishwives, he would scoop out from the bottom of his hold a fresh cargo of insults and injuries, which he would heap upon her as they walked to their house, with her in front, weeping all the way, and him behind, shouting all the way.

And then, when he had her all to himself, he would slap her at the least excuse. Anything would do as a pretext to raise his hand to her, and once he began, there was no stopping him. He would go on and on spitting out the real reasons for his hatred. With every clout he gave her, with every thump of his fist, he would yell: 'Ah, you penniless beggar! You ragamuffin! You empty-bellied bitch! I made a right mess o' things the day I swilled mi mouth out with that rot-gut liquor yer swindlin' father sells!'

And the poor woman lived in a constant state of terror, in a never-ending tension of body and soul, in the panic-stricken expectation of insults and thrashings.

This went on for ten years. She was now so timid that she could hardly talk to anyone without turning pale. Her mind was constantly filled with thoughts of the beatings which were waiting for her, and she had become as thin, as yellow and as withered as a piece of smoked fish.

II

One night when her man was at sea she was suddenly awakened by a fierce growling noise – the sound of a gale getting up, for all the world like the growl of an unleashed dog. She sat up in bed, feeling very upset. Then, as the sound had died away, she lay down again. But almost immediately there came down the chimney a roar which shook the house from top to bottom, and then it seemed to fill the whole sky, as though a herd of wild animals were stampeding through the air, snorting and bellowing.

So she got up and ran down to the harbour. Other women were hurrying along from every direction, carrying lanterns. Men came running up, and together they stood and looked at the sea, watching the crests of the mountainous waves flashing white in the darkness.

The storm went on for fifteen hours. Eleven sailors were lost at sea – and Patin was one of them.

Somewhere near Dieppe they found part of the wreckage from his boat, the *Jeune-Amélie*. Somewhere along the coast towards Saint-Valéry they recovered the bodies of his crew – but Patin's body was never found. The hull of his boat seemed to have been cut in two, and if there had been a collision the other boat might possibly have picked him up and landed him in some distant port. So for a long time Patin's wife expected – and dreaded – that her husband might return.

Then, gradually, she became accustomed to the idea that she was a widow. Even so, she would still tremble with fear if a neighbour, or a beggar, or a pedlar, happened to enter her house unexpectedly.

Now, one afternoon about four years after her husband's disappearance, she was walking down the rue aux Juifs, and she stopped in front of the house of an old sea captain who had recently died, and whose belongings were being sold by auction.

At that particular moment they were auctioning a parrot, a green parrot with a blue head, which was eyeing the little crowd with an air of uneasy displeasure.

'What about three francs?' cried the auctioneer. 'Three francs for a bird that can talk like a lawyer!'

One of Mother Patin's friends jogged her elbow. 'You ought to buy that,' she said. 'You've got plenty of money. That bird'll be a bit of company for you. It's worth more than thirty francs, is that bird. I bet you could sell it again for twenty or twenty-five, easy!'

'Four francs, ladies. Four francs!' the man went on. 'He can sing vespers and preach as good a sermon as the vicar. I tell you, he's out of this world . . . a real marvel!'

Mother Patin bid another fifty centimes, and soon she was carrying the hook-nosed bird home in a little cage.

She set the cage down in her house, and as she was opening the wire door to give the parrot a drink, it pecked her finger viciously, breaking the skin and drawing blood.

'Ah! He's a bad 'un,' she remarked.

Still, she put some hemp-seed and maize into his cage, then left him to preen his feathers and glance shiftily around him as he took stock of his new home and his new mistress.

The next morning, just as it was beginning to get light, Mother Patin heard with the utmost distinctness the sound of a human voice, loud, echoing, rumbling. Unmistakably, it was the voice of Patin shouting: 'Get up, you stinkin' bitch!'

She was so terrified that she buried her head under the bedclothes. In the old days, every morning, the moment her husband opened his eyes, he used to yell in her ear those very same words.

Trembling, cringing, huddled up into a ball, with her back braced to receive the thrashing she expected at any moment, she mumbled with her face buried in the pillow: 'God Almighty! It's him! God Almighty! It's him! He's come back! God Almighty!'

Minutes went by, but no further sound disturbed the silence of the bedroom. Then, still trembling, she looked out from under the bedclothes, feeling convinced that he was there, ready to pounce on her and beat her.

She saw nothing, nothing apart from a ray of sunlight coming in through the window-pane. She thought: 'I bet he's hiding somewhere.'

She waited for a long time, then, gaining a little more confidence, she thought to herself: 'I think I must have been dreaming – for there's no sign of him at all.'

She was just closing her eyes again when, suddenly, from somewhere very near to her, the furious, thunderous voice of the drowned man burst out again, bellowing: 'Damn you! Damn you! Damn you! Are you never going to get up, you bitch?'

She jumped out of bed, impelled by the instinctive, passive obedience of a woman who has been beaten black and blue, and who still remembers, four years later, who will remember for the rest of her life, and who never fails to obey the terrible voice of her master.

'Here I am, Patin,' she said. 'What is it you want?'

But Patin did not answer. In a state of bewilderment, she gazed all round her. Then she started to search everywhere – in the cupboards, up the chimney, under the bed. But she found nobody, and at last she allowed herself to drop into a chair, terrified to the point of anguish, absolutely convinced that Patin's ghost was there, quite near to her, and that he had come back from the dead to torment her.

Then, suddenly, she remembered the hayloft which was reached from outside, by means of ladder. That would surely be the explanation. Patin had hidden up there so he could take her by surprise. He must have been kept prisoner by savages on some distant shore, and not been able to get away until now. And he had come back more wicked than ever – as she could tell for certain, by the mere tone of his voice.

She looked up at the ceiling and asked: 'Are you up there, Patin?'

Patin did not answer.

So she went out of the house and, with her heart palpitating in the grip of the most appalling terror, she climbed up the ladder, opened the loft-door, looked in, saw nothing, went in, looked around . . . and found nothing.

She sat down on a truss of straw and began to weep. But in the midst of her tears she heard from her bedroom, just below, the voice of Patin talking away. Pierced through by a sharp, supernatural dread, she heard him say, less angrily and more quietly than before: 'Filthy weather! . . . Strong gale! . . . Filthy weather . . . And I've not 'ad mi breakfast, dammit!'

She called out through the ceiling: 'I'm here, Patin! I'll make you some nice soup, Don't be angry with me! I'm coming!'

She scrambled down the ladder, and rushed into the house. There was nobody there.

She felt ready to faint away, as though the icy hand of death were upon her – and she was on the point of running out to ask the neighbours to help her, when the voice cried out, quite close to her ear: 'I've not 'ad mi breakfast, dammit!'

From its cage the parrot was glaring at her with its round, shifty, malevolent eye.

And she stared back at it in bewilderment. 'Ah!' she murmured. 'It's you!'

The parrot spoke again, cocking its head on one side: 'Just you wait! Just you wait! I'll teach yer to idle yer time away!'

What was happening to her? She felt certain, she understood now, that it was Patin, that the dead man had come back and concealed himself in the plumage of this creature. He was here so he could start torturing her again, so he could curse and swear at her all day long, so he could bite her, squawk insults at her, so that all the neighbours would hear and gather round to laugh at her . . .

She flung herself upon the cage, opened it and pulled out the bird, which struggled to defend itself, lacerating her skin with its beak and claws. But she held on to it with both hands, squeezing with all her might, and then she threw herself on to the floor, rolling there in a demented frenzy, until she had crushed the life out of the parrot beneath her, and turned it into a ragged lump of flesh, a little soft, green thing, which no longer moved or spoke, but hung limply from her hand.

Then she wrapped the dead bird in a duster for a shroud, and went out of the house, still barefoot and wearing only her nightdress. She went to the quay-side, where the waves were gently lapping and, shaking out the duster, she dropped into the sea this little dead body which looked like a handful of grass.

Then she went back home, fell on her knees in front of the empty cage and, heart-broken over what she had done, she prayed that the Good Lord would forgive her, sobbing away as though she had just committed some horrible crime.

Who Knows?

I

My God! My God! So at last I am going to put down in writing all that has happened to me! But how can I do it? How *dare* I do it? It's all so bizarre, so incomprehensible, so crazy!

If I were not certain about what I have seen, certain that there has been no weak link in my logic, no error in my investigations, no lapse in the relentless progression of my observations, I would consider myself simply the victim of some hallucination, deceived by some strange fantasy. After all, who knows?

I am writing this in a private mental hospital. But I have come in here of my own free will – as a precaution, and because I am afraid. Only one living soul knows my story: the doctor in charge here. And now I am going to write it down – I don't really know why. Perhaps it is so I can get it out of my system, for I can feel it constantly rising within me, like an unbearable nightmare . . . Well, here it is.

I have always had a solitary disposition, always been a dreamer, a sort of lone philosopher, kind to others, content with little, bearing neither bitterness towards men, nor resentment towards heaven. I have always lived alone, as a result of a kind of uneasiness which comes over me when I am with other people. How can I explain this? I don't suppose I can explain it. It's not that I refuse to see people, or to chat to them, or to have dinner with friends, but when I've been with them for some time, even with the people I know best, I find that they weary me, tire me out, get on my nerves – and with a growing feeling of exasperation I long to see them go, or go away myself, so that I can be alone.

This feeling I have is more than a desire: it is a compelling necessity. And if I had to endure the continued presence of other people, if I had to go on listening to their conversation for any length of time, something would certainly happen to me. What exactly would it be? Ah, who knows? Perhaps I should faint – something like that.

I am so passionately fond of solitude that I can't even tolerate other people sleeping under the same roof. I can't bear to live in Paris because, for me, it seems like a lingering death. Not only do I suffer a spiritual death, but I also find that my body and nerves are tortured by the vast, swarming crowds of people who are living all around me, even when they are asleep. Oh, yes, I find the sleep of other human beings even harder to bear than their endless talking. And I can never get any rest myself when I know – or when I suspect – that on the other side of a wall there are lives being interrupted by those regular eclipses of consciousness which we call sleep.

Why do I feel like this? Who knows? Perhaps there is a very simple explanation: perhaps it's because I tire very quickly of anything which takes place outside of me, as it were. There are a lot of people in my situation . . .

One of the results of all this is that I become deeply attached to inanimate objects, which seem to me to take on the importance of living creatures. My house has become – or rather, *had* become – a whole world in which I lived a solitary yet active life, surrounded by physical things – familiar items of furniture and other odds and ends, which seemed to me to be as warm and friendly as human faces. I had gradually filled and adorned my home with these things, and when I was safe inside I felt as content and satisfied and genuinely happy as if I were in the arms of a loving woman whose familiar caress had become a gentle, tranquilizing necessity.

This house stood in a beautiful garden which isolated it from the roads; yet it was within reach of a town where, if I happened to feel like it, I could find all the social activities in which I took an occasional interest. All my servants slept in a building some distance away at the bottom of the kitchen-garden, which was surrounded by a high wall. The embrace of sombre nights in the silence of this house of mine, lost, hidden, submerged amongst the foliage of great trees, was so restful and so good for me that every evening I would delay going to bed for several hours, just so that I could enjoy it even longer.

On that particular day there had been a performance of Ernest Reyer's *Sigurd* at the theatre in town. It was the first time that I had heard this beautiful romantic opera, and it had given me the greatest of pleasure.

I was walking back home, at a brisk and cheerful pace, with my head full of rich melodies and pretty, fairy-tale scenes. It was very dark indeed – so dark, in fact, that I could hardly make out the edge of the main road, and several times I nearly fell into a ditch. The distance from the toll-gate to my house is about a mile, perhaps a little more – let us say twenty minutes at normal walking pace. It would be about one o'clock in the morning – possibly as late as half past one. As I walked, the sky ahead of me seemed to grow a little lighter, and a slender crescent-moon appeared, the melancholy crescent of the moon's last quarter. The crescent of the first quarter, the one you see rising at four or five o'clock in the evening, is bright, cheerful, glistening with silver, but the one you see rising after midnight is reddish, dismal, disturbing – the sinister moon of the Witches' Sabbath. All those who are out late at night must have noticed this difference. The crescent of the first quarter, even if it is only as slender as a thread, sheds a cheerful radiance which gladdens the heart and lights up the earth sufficiently to leave clear-cut shadows. The crescent of the last quarter struggles to shed its dying light, which is so feeble that it hardly casts any shadows at all.

In the distance I noticed the gloomy mass of trees surrounding my garden, and for some reason or other I felt uneasy at the thought of entering it. I slackened my pace . . . the night was very mild. That great cluster of trees had the look of a tomb in which my house was buried.

I opened my gate and walked down the long avenue of sycamore trees which led up to the house. It was arched overhead, like a huge tunnel, and ran past dense masses of shrubbery and dark, moonlit lawns on which flower-beds superimposed their oval patches of wan colours.

When I got near the house I was overcome by a strange feeling of agitation. I stood still. There was not a sound to be heard. There was not a leaf stirring in the breeze. 'What on earth's the matter with me?' I thought. For ten years I had been coming home like this without feeling the slightest bit of anxiety. I was not afraid – and I never have been afraid – when coming home late at night. The mere sight of a strange man, some prowler or burglar, would have made me furious, and I would have leaped upon him without a moment's hesitation. Besides, I was armed: I had my revolver with me. But I did not touch it, because I was determined to master this nervousness stirring within me.

What was it? Some kind of premonition? Was it the mysterious foreboding which takes possession of a man's senses when he is about to see something inexplicable? Possibly. Who knows?

As I moved slowly forwards I felt my skin tingling all over, and when I got to the wall of my vast house with its closed shutters, I knew that I would have to wait a few minutes before I could open the door and go inside. So I sat down on a seat under the windows of my drawing-room. I stayed there for a while, trembling a little, with my head leaning back against the wall of the house, and my eyes wide open, staring at the gloomy foliage. For the first few moments I noticed nothing unusual. There was a sort of rushing sound in my ears – but I often get that. It sometimes seems as though I can hear trains going by, or bells ringing, or marching footsteps.

But soon these head-noises become louder, more distinct, more recognizable. I had been mistaken. It was not the usual surging in my arteries that was filling my ears with this murmuring sound, but a very peculiar, rather jumbled noise. And there was no doubt whatever that it was coming from inside my house.

Through the wall I could make out this continuous noise – more like a vibration than a noise, the sort of confused sound you would expect if a number of things were being moved about. It was as though all my articles of furniture were vibrating, being moved from their accustomed places, being gently dragged about the house.

Oh, I can assure you that for an appreciable time I doubted the evidence of my senses. But when I had pressed my ear against a shutter so I could get a better idea of what was going on inside, I became absolutely convinced that something abnormal and incomprehensible was taking place in my home. I was not exactly afraid, but I was . . . how can I put it? . . . stunned with astonishment. I didn't even release the safety-catch on my revolver, because I felt sure there would be no need to use it . . . I simply waited.

I waited for a long time, unable to come to any decision, thinking very clearly, but beside myself with anxiety. I waited, standing there, listening all the time to the noise which was now growing louder, occasionally reaching a kind of violent intensity, which seemed like a growl of impatience or anger – a sort of mysterious rebellion.

Then, suddenly feeling ashamed of my cowardice, I took my bunch of keys, found the one I needed, pushed it into the keyhole, turned it fully in the lock and, pushing on the door with all my strength, I swung it open so violently that it banged against the inner wall.

The noise it made rang out like a gun-shot – and, instantly, as if in reply to this loud bang, from the whole of my house, from top to bottom, there came the most tremendous uproar. It was so unexpected, so horrible, so deafening, that I recoiled a few steps, and – though I still knew it was useless – I drew my revolver from its holster.

I waited – but not for long! Now I could hear an extraordinary stamping noise on the stairs, on the floors, on the carpets – not the stamping of shoes worn by human beings, but the stamping of crutches – wooden crutches, and iron crutches which made a noise like the clashing of cymbals . . . And then it was that I suddenly noticed an armchair on the threshold of my front door – the big armchair I always used when reading – it was actually going out of the house, swaying and waddling as it went . . . There it was, going off into the garden . . . Other chairs followed it, the ones out of my drawing-room. Then came the low couches, dragging themselves along like crocodiles on their short legs. Then out came all the rest of my chairs, leaping about like goats, and the little stools, bounding along like rabbits.

What a state I was in! I ran out and hid in the shrubbery, crouching down, unable to take my eyes off this march-past of my furniture – for every stick of it was going, one item after the other, some quickly, some slowly, depending on the size and weight. My piano, my huge grand piano, galloped past like a runaway horse, rattling and tinkling with music. The tiniest little objects were running over the gravel: the glasses, the goblets, in which the moonlight gleamed with the phosphorescence of glow-worms. The curtains and carpets were writhing and slithering along, like octopuses . . . Then I saw my writing-desk appear. It was a valuable antique from the eighteenth century and it contained all the letters I have ever received, the entire story of my personal life, a long story which has brought me much suffering! And there were photographs in there, too.

Suddenly, I was afraid no longer. I rushed forward and flung myself on this desk, grabbing hold of it as if I were tackling a burglar. But it continued irresistibly on its way, and in spite of all my struggles, in spite of all my anger, I couldn't even manage to slow it down. Struggling like a desperate man against this terrifying strength, I was flung to the ground, still wrestling to hold it back. Then it sent me rolling over, dragged me along the gravel – and the furniture that had been coming along behind it started to walk over me, trampling on my legs and bruising them badly. Then, as soon as I had let go of the desk, the rest of the furniture passed over my body, just like cavalry charging over a dismounted soldier.

By this time I was beside myself with terror, but I managed to drag myself out of the drive and hide once again amongst the trees, from where I watched all my possessions disappearing into the night – every single one of them: the lowliest, the smallest, the most ordinary, even the ones I had never paid much attention to, but all of them belonging to me.

Then I heard, some distance away, the tremendous clatter of doors being shut. It came from my own house, which was now filled with the sonorous echoes of an empty house. The doors of the building slammed shut from top to bottom until finally the front-door, which in my folly I had opened to permit this mass escape, slammed shut last of all.

I took flight myself, running all the way to the town, and I only recovered my self-control when I got into the streets where there were a few people about, coming home late. I went and rang at the door of a hotel where I was well known. With my hands I had dashed the dirt off my clothes, and at the hotel I told the story that I had lost my bunch of keys, which also included the key to the kitchen-garden. I told them that this was where my servants were asleep in a detached building surrounded by the high wall which protected my fruit and vegetables from prowlers.

They gave me a bed, and though I buried myself under the sheets I couldn't sleep, but lay there waiting for daybreak, listening to the pounding of my heart. I had told somebody in the hotel to inform my servants of my whereabouts as soon as it was light, and at seven o'clock in the morning my valet banged on my door. From his face I could see that he was terribly upset.

'Something dreadful has happened during the night, monsieur,' he said. 'All your furniture has been stolen, monsieur – everything, absolutely everything, even down to the smallest articles.'

I felt pleased when I heard him say this. Why? Who knows? I was completely in control of myself, certain that I would be able to conceal my feelings and not tell anybody about what I had seen, certain that I could hide this thing, bury it deep in my mind like some frightful secret. I answered him by saying: 'It must be the same people as the ones who stole my keys. We must inform the police immediately. I'll get dressed and be with you in just a few moments.'

The investigations went on for five months. The police discovered nothing whatever. They could neither trace the smallest of my possessions nor uncover the slightest clue about the thieves. My God! If I had told them what I knew . . . If I had told them . . . they would have locked me up – me, not the thieves – me, the man who had been able to see what I had seen.

Oh, I knew how to keep my mouth shut. But I didn't start re-furnishing my house. It would have been quite pointless. The whole business would have started all over again. I didn't want to go back to my house. I never did go back. I never saw it again.

I came to Paris and stayed in a hotel. I consulted various doctors about the state of my nerves, something which has been worrying me a great deal ever since that appalling night.

They strongly advised me to travel. I took their advice.

II

I began with a trip to Italy. The sunshine there did me good. For six months I wandered from Genoa to Venice, from Venice to Florence, from Florence to Rome, from Rome to Naples. Then I travelled through Sicily, a place which has both wonderful scenery and wonderful historical sites, relics from the days of the Greeks and the Normans. I went over to Africa and made a safe journey across that great, calm yellow desert, peopled by camels, gazelles and nomadic Arabs, and where in the crystal-clear atmosphere there is no suggestion of any haunting vision, either by night or day.

I returned to France by way of Marseilles, and, in spite of the Provençal gaiety, the fact that the skies were less bright than in Africa made me rather depressed. On returning to Europe I felt as a sick man must feel when he believes himself to be cured – and then a dull pain reminds him that the focus of infection has not been eliminated.

I came back to Paris, and after a month here I became bored. By now it was autumn, and before winter set in I wanted to take a trip through Normandy, where I had never been before.

I began by visiting Rouen, of course, and for a whole week I wandered in a state of ecstatic enthusiasm through this medieval city, this amazing museum of extraordinary Gothic buildings.

Now one afternoon, about four o'clock, I turned down a most peculiar street, along which flowed an inky-black stream called the Eau de Robec. I was gazing up at the queer, ancient façades of the houses, when my attention was suddenly caught by the sight of a whole row of shops dealing in second-hand furniture.

How well they had chosen their site, these sordid dealers in old junk. There they were in this weird alley, perched above this sinister-looking stream, and above them were the angular roofs of tiles and slates on which there still creaked the weather-cocks of a bygone age.

In the depths of these gloomy shops you could see a higgledy-piggledy assortment of carved chests, pottery from Rouen, Nevers and Moustiers, statues of various kinds, some painted, some in oak, images of saints, church ornaments, garments worn by priests; there were even holy chalices and an old wooden tabernacle painted gold, in which God no longer resided. Oh, what strange, mysterious grottoes there were in these tall houses crammed from cellar to attic with objects of every conceivable kind, objects whose life seemed to be over, and yet which had outlived their mortal owners – even outlived their century, their period and their fashion, so they could be bought as curios by new generations.

My passion for antiques was being aroused again in this stronghold of antique-dealers. I went from shop to shop, taking quick, light steps across the little bridges made from three or four rotten planks which lay across the evil-smelling water of the Eau de Robec.

Gracious God! What a shock! I found myself looking at one of my own wardrobes – one of the finest I had. It was standing at the side of a vaulted gallery which was cluttered up with antiques, a place which looked like the entrance to the catacombs of a cemetery for old furniture. I went up to the wardrobe, trembling all over, trembling so much that I hardly dared touch it. Hesitantly I reached out my hand. And yet it really was mine: a unique Louis XIII wardrobe, which would have been recognized straight away by anyone who had seen it even once. Suddenly looking a little further into the gloomy depths of this gallery, I noticed three of my armchairs, the ones upholstered in *petit point* tapestry, then, still deeper in the gallery, my two Henry II tables, so rare that people used to come all the way from Paris to see them.

Just imagine how I felt! Just think of my state of mind!

I moved further into the gallery. I was almost petrified with fear, but I am not a coward, and in spite of my agony of mind I moved forward, like a knight from the Dark Ages thrusting his way into a place that is haunted and bewitched. I went on, and at each step I took I found something that had belonged to me – my chandeliers, my books, my pictures, my curtains, my antique weapons – everything was there except the writing-desk containing my letters, and this was nowhere to be seen.

I went on, going down steps leading to lower floors, then climbing to ones higher up. I was all alone. I called out; but nobody answered. I was all alone – there was not another soul in this vast labyrinth of a building.

Night fell, and I had to sit there in the darkness on one of my own chairs, for I was determined not to leave the place. Every now and then I shouted out: 'Hello! Hello! Is anybody there?'

I must have been there for more than an hour when I heard the sound of footsteps – light, slow footsteps – coming from somewhere in the gallery. I nearly jumped up and ran out into the street, but, bracing myself, I called out once again, and I saw a light appear in an adjoining room.

'Who's there?' asked a voice.

I replied: 'A customer.'

The answer came back: 'It's very late for you to be coming into a shop, isn't it?'

'I've been waiting for more than an hour,' I rejoined.

'You could come back tomorrow.'

'Tomorrow I shall have left Rouen.'

I simply dared not go towards him – and he was not coming out to me. The bright glow was still coming from his lamp and lighting up a tapestry which depicted two angels hovering over the corpses on a battle-field. This item, too, belonged to me.

I called out: 'Well, then? Are you coming?'

He replied: 'I'm waiting for you.'

I got up and went towards him.

In the middle of a large room there stood a little man, very short and very fat, phenomenally fat, like some hideous freak.

He had a thin, straggling beard, which was patchy and yellowish – and there was not a hair on his head! Not a hair! As he lifted up his candle at arm's length in order to see me better, his skull looked just like a little, round moon in this enormous room cluttered with old furniture. His face was wrinkled and bloated; his eyes were so sunken they could hardly be seen.

I bargained with him for three chairs which belonged to me, and paid him a large sum for them in cash, giving him only the number of my room and the name of the hotel. The chairs were to be delivered the following morning by nine o'clock.

Then I left. He saw me to the door, behaving very courteously.

I then went to the local superintendent of police and told him about how my furniture had been stolen and what I had just discovered.

He immediately sent a telegram to the department which had been investigating the burglary, and asked me to wait until he received the information he required. An hour later the reply came, confirming my story.

'I'm going to have this man arrested and questioned,' said the superintendent. 'And it must be done straight away because he might have got suspicious and had your belongings removed . . . If you can go and have a meal and come back in a couple of hours, I'll have him here by then, and I can question him again in your presence.'

'I can certainly do that, monsieur. I am extremely grateful to you.'

I went to my hotel and dined with a heartier appetite than I could have believed possible. I suppose I was feeling rather pleased about the way things had worked out. At last we had him.

Two hours later I went back to the police officer, who was waiting for me.

'Well, now, monsieur!' he said as soon as he saw me. 'We've not found this thief of yours. My men haven't been able to get their hands on him at all.'

'Ah!' I gasped, and suddenly felt as though I was going to faint. 'But,' I asked him, 'surely you've managed to find his house?'

'Yes, indeed. And I'm going to have it kept under surveillance until he gets back. But as for the man himself . . . disappeared!'

'Disappeared?'

'Yes, disappeared. He usually spends his evenings at the house of a neighbour, a woman who is a second-hand dealer, like himself – a queer old witch of a woman, a widow by the name of Bidoin. She hasn't seen him tonight, and she can't tell us where he is. We shall have to wait until tomorrow.'

I left the police station. Ah, those ancient streets of Rouen, how sinister, how disturbing, how haunted they now seemed to me!

I slept very badly that night, with a nightmare at the end of each brief interval of sleep.

The next day I waited until ten o'clock before going to the police. I didn't want to give them the impression that I was too anxious or in too much of a hurry.

The dealer had not turned up. His shop was still closed.

The superintendent said to me: 'I've taken all the necessary steps. I've been in touch with headquarters. I want you to come with us to this shop. I'll have it forced open, and then you can show me what belongs to you.'

We drove there in a carriage. Policemen were standing in front of the shop, and with them there was a locksmith, who soon opened it for us.

When I went in I could see neither my cupboard, nor my armchairs, nor my tables, nor anything at all that had once furnished my house – nothing whatever, and yet the night before I could hardly move a step without coming across something of mine.

The superintendent was surprised, and at first he looked at me rather suspiciously.

I said: 'My word, monsieur, it's a remarkable coincidence that the furniture has disappeared at the same time as the dealer.'

'That's certainly true,' he said with a smile. 'You know, you were wrong to buy those things of yours yesterday – and pay for them as well. It'll have aroused his suspicions.'

'What I simply can't understand,' I said, 'is that every single space that was occupied by my furniture has now been filled by other articles.'

'Oh,' replied the superintendent, 'he's had all night – and probably been helped by accomplices as well. And I dare say this house communicates with the ones on each side . . . Don't worry, monsieur. I'm going to give this case my personal attention. Now we know his hide-out it won't be long before we get our hands on this villain.'

Ah, my heart, my heart, my poor heart, how madly it was beating!

I stayed in Rouen for a fortnight. The man never came back.

My God! My God! Who could ever have been any problem to a man like that, or caught him off his guard?

Now, when I had been in Rouen exactly a fortnight, on the morning of the fifteenth day, I received from the gardener who had been left in charge of my locked and empty house the following strange letter:

Dear Sir,

I beg to inform you that last night something happened which none of us can understand, not even the police. All the furniture has come back – all of it, with not a single thing missing. It's all here, down to the tiniest little things. The house is now exactly the same as it was on the night of the burglary. It's enough to drive you out of your mind. It happened in the middle of the night – between Friday and Saturday. The whole drive has got deep ruts in it, and it looks as though they'd dragged everything from the gate right up to the front-door. It was just like that the day everything disappeared.

We're waiting for you to come back, monsieur, and I remain,

Your obedient servant,
Raudin, Philippe

Oh no! Oh no! No! No! No! I shall never go back!

I took this letter to the Rouen superintendent.

'It's a very clever piece of restitution,' he said. 'We'd better lie low for the time being. Don't worry; we'll nab this fellow one of these days.'

But they haven't nabbed him. Oh, no. They haven't nabbed him – and I'm as scared of him now as if he were a ferocious beast about to spring on me from behind my back.

Untraceable! That's what he is – untraceable. Nobody can possibly find him, this monster with the moon-like skull. They'll never catch him. He'll never go back to his shop. What does *he* care? I am the only person who could possibly confront him – and I don't want to!

No, I don't want to! I don't want to! I don't want to!

And, anyway, what if he does come back, what if he does return to his shop, who will be able to prove that my furniture was on his premises? Mine is the only evidence against him, and I'm well aware that the police are beginning to treat it with suspicion.

Oh, no! I couldn't go on living that kind of life. And yet I couldn't keep quiet about what I have seen. I couldn't go on living a normal life so long as I dreaded the possibility of this business starting all over again.

So I came to see the doctor who runs this private mental hospital, and I told him everything.

After he had spent a long time asking me questions, he said: 'Monsieur, would you be willing to stay here for a while?'

'Yes, monsieur.'

'Would you like a private suite of rooms?'

'Yes, monsieur.'

'Would you like any of your friends to come and visit you?'

'No, monsieur! No! I don't want anybody! The man from Rouen might try to get at me here – out of revenge.'

And I have been alone, all alone, for three months. My nerves are more or less calm now. I have only one fear . . . Suppose the antique-dealer went mad . . . and suppose they brought him into this place . . . Even prisons are not safe . . .

NOTES

The Horla (Le Horla) Published in January 1887, this is infinitely superior to a first draft of the story written the previous October. The setting is almost certainly Flaubert's house, in its fine position on the Seine at Croisset. Based on Maupassant's own terror of insanity, this is also an early example of science-fiction, as is suggested by the name *Horla*, possibly from *hors* (outside) and *là* (there), or *hors-la-loi* (outlaw), and perhaps from Normandy dialect. This invented name became so familiar that Maupassant christened the balloon in which he sailed from Paris to Holland in July 1887, 'Le Horla'.

The Devil (Le Diable) Told with remarkable simplicity, this story illustrates Maupassant's sharp, unsentimental observation of the peasants of his native Normandy. It is typical of his general theme that their hard life has made them tough, cunning, and thrifty to the point of shocking miserliness.

Two Friends (Deux Amis) This fisherman's tale with a difference combines Maupassant's love of the River Seine and his own experience of the Franco-Prussian War of 1870. One of many stories in which he depicts callous Prussian officers and the dignified sufferings of ordinary people. First published in *Gil Blas* in 1883.

Fear (La Peur) Published in 1882, the first of two *contes* with this title. Maupassant here uses his favourite device of a story-within-a-story, to ensure a realistic narration. Note the contrast between the scorching Sahara, which Maupassant had recently visited, and N.E. France in winter.

The Hand (La Main) A revised version of a story published in 1875, which Maupassant had based on the mummified hand he had been given by Swinburne. (See Introduction). Maupassant had visited Corsica in 1880, three years before this appeared. The Englishman, getting his genders wrong, should have said *'ce'* rather than *'cette'*.

Coco Skilfully constructed and swiftly narrated, this is another cameo of country life in Normandy, with an implicit condemnation of this brutalized lad, and powerful sympathy aroused for the old horse, especially in the superb, ironical ending. First published in *Le Gaulois* in 1884.

The Mannerism (Le Tic) Set in the little spa of Châtel-Guyon, about 21 km north of Clermont-Ferrand, this somewhat unlikely tale (1884) is based on Maupassant's visit there in a vain attempt to improve his health. It also owes something to *The Premature Burial* and similar stories by E. A. Poe.

The Madwoman (La Folle) A horror-story from the Franco-Prussian War, possibly based on an actual incident, the whole forming a restrained yet powerful protest against the brutalizing effect of war.

Mohammed-Fripouille One of the stories inspired by Maupassant's stay in North Africa in 1881. Here is cruelty, even sadism, but also compassion for the Arabs, especially the women. First published in 1884.

The Blind Man (L'Aveugle) Were the peasants of Normandy capable of such inhumanity as portrayed here? Maupassant testifies that they were, and his simple tale is in protest. Similar ending to *Coco* and *La Folle*.

At Sea (En Mer) One of several stories based on Maupassant's accurate knowledge of the fishing communities of the northern coast of France. The chance reading of a newspaper report provides a convincing opening, and the whole tale reads like an eye-witness account. The opening is based on an actual news item (Boulogne, 28 January, 1883).

Apparition Published in 1883, the same year as *He?*, but here the narrator only gives us a hint about the nature of what he has seen – a case of sequestration (hiding away)?

Saint-Antoine In this story of occupied France the villain is one of Maupassant's gallery of unsavoury peasants, rather than the Prussians, with whom we sympathize. The allusion is to St. Anthony (251–356) who became the patron saint of swineherds. A pet pig, the smallest of the litter, is traditionally called 'St. Anthony's pig'. The sudden switch from humour to horror is clever, and true to life.

The Wolf (Le Loup) Maupassant was as fond of hunting as of fishing. Wolves were still to be found in eastern France at the time of writing. Notice how the narration, unbroken by dialogue, conveys the gathering momentum of the hunt. The giant Gargantua, according to Rabelais, laughed when his son Pantagruel was born, but wept because the mother died in childbirth.

Terror (La Peur) Like the earlier story with the same title this has two contrasting parts. Maupassant here claims to reproduce what Turgenev had actually told him at Flaubert's flat in Paris in 1876. The second anecdote is derived from Maupassant's visit to Brittany in 1879.

The Diary of a Madman (Un Fou) Published in *Le Gaulois* in 1885. The author's favourite device of a chance discovery leading to the exposure of the terrible truth. The contrast between the judge's reputation and the reality could not be greater. Maupassant loved to unmask hypocrisy and to remind us that things and people are rarely what they seem.

A Vendetta (Une Vendetta) The best-known of the stories arising from Maupassant's stay in Corsica in 1880. The theme of fearful vengeance is common in his writing. He loved dogs, but was not sentimental about them. Here he chooses a bitch to symbolize the avenging Mme Savarini. The curt ending is perfect, and says everything.

The Smile of Schopenhauer (Auprès d'un Mort) Little more than an anecdote, this is another example of Maupassant's obsession with corpses. He genuinely admired the German philosopher Schopenhauer, whose profound pessimism he shared. (See Introduction).

On the River (Sur l'Eau) Based on Maupassant's fascination with the Seine and his love of fishing. The mysterious atmosphere is wonderfully conveyed, and then rounded off with one of the surprise-endings for which he was famous. Though remarkably mature in style, this was one of his earliest stories, first appearing in 1876.

He? (Lui?) Probably based on an actual experience, as Maupassant's friend, Paul Bourget, tells us that he began to suffer from hallucinations in 1883, when this was published. In any case, a moving insight into the mind of a lonely, fear-ridden neurotic.

Old Milon (Le Père Milon) More sympathetically drawn than many of Maupassant's Norman peasants, le père Milon, though shrewd and ruthless, has dignity and courageous patriotism. Neither he nor the Prussians are condemned – only war itself.

The Head of Hair (La Chevelure) Maupassant, long before his own insanity, was interested in asylums. This story (1884) also reflects contemporary discussion of the nature of mental illness, and is a powerful account of fetishism.

The Inn (L'Auberge) As usual, Maupassant describes what he has actually seen – the dramatic alpine region above Leuk (called Louèche-les-bains by the French), a Swiss spa, where he had been for treatment in 1877. Once again a dog is used to enhance the supernatural effect, and the invisible terror anticipates the Horla.

Mother Savage (La Mère Sauvage) The central character is the French equivalent of the Corsican widow in *Une Vendetta*. Her calculated vengeance is, however, swift, and even more terrible, so that here we sympathize with the 'four quiet lads'.

Was he Mad? (Un Fou?) Published in *Le Figaro* in 1884. Three of Maupassant's interests are reflected here: insanity, dogs and hypnotism. (See Introduction).

The Dead Girl (La Morte) This is an original use of the traditional theme of skeletons taking over a churchyard at night – the *danse macabre*, depicted in sculpture at St. Maclou, Rouen, and in music by Saint-Saëns. Here we see Maupassant's bitter disillusionment with humanity in general, and women in particular.

Mademoiselle Cocotte What is so skilful in this story is the way exquisite comedy suddenly turns to pathos, then horror. Once again, Maupassant seems to foresee his own madness. Published in 1883, this was a revision of his earlier tale, *Histoire d'un Chien*.

A Night in Paris (La Nuit) One of the most weird of Maupassant's tales, yet based on simple experiences known to anyone who walks alone late at night. Electric light was still a novelty in Paris, with arc-lamps first introduced at the Paris Exhibition of 1878. The *Halles centrales* was the famous covered market near the Seine, now transferred to the outskirts.

The Case of Louise Roque (La Petite Roque) This is a long *nouvelle*, as distinct from a *conte*, but moves with such pace that it seems like a short story. Cleverly constructed and brilliantly observed, this is not only a crime-story, but an anticipation (1885) of Maupassant's own paranoid hallucinations and attempted suicide (1892). Again he refers to St. Anthony – this time to his temptations.

The Drowned Man (Le Noyé) One of Maupassant's later stories (1888), this is set in the Normandy sea-port of Fécamp, which he knew well. Here humour is a preliminary to another case of persecution by an invisible, supernatural being, though a natural explanation is still possible.

Who Knows? (Qui Sait?) This was published on the 6th April 1890, less than two years before Maupassant himself was admitted to an asylum. Yet it is a masterpiece of lucidity, related with such conviction and vivid detail that we feel we are listening to a man who really has lived through this incredible experience. To some extent it is autobiographical, Maupassant describing his head-noises, his own furniture, the familiar streets of Rouen, and especially his dread of encroaching insanity. The ending is a remarkable foreshadowing of his last days, spent in the private mental hospital at Passy, Paris, run by the best-known psychiatrist in France, Dr. A.-E. Blanche.